C. M. Ward was born and raised in Hanworth, five miles from Heathrow where he began work. Two years later he joined the Royal Navy for almost eight years. He visited various places between Hong Kong, North Borneo, Australia in East to Londonderry in West... he is fairly well-travelled.

After leaving the Royal Navy he moved to Norwich in 1970 where he began writing *Whyte Island*. He has a daughter and loves reading.

Whyte Island

(Part Two)

To Julie Clare Russell, the only young woman to want me mostly for myself rather than for what I possessed.

Acknowledgments

To my wife Margaret for her support, our daughter Helen for teaching me to use a laptop, and the staff at Austin Macauley.

C M Ward

Whyte Island

(Part Two)

AUSTIN MACAULEY
PUBLISHERS LTD.

A CIP catalogue record for this title is available from the British Library.

ISBN 978 1 84963-333-8

www.austinmacauley.com

First Published (2013)
Austin Macauley Publishers Ltd.
25 Canada Square
Canary Wharf
London
E14 5LB

Printed & Bound in Great Britain

As their train glided into the station the passengers, mostly men but with a good number of women amongst them, prepared to leave, but Harry Larke motioned to his companion to remain seated. 'We'll let the others get off first as there isn't any rush. Besides, I thought it would be nice if we strolled down to the park before we begin our tour, then I'll be able to explain something of our aims to you'.

While Harry used the station's telephone in order to inform his secretary he'd arrived, Andrew watched the locomotive draw its train into a refuge siding, uncouple and then steam off, presumably toward the engine sheds. He then turned his attention to the station. This merely consisted of a pair of platforms, each with a set of tracks on either side. Unlike the previous stations he'd seen on the island, there was nothing architecturally interesting about the platform buildings; they were merely oblong glass boxes containing upholstered bench seats, tables and toilets, having apparently been designed to require only the minimum amount of attention.

Although there were no trains in sight, Harry, when he returned, took him down a subway at the far end of the platform; opposite some underground washrooms they turned to their left along a short tunnel. 'Where do they go to?' Andrew asked at the bottom of a slope taking them up to ground level. He gestured toward two tunnels.

'The one nearest us leads to the factory and the other ends up inside the railway centre, but they're only used in times of bad weather.'

'Talking about bad weather,' the young man said recalling a thought he'd had as they'd travelled through the cutting, 'what happens when you have a really severe winter? Isn't the cutting liable to blockage by snowdrifts?'

Mr Larke shook his head vigorously. 'Very rarely. As I recall, it's only happened three times since it was constructed.' He smiled. 'But we were prepared for such an event. Alongside the railway centre is a tunnel which carries the railway right through the down land. When it emerges, the route continues on a viaduct and an embankment until it rejoins the mainline. So even if the cutting becomes blocked, it's still possible for the complex to function normally.'

By the time the pair emerged from the subway, there was no sign of the large number of people who'd alighted from their train's five carriages. Although Andrew glanced about him, he couldn't, in fact, see anyone or even a sign of activity anywhere.

'Don't worry,' his companion said upon noticing his look of surprise, 'there'll be plenty of hustle and bustle soon. The trains from other parts of the island probably haven't arrived yet, and work won't begin until all the first body of staff have changed into their working clothes and settled themselves in'. Harry paused and turned in the direction of the station. 'Look', he said, pointing, 'here comes another train.'

'Isn't it somewhat unfair on the people who've come on the earlier trains? They'll have lost some of their spare time in arriving early, surely?'

Harry chuckled. 'No one would worry much if they did; our working hours are overgenerous when compared to those of most other countries. When you consider that, on the mainland for example, employees arrive and leave by cycle, bus, train, motorbike and private car, each of which are fraught with all kinds of delay, our system is overly fair. However, the order in which our trains arrive is just a matter of luck, because all four set off at exactly the same time and so the first to arrive at each of the end junctions naturally gets the right of way. I know it sounds dangerous, but it isn't really because there's plenty of communication between the locomotive footplate men and the signalling staff.'

Andrew was reminded of the driveway up to the green school as they strolled along the shrub lined road and similarly, Harry led the way along a path diverging to the right well before they reached the factory building. The older man's brief allusion to a park had intrigued him, because he couldn't comprehend what use a recreation space would be to an isolated area without benefit of housing; to his mind an industrial complex was intended for working in and could be for no other purpose. He was therefore surprised at the extent and character of the area revealed to him just beyond the end of the path. Basically, the park consisted of a wide and deep depression whose well-mown grassy slopes were dotted with trees, shrubs, flowerbeds and several enormous rocks. On one side a substantial stream spouted from a rocky cleft to flow in a series of waterfalls down to a substantial lake containing four quite large islands.

He couldn't prevent himself from stopping to gaze upon the scene before him. 'It's beautiful,' he said in wonder, 'but what's it for? This park would rival some of the best municipal equivalents in my country but if, as you say, there aren't any homes here, who's to enjoy it? Surely families wouldn't normally come out this far?'

Mr Larke shrugged. 'Does there always need to be reason for everything?' He nodded in the direction of the lake where a collection of waterfowl swam, while swallows and other small birds flew about. 'I'm sure those creatures are enjoying the fruits of our labours. Actually, Andrew, like so many other things on our island, this park has several roles.' They recommenced walking down toward the lake while Harry explained. 'An area of almost two square miles of chalk was excavated for our complex. Now, the reason why we wanted it below ground level was because we wished to escape the full force of the wind, and also to reduce the railway gradient up from the coast. Unfortunately, we'd overlooked the problem of frost; just like water, frost tends to flow into hollows where it will stay longer and obviously make that area colder than elsewhere.'

Having reached the lakeside, Harry leaned against the back of a park bench and faced the slope they'd just descended. 'So what was done was to excavate the lake site to a further depth of thirty feet to form a depression, then numerous pipes were laid to drain and collect the rain, and water seepage through the chalk.' He gestured toward a jet of water emerging from a rocky area. 'Hence our stream over there. As frost seems to be attracted to water, especially when it's moving, you can see why we've got a lake and a stream. Unfortunately, they then had the problem of boring a tunnel through the chalk to make an overflow outlet for the lake, but in the event it wasn't too difficult, and besides they were able to make use of the railway tunnel to eject the water over the valley which the viaduct crosses.'

Both men sat down to face the lake while several waterfowl began to wander across in their direction. Despite the muted sound of machinery, the occasional noise of banging and the incomprehensible tones issuing from tannoys, it was difficult for Andrew to believe he was elsewhere than in an urban park. 'So there we were,' continued Harry, 'with an outsized hole on our hands and a giant puddle in the middle. Maybe the mainland people would have left it as it was, but we certainly weren't going to, and that's why we've created this park. We brought in tons of good humus, some massive rocks to create miniature crags and even made those islands. After planting all these bushes and deep rooted alkaline tolerant trees, laying paths and stocking the lake with goldfish, as well as introducing exotic birds, we were ready to admit the public.'

'The public?' echoed the younger man incredulously.

Harry laughed. 'Well, not exactly. The temporary citizens of our little domain, really. The statutory period for a dinner break is one hour, with twenty minutes each for morning and afternoon breaks. This holds true for just about every working person on Whyte Island. Well, naturally, our people couldn't get home and back over such a short period, so we've tried to create a home from home atmosphere for them here, hence the park. We've even laid on some outdoor and indoor entertainment to occupy them, but I'll try to explain that later.

'However, for the moment I'd like to outline our industrial policy to you before we take a look around. As you doubtless know, Andrew, we've had plenty of experience in manufacturing cars and a variety of other small road vehicles in our mainland factories. Our original plan was to produce strong, well-made machines, which would be durable yet cheap to make and retail. The kind of vehicle which certain motorists would buy, find reliable and want to purchase again. We weren't interested in pointless gimmicks or ostentation, nor did we want to flood the market with our products as other companies in mostly foreign lands have done with theirs.

'We were happy to fill a niche and to know we could rely on selling our products to regular customers. In brief, we desired to create machines which would be unbeatable in their field, and we believe we've achieved that aim. Our policy has remained basically the same, despite the subsequent opening of this plant. Instead of increasing our production rate in vehicles or lowering the output of our mainland factories to make way for this factory's products, we widened our range of vehicles and developed new ideas.

'Now that much of the so called developed world is panicking about global warming, the rise in sea levels and changing weather patterns, we've been experimenting with reducing harmful gas emissions and more fuel efficient vehicle engines, just as we've reduced our birth rate. I expect you'll remember we introduced our basic flat top design kit which could be used to convert into various roles, from low loader into estate and, by blocking in the side windows, would then become a van? Well, it caused a sensation at the time, and though the idea has been much-copied over the years, it has never been surpassed; but we resisted the temptation to increase production in order to exploit our invention, because we were unwilling to take on extra labour only to have to discard them whenever the bubble burst.

'As we're happy to manufacture vehicles at a steady rate without overproducing, you'll no doubt find the activity in our workshops almost leisurely, Andrew; but when you consider we put quality before quantity then you'll perhaps understand why our pace isn't particularly fast. Whenever an item has to be produced in quantity, it's left to the relevant senior member of staff to set the minimum number to be manufactured on an hourly basis by making them themself. If a subsequent operator feels the quota is too high, then they're at liberty to summon an enquiry'.

'And do they often get their way?' Andrew asked.

'Rarely', Harry grinned, 'because no one ever requests one; the quotas are always easy to maintain. We don't want our staff sweating blood, as it only leads to slap dash work, accidents or lost tempers'.

'What about automation? Do you have any robots or computers here?'

Mr Larke grimaced thoughtfully. 'The only automatic machinery we have here is used to replace people on those mind numbing, tedious repetitive jobs which are necessary to the production of motor vehicles and where micro-accuracy is essential. Office computers are, of course, a great help in ensuring calculations are perfect. Otherwise, we prefer to use manual work. This is because at first sight computers and robot machinery appear ideal. After an initial outlay, they're cheaper than paying a regular salary or wage to a manual workforce, they don't worry about working conditions, they don't require feeding, they can work all hours, and they're more reliable because they don't fall sick, strike, grow idle or take holidays.

'However, if automation is employed to too great an extent then trade will eventually come to a standstill, because all former customers will no longer be earning a wage due to their jobs having been lost to automatic machinery. Many employers globally are finding it profitable to install sophisticated machinery, produce as many of the completed products as quickly as possible while they're still in demand and then close down: an activity which benefits themselves but no one else. Such people consider a business as a means of lining their own pockets at the expense of others!

'We, though, think of a business as a place where people are given the opportunity to earn money to enable them and their dependants to enjoy life. On the other hand, if you deprive people of their employment they become nuisances, they turn to crime, drugs, drink and practice other unpleasant activities, while others might take their own lives. It's obvious to all Whyte Islanders at least, but apparently not to global politicians and others who are in a position to take action to prevent or remedy such inanity.' Harry paused, and glanced at his watch. 'We'd better be making a start on your tour,' he said, getting to his feet. Andrew joined him, and together they made their way to the factory.

'Anyway, to return to a description of our employment conditions,' the older man continued. 'As well as providing jobs, our intention was to ensure everyone was happy in their employment, and so we ensured our working conditions were of the best. As you can possibly guess from your experiences of the Whyte Line, Andrew, we haven't any unions; they're unnecessary because they wouldn't have anything to do. There aren't any pay negotiations to bother about, and our health and safety standards are beyond reproach, as you'll no doubt see.

'But what we do have is a Work's Council. This is comprised of elected representatives from every department and from all grades, and it's their job is to listen to, and judge, all complaints, suggestions and any other matters concerning our workforce. The task of the Council is relatively easy when you consider there are no jealousies caused by different pay structures, working conditions, hours worked or class distinction to worry about, all of which are obvious factors which can result in dissention where people work together. If you take into account that all our employees have been well trained before they come here, that they're only required to work for a certain period before commencing one of their secondary occupations, and that while they're employed here they automatically go from one task to another just to alleviate boredom, then you can see why there's little cause for complaint on either side.

'I recall when I worked on the mainland any superior, from the foreman up, held your job in their hands; if they didn't like the way you worked or acted, or even if you lived in a better house than them, or a workmate told them something to your discredit, then you could be dismissed without warning or reason.' Harry smiled. 'On the other hand, in a factory where there was a strong union presence, you could be worthless yet the foreman, or management for that matter, would be unable to touch you.

'But instant dismissal would be impossible in any factory or other place of employment on Whyte Island, if only because of the work of the Councils. In the unlikely event of a misdemeanour by a member of the workforce, an enquiry would be summoned, and if the transgressor were found unsuitable for further employment then she or he would be found work more agreeable to their temperament elsewhere. Of course, persistent malefactors would eventually be exiled abroad as worthless.' Before they entered the first of the buildings forming the complex, Andrew made a passing reference to the large number of trees to be seen everywhere.

'Why not?' Mr Larke exclaimed. 'We love trees; they're not only beautiful and help to give character to an area, but they're also very useful. To begin with their leaf fall helps to maintain the humus soil overlying the chalk and, like the depression and the lake, they help to provide a defence against frost by warming up the atmosphere in the area slightly. You should have seen the complex before these trees and shrubs were planted. It was lifeless and bleak; now it's interesting and full of life.' He paused. 'Listen to that birdsong, and look at those butterflies. A place of employment should be somewhere which people enjoy going to and working in, and shouldn't be some kind of prison'.

The manufacturing area was so big and there was so much to see that afterward Andrew had only the vaguest recollection of the greater part of his tour; only a few individual scenes stood out in his mind with any clarity. His main memory was of neat, well-designed workshops full of immaculate machinery, tended by cheerful people who invariably greeted Harry as though he were an old friend. At time their progress was almost painfully slow due to his frequent conversations with employees who, in their turn, were more than pleased to make Andrew's acquaintance, especially upon learning he was a visitor from the mainland.

'My primary task appears to be concerned with chatting to the factory personnel,' Harry confided after yet another lengthy conversation, 'but it's an essential job as it does wonders for morale, even though it may occasionally appear pointless. They know what I think and vice-versa. Having worked in mainland factories, I can assure you there would be far less conflict between management and employees if the same method was adopted in your country, Andrew'.

As Harry pointed out later, the main manufacturing area was unusual in that it was divided up into comparatively small buildings arranged in an arc. Each building was connected to the next by a wide, high passageway closed at either end by double doors, with a smaller, lower door set midway along the passage allowing egress to outside.

'The layout of our complex might seem unnecessarily extended at first sight', Harry commented, 'but after our experiences with mainland factories as well as with those we established over there, Andrew, we realised this system would have much to recommend it. As you can see, each workshop has large windows on either side and these ensure the maximum amount of natural light is able to penetrate, which is why they're kept scrupulously clean. You'll possibly also notice they're designed to open in a manner which will keep draughts down to a minimum.

'The reason why we have our buildings quite small is so they would be easier and cheaper to heat in winter, but also to keep cool in summer. Below ground level at the side of many of the workshops is a pulverised coal powered boiler which circulates piped hot water beneath the floors and these, together with the double glazed windows and the closed passageway doors, ensures the ambient temperature is well above discomfort level on even the coldest days. However, during hot days, fresh air can be circulated via air ducts power fed by fans, supplemented by the open windows'.

'I must say', said Andrew looking about him in admiration, 'you really look after the comfort of your workforce'.

'As I've mentioned before', Harry smiled, 'it isn't just for the sake of being humane, though that is a prime factor, but we believe in a quiet, easy and simple life. I well remember the disgusting conditions in most mainland factories; buildings sited too close together in a disorderly fashion making them too gloomy inside and out and also preventing adequate ventilation, buildings which could become unbelievably hot in summer and freezing in winter. So under such circumstances, it's quite surprising many employees managed to set such high standards of workmanship, but not quite such a surprise that others failed to give of their best, that anger was often generated and industrial disruptions frequent.

'This complex, however, having been laid out in such a way as to take advantage of sunlight and the ventilating properties of even the lightest breeze, is thereby well on the way to providing suitable working conditions which, in turn, encourages maximum effort. With the addition of the other little extras I've mentioned, such as a reasonable workshop temperature, we've ensured that we have a happy workforce which won't cause disruption, can be relied upon to give of their best and will produce the right number of vehicles required of them each day'.

It soon became evident to the visitor that the ground floor area of each building was devoted mainly to the relevant process of assembly, painting and fitting out of the various vehicles, as well as the production of the heavier components, while the upper floor, or floors, contained workshops for the manufacture of smaller items, storerooms, an electrical and maintenance department, and the main offices. In the centre of the circle of workshops, a building housed a medical centre and dental surgery on the ground floor, with a large cafeteria on the upper one. This arrangement resulted in an interesting tour for Andrew because Mr Larke led him around each building in turn, and often the difference between ground and upper floors could be quite startling.

The layout of the main workshops left nothing to be desired; the space around the exterior walls was always utilised as a gangway in order, Harry explained, to discourage people from leaning tools, material or items of machinery against the walls as so often happens in many other factories abroad, to provide a safer through route and also allow access to the windows. Each machine was placed as far as possible away from neighbouring machinery to permit all parts to be reached for maintenance and cleaning

23

purposes. 'So often the spaces around fixed machinery are difficult to get at,' observed Harry, 'thereby encouraging piles of rubbish, metal shavings and oil to accumulate which, as you can appreciate from the neatness of this shop, is unacceptable to us'.

Although there was plenty of activity in evidence about the two men, the noise level was surprisingly low, and when the young man mentioned this fact he was told that not only were the machines and other mechanical tools chosen for their comparative quietness, but each workshop had been constructed with materials which helped to absorb sound. 'After all,' Harry added with a grin, 'if it were too noisy, people wouldn't be able to hear the music being broadcast, would they?'

Down the centre of each workshop was a wide gangway which connected with the end passageways. Beside the electric trolleys which carried pallet-loads of components about the complex, they provided room for the overhead railway which transferred vehicle bodies, engines and other heavy or bulky items from one shop to another well above head and end door height and to one side. In the centre of each workshop the shop manager, foreman and charge hands' offices were situated, and after Harry had shown his guest around those in the first shop and introduced some of the present occupants to him, he described their respective tasks briefly. 'Basically, the charge hands are responsible for ensuring the shop is kept clean and tidy and that everyone is contented and has everything they need. The foreman's job is to keep a check on output and the supply of components. He also has to ensure all machinery is working well and is adequately maintained. The manager, naturally enough, oversees the entire workshop and checks everyone is doing their job properly. He is ultimately responsible for the wellbeing of the shop, and so takes the blame should anything go wrong'.

'Not much of an exertion, surely?' interjected Andrew.

'Not really,' Harry Larke agreed, 'which is why he's often to be found operating the various machines in his department. In fact, all the supervisory staff are expected to be able to handle the machinery and processes under their control, so they can step in at a moment's notice to relieve people who've had an accident or are otherwise suddenly indisposed. What you might wish to take into account, Andrew, is the fact that even the most intelligent graduate wishing to take up employment within our industry has to be proficient in every machine and process within the scope of his occupation and subsequent responsibility. We don't have what you call "whiz kids" over here, who move from college straight into positions of responsibility on the evidence of their degrees. A certain amount of experience is essential on our island.'

'What's that place over there?' Andrew, who after giving himself time to take this information in, asked upon noticing a large square structure which stood over toward one corner.

Harry turned to see where he was pointing then, checking his watch, he replied, 'you'll be finding out in twenty five minutes, but we've just got time to have a look at the offices upstairs'.

In many ways, the office space was laid out in a similar fashion to the workshop below, with walkways alongside the walls, frequent transverse gangways with a wider one down the centre, and a few individual enclosed offices in the middle of the open plan floor area. However, there was no access to the adjacent buildings, nor was there a structure in one corner resembling the one Andrew had remarked upon downstairs.

It was soon obvious that Harry was as popular with the office personnel as he had been with the workshop staff, for, as he and his companion moved from one desk to the next, they were warmly welcomed by the occupants, and they too immediately took an interest in Andrew when they found he was a visitor to the island. As most of the office staff were women, he found this regard for him more than a little flattering.

During their tour of the workshop, Harry had invariably permitted the machine operators to explain the nature of their labour to his guest, a consideration which he now extended to the office personnel. However, whatever type of device the person in question was using the explanation of their activity was usually well beyond the young man's comprehension, and so he could only look on, attempting to appear knowledgeable. But when one girl operating before a screen had finished outlining her present task to him, Andrew asked her whether it strained her eyes.

'Goodness, no,' she replied with a smile. 'We're only permitted to use it over periods of three hours each per day, then someone else takes a turn. But I daresay it could cause quite severe eye problems over time otherwise'.

Andrew was introduced to the manager of the department in her office and, after she'd told him of the work undertaken by the different sections within her control, he exclaimed, 'how do you cope? There doesn't seem to be enough people up here to cover all those sections.'

'If this was a mainland office then we probably would be understaffed,' the manager replied, 'but as far as the employment sector is concerned, we have nothing like as complicated a system as you would have over on the mainland. We haven't different rates of pay or wage rises to worry about, and all the various deductions taken from mainland earnings don't occur on Whyte Island. And as far as production is involved, well, our vehicle output rarely varies, so we know exactly what components, materials and spare parts will be required from outside sources; and as those suppliers are nearly always our mainland factories, and we have a substantial store of those of those items anyway, we hardly ever experience difficulties in that direction. So, again, we're able to get by with a small office staff'.

Before the manager could explain further a loud buzzing sound reverberated throughout the upper floor. 'Everything stops for tea,' she smiled. Turning to Harry Larke she asked, 'will you be coming back up?'

The factory manager shook his head. 'You've explained more than adequately, Mary. We've scarcely started our tour yet, and there's so much to see.'

When the two men re-entered the large office area there was hardly anyone in sight. 'Someone's got to stay behind,' Harry remarked, nodding over to where a couple of women and a man were seated at their respective desks, 'just in case a call comes through or a problem arises; but the rest will have gone down to the place in the corner you asked about. Which is where we're going.'

As they made their way through the equally deserted and now almost silent workshop, Harry remarked, 'it's actually a canteen, but I think you'll be somewhat surprised by what you'll find inside. Every workshop contains one, but they're only used for morning and afternoon tea breaks. This facility is an entirely new departure from the usual practice in mainland factories I've worked in or visited. In those places, people were expected to take their breaks in situ, but we felt such a procedure encouraged vermin, besides being generally unhygienic. On the other hand, the provision of a proper tea break area where office and workshop staff could mix together would bring great psychological benefits. I know when I worked as a welder in dirty old factories, the vision of a pretty young girl walking past would linger on in my mind for the remainder of the day, so how much nicer would it be if one were given the opportunity to sit and drink tea, even talk to such a girl.'

Harry Larke's observations raised several questions in the young man's mind, mainly with regard to the problem of cotton dresses accidentally rubbing up against greasy overalls, and of the question of unseemly banter, but as a similar problem must have once occurred and, as he knew, been overcome aboard Whyte Line ships, it was obviously not insoluble. But before he could voice his thoughts on the matter they arrived outside the canteen, and so it was left to his eyes to provide the answer to his thoughts.

At first sight he could be forgiven for assuming they'd entered a rather expensive tea shop. Of overall clad figures there was no sign; instead, almost every table was occupied by people wearing ordinary casual clothes, forcing Andrew to briefly wonder where all the workshop staff had gone to. Because the structure had been sighted in a corner, the two exterior walls contained large windows overlooking the park, while the pair of walls situated within the workshop were windowless, one having a large land and seascape pictures hung upon it, the other one the shelves and cupboards of a substantial food counter. The décor of the big room was well up to the standard set by many of the better types of café on the mainland. 'Come on,' invited Harry above the noise of numerous conversations, 'help yourself to what we came here for; it's all on the house'.

Arranged on the counter, and presided over by a woman and a man, were plates of individually wrapped sandwiches, each labelled with their contents, as well as cakes and biscuits. When Andrew selected a ham sandwich the woman, apparently sensing his visitor status from his uncertainty, chidingly urged him along by saying, 'Go on, love, take something else; you're a growing lad!' And she threw several more rounds on his plate, after which she asked him if he wanted tea, coffee or cocoa.

Upon leaving the counter, Harry didn't bother to glance about to see if there was any one in particular he wished to sit with. Instead he led the way over to the nearest table with two vacant seats. The couple already occupying the table, a dark haired, thin-faced man in his mid-thirties, and an auburn haired, somewhat younger woman with a much-freckled face, greeted them with some enthusiasm, and almost immediately Harry and the man were in deep conversation. This left the young man with the problem of talking to the woman facing him but she, on her part, didn't seem particularly bothered by her erstwhile companion's desertion of her. Instead, she stared boldly at Andrew for a few moments and then asked, 'will you be staying to dinner?'

As soon as she noted his uncertain nod, she picked up a plastic covered folder lying on the table next to a bowl of flowers and handed it across to him, after which she pushed over a small notepad containing a biro. 'Just put down what number dish you'd like, along with the your name and the number of this shop, which is "one"; then pass it along to Harry.'

'What happens then?'

The woman smiled. 'Don't worry, he'll put your choice in the post box by the door.' She paused. 'My name's Joyce, and I'd recommend the trout – either the brown from the lake, or the rainbow from the river below, they're equally delicious'.

'Exactly what my girlfriend said,' he murmured. He was grateful for his present companion's advice, for each of the four dishes listed in the menu seemed as appetising as each other, and so her recommendation helped him come to his decision.

'Do you like it here?' Joyce enquired as soon as he'd introduced himself.

Assuming she meant the factory, he answered, 'I've never been in a mainland factory, but from what Mr Larke's been telling me this one's a paradise compared to most industrial places over there.'

'You're quite right there', the woman laughed. 'My dad's always talking about the working conditions he and his mates had to put up with, as well as the management's attitude to their employees.' Her face grew serious as she continued. 'In my dad's last mainland factory, everyone knew the management was cutting back on production, so they were all surprised when several men, including my dad, were promoted to foremen. But all the foremen were then told to make the workforce more efficient, which was a polite way of saying "get everyone to sweat". Well, everybody soon realised what the management was up to, because after a few months of sky high production and profits, there came a slump and the factory almost immediately closed down; but well before that happened nearly all the foremen, which included my dad, were made redundant.'

Andrew's face must have looked blank because Joyce went on to patiently explain, 'the management were aware there weren't any more orders on the book, so they wanted their outstanding work completed as quickly as possible because they'd lose money, otherwise, in keeping the factory open unnecessarily; but they didn't care about their employees, they were just there to be conned. My poor old dad thought he had a secure future as a well-paid foreman. Instead, he thought himself lucky to take any menial task going, and he was a craftsman.'

'Does he work here now?' he asked, sensing her distress.

Joyce shook her head. 'He used to, but he's been retired a long time.'

Thinking to change what now appeared to him to be an embarrassing subject Andrew enquired, 'do you work in this building? Only I didn't notice you when we were up in the office just before the break.'

Instead of replying, she offered her hands to him. 'Go on, examine them', she insisted. 'Take them.'

Glancing uncertainly at her thin-faced companion and noting he was still engaged in conversation, Andrew did as he was bidden. Joyce's hands were rough, the fingers lined and ingrained with dirt; the nails short, often cracked and black rimmed. 'My husband says he thinks he's in bed with one of his male workmates when I lay hands on him,' she giggled.

'But only with regard to your hands, I hope.'

She laughed louder, 'So do I.'

'Presumably, then, you don't work in an office?' he suggested, belatedly releasing her hands. The alternative, that she was employed in the workshop, shouldn't have surprised him much; he'd worked alongside plenty of women of all ages and in all departments aboard Whyte Line ships, but somehow it seemed rather unpleasant when practiced in a factory. 'So, what work do you do?'

'All kinds. Like most people here I can do just about everything. It's much more interesting when you keep changing round.'

'Do you ever work alongside your husband?'

Joyce took a drink of her tea. 'Quite often,' she replied, 'and we get on like a house on fire, but it still makes a change to get away from him occasionally'.

The candid way in which she answered his questions, together with her apparent lack of aversion to his interrogation, made him ask, 'who looks after your child or children when you're at work?'

The woman laughed again. 'I take it you haven't been on our island long. Women aren't permitted to work full time when their children are under fifteen, and I'm not even thirty yet so I wouldn't have any youngsters. But I much prefer working to motherhood; my younger sister has two children, and I'm most welcome to share them any time I wish.'

'And you don't really mind?'

Joyce shook her head emphatically. 'I'm not really the maternal type. Better I should forego the experience than deprive some young couple of a baby or two which they really yearn for. I'm sure many women have babies because they feel it's expected of them, not because they particularly want them. I occasionally write to a couple of cousins living on the mainland, and the things they tell me about their children often make me wonder what they had them for in the first place. They're nothing but worry and pain to them. The Whyte Island policy which ensures couples only have children because they really want them, and because they'll be certain their offspring will live happy and fulfilling lives, is definitely correct as far as islanders are concerned.'

'I suppose you must watch what you write to your cousins about life over here,' Andrew said, adding, 'only I've worked for years on Whyte Line ships, yet everything was kept a secret from me.'

'People quickly form an opinion from things you tell them, and usually they keep that imagine in their mind permanently; so after informing those cousins that I worked in a factory workshop and had no children, they're convinced Whyte Island is some form of police state. Their letters are therefore rather pitying toward me, and they tend to confine themselves to information about their own lives. I never try to correct them in their appraisal of our country, as it would be a waste of time. Anyway, tell me what you think about the island so far.'

For the remaining five minutes of the tea break, Andrew talked about his feelings for the island to his three companions, who were left in no doubt as to his enthusiasm for most of the things he'd seen and heard since he'd first landed.

'Do you have many women engineering workers here?' Harry

was asked by his young companion as they followed the last person out of the canteen.

'About a dozen or so; most women are too careful of their appearance to make a career out of machining, but a few take to it like a fish to water. We'd rather they didn't, but that's their choice. We never stand in the way of the individual's preferences if we can help it.'

The upper floor of the next building contained the electrical and maintenance departments which, as the factory manager explained, were rather more important than might be supposed from a visit to many of the mainland factories. 'Goodness knows how many hours are lost through machinery breakdowns or lack of replacements of vital tools or spares,' Harry declared. 'We however not only ensure maximum utilisation of all our plant and equipment by the application of a vigorous and meticulous maintenance programme, but we also keep a comprehensive stock of spares, so that if an item breaks or becomes worn we can replace it immediately. As soon as the new item is fitted a fresh one is either ordered, if it's particularly intricate, or else manufactured within this factory or on the mainland. The production of spare parts is a task frequently undertaken in the engineering college because they usually make ideal test pieces.

'Our electrical department is also kept on its toes. Apart from its role in production, any piece of equipment or apparatus which breaks down, no matter how insignificant it might seem, needs to be repaired or replaced immediately. After having worked in one particular factory with a terrible smoke problem due to the welding of pre-painted metalwork and noticing most of the ventilation fans were inoperative or absent because of incompetence, I vowed I'd never allow a similar shortcoming to occur in a Whyte Island works. Neither would I expect employees to have to wait whilst their electric machinery or tools were repaired because the management were inefficient and wouldn't pay for replacements or spares.'

Andrew, well used to the standards set in the storerooms on board Whyte Line ships and the one in the green school, wasn't overly surprised to find the stores in the maintenance and electrical shops spotless, every item being labelled and stowed away neatly in its own compartment or drawer. The personnel in both departments, Harry informed him, took turns in manning their respective stores, and when they weren't engaged in maintenance or repair work they helped keep the workshops tidy. 'Because machinery has to be motionless before it can be serviced properly, the maintenance and electrical people employed in this plant are rather unique among Whyte Island factory personnel, because they regularly work at weekends. Due to our isolated situation, there are few trains running outside weekday working hours, so they and their families have to stay here over the relevant period'.

'Presumably, then, as I recall, you don't operate the factory at night.'

'Goodness, no,' answered Mr Larke in a tone which almost suggested horror. 'We wouldn't even contemplate doing so. Night work is a family wrecker. Very few people over here have jobs which entail being away from home overnight, and when they do, they have a very long break between each duty as compensation. I had a period of night work on the mainland once and although the total number of hours each week was less than on day work, I never seemed to get any spare time to myself; it was all work, sleep and eat. Even my days off were spoilt because it was difficult to adjust to a new time scale. Fortunately I was unmarried at the time, but I heard plenty of stories about other men keeping night working husband's beds warm; even faithful wives often found the loneliness impossible, and so marriage failures weren't uncommon.'

Proof that the authorities cared as much for physical health as they did for moral welfare was to be found in the paint shop, shot blasting and the welding sections, because each was fitted with a first rate ventilation system complete with adjustable temperature controls. In addition, as in the case of the computer operator in the office, the hazard to health was thought serious enough to warrant a frequent change over in the personnel using the equipment. 'The painting, welding and shot blasting sections have another connection,' Harry explained, 'which helps to give our products just that little bit of extra quality, besides making the work much healthier to do.

'As I mentioned before, our vehicles are particularly robust, and especially so in the case of the chassis; this is built of extra thick metal and held together with really strong welds, and we also pay special attention to long life with this component. Unlike many of our rival motor manufacturers we ensure the paintwork on our vehicles endures, because once rust starts to get onto bare metal it means the eventual end of the item in question. I've known of many superior vehicles, for instance, which have been spoilt because they've been badly painted where they're not easy to examine, and not through oversight in many cases.'

'Why?' Andrew enquired.

Harry shook his head. 'I'll explain later. Now, in many countries to prevent steel in bulk from becoming rusty during storage, it's usually customary to spray protective paint over it. We, however, don't paint our steelwork because we store it under cover and not outside as elsewhere. This is because we don't want our welders breathing in the extra smoke which arises from painted metal, the amount of which has to be seen to be believed. After the item in question has been welded up, and where a fine paint finish isn't required, it's shot blasted with minute granules to remove any traces of rust or other substances. This process also provides an excellent key for the paint to adhere to, therefore ensuring the product lasts.'

Harry Larke had an anecdote for each of the relevant three departments; in the shot blasting shop which, although noisy, was much cooler and cleaner than might have been expected from the nature of the work, he described a factory on the mainland where the shot blaster had been sat in a large corrugated iron shed which was open to the elements at one end. 'During the winter it was almost as bad as being in the open. Icy winds would be funnelled between the two side walls and the high roof, and when a gale was blowing in the wrong direction the effect could be devastating.'

In the welding department, Harry told of a mainland factory where the build-up of fumes was so great on damp days when the air was heavy, that it looked as if there was a smog inside; and of windless days when a band of smoke could be seen floating motionless at head height throughout the shop. 'There weren't any supply fans,' he explained, 'and the extraction fans were too few and too high up in the roof to be effective. Of course the management claimed the fumes weren't dangerous, but there were many occasions when my lungs ached like mad and I had coughing fits. I was actually on the point of giving up my trade when Charlie won his fortune, so you can see it was my fortune as well'.

'He laughed and slapped Andrew on the back. 'But there's more than adequate ventilation in here' he went on, 'not that there's much smoke coming from the welding. Try not to look directly at the light, though,' he warned, 'because it can hurt your eyes temporarily. For some unknown reason, eyes seem to become used to it when welding all the time; however, it's claimed welders often suffer from eye damage later on in life, which is why we restrict the time each person spends at the work as much as possible. No profession is worth unnecessarily risking future health for.'

In the paint shop Harry told his companion about a small factory he'd once worked in. 'Their paint bay was just a lean-to built onto the main part of the factory which, incidentally, was constructed from corrugated iron throughout. The bay was permanently open at one end and there was, of course, no ventilation or heating provided. The factory's main product was road making equipment, and this was prepared for painting by being washed with petrol. I remember often seeing one of the painters engaged upon this task holding a gallon can of petrol in one hand and a rag in the other, and with a lighted cigarette in his mouth. They used to clean out their spray guns at the end of the day by spraying petrol through them. The partition between the bay and the main factory area was full of holes, and can you guess what job was done on the other side?'

Andrew shook his head. Harry chuckled. 'Welding!' he exclaimed. 'I can never understand why there wasn't an explosion, or at least a serious fire. The company also used to store their unpainted machines in a muddy field where, if they weren't ordered fairly soon, they began to go rusty. Eventually, to prevent this occurring, someone had the bright idea of applying a layer of oil all over the machines as soon as they'd been constructed. Well, this method stopped the corrosion alright, but when the painters tried to clean the oil off, they found that all the petrol and rags in the factory couldn't do the job adequately. Matters came to a head when a lorry driver, making a check of his load during a stop, discovered the paint on the machinery peeling off like skin on a banana. The next thing the company tried to get rid of the oil was steam cleaning, but this proved to be expensive and time consuming. Of course, it was all due to bad organisation; either the production team was turning out too many machines or else the paint shop staff needed more help. There was really no need to store unpainted machinery outside.'

To avoid having to wear protective clothing and masks, Harry and his guest viewed the painting process from an upstairs office within the shop. One of the senior painters, who spent exactly one third of his working week in administration and paperwork, another third in painting and the remainder elsewhere within the complex, explained the workings of the paint shop in some detail to Andrew.

He dealt with the health aspect of paint spraying first. 'Can you see the water curtain by the walls and down the centre of the shop? This takes away the residue paint dust from the air, the dust is filtered out and the water re-circulated. This ensures the air is much cleaner than otherwise, making it healthier to breathe, and it also means there's less possibility of the vehicle bodies picking up dust from the ceiling, walls and other surfaces. The presence of large steady volumes of water serves another useful purpose, as it's a means of keeping the temperature of the shop at a comfortable level. Naturally it's hot in winter, though not enough to cause excess condensation, and much cooler in summer. This is in addition to the under floor heating, of course. As you can imagine, Andrew, painting is usually an unhealthy and uncomfortable job, so conditions have been made as pleasant as possible with as little time spent in actual spraying as feasible.'

He paused to show his visitor a chart with the range of colours available together with the appropriate undercoats. 'Due to the number and variety of coats applied, we require several paint shops for different items, and also because the whole painting process takes some time to complete, but they're all basically the same in layout and routine.' The senior painter had very little else to add, and after watching the sprayers at their work a little longer Harry and Andrew continued the tour with a visit to the medical centre.

'You were going to explain about why some vehicle manufacturers deliberately painted their products badly,' Andrew said as they crossed a lawn to the building in the middle of the ring of workshops.

'So I was,' Harry smiled. 'Well it's just a ploy to ensure certain components or even entire vehicle bodies didn't endure as long as they ought. Another trick is to use poor quality metal, which is especially reprehensible when used for the manufacture of tools, or bolts and screws, et cetera. But as far as paint is concerned, as I believe I've already mentioned, there are certain areas of vehicles and other large metal items which are difficult to reach after construction, and if they've been left badly painted or unpainted, they'll eventually lead to a deterioration which is impossible to check. Common places for corrosion to set in on vehicles are beneath the wheel arches, various parts of the chassis and at the bottom of doors.

'The idea behind this policy of self-deterioration no doubt came about when mass production began to outstrip demand, and customers became fewer as a result. Obviously, the longer products lasted, then naturally fewer would eventually be required. By encouraging corrosion in a product, the manufacturer ensured his customer would sooner or later need a replacement. The entire process suggested collusion between companies, otherwise if one particular manufacturer were to get a bad reputation for rust in its products it would quickly lose customers, but apparently nearly all vehicle companies had similar life expectancies with their products.

'This deplorable state of affairs meant that many components were scrapped long before they need have been, simply because a relatively minor part of the entire structure had failed. If you consider the large number of different materials, components and additional parts to be found in the average car, Andrew, you will understand the wastage involved. Presumably many vehicle manufacturers have now realised the extent of their combined wastefulness, for emphasis on anti-corrosion methods does seem to be more widespread nowadays. Fortunately though, their early policy of producing limited life vehicles, whether deliberate or not, allowed us a foothold in the industry with our more reliable products.'

Much to Andrew's surprise, the first thing he noticed upon entering the medical centre was an obvious boxing ring. 'What on earth is that doing here?' he exclaimed.

'I can think of no better place for it to be; after all, people have been known to get hurt during fights, in which case here they'd be able to receive prompt and expert attention from the medical staff.'

'Presumably it's used for recreational purposes?'

The manager shook his head. 'We wouldn't encourage our personnel to practice martial arts during meal breaks; they'd only tire themselves out, or perhaps hurt each other, which wouldn't benefit production. No, that piece of equipment is insurance against ill feeling developing between individuals. Everyone knows it's here and freely available on request.' He glanced shrewdly at his companion. 'But surely you saw one during your tour of the green school and so had its usage explained to you? And I'm aware people are always given the chance to settle their differences on board Whyte Line ships in a responsible manner.'

Andrew agreed, but added, 'I just didn't expect to find one in a mainland factory.'

'Every large place of employment should have an area where opponents can fight each other under a measure of control and in a reasonably safe environment. Adults can often be as puerile as juveniles, they can bully, show off and be just as contemptuous toward others, so it's only right that victims of intimidation should be given the opportunity to strike back. I saw some terrible scenes and fights when I was working on the mainland, often caused by bullies taking their troubles out on someone weaker who just happened to be handy. Frequently the scraps took place amongst machinery or where there was a lot of steelwork lying about. There was therefore always the possibility that a fight could get out of hand and so result in serious injury.

'So what could be better than the provision of a boxing ring and a competent referee? Not only could opponents then work off their grievances in a comparatively harmless fashion, but it would also tend to show up the bullies within a workforce. Such people are well aware that others are usually unwilling to risk their jobs or their physical health in unofficial and uncontrolled fighting. However, if it were a case of having an authorised and refereed bout then many more people would agree to a fight if picked upon. This option wouldn't suit most bullies, who are generally bluffers, but where they were willing to fight their frequent appearance in the ring would soon show them up for what they really are.

'As you might imagine, Andrew, fights in this and other Whyte Island places of employment are few and far between. Not only are we educated to live and work amicably with each other, but because of our training in the martial arts, most conflicts would be extremely lengthy and tiring affairs. However, when a fight is unavoidable, it's always held in strict privacy with only a referee, a nurse or doctor and a member of the management present to see fair play and to render assistance where required.'

'Would it always be boxing?'

Harry chuckled. 'They can fight how they like, as long as they use what nature provided them with, but not too unsportsmanlike, though.' He glanced at his watch. 'Look,' he said decisively, 'it's not far off dinnertime. I'll introduce you to the sister and she'll show you around, then if you'd like to go upstairs to the canteen, I'll meet you there.'

The sister was everything a senior nurse might be expected to be. A tall, grey haired woman of about fifty, she emanated quiet confidence, and as she explained the work of the medical centre and its staff duties, and conducted Andrew about, it soon became apparent she was a very competent and knowledgeable person.

'Because we have such a large workforce and the factory is so isolated, it's thought necessary to have a doctor in regular attendance,' she told him. 'Normally there isn't much need for one, so the position is worked by most of the island's practitioners on a weekly roster system.' The sister smiled. 'Apparently it's thought of as something of a holiday because we rarely have emergencies or accidents here, but twice a week the doctors hold surgeries to keep themselves occupied. On two other days each week we have a visit from a dentist as well.'

'Is that usual for a factory? Having a dentist, I mean.'

'Well, the fact that we have a regular doctor would in itself be unusual enough if this were a mainland factory, so having dental facilities would be classed as being phenomenal. But as we are also a long way from any dentists, that's reason enough for having our own surgery. Even where workplaces are situated near relevant surgeries, much time is wasted by people taking time off to visit them. Often on the mainland, a patient would take a whole morning, afternoon or even day off because the appointment would be at an inconvenient time, there was a long wait involved or the surgery was difficult to get to. So it was thought a good idea to have a fully equipped surgery in the actual workplace, where the doctor, dentist and patient were close to hand, thereby eliminating waiting and travelling problems.'

The centre consisted of separate medical and dental surgeries, a combined reception and waiting room, a restroom with two beds and a couch, and a dispensary-cum-treatment room with a well stocked store. 'We don't normally issue a wide range of medicines here,' the sister explained in the latter room, 'because we're mainly concerned with injuries or temporary discomforts. Any prescriptions issued by the doctors are usually dealt with at chemists in the towns and larger villages.'

Although Andrew was to meet neither doctor nor dentist he was introduced to the assistant nurse and also a probationer who, unlike the two experienced full time female nurses, was a young man, present only on a temporary basis. 'This industrial complex, together with the railway centre for which we also provide medical facilities, is ideal for student nurses,' Grace, the Sister mentioned. 'Because not only might they expect to gain experience with various injuries and accidents, but normally there's so little activity occurring that there's plenty of time to study for exams and specialised subjects; and, of course, both Yvonne and I are always ready to help them where necessary and,' she emphasised with a smile, 'to keep their noses in their books!'

Although the spotless medical centre was comparatively small, it contained some very sophisticated surgical equipment. 'This,' Grace explained, 'is a very useful gadget. Even though workshop people are encouraged to wear protective clothing and equipment whenever necessary, we still get the occasional accident. Nothing is one hundred per cent effective all the time. This instrument is an extremely powerful electronic magnet designed specifically to extract metal from eyeballs, but it has also been found to be equally useful in removing metal splinters painlessly from other parts of the body.

'When I worked in a mainland hospital, I once talked to a young chap late one afternoon who'd caught a minute speck of steel in one of his eyes that morning and still hadn't had it removed. They'd tried freezing his eyeball and teasing the object out with a needle, but it was too deeply embedded. Because of economy measures we didn't have an electronic magnet there, otherwise it would have been out in an instant. Not only was it extremely uncomfortable for the young man every time he blinked, but he also told me his firm would probably only compensate him for losing that morning's pay.'

'Wasn't he wearing safety goggles or glasses?'

The sister shook her head. 'As I recall, he was using a fixed grinding machine which should have had some goggles hanging up nearby, but they were missing, there were none in the stores and no one seemed to have a pair.' Andrew was shocked, and said so, but Grace continued. 'That's nothing. Harry Larke once told me about the medical staff and centre in one large factory which employed him that consisted of one qualified nurse and a small room. Presumably the pay was low and the job rather boring because nurses never seemed to stay very long. He said that as soon as a new nurse arrived, an outbreak of minor accidents and ailments would ensue so the men would have an excuse to see her, especially if it was rumoured she was young and attractive. I can't say I'd blame the nurses for being bored while on their own. An industrial nurse's occupation can be dreary for weeks on end with nothing happening, and then suddenly there'll be a spate of accidents; but it's the nurse's job to be on hand whenever required. But, according to Harry, most of the nurses at his factory used to be away for entire mornings or afternoons at a time, which meant medical care would be delegated to amateurs on the shop floor or in the offices who'd merely received basic training in first aid.'

'Wasn't the factory close to a town where professional help was readily obtainable?'

'I've no idea,' replied the Sister, 'but with some accidents, immediate medical aid can mean the difference between life and death, or permanent injury. First impressions might make our centre seem over-manned, but having a doctor, two nurses and a trainee means there's little possibility of any of us becoming lonely or bored, and it also means there's always someone in attendance when required. The rest of the staff can be readily summoned over the loudspeaker system which extends over the whole complex, but on the rare occasions when one of us is alone on duty we can find plenty of things to do, because to be accepted for industrial medical work we need to prove we can keep ourselves amused.

'I, for example, am a fanatic when it comes to embroidery or knitting, while Yvonne loves reading and jigsaws. The secret is to have a hobby which can be dropped at a moment's notice so as to attend to a patient, otherwise we could become quite annoyed at interruptions and forget what we're really here for; but what with keeping the dispensary well stocked, maintaining the medical records, attending the surgeries, refreshing our memories with medical books and being engrossed in our pastimes, we haven't got time to feel bored and frustrated. I wouldn't exchange this job for any other, and I'm sorry when I have to go off to one of the other jobs.'

'Which will be?' Andrew impertinently asked.

'I believe the next one will be labouring in one of our stately mansions. Gardening in fine weather usually, but inside when it's wet, windy or cold; polishing the silverware, woodwork, floors and any other tasks which need doing.'

'Do you like doing that?' he enquired, trying to sound contrite.

'Very much so. I like housework almost as much as gardening and nursing. Now that our son has left home there's not enough in our house to keep me occupied. My husband and I both share our secondary jobs whenever possible, and we each take a hand in keeping our own place neat and tidy.'

The canteen was so plush that Andrew found it difficult to believe it wasn't intended for the exclusive use of the managerial staff. The walls, where they weren't glazed, were fitted with dark wood panelling upon which were fixed wall lamps and small pictures; a dark green carpet covered the vast floor area and upon each of the innumerable linen clad tables there stood a vase of flowers. Large sub-tropical shrubs, small palms and large ferns occupied spaces against the walls, and to add to the air of gentility, subdued music permeated the room.

'We've come up here early so we can take a table overlooking the park,' Harry said while his companion surveyed the empty room with some awe. 'Normally I'd be one of the last to arrive so that each day I can sit at various tables and so chat with different people, but I'm sure you'd rather see our view instead of just conversing with others.'

Before selecting an appropriate table, Harry took his guest over to the servery in the centre of the room where he gave Andrew's and his names and the number of the shop where they placed their meal order to the young woman at the counter. 'Alright, Harry,' she replied brightly before crossing to a hatchway behind her. She returned almost immediately, carrying their meals upon a tray.

'That was quick,' the young man observed in an undertone as they continued to where a man was in charge of an apparent wine bar.

'They need to be pretty fast. In a few minutes time the bulk of the workforce will be arriving, and for a quarter of an hour or so it'll be mayhem for the kitchen staff, which is why this pre numbering of dishes system was devised. It speeds up cooking and serving and eliminates waste. What would you like to drink?'

Andrew glanced from Harry to the man behind the bar. 'What would you recommend?'

'For trout, this,' replied the latter, quickly pouring out a generous glass of white wine.

Seated at a table next to a widow allowing a magnificent view of the park, much of the top of the factory complex and an area of white cliff surmounted by down land, Andrew sipped at his drink. He was no connoisseur of wine but he thought the flavour better than anything he'd ever tasted before, complementing the grilled trout and accompaniments perfectly. 'This is beautiful wine,' he told Harry, 'but it seems rather wasteful for daytime use. It's the sort of drink to have for a romantic evening'..

The factory manager stopped separating some flesh from the leg bone of his roast chicken. 'I don't wish to spoil anything for you but that isn't real wine, it's merely flavoured and textured water. You won't, I hope, find a thimbleful of alcoholic drink in the entire complex. Alcohol encourages accidents and oversights, and anyone drinking here could be liable to exile.'

Harry's revelation should have spoilt Andrew's drink for him but it didn't, and he was pleased when the older man later went off to fetch a passable sherry to accompany his blackberry pie and ice cream dessert. Long before that, however, the dining area had begun to fill up with astonishing speed and soon he and Harry were joined by a young couple. The girl, with her jet black shoulder length hair allied to a skin so delicately pink as to appear translucent, and big blue eyes, was so beautiful and poised that the young visitor could only mumble in monosyllables every time she addressed him, which was frequently. He resisted the temptation to ask her what kind of work she did in case his illusion of her as an angel was shattered and she revealed herself as a fitter, a welder or engaged in some other traditionally unfeminine task.

Instead of taking the lift to the ground floor after their meal, Harry took him to the floor below the canteen, which was laid out as a recreation area. 'As you've doubtless noticed, Andrew,' he said as they made their way between snooker and bar billiard tables, past dartboards and numerous tables suitable for a variety of games and other amusements, 'all these pastimes are of a less active nature because, as I've said before. We don't want anyone tiring themselves needlessly.'

After showing Andrew a bowling alley, Harry took him to a theatre capable of seating an audience of a hundred and fifty. 'We have film shows, concerts, plays and lectures in here. They're all only about half an hour long but it helps people to relax after dinner. Everyone gets a chance to see the shows on a roster system and, of course, they can take part if they want to.'

'What sort of films do you show? Only Charlie said there aren't any cinemas over here.'

The manager chuckled. 'They're nothing spectacular, much the same as those shown in our schools: educational, travel, history and wildlife films; and other similar kinds of subjects.'

'I'm very impressed by all the various amusements you've catered for,' Andrew observed, 'but weren't you taking a chance that your workforce would want to use such facilities, that they'd really prefer to just sit around resting?'

'We balloted them on what they'd like to do during their hour's break, and this is what they came up with.' Harry motioned with his arm around the rapidly filling recreation area, adding, 'and, as you can see, they knew what they wanted.'

Next, the young man was taken out into the park once more where, hidden amongst the trees, were putting, bowling and crazy golf greens. 'Most people, however, prefer to stroll about, feed the ducks or sunbathe,' Harry commented as they wandered round the lake perimeter. He nodded across to where an obvious bandstand had been sited, 'all of which they can do to the accompaniment of a variety of styles of music'.

As he spoke Andrew noticed a small group laden with string instruments heading down a path toward the bandstand. Already, the park was beginning to fill with employees bent on relaxation after their meals, many of whom were couples holding hands, and soon the air began to fill with music more appropriate to the drawing room than a park, but eminently suitable all the same.

'I can think of one strenuous exercise which would be difficult to prevent,' Andrew remarked.

Harry grinned. 'The woodlands you mean? Well, that's up to them; as long as they're back in time, can do what's expected of them, are discreet and aren't being unfaithful, then no one's bothered.'

'What if they are being unfaithful?'

The manager snorted. 'Then I hope someone's got the decency to tell their spouse or regular lover. After all, you wouldn't like it if your partner was cheating on you, would you? Don't worry, though. Just about every Whyte Islander is reliable; and besides, we're all keepers of our friends and neighbours' morals.'

After the dinner break, Andrew was taken to see more offices, the printing and advertising department, and also Harry's personal office. Presumably, the young man reflected later, the visit to the latter room was meant to demonstrate the lack of privilege attending the managerial position, for Mr Larke's office was small, strictly austere and shared with his secretary, a pleasant middle-aged woman who was far from glamorous. The adjoining boardroom, intended for all types of meetings, was hardly more comfortable than the manager's office, being rather plainly decorated. Even the ubiquitous lengthy table with its great number of matching chairs was unprepossessing.

Between visits to the upper floors in the different buildings, Andrew was able to follow the construction of the various vehicles as they passed from one stage to the next, until at last Harry took him to a large shed where the finished machines awaited shipment. After a quick word with one of the attendants, the manager led his charge to a green saloon at the front of one of the lines of vehicles. 'Get in,' he urged after explaining it was ready for testing, and seating himself behind the steering wheel. With a casualness bordering on recklessness, Harry drove the car out of the shed and down a road which seemed to end at the cliff face. However, as they neared the prominence, Andrew saw a steep roadway had been built up the side.

For the following fifteen to twenty minutes they drove along a metalled down land road which was obviously designed to test the mechanical soundness of the vehicle, because the route took them over hills and into valleys containing inclines of varying degrees, and bends and curves of different radii. Although the road was apparently empty, Andrew was nervous at the way in which the car was being driven, and after Harry had veered right over to the other side upon negotiating a sharp curve, he exclaimed, 'won't there be any traffic coming the other way?'

Obviously enjoying himself immensely, the manager laughed as he changed gear in preparation for a steep climb. 'No,' he replied, 'the circuit is one way only. Every vehicle has to travel in this direction in order to reach the railway. It's a means of ensuring it's ready for export. As you can imagine, Andrew, we get no shortage of volunteers for this job. I don't suppose there's a single person within the complex who hasn't driven a vehicle round here at some time or another. On summer weekends, when the park is sometimes open to the public, the biggest attraction is the opportunity for anyone above the age of fifteen to learn to drive and, eventually, to take a vehicle over the circuit.'

'Don't you have a lot of accidents?'

'Never,' Harry replied emphatically, 'but we have some old cars especially for novice drivers, just in case. We also rarely have breakdowns. But you can see a further reason why we've sited the factory well away from residential areas, there's no one to complain about noise and pollution out here.'

By the time they'd reached the sidings, where they left their car in another large shed, the afternoon tea break was almost due and so they made their way back to the main part of the factory. During the walk Andrew asked, 'how can you produce motor vehicles in bulk whilst denying their personal use to your own people? I mean, isn't it a bit hypocritical?'

His companion seemed highly amused by the observation. 'I think you'll find,' he replied eventually, 'we've implanted all the horrors of private ownership of vehicles so completely into the minds of our countrymen that they wouldn't want them even if they were each given a free car tomorrow. As for building and exporting them ourselves, well, we'd rather we hadn't been put into a situation which forced us to produce them, but we saw an opening for ourselves in the industry so we exploited it.'

He shrugged. 'Anyway, we salved our consciences by producing vehicles which were carbon friendly and extremely strong, for we were horrified at the way the average small vehicle folded up in even comparatively minor collisions; and don't forget we were pioneers in the fitting of audible speed warning indicators for use in built up areas. So, even though we disapprove of private vehicle ownership, we can congratulate ourselves in the knowledge that we've helped to make the practice just that little bit healthier and safer.'

This time, Harry chose a rest room in another workshop. It was of a similar size and layout to the one they'd visited that morning, but the décor was entirely different. During the snack, which consisted of tea and the cakes which replaced the sandwiches of earlier, Harry paused in his conversation on the merits of various sailing rigs with the two men sharing their table, and stared pointedly at Andrew. 'So what do you think of our factory and the working conditions?' he asked.

Caught off guard, the younger man could only say what he

thought. 'I doubt if the production side, and the way the machinery, the workshops offices and stores have been arranged could be bettered, even though I know nothing about the manufacturing industry apart from what I've seen today. From what you've told me about the questionable working conditions in my country, though, this place has to be a great improvement, but I think you might have gone a little too far in the opposite direction.'

Harry chuckled and patted him affectionately on the arm while the other two men grinned. 'So you think we're overindulgent, do you? Well Whyte Islanders appreciate frankness, Andrew, so you'd be alright over here. However, we believe that if it's permissible for executive staff to work in near luxury, then it should be equally so for employees too. In actual fact, all we've done is to upgrade the manual personnel and downgrade the office and managerial staff for the sake of peaceful relations; to be completely mercenary about it, the expenditure on places like this and the main canteen more than compensate for the hours which could be lost through industrial disputes and imaginary illness.' The other men nodded in agreement.

As they left the restroom, the manager said, 'I think you've seen just about everything now, Andrew, but unfortunately we'll have to wait until the first group leaves as there won't be a train until then; so perhaps you'd like to meet some more staff, and then we can watch vehicles being loaded onto a train.'

During their seemingly endless journey through the railway tunnel on the alternate route back to Harbourtown, Andrew asked his companion whether he thought the factory had a secure future. 'I doubt it somehow,' was the candid reply. 'I've already mentioned the cause of the present recession as we see it, and so you'll probably understand why we're pessimistic about a permanent end to the depression, and why we're prepared for the worst.' He paused, then said, 'strangely enough, if a birth control policy were to be adopted on a global scale it would, paradoxically, result in the opening up of new markets to industry which, if planned intelligently, could mean work for all industrial nations. If, for example, all the manufacturing companies agreed not to compete too strongly against each other by overproduction and undercutting, and instead employed people rather than automation, then there would probably be employment for all for a very long time to come.

'Time in which to prevent a return to the uncertainty which we have at the moment, but with all the world's nations getting together, sorting out their differences and coming to a common decision on what they collectively want for the future; rather like survivors in a lifeboat, having been swept onto a desolate coast, re-launching their craft after discussing where they ought to attempt to land next.'

Slightly incredulous, Andrew enquired how birth control could bring about such a revitalisation in the global economy.

'Most of the world's nations have little else more profitable than their soil upon which to base their economies, but that soil could bring them untold wealth if utilised properly, because the earth yields countless materials of benefit to mankind: items such as timber for furniture and house construction, cereals and vegetables for food, herbs, medicines, spices, rubber, paper, various beverages, meat and clothing. Such items are not only invaluable to the native populations, but are also highly valued by industrial nations who, due to climatic considerations, might not be able to grow them.

'The big problem is that ignorance prevents these riches from being grown, let alone harvested, due almost entirely to overpopulation. What happens is that the natural vegetation is cut down for fuel and in order to clear areas for cultivation, but because little fertiliser is put back into the soil the plots become barren eventually, thereby compelling the farmers to move onto another section of forest. Now, when you realise each of these families might include at least five children, then you'll perhaps comprehend the extent of the problem. Entire populations can move over a nation like a swarm of locusts leaving desolation in their wake, and increasing in size as they go. Eventually, a complete country can be turned into a worthless desert, wholly reliant upon outside aid for the sustenance of its people instead of being a self supporting, exporting nation able to create wealth through its natural home-grown produce.'

As if to endorse Harry's point, the train suddenly burst from the tunnel onto an embankment bounded on either side by dense woodland through which a stream flowed, forming a marshy area full of grasses, reeds and tall flowering plants.

'So why don't the more intelligent nations explain to the developing ones the folly of their ways?' Andrew asked.

'Probably because it would be too embarrassing for them. Of all the world's nations, only a few recognise the necessity of a controlled level of population and the mainland isn't one of them. So the remainder could hardly insist upon compulsory birth control for other nations while failing to practice it themselves. As you're possibly aware, Andrew, some senior members of your country's government have large families, so they're unlikely to encourage others to cut back on the size of their future families.

'Because of a mixture of pride, greed and dislike of change, governments, religious bodies of most beliefs, the management of companies, economists, certain criminals and the general public as a whole – in fact, just about everybody – wouldn't entertain the idea of compulsory birth control. I'm afraid world society has become rather like a juggernaut moving down a hillside – slowly at first and so relatively easy to stop, but now gathering speed until it can no longer be halted, doomed to destruction eventually because it had become uncontrollable. Global warming, which will inevitably alter our planet for the worse, is caused not so much by aerial pollution per se, but by the amount created by a grossly overpopulated world.

'But you see, Andrew, if the planet's poorer nations were persuaded to reduce their populations to a level which would ensure not only self support but an ability to export replaceable produce rather than just minerals, then new markets would begin to open up to the industrialised nations. Because the formerly impoverished people of those once deprived countries would then be able to afford the manufactured wares which they would be unable to make on their own account.

'This is what the economics of trade is all about. You export the type of products you are able to make or grow successfully, and import that which you are unable to manufacture or cultivate; nothing is to be gained in the long term by exporting and failing to import, or vice-versa. One unfortunate effect incidentally of no longer having poor nations, is that they would begin to compete with the erstwhile richer nations in the consumption of essential home or imported products such as tea, cotton, rubber and timber, for instance, thereby forcing up prices; but unless the problems of global overpopulation are solved, the increasing loss of cultivatable land will ensure the scarcity of such produce anyway.'

As the train crossed over from its single track onto the mainline,

Andrew said, 'I think you forgot to mention one important source of income for poor nations, Harry, which is tourism.'

'Yes, that can be extremely important, and serves to illustrate why it's so essential to limit the size of the relevant population. Few sightseers are going to travel hundreds or thousands of miles to view a wasteland devoid of flora and fauna, but they will be interested in a varied countryside teeming with life and full of beauty. And tourists will be discouraged from visiting a crime ridden nation which has ruinous buildings, beggars and other signs of grinding poverty. However, unless world trade begins to pick up soon, then tourists will become increasingly uncommon.'

After a brief pause the younger man enquired, 'are many other items manufactured on Whyte Island besides vehicles?'

The manager nodded. 'Quite a number. Where our research and development group have noticed an opening in the market, they've been inclined to exploit it. A few of these developing nations, for example, have been flooding the market with various devices and tools which have often been quite ingenious but spoilt by poor workmanship and inferior materials. So we've occasionally developed some of these items and made them into more reliable articles.

'Another device of ours is to provide backing and amenities to people whom, we feel, have potentially successful ideas. Your country, especially, Andrew, has been blessed with inventive people, yet when they attempt to find support for those ideas they're often met with apathy or disbelief, and even when they do receive funds they often have to struggle on their own in order to produce their device. Such people, having turned to us, not only receive a generous sum but are given a percentage of each item sold, as well as the opportunity to oversee its development and manufacture.

'But all our products, regardless of their origin are, as with our vehicles, of high quality but low in price and we offset our under-pricing by regulating our output. One field we've moved into is the production of double-glazed aluminium windows and doors with strengthened glass. With the rise in the crime rate on the mainland and elsewhere, it seems extraordinary to us that affluent people, who can afford to lose valuables in break-ins, should be able to buy expensive burglar proof windows and doors, while the majority who couldn't afford insurance or the replacement of stolen property, could not. So our output has been aimed primarily at those customers.

'We also manufacture reproduction furniture at low cost, though this industry is only in its early stages at the moment as the bulk of our home grown softwood timber isn't fully mature yet. We're well known too for our fashion industry, which produces relatively inexpensive but good quality clothes. As you saw, we're engaged almost entirely in the manufacture of motor vehicles at the complex, but we're quite prepared to change over to other products should the need arise and as global trends demand.' The remainder of their journey, which was interrupted by frequent station stops, was spent in general conversation.

At the harbour station, Mr Larke took his leave of his companion, explaining that he had a visit to make and adding that if he could be of future assistance to him then Andrew had merely to contact him. The prospect of continuing the rest of his journey alone held little appeal for the young man. However, standing in the bus queue in front of him, he recognised a married couple whom he'd met in the factory and they were only too delighted to renew their acquaintance with him, and so the whole of the bus ride was passed in chatting to them.

Mr Maynard, when he answered the front door to Andrew's knock, greeted him with a concern which seemed almost sarcastic, making it appear as though his guest had performed some particularly wearisome feat. 'Come in,' he exclaimed, 'you must be tired'. He led the way through to the lounge and made his guest sit down in one of the armchairs. 'We're just waiting for Linda to come back and then we'll have dinner,' he explained after bringing a cup of tea, 'but in the meantime just rest yourself, you've had a long day.'

The young man, however, said, 'I've been wondering if you could organise some sort of allowance for me while I'm on the island, Charlie, as I've brought only a little money with me. I can't keep allowing people to pay for me, despite what they say. Perhaps it could be drawn against my future salary.'

Mr Maynard smiled understandingly. 'I'll see what I can do,' he replied.

During the evening, which was spent in relaxation, Andrew related his day's experiences to the Maynards, and they displayed the usual amount of interest by asking him various questions, mostly about what he thought of different features of the complex. Unsurprisingly, Charlie was more interested in the young man's views on the engineering aspect and the finished product, while Helen asked about the catering and welfare, and Linda wanted to know about the secretarial side. It was almost as if he'd been visiting a factory in a foreign land instead of one of Charlie's and Harry's own devising. But Andrew had been on the island long enough to realise such inquisitiveness came from a desire to know exactly what an alien, and therefore disinterested, mind thought about the factory complex in the hope that shortcomings would be revealed, so allowing improvements to be made. But he had nothing new to add in the way of suggestions, for as far as he was concerned the complex was impossible to fault.

Eventually the conversation turned to the subject of Helen's hobby and, with a little persuasion on Andrew's part, she brought forth albums of natural history photographs; there were three in all, enough for one each with Helen seated on the sofa next to Andrew, explaining about each coloured picture. They were, for the most part, really marvellous shots and she had some interesting stories to relate about many of them. Typical was an account of how she'd obtained a photograph of a stoat which was sitting up with its front paws raised in the manner of a begging dog.

'This was one of my earliest snaps,' she explained, 'and also the one which gave me the idea of taking up painting as a hobby. I went out for a walk early one morning, and as I was strolling along a wide down land track between fields of half-grown wheat, I heard a rustling noise in the grass verging the path. Being curious, I stopped and stood motionless. Suddenly, out popped a small reddish brown animal which then ran across the track and disappeared into the cereal on the opposite side. No sooner had this animal, which I recognised as being a stoat, vanished than another emerged from exactly the same place as the first. However, this one came loping along the path toward me. Its route took it right up to my feet and it stopped in order to sniff at one of my boots while I stared down at it in fascination. Then its eyes began to follow up the lines of my legs and body until it was gazing straight back at me...'

'And then you took its photo,' Linda finished off. Both she and Charlie were staring at Helen attentively. Surely, Andrew thought, they must have already heard this story, just as they would have seen her photographs and paintings.

'No,' replied her sister, 'I didn't have a camera with me. Anyway, as soon as our eyes met it casually loped off in the direction its companion had taken. Apparently it's typical of stoats and weasels that, when they realise they've been discovered, they depart in a very nonchalant manner; at least that's what I've subsequently found. But when I got back to the cottage I borrowed dad's book on native wild animals, which I've still got,' – father and daughter exchanged smiles at this remark – 'and I looked up the information on stoats. I discovered, among other facts, that they're reputed to frequently appear at the same place within the hour each day. So twenty three hours later, I waited at the same spot, and along they came; but this time they darted across from one field to the other and so I barely glimpsed them.

'Anyway, this visit was only so I could have proof that the information was correct. But to shorten a long story, I began leaving pieces of raw meat and then hiding beneath a blanket on the verge, as there weren't any bushes or other cover in the vicinity.' She laughed. 'I would have seemed peculiar if anyone had come along. My stoats found the meat immediately the first day I positioned it, although they were very wary to begin with, sniffing at it and then jumping away, but eventually they dragged my offerings off, presumably to devour them elsewhere. At first I just got a thrill out of watching them, but then I thought how nice it would be to take some photos so I could remember them forever. I was quite pleased with the result and decided that these, and others which I subsequently took would be nice to paint. Of course, I'd only received a basic education in art, but I went along to evening classes where I was able to improve my technique considerably.'

During this narrative, Helen had continued to turn over the pages of the album, showing further excellent photographs of wildlife subjects. 'It must take plenty of patience to snap these animals, especially,' Andrew said with admiration, the album in question apparently being entirely devoted to mammals, 'but how on earth do you do it?'

The girl exchanged books with her father and began to show her companion the new set of photographs which appertained to all kinds of plant life, from giant trees down to mosses and lichens. 'Patience, yes,' she replied, 'but also a fair amount of knowledge, in addition to plenty of optimism. You need to be able to judge which places and times of day and night are best for seeing a particular species, especially most animals and a few birds, but above all you need to have the confidence that what you're waiting for should eventually turn up, although you ought to be prepared for disappointment. When I began to take up the pastime in earnest, I was often filled with self doubt, but after I'd seen most of the island's species of mammals once or twice due to my efforts my pessimism soon faded, because I then knew I could see them any time I wished.

'But it's thanks to dad and the rest of the island's administration that I and anyone else who's keenly interested in natural history, can observe all these creatures whenever we want to. Because you see, Andrew, none of our animal species is particularly rare, for not only have the various habitats been preserved but no hunting as such is permitted over here. Nature has been allowed to balance itself. One often hears the term vermin applied to different animals in other countries which encroach upon human food sources, et cetera, but it's often conveniently overlooked that it's we humans who are causing all the problems. Many creatures do take advantage of what we have to offer, but we also take advantage of them, just as we do of our fellow humans; but because we continually destroy their own food sources and habitats they can be blamed even less for trying to survive at our expense.'

'Don't you destroy any wildlife then?' Andrew enquired.

It was Charlie who answered. 'Some rabbits and hares are taken for food in rural districts, and deer, being too big to be predated, naturally have to be culled to check their populations, while pigeons, rats and mice are trapped in urban areas. But the work is carried out by professionals as local people aren't allowed to own guns. That's how accidents happen. Nature, though, generally provides its own antidotes for small creatures. Foxes and members of the weasel family, as well as birds of prey can be relied upon to keep them down to reasonable levels if they aren't disturbed. Unfortunately, mankind has still yet to learn the consequences of interfering too much in the balance of nature.'

He smiled wryly to himself. 'It can be quite amusing when you consider the relationship between a mainland farmer and the owner of an adjacent shooting estate, for example; as a reward for allowing fox hunting, the trapping of predatory animals and the shooting of aerial predators, all creatures traditionally dangerous to game birds, and also for returning those birds having fallen on his land, the farmer is often given the benefit of some shooting on his neighbour's preserve. However, he might then scratch his head and wonder why he has a surfeit of rabbits, voles, rats, mice and woodpigeons, all of which are busily consuming his produce at a great rate.

'But I ought to add, Andrew, that although we're quite content to allow nature a free hand, we do take a regular census, undertaken by people like Helen and school children, which gives us a rough idea of the numbers of our various creatures, and this ensures none of them increases beyond a reasonable level. If they did, then we'd be more than willing to take remedial action.'

'Our way of combating so called pests,' Helen said, 'is not only by merely allowing their predators to get on with the job, but we actively encourage their presence by providing nest sites and perches for owls and other birds of prey, and dense woodland and hedge runs for foxes, stoats and other such creatures. On the other hand, we make certain that neither the predators or the prey make nuisances of themselves by ensuring both our urban and rural environments are kept clean, and free from places which they can exploit to their own advantage.' Obviously noticing an expression of perplexity on Andrew's face, she went on hurriedly. 'We don't have open rubbish tips throughout town and country, nor do we have deliberately ruinous buildings or abandoned machinery lying about, all of which are palaces to rodents. On farms the barns and henhouses, for instance, have been especially designed to keep out potentially harmful creatures.'

'This is one very good example of where our form of dictatorial government can prove superior to your system, Andrew,' Charlie interposed. 'On the surface, it can be laudable to be able to do whatever you wish, including having a home and garden which are both untidy, or running a farm which is tumbledown, filthy and uneconomical, but it would be impossible for the government of a country wherein such owners dwelt, to take any real and permanent action to improve the health and wealth of its citizens. But our method by which we ensure that only the most suitable people fill the positions and employment particularly appropriate to them means we can almost move mountains, because if they weren't compliant with our wishes then they wouldn't be suitable, would they? In the case of our farmers and others who work the land, they exchange their freedom to manage their holdings well or badly for security. As long as they continue to run their establishments efficiently and properly according to our precepts then they needn't worry about bad harvests, diseased stock, building repairs, new machinery, labour problems, overwork or poor soil, because it'll all be automatically taken care of.'

While Mr Maynard had been explaining, his guest had continued to look through Helen's album of plant photographs, and so he'd scarcely taken in the information aimed at him. However, following a pause, he thought he ought to make some comment so he said, 'going back to what you said about nature controlling itself, Charlie, have you any real proof? Can you give me any instances?'

The older man laughed. 'The mere fact that our planet hasn't been entirely overrun by just one given species is surely proof enough, though we humans appear to be trying our best. But one very good example is the case of the field vole. You explain, Helen, while I make some tea.'

'Well, occasionally in former times this little rodent,' the girl began, 'reached such large numbers that it attained plague proportions; but almost as soon as that happened all kinds of predator moved in and began to devour them. Especially evident were birds of prey, and these began to lay far bigger egg clutches than would otherwise be the case. Of course, the vole plague would only be a brief phenomenon, and so the predators would have needed to move away or else die.'

'Nature's wonderful, but cruel,' sighed Linda who hitherto had been too interested in examining the contents of the albums to say anything.

When Charlie returned with the tea, he suggested that his older daughter might like to take their guest up to her room to show him her paintings. 'As you can perhaps imagine,' she said as she preceded Andrew out of the room, 'they're a bit too big to bring down, and there are quite a few of them.'

To the young man, Helen's room was full of character; that it was some kind of studio was evident from the large skylight, as well as the big window in the end wall both of which helped the room seem much larger than it actually was. One wall was almost covered in paintings of different sizes, while the latest as yet unfinished, reposed on an easel in one corner. All, without exception, were devoted to natural history subjects. The room also contained a divan which doubled as a bed, a pair of wardrobes, a chest of drawers, a dressing table and several easy chairs. Immediately he saw the paintings, Andrew went over to study them. He knew virtually nothing about art, but it was obvious that many of the pictures were in different styles. In each case, though, the texture was similar: the paint being spread very thin and smooth, the exact opposite of the coarse daubs so often to be found in oil paintings.

'I've arranged them in chronological order,' Helen mentioned as soon as she'd joined him. 'Look, you can see how my style has developed.' She went over to the far corner and returned with a fine study of a bird of prey which she then held alongside the first picture on the wall. The comparison was truly remarkable, for not only was the colour far brighter than on the latter example but the clarity and detail was also a great improvement. 'You'll notice how I've only roughly coloured in the background of this latest picture but increased the foreground detail, whereas I tried to make everything appear equally clear in my first attempts, thus ignoring the examples of the old masters.'

'You've also made your studies more interesting,' Andrew declared, hastily adding, 'I mean given them some activity instead of being just mere portraits. This one for instance.' He was standing before a picture featuring an animal in an upright stance with a mass of flowers and foliage dominating the background. Perched upon a twig just out of reach of the animal was a small bird displaying a mixture of curiosity and fear in its posture and eye. 'It's fantastic,' he exclaimed in admiration. 'Is that a stoat?'

She shook her head. 'No, it's a weasel. You can tell by the absence of a black tip at the end of its tail and the small brown island below the main brown upper colouring on its cheek.'

Without thinking, he replied, 'the people whose house we stayed at the other night had a weasel in their garden.' There was a moment's silence then, in order to cover his embarrassment, he asked, 'but how did you manage capture that moment's action?'

She smiled. 'By trickery. I chose a photo of a weasel from my collection, and another of an appropriate bird, then I went out and looked for a suitable backdrop to the drama. It was then relatively simple to compose a picture featuring all three subjects.'

'I think your paintings are marvellous', he answered, then

asked, 'this isn't all your work, is it?'

'No. I've given away most of my pictures,' she laughed. 'I wouldn't have had room to move if I'd kept them all.' She'd scarcely finished speaking when Linda called up to tell them there was a snack awaiting them downstairs.

During the meal, Andrew looked through the album dedicated to bird photographs, and while he was doing so Charlie said, 'I believe you haven't got anything planned for tomorrow, have you Andrew?' He shook his head. 'Then why don't you take the day off, Helen, and both go on a nature ramble?'

She considered the idea for a moment. 'I'll see if I can think up something,' she replied.

Shortly before the family retired for the night, Andrew managed to get Linda alone. 'Would it be alright if I called on you later?' he asked, wishing to know whether her coolness toward him was real or imaginary.

She passed a hand across her brow in a significantly weary manner. 'I'd rather you didn't,' she answered, 'because I feel a bit tired and I'm expecting my period at any moment. Still, if it's a cuddle you want then you can drop in by all means'.

This reference to a most feminine function had an almost inevitable effect upon him for, although being far from prudish, he felt that his presence in her bed at such a time would be an unjustified intrusion. So as she eyed him covertly, obviously awaiting a decision, he replied, 'well, if you're tired I won't trouble you.' He placed a hand on each of her shoulders to show he didn't really mind, kissed her on the forehead and then went off to sleep alone.

Andrew was awoken next morning by Helen knocking at his door. He glanced across at the clock, six fifty five his mind half registered. 'Oh, no,' he muttered to himself as he crawled wearily out of his bed. He was fully aware by now that the older Maynard daughter was something of a fanatic, but he had expected to have a lie in on a free day, at least. Half asleep, he went off to have a shower and then dressed, choosing sweater and jeans as being most suitable.

Helen awaited him in the kitchen. 'Come on you lazy devil,' she chided cheerfully. 'I've been up ages, and I've made a pile of sandwiches'. He was gratified to note she wore clothing similar to his own. 'The others are still in bed,' she told him as she placed a

57

bowl of porridge before him, 'but dad said you can borrow his binoculars, as I'll be using mine.'

'Where are we going, then?' But she wouldn't tell him.

Expecting to be taken for a stroll along one of the adjacent lanes or tracks, he was therefore quite surprised when she took him outside and showed him two cycles. 'You've got dad's bike,' she said.

It was another bright sunny morning with a slight breeze as they set off along the little lane in the direction of the village in the valley. Andrew, who had been burdened with a rucksack, found it hard work pedalling up to the summit of the ridge while his companion, leading the way without a load, cycled merrily along calling back the names of various birds to him. 'Bullfinch, and tree sparrow,' he heard her call, but other names were lost to the moving air.

Once over the ridge, however, and the ride became a joy. With Helen still leading, they freewheeled down the hill, brakes partly on and bells sounding. 'Just in case of people or traffic,' she shouted back, though there was little possibility of either at that hour of the morning he'd considered ruefully as the wind whistled past him. He also thought of the ride back, which wouldn't be quite so fast or easy. At their breakneck speed, it wasn't long before they reached the village, but to his surprise they didn't cross the railway bridge. Instead, Helen led the way down the road to the station.

Following his companion, Andrew walked his cycle through the station entrance. Unlike his previous visit, there was someone behind the glass of the booking office. 'Two returns to Parlam, please Ken,' the girl requested.

'Hello, Helen. Off to the reserve, are you? You've got a nice day for it.' Recognising the name and voice of his erstwhile companion, Andrew peered into the narrow window of the office and greeted him. 'Oh, I didn't know you two were acquainted,' the railwayman continued. 'I've been trying to run off with Helen for ages, and you manage it within a few days!'

'Andrew's staying with us,' she replied soberly, though still enjoying the banter. 'Besides, he belongs to Linda. I've only got him on loan'.

'I thought everyone belonged to your sister,' Ken answered shrewdly.

After parking their cycles in the racks provided, they crossed over the footbridge and took a seat on one of the many benches. There were about a dozen passengers on each platform, but no one paid them the slightest attention, doubtless assuming them to be a couple of lovers wishing to be left alone. Andrew, however, was thinking about the recent exchange which had taken place between Ken and his companion. He was annoyed because the reference to Linda's easy virtue had seemed an insult to his ability to obtain a decent girl; and besides, he considered Helen's comment about her sister to be disloyal. Eventually he voiced his thoughts. 'I thought you once told me Whyte Islanders don't talk about others behind their backs?'

She replied, somewhat casually, 'you mean what Ken and I said about Linda being free and easy with her favours? Everyone knows it and she admits to it, so it's quite legitimate to mention it. We were only having a joke you know, and there's no stigma attached to what she's doing. She's actually doing a social service.' She glanced at him and, noticing the expression of anguish on his face, took hold of his hands. 'You don't need to take it to heart, love. She's only one of lots of island girls free at the moment. If you got on well with her then you'll succeed with one of them. She just doesn't like to tie herself down. I bet within a week or so you'll have a regular female companion. Have you come across any likely candidates yet?'

He was about to shake his head when he remembered the auburn haired slave girl, so he told his companion about her, though he omitted to mention how he'd put her off. She listened intently and when he'd finished observed, 'you know, Linda's quite a caring person underneath her casual manner, so don't be surprised if your slave turns up out of the blue, but don't say anything to Linda. In fact, forget all about it. Look, here comes our train.'

Despite his assumption that he'd lost the redhead for good and the sadness it brought him, he always looked forward to seeing one of the many railway locomotives the island seemed to possess, so with his companion's last words he turned his head expectantly to watch the approaching train. The engine was similar to the one which had hauled the train upon his visit to the Education Centre and green school, though this machine was painted green. Its most striking feature was a fitting like an upturned flower pot on top of the boiler and this, together with a number plate on the cab side, beading on the wheel splashers, with a large nameplate on the middle one, and a wide band below the chimney rim, was made of gleaming brass which the paintwork set off beautifully. As the locomotive steamed slowly past them he thought he'd rarely seen a more magnificent sight.

During their somewhat brief journey on the train, Andrew, his spirits rising a little, couldn't refrain from imparting some of his enthusiasm for the railways to Helen. She in turn displayed great interest in what he had to say, and eventually said, 'would you like me to ask dad if you could visit the sheds tomorrow? I think they're pretty quiet on Sundays.'

'I'd like nothing better,' he replied, 'but wouldn't it be difficult to arrange at short notice?'

She smiled and shook her head. 'It'll only take a phone call to one of the many enthusiasts. Apparently they have the run of the place at weekends. I'll call dad from the station, if you wish.'

On the walk from Parlam station down to the reserve, she told him about the current warden. 'Brian's a very nice person, but he spent quite a lot of his life on the mainland and certain aspects of that experience gave him severe depression.'

Without considering his question, Andrew said, 'Why? Was he a drug addict, then?'

She replied with an expressionless face. 'Not quite, he was a clergyman. But all I'm going to say is that he's inclined to run on a bit, so be warned.'

The station had been sited on the outskirts of the village and so there were no houses on the lane leading down to the reserve. Through the hedgerows bordering on either side he could see the yellow brown of the reed beds stretching away into apparent infinity, though topped here and there by willows and other water tolerant trees and shrubs. Far away in front of them were more substantial stands of trees. Every so often he stopped to test his binoculars on objects near and far while Helen talked about the reserve with obvious enthusiasm. 'We not only get a lot of rare birds here,' she finally said, 'but some of the plants and insects which used to be common on the mainland, especially in marshland areas, are flourishing.'

After some two hundred yards the lane ended at a double barred gate, beyond which could be seen the thatched roof and upper floor of a brick built cottage, and nearby was a white painted wooden footbridge which, Andrew presumed, spanned the river. Seated on a bench outside the cottage, smoking a pipe, was a bearded man whom he judged to be about fifty. 'I thought you'd might be on one of the early trains, Helen,' he said as he rose to meet them, 'so I decided to wait for you before I set off.'

After introductions had been made Helen asked if there had been anything special observed in the area lately. Brian reeled off a list of names from memory which meant nothing to Andrew but obviously a great deal to the girl for she frequently raised her eyebrows in surprise, and said, 'good', or 'that's nice', as she did so.

Immediately afterwards the warden led the way over the bridge. The young man noticed as he crossed that the river had been channelled between raised banks on either side for a considerable distance, a fact of which he'd been previously unaware due to some concealing thickets. 'That's because the marsh is below river level,' explained Helen. 'The construction of these banks was only the first of a number of jobs which had to be completed before this area could become a wildlife reserve.'

'Yes,' agreed their guide. 'When we first arrived, this was all flat marshland, so machinery such as diggers, earth movers and lorries were brought over on pontoon bridges. It was really hectic at first because an earth moving vehicle had to take soil from the marsh bottom in order to make a path for itself, and when you consider, Andrew, there are twenty three miles of path this side of the river and another nine on the other, not counting the tops of the dykes, then you can imagine how slow and difficult it all was.

'What we've tried to do is have a series of different habitats connected by paths. We've built deep lakes and shallow ones, some large and others small. Some further down the valley are tidal, connected to the river by inlets, and others are not. We've raised some parts so they're permanently dry, while other areas are semi- or continuously wet woodlands. Most of the trees you'll see are marsh tolerant species such as birches, willows and alders, many varieties of which are exotic to this part of the world, but we've also planted other types of trees and shrubs from different regions, and this is one of the reasons why this reserve is unique. We want to make a scientific study of not only what different habitats various plants like, but also what plants different birds, animals and insects prefer. Just imagine, in about twenty years time this place will be really exciting, a botanical garden as well as a nature reserve!'

Brian's enthusiasm was curbed only by their arrival at the first of many viewing stations. Andrew was full of admiration at the way the reserve had been laid out. The path they were on was dead level, packed hard with surface shingle and wide enough to take a large vehicle. On either side was a ditch from which grew rows of tall reeds which, Helen explained, helped to keep them concealed from the wildlife surrounding them, besides helping to muffle visitor noise.

Each time they reached a habitat, a path led off to a hide, the name for an observation hut, which enabled them to watch the wildlife without being seen in return. To Andrew, the glass in the picture windows seemed perfectly clear, but Brian mentioned the panes had been fitted at an angle from top to bottom to create a reflection from the outside through which the wildlife couldn't see. All the hide interiors they visited were comfortable with upholstered seats, tables and even coat hooks, so the temporary inhabitants could feel really relaxed for many hours study if they so wished. At least one of the walls would have a diagram of many of the birds and other creatures which might be expected to visit the relevant hide, and a list of the more notable animals was provided for visitors to tick off to aid study of the given site. In this way, the young man was able to watch the denizens of fenland, sea marsh, lake, pond, heath and meadow, as well as coniferous, mixed and deciduous woodland in comfort and ease, and with two experts to tell him the names and habits of every living creature he saw.

As it was mid-spring, the sound of birdsong was only too obvious, every bush and tree seemed to have its own songster, while waterfowl called and gulls screamed incessantly on the lake and marshland sites. The most melodious habitat was where the hills came down to reserve level. A hide had been built to look down over woodland which had plenty of undergrowth in the form of bushes, briars, brambles, gorse and nettle beds. This seemed to be an area much favoured by small birdlife, for the different species appeared to be rivalling each other in the intensity of their song.

'Listen, Andrew!' Helen exclaimed excitedly. 'Nightingales.'

With much description and instruction he was eventually able to identify the song of the birds, two in all, even though he couldn't see them. 'They often sing by day despite their evocative name,' Brian said, 'though thanks to man's thoughtlessness they're rarely heard by day or night on the mainland now.' Andrew asked why. 'Like many birds they're very choosy about where they live; they're very shy and like to skulk in dense undergrowth. It's possible to stand within feet of them when they're singing and not be able to see them, and then you'll get just too close and they'll fly off. You probably won't see them even then. But the wild scrubland which they and many other small birds prefer is becoming very rare in your country. Mainlanders seem to consider land which isn't making money for them to be worthless, so it has to be utilised.

'Do you know what one of the most important aspects of this reserve is, Andrew?' He shook his head. 'Propaganda,' Brian stated. 'For children, especially. To show them how beautiful, interesting and useful nature can be, to stop them from becoming like, I'm sorry, Andrew, morons in your own country, where overcrowding and greed means intensive farming, huge industrial sites and massive housing estates. These are wanted more than hedgerows, woodlands, heaths and marshes; your people are becoming selfish introverts playing with computers and other...'

'Andrew is a guest, Brian,' Helen reminded him.

But the warden, not to be stopped, tried a different tack. After apologising he asked, 'do you know I used to be a cleric?' The younger man thought it politic to deny that knowledge. 'Well, I was brought up to believe God created the world and everything in it. Therefore I reasoned the world with all its living creatures was sacrosanct. When I first became a clergyman I didn't think for myself but followed the creed of my religion to the letter. I subsequently volunteered for overseas service where I eventually witnessed scenes of terrible squalor. Men and women were starving and dying of disease. They would procreate and while their children died of starvation and illness, they'd have others. They would cut down trees for fuel and to clear patches to scrape a living for a few years, and when the land became exhausted they'd cut down more jungle.

'I saw whole rainforests with swamps and rivers become dry, dusty deserts. Birds and animals, insects and plants quickly disappeared, and soon there was little life evident. My mother church didn't seem to be at all worried by this aspect but continued to pour torrents of money, donated by well meaning but unworldly people residing in the richer nations, in the form of food and medicine into the natives, when all they really wanted was advice on contraception, the useful herding of cattle and the correct methods of farming. In some cases, my church even encouraged them to continue reproducing children.

'Eventually I was so sickened by all the single-minded destruction that I applied to return home. My request was quickly granted and, perhaps as a punishment for being a nuisance, I was subsequently given a living in the middle of a slum where my flock were all ardent church followers, at least as far as reproduction was concerned. Ten or eleven children in a single family wasn't unusual; none of these would die of malnutrition or disease because this was a civilised country and so the state paid for welfare, but when the children grew up there would inevitably be no work for them. There could never be, as there wasn't the industrial demand to encourage the building of factories. So such fresh adults turned to a variety of crimes for a living, and violence and vandalism as a relief from boredom. Because these people received a meagre allowance from the state, they couldn't afford to pay rates, and so neglect and vandalism turned the area into a nightmare. I reasoned that smaller families would work wonders, but no one in authority in my church would listen to my argument as it was against the creed. So because they wouldn't pay attention I left the church and as I couldn't obtain suitable work I fell upon hard times. One day I was sitting on a park bench feeling very depressed when a man came along, and suddenly I was pouring my heart out to him.'

'Mr Maynard?' Andrew suggested.

Brian nodded. 'It was a miracle', he laughed, adding, 'if I still believed in such a phenomena anymore, as he was only on a flying visit to a nearby factory and had decided to take a stroll before returning to Whyte Island.'

At the next hide, which allowed views over an area of gorse, heather and brambles, Helen, whom Andrew could see was annoyed, laid out sandwiches and coffee. 'This habitat,' observed Brian, apparently unaware of her mood, 'can be quite disappointing as little ever seems to happen, but if we're lucky we might see a very uncommon little bird which has more or less been driven off the mainland because too much of its heathland home has been built upon.'

But although they stayed for half an hour while they ate their meal they were disappointed, the most interesting birds being several pairs of linnets and a whitethroat. Pointing to this last bird, the warden said, 'one of the legion of birds, like swallows and swifts, which visit our continent in order to breed during the warm months and to consume an enormous amount of insects and their larvae. Having seen the destruction of rain forest and the resultant spread of desert, I can't help wondering what sort of affect it'll all have on such useful creatures, because many have to pass through, or live in that desolation. It also makes me wonder what might happen to global weather, because jungles create damp, humid heat day and night thereby maintaining a steady average temperature, while deserts fry during the day and freeze at night. No doubt when all the forests have gone and terrible things start to happen climatically, then scientists will start making regretful noises, just as they did after the nuclear bomb tests'.

In all, Andrew saw twenty five different habitats during his tour. Two were especially impressive. One was where a tree top walk took them around a splendid oak. Brian explained that it was intended primarily for viewing special kinds of butterflies later on in the year, but that it was also to enable tree dwelling warblers and flycatchers to be observed. 'Eventually,' he explained, 'the walk will be extended, as the whole of this area has been planted with many of the different species of oaks to be found throughout the world, but it'll take ages for them to attain maturity, of course.'

The other exceptional site was a hide set in the middle of a lake, which was reached by way of a tunnel of concrete pipes some six feet in diameter. The viewing position was a circular building also constructed of concrete but with tinted plate glass windows which allowed observation in all directions. 'When people go bird watching specifically for wildfowl,' said Helen, 'it can be very frustrating because the birds are often in the middle of a stretch of water or mudflat; but here you can see them at point blank range, and at water level. It's a little quiet at the moment, but later on it can be really thrilling for those hoping for a rarity when the birds are over-wintering.'

At last they arrived back at the footbridge, Andrew's aching feet telling him he'd covered many a mile during their tour. The trip had taken so long that it was now early evening and a few bats had joined the swallows and martins in hawking for flies along the river and paths. Outside his cottage, Brian invited them to be seated on the bench and, going inside, he shortly returned carrying first one, and then a second bowl of hot soapy water, into which both his visitors gratefully plunged their feet. Helen even delved into her rucksack and brought forth a change of socks each. 'I'll be having a shower later,' Brian commented by way of explanation, then added, 'since you shared your food with me, I'm compelling you to have supper with us.'

Angela, the warden's pretty and charming wife, had obviously taken their acceptance for granted because the table was already laid for five, and almost as soon as they were seated plates containing generous portions of steak and kidney pie, mashed potatoes and Brussels sprouts were placed before them, but no one started until Angela had taken her seat. Andrew was able to appreciate at first hand the self discipline of Whyte Island children, for Wendy who, like her mother, had glossy black hair and large brown eyes, was perfectly correct being neither shy nor inclined to show off. He was only too aware that a similarly aged girl on the mainland would naturally be guilty of at least one of the misdemeanours when in the presence of a stranger in her home. Whilst he ate, he couldn't refrain from admiring the room they were seated in, a comfortable, cosy place quite in keeping with the rustic exterior of the cottage, and as homely as the meal he was consuming.

During the main course everybody remained silent, but after Angela had served up apple pie and cream followed later by coffee, conversation began. 'You liked the reserve then?' Brian asked.

'Very much,' Andrew replied, 'and judging by the large number of people about later on, I wasn't the only one. But it's the first reserve I've ever visited so I won't be able to draw comparisons for you.'

'In that case, you've been most fortunate,' Helen remarked, 'because you'd probably be disappointed if you went to the average one on the mainland, wouldn't he Brian?'

The warden nodded. 'When I was working in my slum parish I used to feel so miserable that on many Saturday mornings I'd get my motorbike out and go down to a marshland reserve on the coast. Well, the people who ran the place charged a fair bit for entry and the use of half a dozen hides. I suppose they'd done quite a lot of initial work to entice the birds and make them easily visible to the watchers, but subsequently nothing ever seemed to change, except the price of admittance always appeared to increase regularly. It was a good site to visit because it commanded a migration route and so there was always the possibility of something unusual dropping in, but the reserve catered almost exclusively for waterfowl and wading birds, so if you saw anything not in those two groups it was a bonus. It could be incredibly boring at times. Some of the hide areas seemed to have been completely abandoned by the birds, and I soon began to wonder just what the warden was doing to justify the price of entry. It made me think of what I'd do if I was in his place.'

'You've just seen the results, Andrew,' Angela stated.

'Do you work on the reserve?' he asked her.

She laughed. 'Mostly in a psychological capacity. My husband gets plenty of help from the island's many nature lovers in addition to other jobbers. He only has to whistle for them to come flocking'.

Andrew turned to Brian. 'But you don't look after the reserve all the time, do you?'

'Oh, no. Just like every other adult male I've got other jobs, but this is our permanent home. The other chief warden lives up in Parlam village.'

'But regardless of whether it's your turn or not, you still seem to disappear across that river every five minutes,' his wife exclaimed ruefully. But Brian merely grinned and shrugged.

While they waited for their train, Andrew asked his companion, 'does Brian still believe in a god?'

'If you can call my father a god, then he does. Otherwise, no. You can hardly blame him. As a professional man of religion, it was his duty to love his fellow creatures, be they humans or beasts. Brian did so passionately, and so he couldn't understand why nearly all living things had to give way to the pressures imposed by an expanding human population; and loving mankind, too, he couldn't comprehend why people needed to increase in such numbers when starvation, poverty, selfishness and crime appeared to be the only result. Presumably, he prayed to his god seeking some form of enlightenment, and like so many others before him his prayers were doubtless ignored, so then he did something which no true cleric should ever do in all honesty and survive – he began questioning the creed in his mind.

'It was just like a Private soldier questioning a General's right to command him in battle; and the outcome was he lost faith in his religion and God. My dad, without realising, changed him into a complete atheist, for he gave him the means to create his own personal paradise, which was something his god and religion were unable to do. Brian's contented now, but he isn't entirely happy because he knows that outside this island the creatures he loves are still under immense pressure, and we all join him in hoping one day all the other nations will emulate our way of life and realise nothing is to be gained by overpopulation.'

For much of the time Helen had been speaking, Andrew had been idly watching a plume of smoke and a pair of illuminated headlamps far down the track approaching in the deepening twilight until, with her last words, the locomotive and its train rolled into the station and came to a halt. 'As it's such a nice evening,' he said when they were comfortably seated, 'shall we have a drink in the Station Arms?'

'What, so you can see the lie of the land for Wednesday?' she smiled, 'or because you want to delay our journey back for as long as possible? As you wish.'

It was obvious to him that the public house had been very aptly named, for the interior of the bar could have passed for a railway museum. Every wall seemed to be covered with wagon work plates, station name boards, engine names and various photographs and paintings of railway subjects, oil lamps were suspended from the ceiling and a red and white painted signal arm graced one wall, while a yellow and black arm was fitted to another.

The young man thought, however, that the most fascinating item in the bar was to be seen inside a glass case fixed, at head height, to the wall. It was a perfect model of a passenger locomotive, and as he was gazing at it appreciatively he was joined by Helen, who had just returned from the ladies room. 'Watch this,' she said and inserted a coin into a hidden slot. Very slowly, hardly perceptible at first, the main wheels began to rotate, whilst the various rods and bars which made up the driving mechanism began to move back and forth or up and down. Gradually the moving parts increased in speed until the wheels and levers were little more than a blur, while the bulk of the model remained stationary, the rotating wheels not being in contact with the short length of track. When the speed had reached its peak, the mechanism began to slow down until eventually it was motionless once more. 'I suppose you could say it's a little twee for this modern day and age,' she commented as they turned to find a seat, 'but once, apparently, similar models were commonplace on the larger mainland stations. Still, it's the craftsmanship which should be admired most, not so much the ability to perform.'

Shortly after they'd sat down with their drinks, Helen, her gaze having casually surveyed the room and its occupants, said, 'that's strange' when she came to the piano which stood beneath the red and white signal arm. Standing up, she went across and sat down on the piano stool. Casually, much to Andrew's surprise, she then began to play. The result was a piece of music entirely in sympathy with the décor of the bar, for it was a boogie-woogie, the notes of which obviously having been inspired by the clanging and clashing of the driving rods on a steam locomotive.

She emulated the model by starting off slowly and then gradually building up to full speed with her right hand providing an appropriate melody, before finishing slowly once more. Her companion was astonished as he'd never suspected her of such a talent; she was by no means perfect as she faltered on several notes, but no one appeared to notice or care, as Andrew ascertained when he glanced at the clientele while she was playing, each one of whom wore a smile of contentment as they nodded, and tapped their feet in time to the rhythm.

When Helen finished the number and rose to go, there was much applause, cheers and cries for more, but apparently much embarrassed she shook her head and returned to her seat. 'That was marvellous,' he greeted her as she sat down. 'I didn't know you could play the piano.'

'Most islanders can manage a musical instrument. That's why I thought it unusual no one else was playing. Look,' she added as someone took her place at the piano, 'I've started them off. Let's go before they think we're being rude by leaving while they're performing.' So they quickly finished their drinks and departed.

As soon as they'd retrieved their cycles from where they'd left them against the public house wall, Helen suggested they have a race to see who could get the furthest up the hill without stopping. Andrew readily agreed, though he realised he probably wouldn't stand a chance. And so it proved for, with a final shout of warning not to forget to engage his dynamo, his companion rode off into the darkness, and he wasn't to see her again until he'd toiled a considerable distance on foot from where his cycle had eventually come to a standstill.

A lesser person would have greeted him with the words, 'what kept you?' or some other semi-derisive remark, but Helen, and presumably most other islanders, was far less insensitive. 'Hello,' she welcomed from the gloom, 'I'm sorry, but it wasn't really a fair contest because both Linda and I, and dad occasionally, used to have races up this hill, so we used to know exactly when to change gears.'

The hill was so steep in places they needed all their energy just to keep moving, and so they trudged along without speaking, while the moon rose in the sky. On one occasion they passed a strolling couple though, tactfully, no pleasantries were exchanged. At last they reached the level area where the woodland commenced and Andrew began to mount his cycle, but she placed a delaying hand on his wrist. 'No, wait,' she urged. 'It's so beautiful here, listen'.

Far beyond the point where the moon-silvered trunks of the beeches stood, a noise like that made by a free wheeling bicycle rose and fell. 'That's a nightjar,' she whispered. And as he listened, Andrew became aware of other sounds. He correctly identified aloud the songs of several nightingales and, not quite so distant as the nightjar, a tawny owl on a hunting foray called repeatedly. There was also much rustling in the roadside herbage, and numerous insects flew about whirring, prey to the several bats which flew along the course of the lane and in and out of the trees. Helen resumed walking and he fell into step alongside her. He couldn't help wishing Linda was present and available or, preferably, the red-haired slave girl, for the still night with its moon and herbal perfume was surely made for love. But he wasn't going to risk making another move toward his present companion as he'd received enough rebuffs at her hands, which he felt was a pity, as she looked even more attractive than usual in the moonlight. And so they walked directly home to the cottage which was in darkness when they reached it, where, after a brief discussion of the day's events over coffee, they retired to their respective beds.

Once again, he was awoken by Helen outside his door, and as soon as she heard his answer she called, 'breakfast's nearly ready, and dad and Linda are both starving.' So it didn't take him long to shower, dress and repair to the kitchen upon receipt of this none too subtle hint.

During the meal, Andrew underwent the usual friendly interrogation about their adventures of the previous day, assisted by

Helen, but when the subject had been exhausted his thoughts turned to his planned outing of the day, and he wanted to know what he ought to wear. 'Will I need a boiler suit?' he asked.

Charlie Maynard smiled. 'No, lad, you'll be alright as you are. It's going to be a lot cleaner than you obviously expect.'

With a forthrightness which surprised even himself, he then turned to a rather subdued and quiet Linda. 'Are you coming with me?' She shook her head, but before she could offer an excuse he went on. 'In that case, as it's a nice day, would you like to walk some of the way with me?'

Much to his surprise she agreed with alacrity, and so some fifteen minutes later he was walking along the lane once more, but this time with the younger sister by his side. 'You're cooling off me, aren't you?' he said eventually. 'That remark about your prospective period was intended to put me off. Well, I wish you could have been a bit more frank with me. I always thought Whyte Islanders were supposed to be candid.'

Her reply was slow in coming, and then only after much consideration. 'I'm sorry, Andy. I admit I should have been more honest with you but I only wanted to let you off gently. You know, I keep on underestimating your dependence upon me, probably because we're so easy going together when it came to forming a relationship. You and I were just having a little fun together and I assumed you realised that, and that now was the time for us to go our separate ways, so I thought my distant attitude toward you would be enough to make you realise.'

They walked on for a time in silence, and then Linda stopped. 'I'd better not come any further. You'll be late.'

He turned and faced her, raising his arms in a gesture of hopelessness. 'But what do I do now?' he exclaimed petulantly. 'You know how much I like lovemaking and feminine company. Helen won't let me touch her, I've lost that little slave girl and now you! So what does a fellow do over here when he needs a girl?'

She smiled kindly. 'Someone will be along very soon, you'll see.' Then she said, as if a sudden idea had come to her, 'if you haven't got a girl by, say… Thursday, then I'll become your lover again until someone turns up. That's a promise. Now, enjoy yourself.' And she turned around and walked off.

Andrew continued down the lane with very mixed feelings, but in order to stem his thoughts he stepped out and so it wasn't too long before he arrived at the station. Fortunately for his piece of mind Ken, the railwayman, wasn't on duty as he was in no mood for banter about girls, or the lack of them. Although he'd been told the time of the train and that a guide would be looking out for him, he had no idea where to ask for, so he told the ticket collector he wanted a fare for the engine sheds. But the man winked at him and replied, 'I think we can turn a blind eye to a ticket. This platform, about ten minutes.'

A good number of people arrived on the platform during his wait. The opposite side was now empty as a train had already come and gone with its quota. It had been hauled by an ancient looking red locomotive with a tall chimney and dome, and only four driving wheels with four carrying wheels in front. Old it may have appeared, but as soon as it was given the signal it accelerated away with startling rapidity, and was soon but a memory. As he surveyed the number of passengers also awaiting his train, he wondered how his guide was going to contact him, but he needn't have worried for the very first carriage of the train, when it arrived, had a head peering out of a droplight, searching for him. Fortunately, Andrew was at the correct end of the platform for the engine so he only had a short walk to the door where his new companion awaited him.

'I'm Peter, and you, presumably, must be Andrew,' the man greeted him in the vestibule. 'Let's sit down before the train starts.' He led the way into the main body of the coach which seemed to contain, as far as Andrew could make out, a preponderance of mostly young men whom Peter referred to rather disparagingly in an overloud voice as the part time maintenance crowd. He preceded Andrew, amid good-natured jeers, to a place which provided single facing seats across a small fixed table.

It was obvious from the start that Peter was a fanatical railway man, for he spoke of little else whilst Andrew was in his company, but his guest didn't find it at all boring for he hadn't realised railways could be so complicated or interesting. Peter, who was in his middle forties, began by speaking about how he'd missed seeing steam power in revenue earning use on the mainland railways, but that his father had been an enthusiast and had so graphically described the system to him that he'd also become a devotee. 'What made steam engines so fascinating was there were so many hundreds of different designs on the mainland built for a variety of jobs, and each railway company had its own designs peculiar to it. But it went further than just motive power, for every company had its own form of architecture, colour scheme and style of rolling stock, especially railway carriages, and the result was a subtle, yet distinctive, variety in everything to do with mainland railways.'

He sighed sadly, then continued. 'But roughly at the same time as they phased out steam they began to standardise on rolling stock throughout the network. They also began to close stations and routes en masse, as well as signal boxes; and the old semaphore signals were replaced by electric colour lights, so instead of there being variety, there was finally just monotony. In their search for economy, because the railways over there were losing money like mad as you doubtless know, Andrew, they managed to destroy the system. The whole story of railways on the mainland has been sad. At one time there was a comprehensive network, but then it became the policy of the various governments to allow road, and to a lesser extent air, transport to compete for passengers and freight, and then the railways didn't stand a chance.'

'But surely no one can stop free enterprise in a democratic state? Besides there must have been areas where railways couldn't penetrate but road and air transport could.'

Peter answered immediately. 'Nominally in an apparent democracy, yes, there should be complete freedom of action, but this was one example by which democracy can be found wanting, for such freedom doesn't necessarily result in a beneficial or wise decision being made. To begin with, before mechanised road transport took a hold, there was, as I've already explained, a large complete railway system in operation. Taken in its entirety, its construction was a major feat of science and engineering, innumerable tunnels and cuttings were blasted, and valleys and rivers were bridged. Who could estimate the numbers of bricks baked, wooden sleepers cut, the miles of steel rails cast, the mountains of ballast and the earth shifted in order to make such monuments to mankind's achievement? Who could reckon the total amount of money spent, the lives and permanent injuries sacrificed, the calculations made and the hopes and tears wasted? Much of it is now gone for nought.

'Democracy is a fine sounding word, but its true meaning wasn't much in evidence when the railways were dismantled. No member of the public was given the opportunity of deciding whether the money to be spent on replacing a perfectly adequate transport system, might not be better employed elsewhere. I remember several years ago, commercial radio was decimated by your authorities because it was regarded as some sort of threat, despite the possible contrary feelings of the public, and no doubt a little research would reveal further examples of bullying tactics in other fields.

'Of course, vast construction programmes like the building of a motorway network are often undertaken due to political pressures, either because it puts the political party in office in a good light, or else because it brings jobs to the workers and generous profits to the employers. Which might be alright when there's plenty of cash available, but unfortunate when money is scarce, people need housing, and the welfare state is crumbling. That's when politicians and the public alike begin to wish treasury funds hadn't been dispersed so thoughtlessly.'

Peter shrugged dismissively, then continued. 'Anyway, regarding your statement about road transport being able to go where railways couldn't – well, you're quite right of course, but the mainland authorities should've done then what we've done since our society was established, because our road and railway system work together, not as virtually opposing networks. We islanders consider it criminal folly to run down a perfectly adequate and useful network, especially after so much trouble has been taken in its construction. You've seen for yourself, I hope, what a boon a well-run and popular railway can be to the public here, so it's sad for us to see what's happened to your system in the name of free enterprise. Now that your population has grown so enormously over the past fifty years, your railway system needs to be revived to cope with the extra travelling public and freight, and so the government is finding itself having to finance two different transport systems, whereas they should have needed to deal with just one.'

While Peter had been speaking, Andrew had been half aware of the passing scenery, and so he was prepared when their train drew into the loop at Laketown station. Within their coach there was some excitement as they came abreast of a locomotive on the other side of the platform. 'Our only two-six-two,' Peter declared after glancing across at it. 'You know, there were only two classes of tender engines with that wheel arrangement in use on the mainland,

and that engine represents the only to go into quantity production.'

'What do the numbers mean?'

'Well, there are a pair of wheels in front to take the weight and guide the engine round curves, then six driving wheels and finally a pair to support the rear. The tender wheels aren't counted.'

'But why all the interest though?'

'Because this is usually the point where one locomotive is sent to the engine shed and replaced by a fresh one. Our coach and the one behind both contain volunteers who are going on to the railway centre, and our present locomotive will be taking us. Meanwhile, the engine over there will reverse onto the remainder of the train as scheduled, and because it's just come from the local shed the enthusiasts are naturally anxious to see it.'

It took just a few minutes to uncouple the other coaches, and soon their journey resumed with the locomotive making easy work of its light load. It was soon apparent Peter hadn't forgotten what he'd been saying before the stop, for he went on. 'According to my dad it was once possible to go to any mainland station and get a ticket to just about any town, and many villages, without needing to enquire too closely about arrival times and connections, so certain was it there would be a readily available service. But when lines and stations began to close, rail travel became too complicated and vexatious. Bus companies didn't always coordinate with rail timetables, and often buses didn't even patronise railway stations. So, many travellers must have stepped off trains and found they couldn't go any further because the line to their destination had been closed and there wasn't any alternative transport available. This, together with the cutting back of refreshment facilities on trains and stations, as well as filthy and unpunctual trains, and ever increasing fare prices, served to ensure loss of custom. Either the management was incredibly stupid and didn't travel by rail and so were unaware of what was happening, or else they were deliberately sabotaging their own livelihoods.'

'What about freight?' his companion asked.

'That naturally suffered as well, but for different reasons. At the beginning of the last century, pay, working conditions and hours of work were really bad on the railways, and so strikes inevitably broke out, but each time there was a stoppage freight was lost to the increasingly competitive road transport. You see, Andrew, most road haulage was in private hands and usually in small companies at first, and because of this the unions weren't very powerful in that sector. So while the railway unions could call upon a large body of members to strike, this never happened with road transport because there was little coordination between employees, the appropriate union membership where it existed being too small and widespread to be powerful.

'Therefore, while railways could be shut down through strikes, road haulage could not and so was more reliable to customers. Perhaps if the old railway companies had cared more about the humane side of operating their businesses and less about profits, their employees might have felt less aggrieved to the point of having to protest in the only way open to them. Just as on our island, if the employers had been compelled to savour the same working conditions as the majority of their personnel, then maybe their railways would still be their nation's prime transport system. Later on, I'll show you the types of locomotive that footplate crew, the drivers and coal firemen would have to work on in the old days, no joke on a hot summer's day but a nightmare in freezing, foggy and stormy weather, especially when running tender first.

'The tragedy of your transport system as it stands at the moment, Andrew, is that due to private enterprise it could never reorganise itself on lines similar to ours, despite the fact our network is far more practical and economical than yours is. Because if anyone tried to alter dependency on road transport it would cause such disruption it would probably bankrupt the country. The oil and vehicle industries would be particularly badly hit. They wouldn't consider it anyway – no political party in government at the time could bear to withstand the ensuing loss of votes. So until the oilfields dry up you'll just have to continue enduring traffic jams, the annual road accident toll, pollution and an unfair transport system. But it goes to prove what problems can arise through adopting the wrong course.'

'You'd feel the pinch with your vehicle industry too,' Andrew pointed out.

Peter grinned. 'We probably would, but we'd simply begin to produce something else equally profitable and worthwhile, perhaps railway locomotives for export.'

There was a pause, which was soon broken by Andrew. 'Tell me about the island's railways,' he said.

'Alright, I'll explain about our network but leave the motive power and other rolling stock until you can see them for yourself, if you don't mind.' He then went on to repeat many of the facts which the railwayman, Ken, had already mentioned, but added some extra items of interest. 'Really it's like a huge life-size model layout, but one which provides an essential service. Apart from the branch to the railway centre and industrial complex and a few other branches, station loops and storage sidings, the system is double tracked throughout. It's never been our authorities' policy to replace men by machines, but they do like to economise by ensuring relevant materials have been made to last, so the tracks are of the highest quality. Rail lengths are very long, thereby preventing wheels from receiving a hammering by too many rail connecting joints, thereby sadly eliminating the old clackety-clack noise which once added such a comforting dimension to rail travel. Every sleeper, the crosswise packing which supports the track and keeps the two rails relative to each other, is made of concrete. The rotting away of wooden sleepers has often been used as a contributory excuse for closing down a rail route on the mainland.

'All track points are electrically heated against freezing, and they can be operated manually in an emergency. The signal boxes, although they appear old fashioned, are completely modern inside, and are fitted for electrical and manual control in case of a local problem. But normally a "mother" signal complex remotely controls the entire island system. Safety is to the highest standards. For instance, in stations the passing loops are all automatically controlled against rolling stock collisions, because to prevent trains from running into stationary vehicles due to points set incorrectly, an electric circuit passing through the latter's wheels prevents the relevant points from being operated. A further device is that when the signal for the platform is operated, it also locks the vital points shut, so the only way in which a locomotive can normally retrieve rolling stock from the adjacent passing loop is by reversing down to it. Of course, as on the mainland, we also have automatic train control all over the system, which prevents drivers from passing signals at danger.

'When I mentioned our network was like a model railway, I also meant aesthetic conditions were taken into account when it was designed and constructed and so no station, signal box or any other railway building is exactly the same, and all have been based upon designs copied from the mainland's railways. There are at least two different station layouts, one with island platforms and the other with facing platforms, but the passing loops are usually allocated on the outside for easy handling of freight. The materials used for the buildings are varied and usually in sympathy with the architectural style of the adjacent town or village; wood, brick, stone, concrete and flint are all represented with the addition of metal on lattice footbridges, signal posts and station canopy supports, and each station has its quota of advertisements which are regularly exchanged with those of other stations.

'As you've doubtless noticed, Andrew, all our stations are tidy, well maintained and are gardeners' delights. The waiting rooms and all offices are double glazed and centrally heated, and all trains are automatically indicated well in advance. Our authorities believe in making travel as interesting as possible and it's thought over here that the subconscious mind picks up much more than is generally supposed, and that's why variety and comfort is so important. Who wants to see the same dreary thing day in and day out on the way to work, the shops or when going out for recreational purposes? One thing we do over here which no one on the mainland seems to bother about is to transform the railway verges into natural reserves, and so wild and garden flowers, shrubs and trees are grown everywhere. It thereby makes not only the railway, but the whole island attractive.'

During the following pause, Andrew glanced out of the window and, seeing nothing but chalk cliff, realised they'd soon be at the factory complex. 'Nearly there,' Peter commented as if he'd read his thoughts.

His companion nodded and replied, 'I didn't expect to be back here again so soon. I was only shown around the car plant on Friday.'

Almost as soon as everyone had disembarked from the train, the locomotive had been uncoupled and steamed off down the track, followed at a far more leisurely rate by the party of enthusiasts. Shortly a track converged from the left, which Andrew knew from his previous visit connected with the factory sidings, and soon afterwards, a series of points allowed three separate tracks to radiate from the single mainline. The first one passed behind a long brick building through which the second track ran, and finally arrived alongside a huge mound of coal where an overhead crane straddled both fuel and track.

'That's where the engine's tender is coaled and watered,' explained Peter, who'd allowed the rest of the party to go on ahead, 'but you can't see the water treatment unit and filling tower from here as they're behind the engine maintenance and storage shed. All the coal is graded elsewhere so it's not too big for the shovel or so small it's little more than dust. Some of the old photographs of locomotives on the mainland are quite horrifying. Often, locomotives had huge lumps of coal in their tenders, while others appeared to be full of dust. No wonder they often steamed badly or belched thick black smoke. Another innovation we have is that in addition to purifying our water it's delivered pre-heated and the temperature is thermostatically controlled whilst in the tender. You can imagine what a boon that must be, especially in winter'.

At first, Andrew had thought the ancient looking engine shed with is large but uncharacteristically clean windows was the main building, but Peter told him it was only the place where the engines were allowed to cool down after coming off their train, where their boilers and fire grates were emptied and they received preliminary cleaning.

'One of the excuses for getting rid of steam locomotion on the mainland,' Peter continued, 'was that youngsters were no longer interested in maintaining steam engines. Judging by the working conditions at the time it was hardly surprising, for the machines were often filthy and there were too many different types, or classes, making maintenance difficult. But what was worse was that engine sheds were also dirty and uncomfortable to work in, for sometimes there weren't any main doors and even when there were, they were often left open all year round. Frequently, repairs were undertaken out in the open. But it doesn't happen here of course because, as you'll see, all maintenance is done inside where it's warm and dry, but even when work such as coaling and watering is carried on outside it's done from an enclosed cab, or some other kind of cover.'

Andrew was a little disappointed as he'd been hoping to see an array of locomotives lined up outside on such a pleasant day, but there wasn't even one engine to be seen as their erstwhile locomotive was absent being, presumably, inside the brick engine shed. The track they were following curved away from the main line, eventually being joined by the one from the engine shed. In front of them now was the chalk cliff toward which the track was heading. 'Quite impressive, isn't it?' Peter declared as they approached the railway centre.

The younger man thought his companion was making an understatement because it was only too obvious that a major feat of engineering had been achieved, for the main building had been constructed within the bulk of the cliff. Only the stone facing with its folding door entrance for locomotives, smaller door for personnel and several storeys of large windows was visible, built flush with the cliff face. 'The architects got the idea from the enormous military installations which were built into some of the chalk cliffs along your coastline, Andrew. Those big windows above the doors let in plenty of natural light, and the entrance for the engines is electrically operated, so there's no excuse for leaving it open. Come on, let's go inside. I think you'll be pleasantly surprised.'

As the door gently closed behind them Andrew couldn't suppress a gasp of astonishment, for he found himself confronted by a massive hall, lit at their end by the double row of windows, and further back by large lights which transformed the interior into day. On either side of the hall great pillars rose to the ceiling where they supported huge arched girders holding up the roof. Slung from these were transverse overhead crane tracks. The railway line from outside had been embedded in the concrete floor for safety reasons, having a groove on the inside of each rail to take the wheel flanges, and about the length of a large locomotive away from the entrance door a turntable was sited from which three parallel tracks passed down the length of the hall. Alongside one of these tracks on either side, were rows of locomotives minus their tenders.

'Before we go any further, I think I'd better start explaining,' Peter suggested. Pointing to their left, he began. 'That track running down the left hand side of the hall leads to a turntable which allows multiple short lengths of line to branch out, on which the various tenders are stored and overhauled where necessary. The floor above contains offices. The centre track leads to where the locomotives are kept, using the same method as with the tenders while above are more offices, as well as a restaurant and toilets. On the right hand side the track leads to the boiler and chassis shops with machine shops for smaller items above.'

Just as Harry Larke had done in the adjacent road vehicle complex, Peter took his companion on a comprehensive tour of the railway centre beginning with an inspection of the lines of locomotives and tenders which, from floor level, seemed even more impressive than when observed from station platforms. Many of the driving wheels, even, towered above him. Andrew lost count of the number of cab footplates he climbed up to in order to examine the seemingly complex set of controls. 'On the mainland railways,' Peter explained, 'there were lots of different types of locomotive classes, and virtually each one had its own individual style with levers, valves and gauges in various places. Some engines were even driven from the right hand side of the cab, but in the interest of safety and simplicity all island locomotives are driven from the left and the control positions have been standardised.'

'One of Mr Maynard's daughters told me you obtained your locomotives from preserved railways in my country. Did you change the controls on them?'

Peter smiled at the implied impossibility of the task. 'I had nothing to do with the modifications I'm pleased to say, but as we've already been on several engines which originated from two different mainland railways, the answer must be "yes". It would have been a terrible head scratching task though, but it's proof of our island's determination to attempt the impossible and overcome when it's deemed necessary.'

On one of the locomotive footplates Andrew's guide said, 'this is one of the old fashioned engines I mentioned earlier. As you can see there aren't any windows in the sides, the cab isn't very long and the tender isn't very high so, except for in the mildest weather, conditions for the crew would've been pretty grim. I suppose the management's reasoning in the old days was that if the enginemen were easy to see, they couldn't be getting up to mischief, which is somewhat patronising in my books.

'Fortunately over the course of time, conditions began to improve. First one and then two windows per side were introduced, the cabs and roofs extended and the tender height was raised, until finally the gap between cab and tender was reduced to a mere split so that everything was enclosed. But due to the often critical level of finances on the mainland railways, many user unfriendly locomotives lasted to the end of steam. If it wasn't for union pressure constantly pushing against the boundaries of human thoughtfulness, there would have been far fewer warm and comfortable cabs on the railways.'

'Why do all the locomotives seem to have different sized main wheels?' Andrew asked as they continued their inspection of the engine fleet.

'Because steam locomotives don't have gears, as electric and oil powered engines do. They're fitted with the driving wheel size which suits the work they're designed to do. The smaller size range makes for strong hauling power, track adhesion and ease of starting off, but restricts the speed limit. The largest wheels more or less provide a completely contradictory set of conditions. They allow the locomotive to travel at high speed with lighter loads, but can make it difficult to start the train and aren't always reliable in climbing gradients. Engines with wheels intermediate in diameter between the two make the best of both worlds. They tend to be superior in pulling passenger trains than the small wheeled types and in hauling freight trains than the large wheeled locomotives, but in both cases they're generally unable to take as much of a load as they can. Ideally, our island requirements would indicate the need for only mixed traffic engines, but variety being one of the spices of our life, we like to see all the different designs.'

'But why did you choose steam power, surely it's obsolete now?'

Andrew's companion nodded and smiled. 'Steam might be old fashioned,' he agreed, 'but it's still loved. Do you know we island railway enthusiasts have our own library? It contains hundreds of books almost all without exception concerning steam engines, which include countless photographs and scale drawings. Now, those books wouldn't have been published or those photos taken if there hadn't been a tremendous amount of interest in the subject. Further proof may be found from the large number of trainspotters who used to frequent the larger railway stations on the mainland. With the supplanting of steam by other forms of traction and the introduction of standardisation, the majority of spotters disappeared – they just weren't interested anymore. In actual fact, the island authorities are being extremely shrewd in employing steam power and variation in equipment and buildings. Having spent so much time, money and effort in constructing a comprehensive transport system, they're not going to allow it to be threatened in any way. Having as many enthusiasts as possible lessens the chance of that happening.'

As they turned to go Andrew remarked, 'it's a wonder you're

not plagued by enthusiasts in other countries wanting to see this railway.'

'We are, even though information about Whyte Island is officially supposed to be non-existent. But on one occasion a referendum allowed the authorities to organise a railway open day for selected visitors from abroad, but because of the dangerous and foolhardy behaviour of some of the guests, the vandalising and theft of property as well as the amount of litter left behind, the experiment was never repeated'

On their way to inspect the rolling stock, Peter explained about the modifications which were made to the vehicles. 'As I think I've already said, we believe in making items last over here and this is reflected in our stock. Virtually all vehicles are fitted with roller bearings and, where possible, constructed from alloys, and just like our locomotives the passenger and freight vehicles have been standardised, but this time the main difference is in size. Some of the vehicles might look very different from each other, but they've been built to the same dimensions.

'Take the coaches, for example. Some have simulated wooden sides with exterior beading, roofs which slope down at the ends, and unusual wheel frames – or bogies as they're officially called – and others have flat metal sides, square ended roofs and more normal bogies, while others have curved sides. Each type has been painted in the authentic colours of the railway which designed it, and many have been made up into train sets of matching coaches, and others are formed into mixed rakes to ape the frequent formation of actual mainland passenger trains. Different designs of carriages with sides of cream and red, maroon or green all mixed together were not unusual at one time, though in the case of our island trains, they'd all be fitted on the same frames.

'Likewise, the wagons all appear to be different, some being faced with vertical wood planking, others with horizontal, whilst many are constructed with metal sides. Some vans have almost flat roofs, others are distinctly curved. Some chassis have been fitted with spoked wheels, some with solid disked. But each body can be easily lifted off its frame and then be replaced by another.

'The reason for this modification is not merely to add variety, but also for ease of maintenance. A chassis is much easier to inspect and work on if it's separated from its body, and also the entire unit won't necessarily be out of commission at the same time. If, for instance, the body is finished being overhauled before the chassis, it can be lowered onto another one, and vice versa. The management puts a premium on maintenance. Each body, chassis and bogie carries a small coloured square with every colour representing a given year, with a date mark in the centre, so it can immediately be known when the item last received attention.'

By this time they'd reached the carriage and wagon section where Andrew was able to examine everything, including five coaches undergoing overhaul, and about twenty wagons, some of which were covered vans, others open trucks. He was especially interested to note how the covered vans operated, for the whole of each side could be lowered on its bottom hinges, so allowing the smaller individual containers which were standard on Whyte Island to be easily loaded and unloaded. He found it intriguing to board the coach bodies at ground level, for each one of them was without a chassis and all were in different stages of renovation from being almost entirely stripped down to nearing completion, the smell of paint, new wood and varnish sometimes being quite overwhelming.

'Although I mentioned some mainland coaches were constructed with wooden sides,' Peter said as they surveyed a particularly handsome carriage which had curved roof ends, large square cornered windows and half round beading, 'it was found to be not very durable material, especially in the corners of the windows, and so it was replaced by pressed steel, as in this case; but it looks like wood, doesn't it?'

Andrew, who had thought it was wood, was compelled to agree. His guide checked his watch. 'Almost time for dinner,' he observed, 'but we've just enough left to look at the main workshops before we dine.'

On the way, they passed several long flat trucks supported on pairs of bogies which the younger man recognised as being similar to the ones onto which the containers were being loaded at the quay, and also an old fashioned-seeming coach body with a peculiar small secondary roof and sides running along the apex of the main roof. 'One of the carriages in our set of eight clerestory stock, all of which are noticeably different from each other, and all much newer than they appear. We use them in service, of course, as a novelty, but they were designed primarily for film work. They look very quaint when hauled by one of our ancient looking locomotives.'

The workshops had all the equipment necessary for the construction, repair and maintenance of steam engines and other rolling stock, and there was even a foundry and jigs for the production of a variety of items including wheels of all sizes. Peter explained that much of the machinery was little used for railway work now as few heavy repair jobs needed to be undertaken, but that when the island railways were first being expanded, the place had been a hive of industry. 'Every so often, maybe two or three times a year, a boiler becomes due for overhaul and so obviously the entire locomotive and tender will get a checking over and receive maintenance and renewal of parts where necessary. But the entire railway complex now serves as an ideal training centre for engineering students as there aren't any reasons for them to be under any pressure to hurry over their learning skills, and they've a whole range of equipment to practice on.'

'So what sort of work do you amateurs carry out?' Andrew asked as they made their way toward the restaurant.

His companion chuckled. 'Nothing particularly technical. You could imagine the confusion which would entail if we were permitted to carry out repairs or maintenance work, so we're confined to cleaning and polishing. It's dirty work, but it's a labour of love. Although most of the staff have the weekend off, there are enough people about to keep an eye on us and let us know what needs doing.'

'So who cooks the dinner?'

'Well, as there are railway employees on duty that means a member of the restaurant staff,' Peter grinned. 'But wives, daughters or girlfriends often come along, especially when the weather is fine, like today, and they can usually be depended upon to lend a hand. Though as all island males receive cookery lessons at school, we're quite capable of looking after ourselves if need be. You may have noticed during our tour there were a number of female railway enthusiasts, some of whom also enjoy cooking as a hobby, so it's up to them if they want to work in the kitchen.'

The restaurant was long, quite narrow and decorated with a seemingly endless display of wall mounted photographs of railway subjects. As Andrew might have expected, all the fittings and much of the décor seemed to have been made of stainless steel or plastic, and although far from soulless, the room gave the impression of being almost utilitarian. The contrast with the decor of the canteen in the factory complex was therefore quite startling. The food was laid out in pans on the self-service counter and, as he was to discover, there was no restriction on what might be chosen, or the amount, and there was no charge. Behind the servery in the open plan kitchen, two women and a man worked cheerfully, cooking and replenishing the contents of the pans.

After taking what they wanted, Peter led the way over to a table where they would be on their own and where, for a change, they talked of subjects other than railways whilst they enjoyed their repast. Once again, Andrew was reminded of the degree of courtesy prevalent on Whyte Island. When they'd first arrived there had been a dozen or so people dining, all of whom had removed their overalls, and during the course of their meal others entered the restaurant in twos and threes, and he'd marvelled that, although some of these were doubtless particular friends of Peter, yet he'd preferred through choice to give his whole attention to his companion. What was equally impressive was the fact that Peter's friends should accept this gesture as being perfectly normal.

Upon leaving the restaurant, Andrew was taken up to the design and drawing offices where Peter explained about how the various problems in building a virtually new railway system were solved, and how the modification of the locomotives, rolling stock and various buildings had been planned and carried out. Adjacent to the offices was a room full of rows of vertical cabinets, which housed innumerable scale drawings of track layouts and everything else pertinent to the island's railways. They spent much of the remainder of their visit in examining various drawings, of which those pertaining to the steam engines particularly interested the younger man.

'Apart from a few small tank engines, which carry their water and coal supply on the same chassis as the rest of the locomotive, and are used on a couple of branch lines, Whyte Island only has tender engines as there is little need for them to run backwards over long distances. Our railway's route system, being in the form of two giant circles joined together, means that once travelling forward, each engine will return to the same point from which it started, facing in the same direction. Tank engines, though, are designed to travel both forward and in reverse which we islanders, being safety conscious, feel to be unsatisfactory as reverse running seriously restricts the footplate crew's area of vision besides being uncomfortable over long periods.'

'But surely the same criterion applies to tank locomotives as it does to tender engines,' Andrew pointed out, 'in that once facing forward they won't need to be turned around?'

Peter smiled grimly at his companion's point. 'You're quite right of course, but there is another reason for just having tender engines. Tenders can carry much more coal and water than tank locomotives and tend to spread the weight of the two vehicles along the length of track supporting them more evenly, whereas tank engines have the additional disadvantage of being less stable with all the weight of the fuel in addition to that of the locomotive itself, making the whole affair top heavy.'

Returning to the drawings Peter said, 'this section contains mainland designs of locomotives which were never built and there are a lot of railway fans over here, especially modellers, clamouring for one or two of the more plausible to be built.'

'And do you think they'll be satisfied?'

'Everything seems to be possible here,' the older man smiled, 'but as you can see for yourself,' he added, selecting several drawings, 'many of them appear to be huge machines, and so well over the top for our requirements. I think they'd best be left to the skills of the railway modeller. Have you seen our model railway, by the way? It's very impressive, and huge. It's one of the additional attractions of Laketown.'

Before they left the interior of the complex for the station, Peter showed his guest one of the three battery powered towing machines, a curious little object with totally enclosed cab, all round vision and very wide tyres. 'This vehicle was especially designed for the railway centre', he said. 'It's got tyres instead of flanged wheels to allow for greater flexibility when it's towing its charges. As you've probably noticed, all the track in the complex is virtually flush with the floor and ground, so having tyred wheels presents no difficulties. When an item of rolling stock is being towed or propelled, an automatic warning alarm is set off, but a guard is also required at the opposite end of the railway vehicle in question to give a warning, though as the top speed is only ten miles an hour there's little chance of an accident anyway.'

As they made their way back to the station Andrew, even more interested in the railway now that he'd toured the centre, asked, 'have you got any idea what type of locomotive we'll be getting on our train?'

His companion grinned and shrugged. 'That's a tall order as it could be one of many. You see, the position of all the engines is recorded on an illuminated track plan at the railway headquarters, and as there are spare locomotives kept in steam in key places throughout the system, it might possibly be one of them. Each engine driver, having a mobile phone, is easily called up and given instructions.'

In the event it was the little four-four-zero which Andrew had last seen leaving the station while he'd awaited his present companion's train that was standing at the platform and, as they were early, Peter was able to persuade the driver to allow them onto the footplate. The crew were only too pleased to explain about the controls and gauges, each one of which had a small explanatory plate attached, and also how the locomotive was driven and fired. 'This particular machine was brought over from the mainland and was built and used by a railway company in the far north,' the driver said after Peter had told the crew Andrew was visiting the island, 'so it needed to have its driving control layout standardised. In the old days, driving a steam engine over there could be a nightmare; some of the controls were operated by push rods resting on ratchets, instead of by screw handles as on our island, and sometimes, due to vibration, they'd fly open or shut as the case might be, with impressive results. Another cause of great trouble were the injectors which forced the water from the tender into the boiler, and these frequently didn't deliver the right quantity or else failed altogether, so bringing the train to a stop. Also, I'm told, many of the engines pitched and swayed so much that bruises and even broken bones weren't unknown.'

'Of course,' Peter added, 'in addition to reliable controls and comfortable cabs you've also got roller bearings, self-cleaning smoke boxes and rocking grates.'

'Yes,' the driver agreed; neglecting to explain the latter two devices to Andrew. He continued, 'as well as radio communications, automatic warning signalling and, last but not least, people to clean, maintain and prepare our machines for the next period of duty for us.'

He had barely finished speaking when one of the enthusiasts appeared at the cab side. 'I'm the last one, Joe,' he said, 'so ready when you are.'

After thanking the engine crew, Andrew and his companion left the footplate and boarded the first of the two coaches where, as soon as they were seated, the younger man asked, 'do the engines finish up here at nights?'

Peter shook his head. 'No, it would be inconvenient all round. Besides, there's little in the way of stabling facilities here. The locomotives are kept at the towns where the crews live. This means the footplate men and guards need to reside close to where there is an engine shed, because no engine can stay out in the open when not in use. Even the carriages and wagons spend much of the time under cover, although not in such elaborate shelters.'

A sudden shriek from the engine's whistle and a brief hiss of steam heralded the departure of their train, the driver gently easing the small load out of the station and into the tunnel at an almost leisurely pace. Two stops of the unscheduled service to allow enthusiasts off brought Andrew to his station, but before they arrived Peter gave him his phone number in case he wished to see more of the railway system during his leave.

As it was still a warm day Andrew, before attempting the hill climb, called in at the Station Arms for a cooling pint of beer, and he was soon having an interesting talk with the publican who, not surprisingly, was very fond of the railways. On his subsequent ambling though still somewhat hectic walk up the hill, he allowed his thoughts to return to the subject of Linda and her surprisingly confident offer to re-associate with him on Thursday if he didn't have a girl by then. He considered the red haired slave girl of the previous Wednesday and it made him wonder again if she tied in with his Folk Club visit. He found it an attractive thought, especially after Helen's comment of the previous day, but decided it would be highly improbable after his rejection of her.

When he reached the cottage he went straight round the back to the garden where he found Linda seated on a chair by the pond gazing at the water reflectively. 'Hello,' she greeted him cheerfully. 'We've been expecting you. Tea's ready'.

'Expecting me?' he replied nonplussed.

'Yes. Peter phoned; he's quite taken with you. Did you have a nice time?'

Tea was indeed ready, a salad prepared in inimitable way by the girls was laid out on the table. Hardly had the four of them sat down when Andrew, without prompting, began to enthuse about his day out on the railway. Eventually, when he'd told them just about everything he could think of, Charlie Maynard said as he poured out their second cup of tea, 'I know you've been extremely active this weekend, lad, but do you think you'd like to continue your visits to the island's schools tomorrow?'

Andrew, upon receipt of these words, couldn't refrain from glancing across at Linda, but noticing the look Charlie quickly added, 'I'm afraid Linda is still doing a filling in turn so she won't be available, but you've met Sandra, I believe?' He turned to his younger daughter in a questioning manner and she silently nodded in reply. 'In that case,' he continued, 'I'm sure she'll be only too pleased to take you on a tour of a blue school, and maybe of a red establishment later on.'

The young man, remembering the very attractive girl whom he'd met that Wednesday on the way to the Education Centre, was in complete agreement with this suggestion, but he couldn't help wondering if this was a way for Linda to be rid of him, and also whether Sandra was to take her place. But he of course, said nothing, apart from expressing the wish to return to the school visits.

It was a great relief to Andrew when, after the tea things had been cleared away and the washing up done, one of the sisters suggested they should listen to some music, for he felt quite worn out and required nothing more than to relax. 'It's our guest's choice,' announced their father. 'Is that alright with you?' Andrew nodded.

'Radio, or our own?' Helen asked.

'Oh yours, if you don't mind.'

As he had no preference for any particular type of music, she chose a selection of classical discs, mostly overtures but with a few sonatas amongst them. With their chairs arranged before the wide open patio windows and with only one lamp behind them switched on, it felt really peaceful and romantic looking out onto the garden in the dusk and hearing, above the sound of the music, the singing of several birds.

Very few words were spoken and when Andrew felt a nudge and glanced up to see Linda offering him a glass of wine, neither said anything. He'd never really paid much attention to classical music before, and if he'd ever thought of it previously he'd dismissed it as the province of the affluent and well educated. But these recordings were a new experience. The overtures were especially enthralling with their periods of melancholy beauty changing within moments to fast sections of excited rhythm. During an interlude, when he helped Helen make some coffee, Charlie asked him if he liked the music. After affirming that he did and explaining why, he added, 'the setting compliments its beauty. Looking out onto the lawn seems to make it even more perfect. The style of music together with the garden – what could be better?'

He was somewhat surprised to see all three Maynards smiling at his remark as though sharing some secret, but upon noticing his confusion Charlie observed, 'a night out appears to be indicated. Who wants to go?'

Linda immediately put up her hand like an excited schoolgirl. 'Me, me!' she cried.

But Helen said soberly, 'why not make a family party, dad? It'd be fun if we all went.'

'Alright,' he agreed. 'I'll see if there's a vacancy tomorrow evening, as long as Andrew doesn't have too tiring a day.'

The young man smiled as he put down his cup. 'Whatever it is, I'm sure I'll have the energy for it,' he said.

With the onset of night the temperature dropped below the level of comfort and so the patio windows were closed, the curtains drawn and the easy chairs arranged round the fireplace; but the light remained low, the CD recital continued, and once again everyone had a glass of wine.

When Andrew arrived at breakfast the following morning, he wasn't too surprised to learn from Charlie that his visit to a blue school with Sandra had been arranged. How it had been managed at such short notice he had no idea, for it wasn't yet eight o'clock, but miracles appeared easy to arrange on Whyte Island.

Sandra, looking just as attractive as on the first occasion he'd seen her, awaited him as he stepped off the bus at Harbourtown station. All the way down he'd pondered upon how he ought to behave in her company. Should he treat her as a prospective lover, or as a guide, just another person? Remembering certain remarks which the sisters had imparted on the subject at various times, he resolved to let his present companion make any of the necessary moves as she thought fit. 'Whereabouts is this blue school we're going to visit?' he asked after greetings had been exchanged.

'Have you been to the far side of the island yet?' When he

shook his head, she went on. 'Well, it'll be an additional treat for you because that's where we're off to.'

On the train, which was hauled by the handsome two-six-two he'd glimpsed the previous day, Andrew's interest was divided equally between his pretty companion and the view, but especially the latter because during the later stage of their journey it was all new to him. Besides, as he'd had quite a conversation with Sandra when they'd first met he felt as though he already knew her, and so he was inclined to treat her as he would an old friend. 'What's the town we're going to like?' he eventually asked.

'It's one of the oldest looking places on the island but in fact it's one of those new towns we mentioned the other day. No doubt you've been told we like to make things appear interesting? Well, this town's been built around a harbour, almost all of which was excavated by the islanders, and all the buildings have been made to look medieval with plaster and lathe, brick and beam and stone exteriors and, in many cases, stepped out fronts all with old fashioned window panes. All varied for interest's sake, but each apparently authentic.'

Andrew grinned. 'But I bet they're not built of those materials. I visited the railway centre yesterday and the chap who showed me around stressed things were built to last over here.'

Sandra smiled. 'Well, there are plenty of really old buildings on the mainland, so the original materials couldn't have been all that bad, but, yes, I believe you'd find the plaster and wood was really concrete, or else the wood will have been especially treated against rot and insect pests. We won't have much time but I think we'll be able to have a quick look at the town before we go to the school, and I'm sure you'll want to explore it more thoroughly with a friend at some later date.'

He glanced at her with added interest when she said the word "friend", but obviously no hint was intended for she went on. 'But if you remember the town is little more than fifteen years old, then I think you'll be impressed.'

'As new as that,' he murmured to himself.

His companion, hearing him, nodded then glanced out of the window. 'See those trees?' she asked. Andrew looked about him and saw woodland flashing past on either side of the track. 'They were planted at about the same time as the town was begun.'

He was surprised for the trees were of considerable height and, where a large area of space permitted a distant view, he noted their girth wasn't very large, but the forest, for such it was, seemed timeless. 'We're only about a mile from the sea here,' Sandra continued, 'and quite high up. This was once all chalk down land but because of the ferocious gales which often come in from this quarter, it was decided to grow a forest here to protect the area. So all the toughest, fastest growing, calcareous tolerant trees from around the world were planted, and subsequent records have shown that it's worked wonders. They've been arranged in alternate rows of deciduous and coniferous with the more salt and wind resistant nearest the coast, and when they're eventually thinned out an interesting and varied forest will result.

'I've explained all this to illustrate how easy and quick it can be to do something worthwhile, even on such a large scale. Most of these tree species were also planted in Newtown, and that's another reason why it seems so old and permanent.'

Shortly afterwards, the train began to descend a bank and the forest was then replaced by the steep chalk sides of a cutting. The brakes were soon applied and Andrew noticed that the pair of tracks had suddenly become four, heralding their imminent arrival at a station. As if to endorse this fact Sandra, as well as a number of other passengers, stood up. 'Our stop,' she smiled.

He couldn't help feeling a sense of wonder once the train had left them standing on the platform to complete the remainder of its journey, for the station was completely different from others he'd seen on the island. To begin with, it had a high, bowed overall roof covering all three platforms for most of their length, while supporting this roof, on the perimeter of each of the outer platforms, were two storey buildings whose upper windows proclaimed first floor rooms.

Sandra mentioned that one of these buildings was a hotel much frequented by those who enjoyed the kind of sounds which emanate from a busy steam railway. Another unusual feature was that the station boasted a wide subway instead of footbridge and, as they walked down this, a small electric baggage trolley came toward them towing several barrows, the driver of which smiled cheerfully at them as he passed.

'Is this station as important as it appears?' Andrew asked as they came up the ramp onto the far platform, then quickly added, 'could we go down to the end of this platform?'

If his companion thought this request strange, she displayed no sign but merely nodded and smiled. 'Yes to both questions.' And as they began to walk along the length of the sizeable platform, she explained why the station had an air of bustle. 'You see, Andy, this was once one of the most desolate parts of Whyte Island and so it was decided it ought to be developed in order to balance the remainder of our nation, but to make it all worthwhile it needed to have a rationale: to be useful and also attractive to holidaymakers.

'First of all, a small bay with a little stream was excavated with explosives to make it into a deep water harbour with large level areas on either side suitable as the foundation of an extensive town. The harbour then became a trading and fishing port, and the town a medieval style community and leisure centre. As this coastline is rather exposed other areas of cliff were demolished to form sheltered bays and inlets for residential and holiday villages, and now, instead of a part of the island being useless except for a sort of wild grandeur of beauty it's been utilised – although, hopefully, no one will say it's been ruined in the process.'

Together they stood at the end of the platform, but Andrew had only been half listening to his companion's explanation for, as they'd walked along, he'd been gazing about him. The station area was similar to the industrial and railway complex but on a much smaller scale, a large hollow some fifty feet deep had been cut out of the chalk and within this the railway, along with various associated buildings including a substantial engine shed as well as a freight yard, had been built. There were only three exits from this arena – up through the cutting from which their train had just descended, through the tunnel at the opposite end of the station and finally, for road traffic and pedestrians, by way of a gap in the cliff which, the young man presumed, must lead to the town.

Because the station complex was situated on the island, nature hadn't been left to its own devices, so, doubtless by design, innumerable ledges of varying size had been let into the cliffs, and plants of bewildering variety from small trees and bushes down to climbing and trailing shrubs covered the almost sheer face until its chalky composition was scarcely visible. Andrew could have quite happily spent hours standing at the platform end, but a nudge from Sandra told him it was time to go. 'So because the town had become so attractive and, therefore, busy with residents, holidaymakers and sea trade,' she was saying, 'a station to match the town's importance was constructed. The two complement each other really, and it can be quite hectic here on a summer weekend with visitors arriving and departing.'

As if to endorse her words, a shrill whistle from inside the tunnel was immediately followed by the appearance of a passenger train, and by the time they'd turned into the station's exit the platform was full of people. Outside there were several buses awaiting the expected influx of passengers, and Sandra commented, 'one of those would have been ours, but as we're going to have a quick look at the town, it isn't worth getting on just yet.'

The road to the town led straight through the gap in the chalk, which was some two hundred feet long and buttressed by a brick wall as a safety measure, to a height of about fifteen feet. Unsurprisingly, both the cliff and the brickwork were covered in vegetation, the latter having a large number of plants which, she told him, were nearly all types of fern. She went on, after noticing him looking up at the foliage on the chalk cliff above them. 'They help to stabilise the face and so make it safer. When it was excavated, pockets of different sizes were dug out and earth packed in, and the same thing was done with the terraces and ledges which helped all the plants to get off to a good start. Some of them are very rare; they can multiply to their heart's content, and because they're high up they've got a good chance of dispersing their seeds or spores and are also immune from interference. I remember seeing some of the work being done when I was little. They used fire engine escape ladders.'

'Our mainland conservationists seem to have a lot to learn,' mused Andrew.

'I suppose they have,' she tactfully replied.

At the end of the cutting, the town began as a wide, tree-lined avenue which inclined gently down to the harbour, with houses built in almost every conceivable style upon either side. 'They don't look very medieval to me,' he dryly commented, drawing his companion's attention to the buildings.

The girl merely smiled. 'Such places might look picturesque but they're hardly suitable for a modern residential area. No, you'll find all the period style buildings in and around the town centre. If you think about it, such an arrangement makes it even more authentic as towns and cities usually spread outwards as the population slowly increased, leaving the oldest structures nearest the centre. In planning the peripheral areas of this and other towns, the authorities, wishing for variety, commissioned photographers to take pictures of buildings from all over the mainland and other pertinent countries, and so thousands of designs were available for the architects to follow. Despite all this variety, I think you'll agree that none of these houses clash with their neighbours'.'

Most of the buildings were residential only, but some shops, cafes and public houses appeared fairly regularly. Usually they lined the avenue, but occasionally groups were set some distance back in order to form squares, whilst many homes were situated a little way back, allowing small front gardens. Looking ahead, Andrew noted that the road continued down to a bridge, enabling access to a further part of the town on the far side of the harbour, for he could clearly see buildings, with down land topped cliffs beyond.

'We've just got time to go down to the quayside and then walk along to the first bus stop,' Sandra said, coincidentally with a bus passing by on its way to the bridge. He was pleasantly surprised at the scene before him as they turned the corner near the bridge. On their left was the broad cobbled area of the harbour side with its long low loading shed, piles of fish boxes, coiled ropes and bollards, its cranes and parked lorries. This was separated from the adjacent road by a line of almost mature trees on the quay, with two fishing boats and a coaster berthed alongside, and looked most aesthetic and peaceful.

On their side of the road, however, the town continued, now appearing to be much more substantial and ancient in character; for many of the buildings had overhanging upper storeys, some of which were several floors high so giving an inverted staircase effect. Between the town and the quayside the wide, tree verged road ran straight, disappearing into the distance where the line of cliffs enclosing the town seemed to block further progress.

Sandra led the way across the road, where they stood by the bridge for a few moments. Andrew, gazing toward the sea, expected to see a gap in the cliffs with blue sky and the ocean beyond, but instead the harbour, although comparatively wide in the vicinity of the town, gradually became narrower to seaward until the actual exit was eventually hidden by a bend. About halfway between the bridge and this bend, a barrier traversed the stretch of water. 'That's one of the pair of lochs,' she observed.

'The other one's nearer the harbour mouth.' Without waiting for his comment, she continued. 'It not only makes it easier for the seamen and the harbour staff if the port is non-tidal, but it also helps the town to be more attractive; no smelly seaweed hanging from the quayside walls at low tide, no unsightly mud banks or stranded boats. It also becomes easier and safer to fish with rod and line within the harbour area.'

She pointed toward the roads which ran along the foot of the cliffs on either side of the harbour and which disappeared round the corner. 'Those continue to the ends of the breakwater forming the substantial outer harbour. Fishing boats and other small vessels can safely moor there until it's time for them to enter the main part, but it can also be used as a temporary refuge in times of bad weather.'

'I expect it's a prime spot for illegal immigrants,' Andrew considered aloud. 'I'd be interested in knowing how you deal with them.'

'According to what we've been taught,' Sandra answered. 'They're housed in suitable accommodation where they're repeatedly informed about the pointlessness of overpopulation in their countries of origin, how their own nations could be far better and fairer if the populations were to decrease, and that it wasn't reasonable to expect a nation which did practice birth control to pay for their lack of foresight. They're indoctrinated ceaselessly apparently, until they're sick of it and move on elsewhere.'

'Don't foreign welfare groups complain about their treatment, though?'

'I should imagine our authorities are pleased if they do, because we wouldn't want the expense of feeding, clothing and housing them indefinitely. Any other nation or body which complains could doubtless look after them as soon as possible. I personally would rather they returned to their various countries of origin and took our message with them.'

After admiring the medieval style bridge which, though wide enough for two way traffic still had passing places cut out of the parapets, they strolled over to view the trawlers and coaster. Being Whyte Island owned all three looked old fashioned, but as he well knew from experience they would be sure to be modern in every way. Although the quayside was practically deserted, great activity on board the fishing vessels heralded their imminent departure. He would have liked to see them leaving the harbour but his companion, on checking her watch, urged haste, and so he was compelled to be content with a brief eye-scanning of the harbour and its long line of buildings and backdrop of cliffs on the opposite side, and to watch the quarrelsome gulls and the dainty terns as they hovered or dipped into the water to pick up a small fish or morsel.

Standing at the bus stop and facing toward the town, Sandra described a little of the place to him. 'It's a great favourite with many of us islanders,' she declared enthusiastically. 'This side of the harbour, being the greater area, is the best; it's riddled with little alleyways leading to bookshops, art studios, pubs, restaurants, coffee houses, and inns and B & Bs, and other such places. And there are squares of varying sizes, each one named after the particular tree planted in the centre, which prevents the area from becoming too claustrophobic or tedious.' She paused, then urged, 'look over there'.

His gaze followed her finger which was directed toward a square church tower rising above the adjacent roof tops. He'd quite forgotten the town was really modern, so he was surprised when he realised the atheistic Whyte Islanders had built a church, and one which even from this distance could be seen to have been authentically constructed in a medieval design. 'Of course,' the girl explained, 'it isn't used as a place of worship. Instead it contains a museum of early items such as clothing, various domestic and workplace utensils and furniture. There's also a library and a display of replica paintings and jewellery of the era, and they also hold concerts of contemporary music and have banquets. All our island churches have been restored where necessary and put to a variety of uses. Don't you think it's sad so many of your religious houses have been abandoned to the attentions of dry rot and woodworm, while others are being used in totally inappropriate ways?'

Sandra went on telling him about the town until their bus, a bright green single decker, arrived. Their destination was situated several stops down the straight road near where a smaller stream emerged from a steep valley, and Andrew's companion chose seats on the side nearest the town, so enabling him to study the different buildings as they passed by. About a third of the way along the road the bus stopped opposite a large paved square, in the centre of which was an imposing plaster and wood structure raised on wooden pillars above an open space. This, she explained, contained the town hall and council offices. Some distance beyond was the great bulk of the church. The remaining two sides of the square were occupied by rows of shops. Judging by the number of passengers alighting at the stop, and by the people with shopping bags constantly crossing the square, the shops were well patronised. It was an incongruous sight, in a town so well endowed with ancient looking buildings and quite unspoilt by the intrusion of modern style ones, to see people wearing various recent modes of clothing.

Andrew could scarcely believe the contrast when they finally stepped down from the bus. Although they weren't far from the town they might almost have been in the countryside, for on one side a narrow road led to what appeared to be a park, while on their left a bridge, over which their bus had departed, spanned the small stream which eventually disgorged into the harbour. Immediately ahead of them a woodland flanked lane climbed up through a wide cleft in the chalk cliff. Turning to watch the progress of their late bus, the young man noted it was heading in the direction of the area of town on the opposite side of the harbour and assumed it would eventually arrive back at the station via the main bridge, for there could be no roadway exit through the cliff beyond the houses.

As they crossed the road, Sandra told him that the school, in order to conform with island policy, had been situated in parkland, but she also mentioned the park extended virtually all the way round to the station yard entrance. 'Apart from making an ideal recreational area,' she explained, 'it helps to safeguard the town from any landslips from the cliffs which, though extremely uncommon, is why you wouldn't find any buildings near their foot.'

'Including the school?' Andrew murmured hopefully.

The driveway, which was long and pleasantly wooded, ran parallel with the only partially visible line of cliffs until it suddenly widened out into a large tarmac area, in the midst of which was situated the school. Further proof that the whimsical nature of island architecture didn't extend to schools was evident in the building which eventually faced them, for far from being medieval in style, it was every bit as modern as the green school Andrew had visited the previous week.

As Sandra led the way through the main entrance doors and up the stairs for the obligatory visit to the headteacher's office, she gave him some idea of what to expect. 'All blue schools have two principals, a man and a woman. This is because the ten to fifteen age range naturally covers the years of puberty when guidance and understanding from a really responsible and knowledgeable person of the pupil's own sex is essential. For the same reason, the numbers of teachers of either gender is more or less equal. As you may know, Andrew, one of the main concerns of the island's authorities is that the sexes should live together in perfect harmony. Married life, we feel, is the fountainhead of all happiness and contentment, and so the opportunity is taken at these schools of teaching boys and girls every aspect of successful coexistence. Also, when the pupils attain blue school age, their special aptitudes and interests have usually become more apparent, and so throughout their sojourn they're gently guided into their best roles in life. But anyway, I think I've said too much as you'll probably hear it all again from one of the headteachers.'

But this was not to be, for when the door to the appropriate office had been opened to Sandra's knock, the girl before them said, 'I'm sorry, but both headteachers are indisposed. I'm just the secretary, but Mrs Grant has left you a programme if you'd care to follow it?'

Sandra smiled. 'That's alright. I've shown visitors around before so there shouldn't be too much trouble.'

Nevertheless, the secretary insisted they should have some coffee whilst Andrew's companion perused the programme, and this she did in some detail, though she managed to involve him at the same time.

'I'm quite surprised there wasn't anyone official to receive us,' he observed after they'd left the office, 'as I always thought the organisation on the island was exceptional.'

She laughed. 'It might well have been done deliberately. They could be testing my ability to deal with an unexpected situation. After all I wouldn't be much use in a sudden crisis if I couldn't cope, would I?' Even though she was only about the same age as Linda he couldn't help being impressed by the girl's self-assurance, for on their subsequent tour of the school she never became flustered or at a loss for words, and she also succeeded in maintaining his constant interest.

In many ways this establishment, together with its layout, was a carbon copy of the earlier school except, naturally, the standards were much higher. Before taking him into a classroom, for example, Sandra would explain what might be happening inside whereupon, just as in the green school, they would knock on the door, meet the teacher and pupils, and then sit down at the back of the room to witness the proceedings.

There were notable exceptions, though; an example being where they arrived at a classroom fitted with two doors. After explaining what would be occurring beyond, Sandra, without knocking, opened one of the doors which was reached by short metal staircase, and Andrew found himself at the back of a miniature theatre in which a play was being staged. The drama, which he soon caught the gist of, was concerned with what happened when a selfish and coarse man moved in next door to a quiet family, and the disruptions caused by the endless home improvements which the former inflicted upon the latter. The stage area had been cleverly halved so that the dividing wall between the two homes was depicted enabling the activity on either side to be seen in detail.

The play seemed quite amusing in places but he couldn't detect any signs of mirth emanating from the young audience below and before him, and he quickly realised what a serious subject it really was. He was very much impressed by the high standard of acting, for the participants' youth didn't prevent them from displaying real professionalism when called upon to do so; and so they were able to portray happiness, annoyance, contempt, rage and fear with complete ease, and they weren't afraid to shout whenever the drama indicated it. Because the audience had its back to them he was unable to see precisely what effect the drama was having, but he was sure the actors where enjoying themselves as much as the youngsters in the green school play had.

There wasn't time to see very much of the drama, but as they moved on to the next classroom Sandra explained what eventually happened to both families; how the peace loving neighbour repeatedly asked the noisy man to be quieter, and how his requests were answered by sneers until the quiet man became deranged and began making noises in retaliation. This prompted the hypocritical home improver to seek legal aid, which so enraged the quiet man that he attacked his perceived persecutor with a hammer.

'To make the play even more complicated and interesting,' the girl continued, 'the effect of each man's personality on their respective families was shown, how the home improver had no time to spare for his wife and children and what was happening to them as a result, and how the peace-loving man's mental instability caused him to direct psychological and, to a lesser extent, physical violence against his loved ones. In fact, the noisy neighbour had been psychologically neglected by his father, and so his self-imposed home improvement was a subconscious desire to show his father, and the world at large, how clever he really was. However, he was totally unaware of the fact that he, in his turn, was doing to his children what his father had done to him.'

Because the blue schools were designed to bring out each pupil's personal aptitude, some new subjects were introduced which weren't found in the green establishments. These included cookery and domestic sciences, wood and metalwork, embroidery and knitting, plumbing and electricity. It amused Andrew to see the boys sitting down to do sewing along with the girls in one class, and then for him to witness a lecture and demonstration on bricklaying with both sexes present.

'Although there are some subjects which the opposite gender, as the case may be, might not be expected to take a professional interest in,' said Sandra in answer to her companion's subsequent query, 'it's felt there isn't any harm in each gender experiencing what is normally thought of as being the province of one particular sex. You'd be surprised at the number of advantages this policy produces. To begin with, it brings the sexes closer together because it creates further topics of conversation, so that a boy might ask a new girl friend how good she was at metalwork, while he would be able to hold forth on the techniques of crocheting. As a bonus it also provides additional defence against snobbery. No woman, no matter how immaculately coiffured and well dressed, can think herself superior to others when it is naturally known she has wielded a spanner to connect up a series of water pipes. On the other hand, a man who has gained top marks for knitting a sweater can't expect to parade himself as a pocket Hercules without ridicule.'

'Aren't there ever any objections from the pupils?'

'Not anymore,' smiled Sandra. 'Quite a number of girls have discovered they enjoy getting their hands dirty in mechanical pursuits, and many boys actually like to do cooking and handicrafts.'

Andrew nodded in recollection. 'That would explain why there are so many women employed in the engineering and electrical branches on board Whyte Line ships, and why I met a woman in a workshop at the factory complex.'

'In theory there's absolutely no reason why women shouldn't do similar work to men. Although we're usually not as strong, we're often equally as intelligent and reliable. The air department of one of the armed services on the mainland has had a long tradition of employing women on aircraft maintenance and repair duties, but somehow until fairly recently the practice hadn't caught on elsewhere.' She shrugged and continued. 'It probably comes down to gender prejudices and attitudes. The lack of faith men subconsciously have in women's engineering ability, the fear of employers that their workforce would spend too much time in having affairs, and frequent absenteeism due to pregnancies, although these last to handicaps could apply equally to office staff. But mostly, I think, the greater percentage of women aren't interested in getting grimy hands and working in dirty and uncomfortable conditions. Personally I found boy's work fun at school, but I wouldn't want to do it permanently.'

From what he could make out, the lack of gender prejudice extended to the playing fields, for their tour of the school next took them out to see the various sporting activities just before the mid-day break. It was a warm though somewhat overcast day with a gentle off-sea breeze, and the sports field was therefore well patronised. Three activities were taking place – on the perimeter a relay race was in the course of being run, while the large area in the centre provided room enough for a game of basketball to be played, as well as to permit a group to practice javelin throwing. The arrangement wasn't as dangerous as it at first seemed, for each party was a safe distance from its neighbours. Each event, however, was made up of teams containing both boys and girls, but to allow for the difference in power and endurance of the genders, each team comprised an equal number of each.

'You'll never see all girl teams playing all boy teams, or even sides consisting of just one sex,' commented Sandra. 'Normally each side is made up of half and half.'

'You don't take sport very seriously over here, do you?' Andrew observed, recalling something Linda had once mentioned, and not being able to remember any of his former shipmates taking part in sporting competitions abroad.

'Well, nowhere near as seriously as it is in your country and elsewhere. We don't, for instance, have cases of crowds of fans going on the rampage because their football team has lost, or people paying large sums of money for a seat at a tennis, cricket or basketball match, or whatever. This isn't merely because it's out of character for Whyte Islanders to form unruly mobs or because we haven't the money to spend unnecessarily, but due to the fact that rivalry, even in sport, seems pointless. So sport is generally thought of as being for personal interest only, to be enjoyed by the participants and not for the benefit of spectators. We believe such activity to be useful as it keeps the player fit and healthy, and helps as a practice of self-control. It encourages the individual to remain calm and civil in the heat of the moment, to be a good winner or loser, and to be fair-minded; in other words, to be a good sportsperson, to use the term in its accepted sense.

'The last thing our authorities want is a cause for any rivalry to become established over here. By studying history and observing what has occurred and is now happening in the rest of the world, we're well aware of how innocuous, well-meaning foundations such as religion and the legal system can remorselessly grow out of control until they eventually make a mockery out of their original altruistic intentions: to bring fairness and justice for all, in the case of the aforementioned examples.

'For the same reason, we realise that allowing just one match between schools, villages or towns would lead to others being requested, thereby engendering the beginning of rivalries, leading to schisms and an eventual breakdown in our carefully built 'all for one and one for all' ideology. Incidentally, we find the necessity of involving vast sums of money in sporting activities throughout our planet quite incomprehensible. We think such amounts could be better directed toward alleviating poverty and suffering. But of course, while people continue to consider such problems impossible to solve, money will always be squandered.' After watching each of the three contests in turn for some time, Sandra mentioned it was time for dinner.

The cafeteria was a fascinating place to Andrew's eyes, for it adjoined a massive swimming pool from which it was separated by a huge plate glass window. He hadn't seen anything like the pool before because, although it was an indoor one, it sheltered palm trees and other tropical plants. This vegetation was set well back from the water's edge, presumably to guard against foliage falling into the water, and there was a large area of patio around the actual pool, which accommodated what appeared to be a grotto with a waterfall, in addition to several fountains. To support the overall tinted glass roof it had been necessary to employ central pillars, and where these entered the water they'd been utilised as islands where swimmers could sit and rest on ceramic tile bases.

The visitor thought it all seemed a bit ostentatious for mere school use, so he wasn't overly surprised when his companion explained that although the pool had been built primarily for schoolchildren, it was also intended, like the green school gymnasium, for the use of the public outside school hours. It was also often used as a nightclub, and was where swimming galas and similar water activities were frequently staged.

After his experience of the green school cafeteria, Andrew wasn't all that surprised to find quite a variable menu, but he was taken aback to note that, apart from a couple of supervising adults, all the staff in the open plan kitchen and servery were children. When they'd taken their food-laden trays over to a table next the plate glass window, he mentioned this fact.

'Yes,' Sandra acknowledged, 'it's a part of their education. When they've passed a proficiency exam in cookery they're permitted to take a turn in the canteen under the minimum of supervision. The attendant kitchen staff mainly ensure nothing gets out of hand, and also lift and carry heavy and potentially dangerous items. As you no doubt noticed while we were being served, the counter and kitchen units were lower than normal and the children involved weren't much smaller on average than the adults.'

'You mean they even cooked this meal?' he asked in bewilderment between mouthfuls of a truly succulent steak.

'Yes, and drew up the menu and even ordered the supplies.'

Andrew stared down at his meat with accompanying asparagus in delicious creamy sauce, his tender roast potatoes, as well as his ice cream with diced pears, and he shook his head slowly in astonishment. 'And all under fifteen,' he murmured.

The dining hall had been about half full when they'd entered, and their subsequent table with chairs for six had been unoccupied, but now they were joined by a boy and a girl of about thirteen and later by another mixed couple some two years younger. All four children greeted them pleasantly enough but confined their subsequent conversation amongst themselves, chatting away happily to each other. Sandra, though, kept her companion amused by describing the swimming pool and its various uses.

'I think I can safely say I've visited this pool for just about all the events because I love swimming and diving. I've given lessons here, been swimming in the evenings and at weekends when it's employed as a public baths, even taken part in and watched galas and displays. You wouldn't think by looking at it now it could become so beautiful, would you?'

The young man, glancing toward the pool, thought it seemed very attractive as it was, but his companion continued. 'When it's used as a nightclub it becomes transformed. A huge curtain covers this window, and a bar and buffet are opened up on the patio in addition to the obvious tables and chairs. You can't see it from here but there's concealed lighting everywhere, even at the sides of the pool, much of which can be focused automatically in various colours and brightness. It's difficult to appreciate how beautiful those palms, fountains and the grotto can look in various shades, and when there's a band or orchestra playing and people are dancing, it's really marvellous.' Andrew felt like asking whether anyone fell in the water on such occasions, but it seemed churlish to deflate her obvious enthusiasm.

After their meal, which was followed by a very tasty cup of coffee each, Sandra took him on a tour of the school grounds while they waited for the afternoon lessons to begin. By this time most of the clouds had disappeared and so there were plenty of children and teachers outside enjoying the substantial recreational area surrounding the school.

Andrew's memories of his own boyhood dinner breaks contrasted entirely with what he saw before him. He recalled there had then been a large tarred playground in front of the school for winter or wet weather use, and a huge playing field, which was utilised on dry summer days. The pupils had been sent out without supervision to fend for themselves, and with no organised games or sports equipment. There had been no seats, and both recreation areas were devoid of bushes and trees, the reason no doubt being so the children could be easily surveyed to ensure they were not up to mischief. As far as he could remember, there had been plenty of devilment going on nevertheless, with gangs of boys wandering about tormenting smaller or weaker children, and generally making a nuisance of themselves.

By the time he'd reached puberty the last school he'd attended had been for boys only, but he'd heard from people who'd studied at co-educational schools that incidents of a sexual nature were quite common, which was probably another reason why play areas hadn't been made visually more interesting.

Here though, the recreational space was more like a park, and even the sports fields had been edged with trees and shrubs. Everywhere children and teachers played or strolled, rested or exerted themselves as the fancy took them. Ostensibly there was plenty of opportunity for the pupils to form gangs, to take part in acts of vandalism, or to go off in mixed pairs to dally, but Andrew couldn't see any signs of mischief taking place. The only visible groups were involved in various impromptu sporting activities, but most of the children were either seated on the benches thoughtfully placed beneath the large variety of trees planted about the grounds, or else made use of the grass to lounge around in a variety of positions; they either studied alone or else gathered in twos, fours or more.

Sandra led the way over to a vacant bench sited beneath a great tree with greenish-blue fine pointed leaves, and flaking bark which gave a matted appearance to the trunk and thicker branches. It shocked him when he realised this large plant couldn't be much older than the school's senior pupil. 'It would be impossible to have all this beauty, tranquillity and discipline in a mainland school,' he reflected as they watched as four children rose to their feet and began to toss a ball to one another. 'Those kids would be bullying, or else be bullied, vandalising or be in the bushes exploring each other's anatomies.'

Sandra was silent for a moment and then asked, 'did you see the miniature roadway system during your green school tour?' When he nodded she went on. 'Well, all this landscaping is an extension of that idea. Once again, we're encouraging our children to be mischievous just so we can punish them when they err. But our educational policy has proved so successful that punishment is rarely necessary now because most pupils have already had self-discipline instilled in them by the time they enter blue schools.

'When Roger and Jane Jones devised our teaching system, they also introduced several provisions to ensure its continuing success, so in addition to our policy of treating our youngsters with respect and giving them every academic benefit and advantage, whilst willing to apply instantaneous discipline should the need arise, we also encourage our children to respect us in return.

'On the mainland, I daresay, when a mischievous child cheeks a teacher, their fellow classmates tend to admire them for their audacity and also because they regard their teacher as an opponent, but on Whyte Island the opposite would probably be true. They'd dislike the naughty child for trying to make a fool of the instructor they admire and for disrupting their lesson. Another provision encourages pupils to confide in their teachers. In your country, Andrew, it's looked upon as telling tales or sneaking, but over here we consider it as an act of responsibility for a child to tell their teacher of any misdemeanour on the part of a classmate or an acquaintance. Misbehaviour is thought of as being unnecessary because our children receive plenty of freedom and understanding, and so a private prank, for example, would be considered dangerous or pointless.'

He began to interrupt but Sandra quickly continued. 'I think I know what you're going to say, but you perhaps ought to take into account the fact that what children are taught they generally soon accept as normal, and so no pupil who confides in their teacher is thought badly of. To make it easy for our children and to create a psychological effect, school staff are expected to approach and converse with each pupil on a regular basis. The result is that despite the conversation possibly being about nothing in particular, the remainder of the pupils looking on might assume it could be with regard to something concerning them, so they wouldn't know whom to trust if they were thinking about doing something wrong. The fact that our youngsters seem to have few disturbing tales to tell these days appears to support the success of the system.

'One further aspect of our teacher-pupil relationship is that parents have no direct control over the treatment of their children during school hours. I'll give you an example, Andrew. It isn't unknown for pupils on the mainland to physically attack their teachers, is it? Or for outraged parents to offer violence?' He nodded. 'Well,' she went on, 'any pupil on Whyte Island who threatened a teacher could expect to face the bully basher, as would their parent if he, or she, came to school threatening violence. A parent wishing to complain about their child's treatment in school would need to see the representative for education or their local member of parliament, or both, to obtain satisfaction which, I can assure you, would be immediately forthcoming. Every islander has seen official films about classroom violence on the mainland, and frankly we're all amazed at the rudeness and lack of discipline displayed by many of the pupils, and we wouldn't dream of allowing such behaviour over here.'

Sandra smiled. 'Jane Jones apparently thought up an idea which might have proved useful in a similar situation. Instead of punishing wrongdoers within a class, what would happen if the remainder of the class was punished in his place? The onus would then have been on the innocent children to administer their own justice. But, of course, the success of our educational system made the experiment unnecessary. It would have been...' She never finished, because a smart middle-aged woman whom, as Andrew had noticed at a distance, appeared to be searching for someone suddenly saw them and came across.

'This is Mrs Grant,' Sandra explained, and after the newcomer had returned his greeting, she drew his companion to one side where they quickly became engaged in deep conversation. He tried to appear disinterested but he couldn't refrain from noting out of the corner of his eye that he seemed to be the main object of their exchange, for they each glanced at him several times. At last the headmistress and Sandra returned to sit next to him.

'Andrew,' the latter eventually addressed him, 'you remember I mentioned that blue schools are concerned with encouraging the sexes to live happily together?' He nodded, wondering what was coming next. 'Well, here's a unique opportunity for you to attend the final sex lesson. The children who'll witness it are later given a written and oral examination which, if they pass, allows them to take a partner of the opposite sex if they wish, so enabling them to live together. They need to be almost fifteen even to view the lesson, though I must warn you that everything bar actual intercourse will be shown, and even that will be simulated in various positions. But, of course, if you think it'll be too embarrassing then we won't go.'

Andrew didn't know what to say. On the mainland the sex act had long been portrayed in films and on the television, and even the radio staged very authentic sounding renditions of it. Somehow, though, no matter how realistic the performances, they seemed impersonal to him. But seeing a naked couple disporting themselves in real life while witnessed by children was a very different matter; it would be like seeing a surgical operation for the first time because he wouldn't know what his response might be. But then he realised the other people present wouldn't care about his reactions. Whyte Island children, he was beginning to realise, would be too sophisticated and polite to show any awareness of embarrassment on his part. 'Yes, I'd like to go,' he replied decisively.

The sex demonstration was the second lesson scheduled for that afternoon, but first they were to attend a lesson for older children which would be different because the teacher asked questions and the pupils provided oral answers if they could, though being helped along by the teacher if they ran into difficulties. Sandra told her companion, as they made their way back into the school building, that the children at the first lesson would be the ones attending the sex demonstration. They were due to go on to the red establishments, and so it was essential they should have a good grasp of what could generally be termed sociology before they graduated. 'You see, Andrew, when these children leave this school they'll be classed as adults and so from then on they'll be pursuing their own vocations, so it therefore has to be taken for granted their characters have been moulded in just the way our society wishes. I know it seems as though we're mass-producing automatons, but I'm sure you've noticed that our youngsters are extremely free thinking people. This first lesson gives both teacher and pupils an insight into what the other party knows, and you should find it most revealing. But in no way is it a substitute for the large number of exams the children have to face, along with their assessments, before they graduate.'

The classroom she took him to seemed especially designed for the lesson and wasn't unlike the theatre in that the floors rose from front to back allowing teacher and children to see each other perfectly. When they arrived the room was empty and so Sandra led the way to the back where their hands would be almost able to touch the ceiling. Soon a male teacher appeared, calling up a cheerful greeting to them, and then the pupils began to enter, each one dipping a hand into a bin on a table near the door and picking out what seemed to be a small white card. 'Every question is identified by a number,' the girl whispered, 'and so there are twenty questions, one for each pupil.'

'A lot of questions to be answered at random,' Andrew observed, also in an undertone.

'They shouldn't experience any difficulty because they've had them drummed into them enough times. Those questions represent the whole basis of our social structure.'

At last all the children had taken their seats. 'Number one,' called out the teacher as soon as they were all attentive. A girl with long dark hair just in front of Andrew stood up and waited expectantly. 'Why are there no hereditary positions of power on the island?' she was asked.

Her reply gave proof she was not reciting a dogma. It was obvious the question had been discussed in her presence on several occasions but her answer was plainly in her own words and so the result of much thought. 'A person who is born into a superior position is naturally out of touch with reality; they have no empathy or sympathy with less fortunate people because they haven't experienced privation. Such a person often becomes self-centred, arrogant, demanding and thoughtless with regard to others.' She hesitated, but the teacher allowed her plenty of time to gather her thoughts. 'Such a person helps to undermine their society, for any society which condones hereditary superiority has to be a hypocritical one because it must maintain one law for rich people and another for the poor. Therefore hereditary power isn't allowable here because hypocrisy is a crime on Whyte Island.'

'Very good, Diana,' the teacher congratulated her, 'but can you add to that?'

The girl thought some more, then suddenly said, 'oh, yes. If hereditary power were permitted, then in time a gap would appear in our island society, and eventually some members of the community would become poorer and this would lead to terrible things happening. Also, if complete power over the island were handed down from parent to child, it wouldn't necessarily mean the child was suitable for that responsibility.'

Apparently satisfied with her answer, the teacher allowed her to sit down to murmurs of approval, and then called out, 'number two, please.' Another girl arose and was asked, 'why is there little social intercourse between islanders and the outside world?'

Although by no means perplexed by the question, the girl

lacked the confidence of the first examinee and so she had to be coaxed by the teacher. She began easily enough. 'Island children get a much better education than most other countries teach; they are brought up to be courteous, honest and polite, but when they grow up they are more sensitive than other people. So if they mix with people of other lands they could either be hurt, mentally, by them or even worse, copy them and bring back bad ways to our island.'

To Andrew this seemed fair enough, but the teacher appeared to expect more, for after a minute or two of pregnant silence he said kindly, 'yes, Shirley, but what about tourists coming to the island?'

'Oh, they have different ways of doing things. They would leave litter about, be rude and might even steal.' Another long pause.

'What else?'

Possibly with the next lesson in mind, Shirley seemed to receive divine inspiration for she continued confidently. 'They would spoil the sex life of the island, the males would think us girls easy to seduce...' – Andrew was sure he could hear some subdued laughter at this – '….. and the island males would find foreign girls difficult to approach.' Nothing more seemed to be forthcoming so the teacher left it at that and called out the third number.

As the session progressed, Andrew began to realise each of the questions interlinked with others until he finally became aware that they were all about living together in a near perfect society. In this way the island authorities ensured every child knew what made up the intricate, to the newcomer, yet paradoxically simple society they lived in, giving them each the opportunity to understand why it was essential for certain lessons to be imbibed and for particular laws to be enforced.

'Does each pupil know what question they're going to be asked?' he whispered incredulously, as a bewildering variety of complicated questions were systematically answered.

'No,' replied Sandra quietly, surprise showing in her voice. 'I thought you realised. What happens is that the teacher takes the twenty standard questions and numbers them in any order he wishes. The children then take a numbered card from that bin, not knowing of course what that number will be. This ensures each pupil gets treated as fairly as possible. They all need to understand the workings of our society pretty intimately, but naturally some of the questions will be more difficult than others.'

To Andrew's untrained mind all the questions appeared complicated, but even Shirley, who gave one of the worst answers, was reasonably articulate and knowledgeable in her reply. He was only too pleased he wasn't expected to answer any of the questions. And so it went on, and subjects as diverse as crime, happiness, welfare, entertainment, politics and education were all answered with varying degrees of competence, until it was obvious to the visitor that these children had absorbed enough information to last them the rest of their lives. Eventually the answer to number twenty was forthcoming, but before the end of the session Andrew was to receive another surprise, for after the teacher had given his verdict on the class' joint effort he added, 'I believe you've all learnt enough to sit next week's paper on the subject. That is all. Thank you.'

Sandra had barely enough time in which to introduce her companion to the teacher after the pupils had gone, but Andrew was able to comment on the high aptitude of the children before asking why it was necessary to question them if they were going to take an examination on sociology anyway.

'As I said to the pupils,' Mark, the teacher, smiled, 'it's partly to test their proficiency in the subject. But giving them an oral is often a bigger eye-opener than when they actually sit the written exam. With the oral test, they have to form ideas straight from their minds, and this gives me a greater clue as to whether they subconsciously know what they're talking about, whereas when they're sitting down to a test they have time to think about the subject, even though there's more work for them to do.'

Andrew was scarcely able to thank Mark before Sandra whisked him away, so allowing them to time to reach the room where the sex demonstration was due to take place before anything had begun. On the way, however, he asked what happened to children who failed to pass their sociological examination. 'In really bad cases,' she explained, 'they might have to stay on for another year, but usually they're permitted to graduate and subsequently receive extra tuition on the subject, in which case they sit the exam annually until they pass. The worst effect of failing is they stand little or no chance of procreating while they're an island citizen.'

'You mean if they want children they have to emigrate?'

Sandra shrugged dismissively. 'That's another way of putting it. It's best for the island and our society in the long term, and a true patriot would recognise that fact.'

If the previous classroom seemed to have been designed for a question and answer session, then the room the young man found himself in had definitely been intended for the kind of demonstration they were about to witness. It was similar to the previous room in one respect as the floor also rose in stages. However, the wide shallow tiers had been arranged in order to form an amphitheatre completely enclosing a central space, within which stood an open sided couch with a backrest and a low combined cocktail cabinet and CD player. Directly above this furniture several large mirrors had been suspended in a way which permitted the audience various angles from which to view the centre floor. The temperature in the room was distinctly warm and this, together with the rich red carpet covering every part of the floor space, the pink furniture and orange pink lighting, subdued but bright enough to see clearly by, made the room very comfortable to be in. For the spectators, though Andrew might have used the description "voyeurs", substantial armchairs had been provided on the three tiers surrounding the central area.

As soon as they'd seated themselves, again at the back of the room he, glancing idly about, remarked, 'there are a lot more than twenty children here, I should think.'

Sandra nodded in agreement. 'The additional pupils have come from various local schools. This will be a rather specialised demonstration taking place in a specialised room, so it's hardly surprising that it should be witnessed by as many children as possible.'

'What's that for?' he asked in the quiet tone which the room seemed to demand, pointing to a small window set high up in the centre of one of the walls.

'That's the commentator's position. Look'. She lifted a lid set flush in the wide arm of her chair, and from out of the box which it concealed she withdrew a headset which she then placed over her ears.

Copying her, all he could hear was a pleasant, dreamy music, but almost as soon as the last of the pupils had donned her headset a compelling husky female voice began to whisper in his ear. 'I should like you to imagine that this is a private room in a building within which a couple are living together. All the demonstrations which you will see this afternoon will have been anticipated by one or both the partners. In each display, therefore, preparations will have been made to ensure the success of the subsequent lovemaking. They will have showered and perfumed themselves and changed into clothing which might easily be removed, the bed or couch will have been made ready, the room scented, a suitable CD placed on the player and a bottle of wine opened to sweeten the breath and relax the senses.

'Generally, with spontaneous sex, the motive is to assuage the desire as quickly as possible, coition being the primary goal. However, today's lovemaking will take place at a more leisurely rate with sexual intercourse being merely the pinnacle of love play. All the senses: touch, taste, vision, smell and hearing will be employed to maximum effect. While you watch the demonstration, I will provide a commentary, paying extra attention to points of special interest. Let us begin.'

Somewhere a door closed rather noisily, and almost immediately a young man with dark, almost black, hair and wearing a blue dressing gown appeared from an opening in the viewing stands. 'I'll just open some wine, darling,' he called. 'Don't be too long'. He selected a bottle, poured some of its contents into two glasses and, when accomplished, he lit a perfumed spill standing in a bowl on the drinks cabinet and watched the smoke for a moment as it curled lazily upward. Finally he knelt before the cabinet and looked at several discs before placing one on the player.

As the music reached Andrew's ears, he found it just as loud and clear as the music and voice which had emanated from the commentator's box. He couldn't help admiring the way in which the man was setting the scene for the demonstration, making it seem more like a play than a lesson. Almost as if the gentle music from the player were a cue, a beautiful girl with shoulder length honey-gold hair appeared, clad in a white dressing gown. She was much shorter than the man, as was evident when she moved over to him where, after putting her hands behind his neck, she stood on tiptoe and whispered something intimate in his ear; whatever it was, was immediately answered with a passionate embrace and kiss. When the two eventually parted, the girl, with wonderful grace, moved across to the couch upon which she lay down with her back resting against the raised end. In the meantime her companion, who had gone to fetch the drinks, returned to sit by her side. As she took her glass they both laughed and pressed their heads together. Andrew then distinctly saw the girl raise her glass to her lips and her tongue dip into the wine. She then deliberately withdrew the tongue and inserted it between her lover's slightly open lips.

During the intense embrace which followed, the man's hand moved to the bow on the girl's belt, which was the only fastening on her dressing gown. A deft tug on the knot caused one half of the his lover's garment to fall away revealing the right side of her body which included a shapely breast, the whole of one leg and a tantalising glimpse of body hair. The man's hand wasn't slow in taking advantage of his companion's exposed flesh for it first caressed her breast, then moved down her side to fondle her leg, before returning once more to her breast.

The sensation was obviously too much for the girl, for she removed her lips from those of her lover and finished off the wine in her glass so her right hand would be free. Once unencumbered by the glass, her hand began exploring her companion's as yet clothed body. Whispered words of love and endearment between kisses came through on Andrew's microphone, and then the commentator's voice was heard once more.

'Notice how both lovers are taking part in fondling and talking to their partner. This is most important in lovemaking, as the bed or couch is not the place for any shyness or reticence. It is difficult to credit the number of relationships which have failed due to one of the partners, usually the female, consistently taking a passive role. Each lover needs to know they are desired, loved, needed and admired, and that the various parts of their body are of interest and are desirable to their companion in love. Notice, too, how the hands caress the body, sometimes gently, often firmly, and how those hands are frequently moved to different areas of sensuality, gradually remaining longer in those areas of greatest sexuality. The position of the couple to each other allows greater freedom of movement to the arms and hands, and also exposes the maximum expanse of body for the purpose of mutual exploration. Only during, and often after, actual coupling is it necessary or even desirable for the two bodies to be pressed together.'

Andrew, who had been experiencing some difficulty in deciding which was the appropriate mirror to watch at any one time, had been afraid he'd think the demonstration sordid and cheap but instead he found it interesting and surprisingly beautiful. The couple below him were obviously deeply in love and perfectly happy about displaying the intensity of their love before strangers.

He glanced sideways at Sandra to check whether she were disturbed in any way by the activity in the arena, but she was simply gazing down in a manner which suggested that she was observing nothing in particular. Obviously noting his interest in her, she simply faced him, smiled and commented, 'it's just life, Andrew.'

Now, with exact timing, the lovers progressed from hand caressing to body kissing, a form of love play necessitating a certain amount of position changing for both participants. Finally, when they'd both reached the peak of sexual excitement, they adopted the most common position for coition. It said much for the lovers that they managed to refrain from actually uniting for they were obviously under some stress, and so it was probably hardly surprising they didn't remain long in their very intimate position because they soon vacated their couch and, after retrieving their dressing gowns, disappeared behind the staging.

Andrew, who'd been wondering if, like Linda and he, they ever managed to slip up, was so impressed by their performance that he quite forgot himself and began applauding. For a moment he was alone but, much to his relief, his clapping was gradually taken up until the entire room, including Sandra, had joined him.

The couple must have immediately taken a cold shower, because it wasn't long before the girl, looking composed and refreshed, reappeared in the centre area. Now it was her turn to pour the drinks and choose a disc and, according to the commentator, to take the leading role. Presumably the subsequent demonstration was primarily for the girls in the audience, for when her beau entered, the honey blonde gave a display of artistry in seduction which would have given hope to the shyest and plainest of females. With the man laying passively on the couch she was easily able to arouse him to an obvious state of distraction with coquettish glances and tantalising glimpses of her faultless body, along with intimate whispering in his ear while allowing her tresses to flow over his face, and with subtle caresses of his body from her hands and fingers.

During her seduction she managed to divest herself of her gown and insinuate a leg over his hips. Soon she had adopted the position of sexual intercourse, but she'd only just begun for at that moment the disc she'd chosen changed to a tune of frantic rhythm and she responded by moving her body in time to the music, flailing her arms, head and upper torso about in violent contortions and by adopting a variety of brief poses as she did so. How Andrew envied and pitied her lover, the sensation he must be undergoing must have been exquisitely unendurable. During his trips abroad on the Whyte Line ships, Andrew had seen exotic dances performed which involved much hip rolling and shaking by women and girls, that he'd assumed were merely part of the dance routine, but now, due to the performance he was witnessing he realised their display was originally intended to advertise their prowess in lovemaking. And here was the proof before him. Eventually the music changed to a more gentle rhythm and became more dreamy, at which the girl became less violent and continued her gyrations at a much more leisurely pace until the end of the disc, whereupon she removed herself from her lover, donned her gown and together the lovers departed.

The visitor could only guess how the younger males in the audience felt, but he was distinctly agitated by the performance and could only wish he had Linda by his side so he might rearrange his senses as soon as possible. 'This last demonstration,' the woman's sultry voice sounded in his ears, 'illustrates how easily the male gender can be aroused and satisfied, and how advisable it is for girls and women to become expert in rotating, as well as reciprocating, their hips as in the position just shown, if the partnership is to be continued further. Males in such a situation should likewise ensure they can trust their lover in such a position if they submit to restraint and muting, as prolonged exercise in this manner may lead to emotional and physical damage in the long term. Now, onto the final demonstration of the day.'

Almost immediately the couple returned simultaneously. On this occasion it was the turn of the man to take the lead, his partner pretending to be sulky and uncooperative. The lovemaking began with the partners standing up, the man merely caressing his partner's hair and the nape of her neck and telling her softly how beautiful she was and how much he loved, admired and needed her. Then he started to comment on the beauty of her eyes, nose and mouth, kissing each in turn as he did so. Gradually he became more daring as he sensed her increasing warmth and interest in him. By having recourse to one of the mirrors Andrew saw the man's hands move from their position on his lover's shoulders down to her back, thence to her waist and finally to her buttocks where he used them to pull her pelvis subtly against his own. As he did so, he gave her a prolonged kiss. He then raised his right hand to the back of her head and stroked her hair. And so he had her completely trapped against him, and in this position he held her until, presumably, he felt some response in sexual desire, for now he had to make a direct assault upon her body and doubtless he didn't wish her sulkiness to return by making her suspect he was more interested in her body than in herself.

By a remarkable coincidence, the voice in Andrew's headset began again for the first time since the previous demonstration, and it said exactly what he'd been thinking, but also added, 'just as a woman has man's desire for her body as a weapon against his flagging sexual desire, as typified by the last performance, so a man has the average female's low resistance to flattery and guile to aid him.'

The man overcame his particular problem of continuity by gradually pulling his partner over toward the couch where, as soon as he felt it touch the back of his legs, he insinuated his hand to the front of her waist where he undid her belt and, using both hands, he carefully eased the dressing gown off her shoulders, sitting down as he did so. After drawing her between his open knees he employed one hand to fondle an exposed breast, his mouth on the other and remaining hand to caress an even more intimate part of her body. By this time, his lover was in a trancelike state and she was therefore finally easily manoeuvred into the third position of intercourse to be demonstrated that day.

'Before we end our display of pre-sexual love play,' announced the headset voice, 'a few words about post-coital courtesy. Firstly, it is always desirable lovers should thank each other for the use of their respective bodies. Secondly, on no account ought partners draw away from each other immediately after intercourse. Men frequently fall asleep within minutes of the end of the sex act and I speak from experience when I state there are few emotions nicer than having the partner you love asleep in your arms. However, should both partners manage to remain conscious, then immediate kisses, caresses and terms of endearment and appreciation will go a remarkably long way to ensuring the long term success of a relationship.

'Finally, this demonstration has been primarily concerned with the arousal of the senses before intercourse. Women, especially, feel used if not enough attention has been paid to this aspect. The actual sex act is, by comparison, relatively simple and straightforward and this has been comprehensively described and illustrated in the book 'Living Together' with which you will all be presented when you graduate from your blue schools. You will also find all the different positions for intercourse, in addition to everything else you'll need to know about forming a successful heterosexual relationship. Good luck with your exams and we hope you all manage to set up homes soon if you wish to. Thank you!'

As they rose to their feet Sandra glanced at her watch and said, 'those two lessons took longer than I thought they would. We'd better take our leave of Mrs Grant or Mr Hetherington, whichever one's available, as it's much too late to attend anymore lessons.'

'What about the children?'

'Oh, they know what to do,' she replied dismissively, then asked, 'look, how do you fancy coming again tomorrow? Then in the afternoon we could perhaps visit the summer camp.'

Andrew was completely agreeable to this suggestion, but emboldened by the recent demonstration and completely forgetting his date with the Maynard family for that evening he added, 'do we have to go home now?'

Sandra paused on the stairs and turned to look up at him, a puzzled expression on her face. 'What do you mean?' she enquired with a frown. Her bewilderment made him realise he'd blundered, forcing him to begin to stammer a reply, but suddenly she smiled, joined him on his step and then pressed a finger tip briefly to his nose. 'If you mean what I think you mean, then the answer is definitely "no".'

It was his turn to look perplexed making his companion laugh, although without malice. 'I'm sorry. You don't seem to understand. Over here it's generally the female who makes the first move, so if I'd been interested in you I'd have let you know long ago. I've already got a boyfriend and so even if I'd fancied you I wouldn't lead you on, because serious island lovers are intensely loyal to each other. I mean, you've got Linda, so you shouldn't be poaching.'

'You mean I did have Linda,' he said sadly as they continued down the stairs bound for the heads' office.

'Oh dear.' She looked back at him with concern. 'She's a bit like that.'

'Yes, she dropped me like a hot brick,' he replied, full of self-pity. 'She wouldn't even accompany me to the Station Arms on Wednesday.'

'What, the pub in the village below the Maynards'?' she asked with increasing interest. 'Now that isn't like her. There's someone down there,' she added with conviction.

'You're the second person to say that,' Andrew replied cheerfully, his gloom now rapidly evaporating.

Sandra nudged him conspiratorially. 'You lucky devil. I bet she'll make me look like an old hag!'

'Well, if she doesn't I'll come and kidnap you.' This remark made the girl laugh all the way to their destination.

Mrs Grant was getting ready to leave by the time they arrived, but she happily dropped everything in order to attend to them, and so the programme for the following day was easily arranged. In some strange way their arrival seemed to drive all thought of departure from the headmistress' mind for, after removing herself a short way from their presence to phone someone called Malcolm on her mobile, she bade them sit down and made them some tea. 'Tell me, Andrew,' she said when they were all comfortable, 'as a stranger, what do you think of our sex policy after seeing the demonstrations? Are they anything like sex lessons on the mainland?'

The young man found the sudden questions extremely embarrassing. He still harboured his country's guilt complex about sexual matters in his veins, so discussing such a subject with a woman old enough to be his mother, along with a young girl both virtual strangers, was extremely difficult for him. However, he felt he'd better make the attempt, so he tried to deflect the question as much as possible. 'Well,' he began, 'the lessons I received were confined to books and diagrams and dealt more with the biological aspect.' Then he added rather pointlessly, 'I only went to a boy's school. But I believe our education authorities and the general public would think you rather immoral encouraging youngsters to have sex, and especially showing them how to arouse their

121

partners.'

He heard a gasp and glanced around to see Sandra staring at him in surprise, but Mrs Grant wasn't in the least perturbed. 'I can understand that you might find our ways a little strange here when compared to your own country, but may I explain further?' When he nodded she continued. 'Now, you've already toured the green schools, so you would have had a pretty good idea of why we teach our children the rudiments of sex at an early age, and you've also just witnessed the sex demonstration for our older children. But that was only a small part of our general policy with regard to sex because there was much more we had to take into consideration.

'I don't know if anyone's told you, Andrew, but before Whyte Island was established Charlie Maynard and Harry Larke set up discussion groups in their mainland factories to which eminent and professional people were often invited as guest speakers. During one of these debates, at which I was most fortunate to be present, a lady psychiatrist who'd had a lot of experience in criminal work related a particularly horrific story.'

She paused briefly, then went on. 'Basically what happened was that a man whom you would probably call a thug, went out one night carrying a knife ostensibly to do a bit of burglary. He eventually chose a likely looking house in the affluent part of his town. Unhappily his choice was rather unfortunate by mainland standards because the occupiers were both celebrated film and television stars, who not only led blameless lives but also did a great deal of charity work. On the day in question they'd returned home in the early evening after a particularly gruelling day's work and, without bothering to lock up, had gone upstairs to rest for a few hours before nightfall. The next thing they were both aware of was it was pitch black outside and someone was shining a light in their eyes.'

Once again Mrs Grant paused. 'Now, I'm not going into any details,' she continued, 'but when I tell you the least vile thing that burglar did was to rape and generally abuse the wife then you might have some idea of what happened next. The subsequent result was the marriage was irrevocably ruined, the wife lost all her self-respect, the husband, now unable to look at another woman, including his wife, entered a monastery and the intruder was sent to an asylum for the criminally insane. Of course, the couple, being celebrities, were able to hush the entire episode up and they quietly faded from public view, just like so many other well-known personalities.

'On the surface, Andrew, this story was nothing unusual, but it was to have a profound effect on the society of the future Whyte Island because the psychiatrist then went on to analyse the underlying cause of the attack for our benefit.' The headmistress smiled ruefully. 'Before her explanation I don't suppose there would have been one of us present who wouldn't have willingly removed that burglar's testicles and then lynched him. But afterwards we actually pitied him. You see, Andrew, that psychiatrist made us realise we shouldn't have been thinking of revenge, but rather of how to prevent that kind of outrage from occurring in future.

'What she then did was to tell us the life experience of the intruder. Apparently he'd been born the wrong colour and into poverty, he'd been neglected and ill-treated as a child and had grown up extremely ugly. Unfortunately in his maturity he was very highly sexed, but experienced great difficulty in being accepted by girls and women. Eventually, though, out of desperation he married a person who, paradoxically, was very promiscuous in her favours but not at all sexually satisfying.

'So, Andrew, if you can take into account all the misfortunes attendant on this man, you might begin to understand how he felt when he found himself gazing down at the bewildered couple lying in bed. He later told the psychiatrist he'd recognised them immediately. He'd been jealous of their fame, their wealth, had envied the man his good looks and had lusted after his wife's half exposed body, and he'd hated them both for their colour, which had always seemed a passport to success to him.'

Mrs Grant shrugged. 'So, under the circumstances, it's hardly surprising that the urge to humiliate them both should become irresistible. Now, when the psychiatrist had finished explaining, we held a grand discussion on the case and the final conclusion was obvious to us, which was that should we ever be in the position to found a society we wouldn't take revenge on wrongdoers, as the rest of the world does. Instead we'd ensure people would no longer have a motive for behaving badly.

'No doubt that unfortunate burglar is still suffering from sexual frustration in some padded cell, a hopeless case beyond salvation whom, Andrew, out of humanity we'd almost certainly have put out of his misery long ago, but if it hadn't been for his crime our moral code wouldn't have been established.

'During our various discussions, many personal stories came to light and significantly concerning sexual matters, the men were more willing to relate their experiences than were the women. I can clearly recall three interesting tales which aptly demonstrated our gender's mystifying, to men, attitude toward them.' Mrs Grant paused and smiled across at Sandra. 'And quite frankly after hearing them I can quite understand why males should sometimes think us females odd.

'The first man stated that often, in his younger days, he used to travel around the mainland a great deal and, as he was fond of both women and dancing, he would frequent the current local dancehalls. However, he told us it wasn't unusual to be refused dances out of hand and for absolutely no reason he could tell. On one occasion he arrived at a dance quite early and found a long line of girls of all ages and degrees of attractiveness seated against a wall, so he went from one girl to the next asking for a dance and at the twelfth refusal he gave up and asked the girl at the bar for the first of a series of drinks.

'At another dancehall in a different town he subsequently equalled the old score, but on this occasion it was well on into the evening and he'd gone to various parts of the room to request dances. The unfortunate man explained that although sexually attracted toward women, he would have been quite happy to have had a girl to talk to if only in the absence of her regular boyfriend; he merely wanted company whilst in a strange town.

'The second man, theoretically, had much less to complain of, but he was equally puzzled by some of his experiences. On at least three separate occasions he could remember being with girls he'd never met before, and each one had lain impassively whilst permitting him to do as he wished with her body.'

Both Sandra and the headmistress laughed when Andrew automatically commented, 'lucky man.'

But Mrs Grant said, 'well, he didn't seem to think so. He did take advantage of them but stopped short of actual intercourse, because he reckoned there didn't seem to be any pleasure to be had from it.'

'Like mounting a sack of warm wool?' suggested Sandra.

The headmistress nodded. 'But according to him he wasn't

particularly successful at dating girls, and so the percentage of similar lifeless women might be quite high on the mainland. I felt really sorry for the narrator of the last story, though, because apparently he was a lonely individual who experienced great difficulty in forming liaisons with the opposite sex. Eventually, however, he managed to get a naïve young girl to go steady with him and, without really planning to, in the course of time he seduced her. From then on sexual intimacy became a regular occurrence but gradually their unions became, let us say, more earthy and cruder, but no matter what liberties the girl allowed her lover it was never enough. He became more demanding, cruder and crueller, until eventually she became convinced that he was only interested in her as a gratification for his outrageous sexual desires. He had shattered her love for him, and so she left him at the first opportunity. The man, who at first reckoning deserved to have been rejected, went back to a life of loneliness and unhappiness, made doubly painful by the knowledge of the treasure he'd lost. Would you like to hazard a guess as to what went wrong, Andrew?'

The young man shook his head. 'I'm afraid I haven't a clue.'

'Well, a prime reason for the break up was that the girl never seemed able to form an opinion upon anything. The man wanted a companion but all he got was a sex object. But the really vital missing element was that, even in the later stages of their union when he was using her in the most intimate of ways, she was still shy with him. She rarely, if ever, began sexual advances, never talked to him in return when they made love, and never of her own accord showed him through her actions she really loved him. Thus she was leaving all the initiative in love making to him. So therefore, ironically, the more he had sex with her the more subconsciously frustrated he became.

'A sad sequel to this story was the fact that, during the course of their relationship, the man's work kept him away from his home a great deal and so a large amount of correspondence took place between the lovers. At the time he did little more than glance through the girl's letters as he received them, but later, after their break up, when he was lonely and frustrated once more, he used to read them frequently and in great depth. He found that not only was she not shy in expressing her love on paper, but that she was also very intelligent and perceptive, so if she could have expressed in words what she had in writing, then the future of the two might well have been very different.

'I think you'll agree, Andrew, that in each of the four stories I've just related, we women don't appear in a very good light, and this fairly obvious fact made us realise that if we should ever wish to improve our moral standards substantially, then women would be required to take a far more active part. The story concerning the burglar, besides numerous other examples of brutality from the entertainment and media industries of other countries, proved graphically how dangerous the male's combined sexual and aggressive drive can be when frustrated. So, instead of leaving the problem to prostitutes, raped or molested females and children, even to men and animals in some circumstances, it was thought far more just if we women shared the responsibility equally between us.'

Recalling something Linda had once said, Andrew asked, 'but you don't force promiscuity on girls, though?'

Mrs Grant shook her head. 'No, that decision is left entirely to the individual. But what our authorities did was to encourage we women to exchange roles with the men. In other words, we were expected to take the initiative with regard to social and sexual activities, and to display more discernment, determination, decisiveness and compassion in our dealings with the opposite sex. The intention was to ensure no male over the age of fifteen should be without the chance to make love to a female.'

'Isn't that rather what they call sexist?' he asked.

The headmistress laughed. 'Well, if it is, no one's complained so far. By the nature of things, few women under normal circumstances need ever worry about lack of sexual gratification while there are normal men available, besides which we seem better able to withstand lack of bodily pleasures, and so create less mayhem when deprived of sex. No, the males were the ones who needed to be taken seriously. Mind you, males had to learn a new set of rules. They were expected to regard promiscuity in a female as being of as little consequence as it would be in a male, neither should they be possessive toward single women against their will, or treat them as mere sex objects. Both genders were expected to honour the sanctity of their own and other people's relationships. In other words they shouldn't poach, especially where their prospective lovers were already parents.'

She paused thoughtfully, then continued. 'To return specifically to us women, I think I'd better give you a further example of what is expected of us, Andrew. Now, supposing you'd just arrived from the mainland and were sitting alone in a park; you knew no one, were ill at ease with females, were untidy, had bad breath and your feet smelled.' Sandra giggled but Mrs Grant merely smiled and remarked, 'Of course, you're not like that, but this is only an example. Now, the first unattached female to notice you would certainly approach you. Ostensibly she'd be little different from any other reasonably well dressed female, but she'd have been the product of our educational system and society. Therefore, she'd be using the tactics she'd been taught at school. Most importantly she wouldn't have any doubts or problems on her mind. She'd be poised and confident, frank and honest and she'd have been trained to overlook your bad points and seek out your good ones. The former she'd learn to live with or remedy in time, the latter she'd exploit to the full.

'She'd be a good conversationalist with a more than adequate command of knowledge, and she'd consider sex as being perfectly natural and would be skilled in its practice. Whilst she conversed with you, she'd be assessing you in a completely impartial manner, finding out everything you were willing to divulge after which, even if she didn't think you were right for her, she'd possibly accompany you for the rest of the day. She might even sleep with you in order to give you confidence, perhaps to prevent you from venting your passion on an unwilling person, but if you didn't "click" together she'd leave you in no doubt your relationship had ended.

'But let's suppose your companion liked you. She'd then make you more permanently attractive to her. As tactfully as possible she'd do something about your bad breath, would try to smarten you up and, on preparing to sleep with you, would probably suggest sharing a shower in order to freshen up your feet and, while in bed would do her utmost to please and satisfy you. If you wanted to play games which weren't too perverse for her then she might play them with you. It would be her decision.'

Andrew, puzzled, asked, 'What sort of games?'

Surprisingly, it was Sandra who replied, 'harmless ones. Dressing up and acting out real life dramas; rapist and victim, for instance. But she'd be advised to have really got to know you before you both indulged in such activities.'

He pulled a face and Mrs Grant hurriedly explained. 'I mentioned perversions in order to illustrate how broadminded island girls could be. In actual fact, real perversions are relatively uncommon over here as far as is known, for our authorities aren't given to probing behind closed doors, due to the success of our radical moral code; they're really the product of a bad society.

'Many perverted people actually feel inadequate and are really in need of encouragement. A man who exposes himself to women seeks to horrify them, of course, because any kind of reaction is better than none, but doubtless he'd much rather they admired his attributes, to fondle and perhaps make use of them. It isn't all that much different from a female stripper on the mainland performing before a crowd of drunken, excited men. She gets similar satisfaction out of their response to her body and, of course, as do women when faced with a male stripper. The difference is that your society condemns the former and grudgingly accepts the latter. Similarly, a man who molests children would almost certainly prefer to molest a mature, willing girl or woman, but he also lacks the confidence or else the opportunity.'

Not really knowing why, Andrew suddenly blurted out, 'supposing such perverts did have their own partners but still continued to be nuisances. What then?'

The headmistress glanced at Sandra who immediately said, 'if my lover were a "flasher" then I'd let him jump out on me in private and pretend to be shocked and frightened, but I'd also dish up the admiration by the bucket load at other times; and if he were hooked on children as sexual objects I'd dress up as a little girl and act like one. But if I found out he pursued youngsters as well then, no matter how much I loved him, I'd report him, even though it might end in his deportation. My first duty would have been to my society, not to my lover. I'd feel I'd done my best for him, and if that hadn't been good enough then he must be incurable.'

'So there you are, Andrew,' Mrs Grant exclaimed. 'We women are prepared to go to any lengths to maintain our relationships and healthy society. Actually, sex games can be quite stimulating and amusing as long as they're not too brutal and are confined to a consenting adult couple in private. However, both homosexual and group sex is illegal over here because they can both be very disruptive to our heterosexual and morally based society, causing unbelievable problems.' She turned and looked at the wall clock behind her. 'My goodness, I'd completely lost track of the time; it's my turn to prepare dinner tonight.' She hastily gathered her things together. 'Do you think you could both be precious and wash up the crockery, then lock up the office?' she said as she prepared to leave. 'Only Mr Hetherington left earlier and the secretary's already gone.' She handed Andrew the key and, with a quick smile, left the room.

As soon as they were alone he commented, 'all that was very interesting but I'd already experienced the friendliness of island girls on board Whyte Line ships, and Linda left me in no doubt as to her skill in sexual matters.'

His companion, after placing the third cup and saucer on the tray, turned and faced him. 'You didn't give her time to finish, you naughty boy.' She wagged a finger playfully before his face. 'You not only interrupted her, but you led her away from the point she was trying to make.' She handed him the loaded tray and then preceded him out of the door and in the direction of the washroom. 'There were at least two things Mrs Grant was probably about to tell you,' she continued as they washed up, 'one being we girls had to be taught to view men dispassionately. I mean, I'm only human and if I was at a dance and a handsome, well dressed, confident man came up to me I'd be so flattered that I'd most likely be putty in his hands. Only the knowledge which training brings would've warned me that such a man would probably have had a surfeit of women and would therefore doubtlessly hold us all in some contempt, a veritable heartbreaker.

'On the other hand, the type of man Mrs Grant described would be a far better proposition. He'd be so grateful for my attention he'd be like putty in my hands, the ideal person upon which to base a relationship and, eventually perhaps, a lifetime. Our greatest criticism of your mainland's outlook on sex is probably this fact, that some men enjoy more females than they really need whilst others experience little or no sexual relationships at all. Meanwhile, the media always tends to assume the former condition prevails and this encourages many of the men who are compelled to do without to take their share how and when they can; hence rape and other kinds of sexual molestation.

'Another point Mrs Grant probably didn't get round to was in the case of the lonely man who increasingly abused his lover. Apparently it didn't seem to occur to either of them, especially the girl, to tell the other how they felt about their crude lovemaking. We islanders have been taught to be frank and outspoken with each other, and lovers over here wouldn't dream of allowing a relationship to sour due to mere lack of communication.' She neatly folded up the drying cloth and placed it over a nearby rail. 'We'll leave everything here,' she said, 'then lock up and be on our way.'

In the corridor Sandra continued to talk about sexual matters. 'When our island was finally established the authorities had to decide upon what attitude to adopt regarding public morality. Should they allow their people to do as they wished rather as they do in your country, Andrew, should they make an active return to Puritanism, or ought they to encourage moral laxity? Pornography, public nudity and anything else certain elements of society thought acceptable, working on the misguided principle that over-exposure, if you'll forgive the pun, ultimately results in indifference. Of course, the final decision was dependant on a referendum but you've probably experienced enough of our society by now to be aware of what that decision was- plenty of sexual licence and opportunity as long as it was practiced discreetly. You won't, for instance, normally find girls and women actively displaying their charms to you in public. Apart from old paintings, the only time you're likely to see half-naked females publicly is when there's sunshine and water about, and then physical freedom, not intimidation, would be the prime motive.'

Later, after they'd deposited the key at the caretaker's house and were making their way toward the station by way of the school path running parallel with the cliff, Sandra suddenly asked her companion a rather surprising question. 'Tell me, Andrew, when did you last make love? It was probably with Linda, so you needn't tell me who the partner was, just when.'

He didn't need to think. 'Late last Thursday morning. Why?'

To his astonishment she seemed to become quite angry. 'I don't know what those two girls are playing at, but it would have been their fault if you'd made a physical pass at me. I'm sure their father, as president, would be most annoyed if he'd known what his daughters had done, or rather hadn't done. Actually, they should've taken one of three courses of action with regard to you. One of them should either have made herself available to you, or they should have explained they'd definitely fixed you up with a date on Wednesday, or else they ought to have mentioned our modern method of introducing the sexes to each other.'

'Well,' replied Andrew, 'to be fair to Linda, she lost no time in making me acquainted with what she had beneath her clothing, and she did mention something about phone dating. I was just somewhat bewildered at the sudden way she dropped me without explanation.'

'In that case perhaps I was a little critical, but Linda had no right to leave you in suspense without explaining her motive. If I were you I'd say nothing to the Maynard sisters for the time being but wait and see what happens on Wednesday night. If you're still on your own by the following day, phone up computer dating – the number will be in the directory – give them your details and requirements, and the rest will be automatically arranged. If you don't have a girl on Wednesday, though, tell Mr Maynard what his daughters have done, because their behaviour is dangerous and therefore illegal. Don't worry about Charlie's reaction, though, because he'll understand. It's your duty'.

Sandra then changed the subject, and by the time they were seated on a bench on the appropriate platform they were discussing child welfare. 'What do the children generally do in the evenings and at weekends?' he asked. 'Only I can't see your society allowing them to run wild as ours does, and I don't recall seeing any youngsters on their own or in groups.'

The girl smiled at him. 'No, you won't; parents over here are expected to be responsible for their children outside school hours until they reach the age of fifteen, when they're deemed mature enough to know how to behave responsibly. That might seem as if it's oppressive toward parents but what usually happens is when the youngsters form friendships at school, the respective parents of those friends often take turns in offering hospitality to the child, or children in question. So even though each family isn't allowed to consist of more than two offspring, it isn't unusual to visit a house and find it full of children, or to see a pair of adults with six or more kids in tow whilst on an outing.'

'Goodness,' Andrew exclaimed, 'parents must find it difficult to arrange for things for their charges to do!'

Sandra laughed. 'You've been on our island scarcely a week, so you don't really know all it has to offer yet. There are an enormous number of places to visit and interesting things to do regardless of the weather, and there are plenty of people, often expert, willing to supervise children. Often all a married couple have to do is deliver their children to a riding school, a swimming baths or theatre, for instance, and forget all about them for a while. Our school buildings and grounds are also probably utilised far more than they are on the mainland, and so parents have even less need to worry about the entertainment of their offspring. As long as children receive some form of supervision they're usually as good as gold, and I'm sure they enjoy themselves much more when left to their own devices.'

'It all sounds idyllic,' he commented.

'It is, I can assure you. A friend of mine first met her fiancé when she was making clay models at the age of five and he began helping her. They then formed part of a friendship group and eventually became inseparable. To date they've only had one disagreement and that was when they were both fifteen – they couldn't decide which set of parents to live with'. She laughed. 'In the end they chose to reside at each house on a yearly basis. And if you want further proof then take me for an example. I loved my childhood which ended just four years ago, so I can vouch for the success of the system.'

Their journey home was uneventful, the large square shaped engine with the peculiar patterned wheels making a fine sight as it drew in under the overall station roof hauling half a dozen matching green carriages, and it was soon rushing them back to Harbourtown station.

Sandra wished him a cheerful goodbye after arranging to meet him at the same time and place the following morning, then she walked briskly away, leaving him to await the bus taking him up the hill. Fortunately he was soon in conversation with a middle aged woman whom, she told him, had just been to visit her daughter and grandchild. Their talk lasted well up the hill where she left the bus, leaving Andrew reflecting that such casual conversation was almost a thing of the past in his own land. Such intimacy between strangers, when it took place, was usually carried out grudgingly and in mutual suspicion. He also thought briefly of some of the information his two mentors had recently given him, but he was soon to forget all about most of it, and it was to be left to yet another female to provide practical reminders.

He'd half expected a meal to be ready upon his reaching the cottage, but although all three Maynards awaited him, the only repast provided was tea, biscuits and cakes which were consumed out in the garden, the late afternoon being so pleasant. However, his hunger pangs were temporarily assuaged when Linda, at an appropriate moment, whispered conspiratorially in his ear that they were all dining out as part of his surprise that night. Without waiting to be prompted this time, Andrew told them about his school visit, and they were naturally especially interested in what he thought about the sex demonstration, but almost as soon as he'd drunk his second cup of tea with accompanying cake, Helen stood up and, beckoning him to follow her, she led him up to his own room.

Optimistic notions that perhaps she'd altered her feelings about him were soon dashed when she motioned toward the bed, for neatly laid out was a formal evening suit, while a dress shirt with a bow tie draped round the neck hung upon a coat hanger on the wardrobe door knob. Nodding toward the suit she said, 'we've hired these for you, Andy, so would you like to check they fit?' After waiting a few minutes to see if she was going to leave, he mentally shrugged when she made no move and then began to remove his shirt followed by his trousers; obviously, he thought as he performed his dressing operation, the island was beginning to affect him, for he'd known this attractive girl for hardly a week and yet here he was treating her like he would a sister or wife. Helen stopped him from trying on the shirt. 'We won't be going for a couple of hours', she explained. 'We only want to see if the suit fits.' He put the jacket on, and after she'd made a few adjustments she stood back and surveyed him. 'You'll do very nicely,' she finally said, a hint of admiration in her voice.

The four of them looked an incongruous sight, Andrew mused as they waited at the bus stop, and even more so when seated two abreast on board the bus. Charlie sported an evening suit like himself, though his shirt was less ostentatious, while both girls wore ankle length gowns in the empire style. Helen's was of a pastel shade of blue, while her sister, who was seated next to her erstwhile lover, had on a pink dress. Both girls wore light evening coats, while their escorts carried coats as insurance against bad weather. Although they were the only passengers dressed in anything like formal clothing, no one seemed to think them worthy of any special attention except that Charlie, as the main founder of the island's unique society, was greeted with more than usual enthusiasm. Andrew, though, couldn't refrain from feeling self-conscious, for he considered his attire would be out of place in any mode of transport other than an expensive car; so it was therefore a relief, when they were standing on Harbourtown station platform, to note several other people similarly dressed awaiting their train.

Despite subtle questioning of Linda on the bus, and of Helen who was now his closest companion on the train, neither would give him a clue as to where they were bound, but he surmised from their record recital of the previous evening and their special clothing that it would probably be a concert with dining facilities. From the direction the train was taking he'd assumed they were destined for the town he'd already visited that day but instead they, and the other passengers clad in evening dress, alighted at a rural station several stops before Newtown.

Much to Andrew's surprise a line of horse drawn carriages awaited them in the station forecourt; some were totally enclosed, others open, but all were different from one another. 'Look, Andrew,' murmured Charlie in his ear, 'which shall we have, Phaeton, Brougham, Landau...?' But the girls had preceded them and were already being handed up into a wide bodied four-seater vehicle by a driver dressed in mid-nineteenth century style costume complete with top hat. As soon as they were seated comfortably, the coachman climbed abroad and then chivvied his pair of grey horses into motion. The young man noticed as they drew away from the station, that all the buildings in the adjacent village were situated beyond the far platform, which gave their side of the track a purely rural aspect. The only other building in the vicinity had the appearance of a lodge gate appertaining to a large mansion, and so it proved to be for as soon as the coach in front drew abreast of this structure, it turned left through a pair of open decorative iron work gates, to be followed by their vehicle and the three others behind.

Immediately Andrew found himself transported back to the eighteenth century, for they were now travelling through country parkland typical of that period. The carriages followed a broad shingle road bordered upon either side by equally wide grass verges liberally peppered with buttercups, daisies and other prostrate lawn-loving plants. Beyond iron railings of the period, cattle and sheep of various breeds grazed amid widely scattered groups of mature parkland trees, and on one occasion a herd of antlered deer lying in the shade of a particularly stately tree watched their progress with listless indifference. Had the road been straight the long ride might eventually have become tedious, but after an extensive stretch just beyond the lodge, the roadway curved to the right and began to ascend a low prominence.

Not for the first time on Whyte Island, Andrew felt utterly content. Once more he was experiencing a sensation which he'd thought scarcely possible for he had one attractive girl facing him and another by his side, while for a friend he had Mr Maynard, the kindest of men in a land of kind people. If that were not enough, they were travelling in a form of transport long since displaced by more mundane modes, and through the type of landscape rapidly disappearing in his homeland. The evening was warm and windless, and across their path swallows, swifts and martins darted, while more than once they passed lone birds perched on the fencing, seemingly unaware of their brief presence and often singing in apparent competition with the combined sound emanating from numerous insects. No one spoke, for conversation at such a time seemed almost sacrilegious. Eventually, at the crest of the hill by a grove of shrubs and birches, the road curved back toward the left and after passing between a pair of wrought iron gates set in a high brick wall, their destination came into view.

Before them stood an ornate, though medium sized, country house, which appeared to match the park in period and style perfectly. Constructed of light grey dressed stone, apart from a pair of tall marble pillars supporting the roof of an imposing porch, the building's main feature was a large central dome, on either side of which was a wing, each containing four sash windows on two floors. Their carriage came to a halt at the foot of a flight of steps rising up to the open front door, through which the erstwhile occupants of the leading coach were already passing. Andrew followed the girls out of the carriage, thanking the coachman for lending his hand as he did so, although he was somewhat surprised to note he was the only one in their particular party to extend this small mark of appreciation.

The first thing he noted upon entering the house was the incredible coolness after the warmth outside, and secondly the wonderfully evocative aroma of furniture polish permeating the hallway. Back in his own country he'd developed quite a passion for visiting stately homes and museums during his leaves, but he'd yet to see a room quite like the one in which they were now standing. For the walls on either side were wood-panelled with a pair of doors set in each, yet facing them, in complete contrast, was an elegant marble staircase wide enough to permit three people to ascend abreast in perfect ease. The stairs allowed access to a colonnaded balcony, above which towered the dome.

After an usher stationed just inside the front door had relieved them of their coats, they ascended the stairway to where another usher waited by a pair of closed doors. As they climbed, Andrew felt his eyes drawn to the decoration on the dome's ceiling far above. Several long narrow windows lit up the interior of the construction while a huge chandelier hung on a long wire from the centre of the ceiling. The remainder of the roof space comprised a floral pattern in plaster relief with leaves, branches, flowers and berries intertwined in marvellous shades of red, pale greens, yellows, blues and pinks, upon which birds, butterflies and exotic insects, finished in bolder and more varied colours, explored and rested. However, he scarcely had time in which to admire the inverted scene in detail before they reached the double doors, which were immediately opened by the usher.

The young man had more or less assumed that beyond would be a ballroom similar in age and design to the hall, staircase and dome, so it therefore came as a complete surprise when he was confronted by what the opened doors revealed. Instead of an eighteenth-century ballroom, he surveyed, upon entering the room, what he could only think of as a massive modern sun lounge. At either end were plate glass windows, while facing him was an open space which, he noted, could be sealed by means of a pair of very long sliding glass doors during cool or inclement weather. Set in the comparatively low ceiling, numerous flush light fittings served to complete the lounge's ultra-modern aspect.

Andrew took in all this detail at a glance before being escorted, along with his companion, to a table close to the open area. Beyond lay a breath-taking view. He had failed to realise their carriage had been taking them in the direction of the reservoir lake, and now they were here at its far end, with the expanse of water directly before them. To the left, in the far distance and dwarfed by the great hill beyond was Laketown, while somewhere on the right, hidden by one of several headlands, and giving the young man more than a pang of sadness, would be the Roman villa. He presumed that somewhere beyond the hill, rising to the left of the garden, the dam was situated.

The sun lounge had been perfectly placed; not too high to be divorced from the lake yet not so close as to allow it to dominate the view. Beyond a grey stone balustrade a lawn, the far end of which merged into trees, sloped somewhat steeply down to the edge of the lake gained by steps on one side. On the right, both lounge and mansion were overshadowed by a higher slope, whilst the left hand side of the lawn was edged by trees, so encouraging the viewer to direct their gaze toward the lake and the panorama beyond.

With some reluctance, Andrew drew his eyes away from the scene and began to examine the room. It was roughly twice as wide as it was long and, apart from a great variety of potted plants spaced around the remaining three sides, was devoid of decoration. Close to the double doors was a stage upon which were arranged seats as well as stands holding sheets of music, and a number of musical instruments including a grand piano. On the far side of the stage was a small servery which, he was much later to discover, was supplied by a large kitchen on the floor below via a domestic lift.

The table at which they sat was one of a row positioned parallel to the open area, allowing each diner an uninterrupted view over the landscape, for although each table seated four people, they had been designed in a way which enabled everyone to face toward the outside. Andrew counted fifteen tables in all. About six feet away a step led down to the same level as the base of the sliding doors, beyond which the patio contained ornate metal tables with a matching chair on either side.

'Do you like it, Andrew?' Helen was asking.

With his mind entirely occupied with surveying his surroundings he could only reply, 'what?' Then he added, 'yes, it's very nice. But a little unusual.'

'You ain't seen nothing yet,' parodied Linda.

Their table had been laid for a full meal, the cutlery and condiments were of sparkling silver, there were several sets of different glasses, and in the centre stood a vase of attractive flowers. They hadn't been waiting long before they were each handed an elaborate menu on the back of which was a comprehensive wine list. 'What aperitif would you like girls? Andrew?' Charlie prompted.

Their immediate replies showed Andrew how confident they were with their situation, and this fact made him feel conscious of his own lack of experience in such matters, so he quickly thrust the menu before Linda who was closest to him, and whispered, 'er, that one seems quite nice.'

'Good choice, Andy,' she replied, obviously sensing his discomfort. 'I think I'll join you.' And she promptly relayed the information to her father.

'Now, what do we want to eat?' Mr Maynard asked when the wine waiter had retired. Fortunately the menu presented the young man with no problems and he was able to order what he wanted from a varied and exotic choice.

The waiter, upon his return, poured a few drops of wine into Andrew's glass and the young man, aware of what was expected of him, consumed the contents then raised his head to nod approval, but much to his consternation he found himself gazing at the face of Harry Larke. 'Mr Larke!' he exclaimed, glancing at his companions in perplexity as he did so, 'what on earth are you doing here?'

'I'm sorry sir, but I think you must have mistaken me for someone else,' came the polite yet distinctly cool reply. Taking this exchange as acceptance of the wine ,the waiter the proceeded to pour out the remainder of the drink and went on to administer to the Maynards. Andrew studied him as he moved round the table, becoming increasingly convinced it really was Harry, but too embarrassed to say anything further.

As soon as the waiter had gone, Charlie rounded on his daughters. 'Didn't either of you warn Andrew this might happen?' he demanded coldly.

Helen was suitably contrite for them both. 'We're sorry, dad, but the thought hadn't occurred to us; after all, Andy hardly knows anyone on the island and you must admit it's a fantastic coincidence.'

Mr Maynard nodded his somewhat reluctant acceptance and turned to their guest. 'I'm sorry, lad, but that really was Harry Larke, but for the sake of appearance we're keeping up the pretence of being affluent people whilst he is assuming a working class background. You see, at one time or another Harry and his wife will have dined here, and we have a rule that at every place where a servant-master situation occurs, then some of the former masters will later have to pose as servants or helpers. This is nothing whatever to do with our practice of having several jobs per person, but only applies at an entertainment level. However, if you never visited a formal place like this where you'd expect to be waited upon, then you wouldn't receive a summons to help out.'

'Well, how does it work?' Andrew asked, looking with difficulty at the three of them in turn, giving each of them a chance to reply, then adding, 'for instance, there will be sixty or so customers here tonight but hardly that number of staff to cater for, or serve, them, and most of the latter, surely, won't be amateurs?'

It was Helen, seated on his left, who answered first. 'In your country you have a lottery which is managed by a computer.' It was a statement rather than a question, to which he replied with a nod. 'Well, that's how it works here,' she went on. 'When dad phoned in our reservation he was asked the names of all the people in our party. Do you know, by the way, that everyone on Whyte Island has their own personal number in much the same way as you have an insurance number? Well, from that information our numbers were found and put into the computer along with those of other guests. From these figures a few will be automatically and impartially selected and the owners will, over the next month, be required to help out here on one occasion only. Of course, all the kitchen and serving staff are professionals and merely supervise the temps. Usually these do jobs like dishwashing and tidying up, but I expect Harry's standing in for an indisposed waiter because he's quite a jack-of-all-trades'.

'Yes, and it's good fun,' interjected Linda. 'Many people get quite upset when they fail to get summoned, you get a drink and the pick of the menu free as a bonus.'

'Have you all done it, then?'

'Dad and Linda have,' replied Helen somewhat ruefully, 'but not here, though. But it's a good idea, don't you think? Everyone has the chance to act the high and mighty as much as they wish and equally, if they begin to think themselves something special, they might find themselves washing up one or two hundred plates and countless items of cutlery.' By this time their orders had arrived, wheeled in on a silver trolley and served out by Harry Larke. Andrew, scanning his face briefly, was sure he detected a slight smile on his features, as though he knew the young man had been advised regarding the incident.

Whilst they'd been conversing, Andrew had been half aware of movement behind and on either side of them, as later arrivals entered and took their seats at the tables. Then the sound of waiters attending to their new guests, of those with meals to eat and that of muffled conversation was interposed by the noise of activity emanating from the direction of the stage heralding the arrival of an orchestra. After a brief preliminary warming up, they began to play a series of early waltzes which Andrew, taking his cue from the Maynards and other diners, paid no attention to, treating it in much the same way as he would if the music had been coming from a sound system. He was surprised, however, by the fact that although they were quite close to the orchestra the waltzes were far from loud. Nudging Linda he asked, after swallowing a mouthful of food, 'why isn't the music as noisy as you might expect?'

'You can't see properly from here,' she answered, turning her head round to face the stage, 'but there are lots of grilles, I believe, which extract most of the sound somehow. As a matter of interest the garden below is fitted with speakers which enables guests to wander down as far as the lake's edge and still hear the music clearly.'

To Andrew the music, although faultlessly played, merely complimented the meal being, like most waltzes, for the most part lively but subtle. As the last of the sweet courses were finished, the tables cleared, and more wine poured and cigars and cigarettes lit, the orchestra, presumably taking its cue from the diners, began to play something more romantic.

It began to occur to him as he sipped his wine that everything had been carefully timed to coincide with the onset of dusk, for as the sun began to set behind the mansion turning the clouds above and beyond the lake to shades of pink and transforming the hills and the lake to a warm orange hue, the music became much more gentle and sensitive, with some wonderful overtures which Andrew had never heard before. 'This is what everyone has come here for,' Helen whispered to him, 'beautiful music shouldn't only be confined to the concert hall or the home lounge but should also be played in order to enhance a lovely, serene view. Look how they all appreciate it.' He turned his head to glance along the line of tables on either side of them, all conversation had ceased while every face was turned to the panorama before them, and it wasn't long before he followed their tacit advice and also began to gaze at the scene.

As each carefully selected melody followed the next without

pause, so the colours of the landscape imperceptibly pushed their predecessors away. Clouds changed from pink to red and finally to grey then black, orange hills became purple and dark blue and the waters of the lake altered to silvery grey and thence to black as well. A myriad of lights in the vicinity of Laketown blinked into existence together with those in villages and isolated homes, whilst the eventide songs of blackbird, thrush and robin was replaced by the occasional calling of owls from near and far.

The swallows, martins and swifts which had graced the skies vanished as darkness advanced to be superseded by bats, made visible by a brightening moon. Eventually, when most of the light had gone, the trees at the end of the lawn were individually illuminated by floodlights, each one a different colour; the effect was garish but remarkably beautiful. Long before this event, however, the flush lights set in the lounge ceiling had been turned on, the subtle colours permitting enough light to see by though not enough to detract from the view.

Perhaps not by mere chance the orchestra had finished playing, their place having been taken by a brilliant young solo pianist who acknowledged the onset of night by the rendering of nocturnes and sonatas. 'Look, Andy,' whispered Helen, nudging him out of his reverie. Following her gaze he noticed a couple dancing in close embrace. Not understanding what she expected of him, he nodded sagely and smiled inanely. 'Well, go on then,' she prompted, and then it came to him that she was, completely out of character he thought, urging him to invite her to dance. After glancing at Charlie and Linda in turn and receiving encouraging smiles from each, he stood up and formerly asked Helen for her company on the dance floor.

Andrew still considered her somewhat formidable after her rebuffs of him, so he took her in his arms in the formal manner, but much to his astonishment and delight she immediately put her arms about his neck, pressed her body intimately against him and laid her cheek alongside his. Still feeling his way he waited for her to speak, but as she remained silent he was perfectly content to allow her closeness, her touch, the smell of her perfume and the sound of the piano music to overwhelm him. Through half closed eyes he saw the dance floor begin to fill with couples until almost every movement meant physical contact with another person.

During a brief glance in the direction of their table he was rather surprised to see a man and woman standing talking to Charlie and his younger daughter and when, sometime later, he next looked the table was unoccupied. Subsequently, through a gap in the crowd, he glimpsed Mr Maynard partnering the woman and presumed Linda would be dancing with the man. Lulled by the wine, the press of other dancers and his companion's close embrace, a notion began to form in Andrew's mind that Helen had begun to change her opinion regarding him and was now trying to encourage a relationship. Soon the seed became a certainty, so he began to kiss her neck and whisper to her in unconscious imitation of the man in the sex demonstration. Although she didn't object in any way, he thought, despite his sense of euphoria that she wasn't particularly pleased, and when he eventually pressed his mouth against her lips and attempted to insert his tongue between, she immediately withdrew her arms and, taking him by the hand, led him determinedly off the dance floor and out onto the, as yet, empty patio.

By the balustrade she turned and faced him. 'Why,' she demanded softly, 'did you have to spoil it?'

'I thought you were trying to encourage me,' he answered lamely. 'I didn't think you'd mind because it was too dark for anyone to see us properly.'

'I'm not talking about whether people could see us or not' she continued angrily, 'but why you should have done it in the first place. I was not trying to turn you on; not deliberately anyway.' She raised her hands and then let them fall to her sides in a gesture of futility. 'Come on,' she urged, 'let's go down and see the lake.'

On the way down to the paradise of coloured trees she attempted to explain herself. 'It's so difficult for some women, girls, at times. You see I just wanted to pretend you were my lover, someone I could relax with and whose company I could enjoy. Perhaps it was thoughtless and selfish of me, but I didn't think or expect you'd take it as a pass. I sometimes think I must be a museum piece; probably ninety nine per cent of the island's unattached girls would have led you onto the ultimate experience quite willingly. But…'

'It's that old boyfriend, isn't it?' Andrew interposed rather angrily. 'That lover of long ago, and you can't forget him.'

He was wide of the mark but Helen, to her eternal personal credit, decided not to disabuse him but instead sighed miserably.

'Yes, I suppose you're right; there's always someone else, isn't there?'

'Well, I think you should get him out of your system.' Significantly, she said nothing in reply to this suggestion, but Andrew, entirely unaware of the opportunity which had been presented to him, and suspecting her of crying, merely traced a forefinger gently along her eyelid and, tasting the salty moisture at the tip, whispered aimlessly, 'Sorry.' Without warning she immediately threw her arms about his neck and burst into tears, sobs wracking her body.

Like many men in such a situation he didn't know quite what to do, he only knew he was shocked by the sudden change in her. She had seemed such a stolid, self-reliant person, quite awesome to him, and now in complete contrast she had apparently gone to pieces, and so all he could think of doing was to hold her tightly until she'd calmed down. The occasion was made even more bizarre by the red glow from the nearest floodlight which bathed their figures, and by the music emanating from an adjacent speaker.

After what seemed to be an eternity Helen's sobs began to decrease until she was eventually able to whisper, 'I feel such a fool, what must you think of me?' And she added in near panic, 'I can't go back in there.'

Andrew pressed his handkerchief upon her. 'Look,' he said, taking charge, 'we'll go back up to the patio, then I'll tell your dad you're out of sorts.'

The remainder of the evening had all the aspect of a weird dream for Andrew. Leaving his companion standing outside, he hurried to their table where he found Mr Maynard entertaining his dancing partner; of Linda and the man who'd been talking to her there was no sign. Briefly explaining the circumstances to Charlie and arranging to meet him at around eleven o'clock by the front steps, he hastened back to Helen bearing their coats and her bag. While she went off to attend to her make-up, he strolled the lakeside away from the other guests, some of whom were now beginning to disgorge onto the lawn and amongst the trees. Helen joined him later, and together they seated themselves on a bench far from the others where the music reached them as a low murmur.

Looking back to that time, Andrew knew that ordinarily his behaviour might have been considered rather churlish because normal experience might have told him his companion was merely awaiting his first move. However, after Mrs Grant's and Sandra's explanations regarding sexual etiquette earlier that day, he was expecting his companion to take the initiative should she wish to. He'd already shown her once that evening he'd been willing to make love to her and been rebuffed for his trouble, so he wasn't going to try any more. Instead, he acted the perfect gentleman, not even attempting to take her hand, while she, on her part, chatted to him of quite serious matters, thereby becoming once more the self-possessed woman.

Charlie's companion replaced Linda in a hard-topped coach on the ride back to the station, and Andrew was only half surprised when they both went off together outside Harbourtown station, leaving Helen and himself to continue the remainder of their journey alone. Having lapsed once again into a somewhat impersonal relationship with his companion he found it impossible to attempt anew their former intimacy; on the surface, at least, she was exactly the same as she'd been before their outing, polite and talkative but just a little distant and when back at the cottage, she made them both coffee but took her cup up to her room, he realised he'd blundered.

It came as a complete surprise to Andrew to be awakened by Linda's voice gaily calling, 'wake up sleepy head. Seven fifteen, school today,' as she banged on his door. While he showered, he mused that for a country in which nobody had personal transport apart from cycles, people certainly got around; he'd remembered wondering, among other things, whether Linda and Charlie would be back in time for their duties on the morrow.

At breakfast Helen was notably absent, but Mr Maynard was seated at the table stirring his tea. Apart from conversational enquiries regarding the night before, nothing was said concerning subsequent activities, and certainly not about sleeping arrangements. The young man, feeling guilty in a complete reversal of what would once have been considered moral in his own country regarding what he hadn't done to Charlie's elder daughter rather than what he had done, asked with false casualness where she was. Linda laughed and glanced out the window. 'As it's a nice morning she went out early with her camera. She left a note,' she added by way of explanation. Then more seriously she winked at him and declared, 'she's a tricky one.' He glanced across at Charlie in some confusion, but he'd elected not to hear.

Somehow, despite feeling more than a little tired, Andrew managed to catch the bus and to reach the train in time where Sandra once more awaited him. 'I'm sorry I had to dash off yesterday but I had to phone up my boyfriend as he begins to fret if he doesn't hear from me. He's at the summer camp and I expect you'll be meeting him this afternoon.' He waved aside her apology and explained about how he'd had the company of a woman during his bus ride home, but he couldn't help marvelling that the girl felt she must excuse herself for abandoning him.

Throughout the train journey he couldn't keep from yawning. 'I'm sorry,' he said eventually after noticing her looking at him in an amused but puzzled manner, 'I had a late and very hectic night.' She said nothing, but the slight raising of her eyebrows encouraged him to continue. 'We went, Charlie, the girls and I to that place at the end of the lake where you dine, listen to the music, watch the sunset and dance.'

'Yes,' she answered, 'I know it.' She mentioned the name, then added, 'did you enjoy yourself?'

'Well, I did at first, but I made a fool of myself and made Helen, Linda's sister, cry.'

'Now that is unusual on the island,' she exclaimed, 'a female crying. We're all expected to take a stoical view of life, especially where it involves the opposite sex.' Then she made a speculation which exhibited further proof to Andrew how advanced Whyte Islanders could be when it came to practical psychology, particularly as it was so close to what Mr Maynard had already conjectured about his older daughter. 'I think Helen might be a little different from most other islanders. She'd have been quite old by the time our educational policy became really effective, and don't forget she'd have been under the influence of adults who hadn't received the benefits of our social system, so she might have a different outlook on life.

'According to Linda they lost their mother when they were both quite young and Helen, being the older of the two, had doubtless bonded more with her mum than little Linda, and so was more inclined to miss her. To add to Helen's problems, her younger sister is by nature a sociable, devil may care sort of person who takes life on the chin, while she, personally, is a solitary creature who takes things to heart and, therefore, is easily upset. Exactly how did you make her cry?'

Andrew described all that had happened, adding that he liked Helen but found her hard to understand or to come to terms with; that on several occasions he'd made passes but had been rebuffed. 'It's quite possible,' mused Sandra, 'that she really is attracted to you but feels she owes her allegiance to her father, and so it would be unfair to both you and Charlie if she took you on. I mentioned yesterday that either one or both of the sisters might have arranged a meeting for you with some girl tomorrow, and it's therefore quite possible she might be jealous, and it's also possible, though unlikely, she is jealous of your relationship with Linda.

'But the big problem for Helen with regard to you is that you're merely a visitor to our island, so you might care to empathise with her dilemma. Being sensitive, she'd be frightened to fall for you if the outcome could be your eventual expulsion from Whyte Island.'

'But being Mr Maynard's daughter, surely she'd be able to influence him?'

Sandra was obviously shocked. 'Keep your voice down,' she whispered. 'You aren't supposed to talk like that in public! It wouldn't be up to Charlie Maynard. The only way you'd get citizenship would be if the authorities approved of you, and no matter how well you behaved yourself, the chances of that are very slim. More likely Helen would be banished to the mainland with you if she were resolute in sharing her life with you.'

'Thank goodness it's all conjecture, then. I wouldn't want anyone here to follow me back to my country. It's paradise here compared to anywhere else, as I well know. I'll be sorry to leave it all behind.'

Sandra said nothing to enlighten him, but veered the subject of conversation round to another topic. After turning to stare at the passing countryside for a few minutes she suddenly faced him and asked, 'have you altered your opinion regarding that sex demonstration yet?'

Andrew had certainly done so the night before. The vision of the blonde girl's faultless body and her capable seduction of her lover, together with the knowledge that he himself was alone in the cottage with a desirable girl who was his for the asking, at the expense of a little skill and temerity, had tormented him in the half hour or so before he'd finally fallen asleep. And he still couldn't understand why he hadn't taken advantage of the situation. However, he knew what his companion's question actually referred to. 'Yes, and I think I was perhaps a little hasty in my conclusions.'

'I'm pleased to hear that. It's impossible to overestimate how important it is for both lovers to use their initiative in ensuring a successful relationship. Naturally, the best way of making sure people comprehend is by teaching them at school while they're relatively unbiased and impressionable; and so, by having actual couples demonstrating love play authentically, the maximum desired effect is obtained. Experience has shown this method is much better than getting the children to study books or to attend films or lectures on the subject.' Sandra smiled to herself, then continued. 'By far the best way would be to persuade the children to make love under supervision, just as with the real life dramas they act in at school, but of course such a lesson would be impractical for obvious reasons.'

'It amazes me how you get a couple to demonstrate in public, especially before youngsters,' he muttered. 'After all, you people are taught that love-making is a private activity.'

'I can assure you, Andy, there is no shortage of volunteers. It's a compliment to our educational system that couples are prepared to overcome their environmentally imposed instincts for the sake of an essential service.'

'Would you and your boyfriend…' he began huskily, which compelled him to clear his throat in mid-sentence, 'be prepared to give a sex demonstration?'

She laughed at his all too obvious embarrassment. 'We've had our names down for quite a while now. We're rather looking forward to it, but we'll have a long time to wait because couples are only required a few times each year.'

Unlike the previous day they didn't linger in the station or town but walked along the path at the foot of the cliffs which led directly to the school. On the way Andrew asked, 'if we're going to the summer camp this afternoon, what's on the agenda for this morning?'

'Normally I wouldn't know because I haven't been in contact with the school since yesterday, but as I've read the prospectus I can tell you it's a lesson nicknamed the "whys".' As he looked askance she went on. 'That's because it's a debate about subjects which all end in the letter "Y", in other words the 'ologies. But to us they're all one – it's all about living together in a state of community, and why we islanders need to tolerate not having so called essentials such as personal wealth and road vehicles. In fact, it's a lesson of which yesterday's oral test, if you remember, is the conclusion. The authorities hold the debate to be so important that mixed age group classes attend each session, and each child has to be present at least once a year. This means, of course, that each pupil takes part in a minimum of five debates on the subject, and therefore becomes well versed in them by the time they graduate to the red establishments.'

The visit to the school office was a mere formality, for once again only the secretary was present, besides which Sandra knew what classroom they were to attend. He wasn't surprised to find the venue to be the same room as that which the oral test had been taken in as it was ideally suited for the purpose of debating, or that the same teacher, Mark, was presiding. But as soon as Sandra and he had seated themselves, once again high up at the back, Andrew was rather mystified upon seeing a large plan view of an aircraft positioned on an easel in the centre area as well as the words "Psychology, "Sociology", "Philosophy" and "Physiology" written upon an adjacent blackboard. Judging by the fact that the children were already present when they arrived he surmised they were only awaiting their arrival before beginning.

As soon as they were comfortable, Mark pointed to the aircraft diagram and said, 'if each of you children were the pilot of this machine whilst in flight, what would you feel to be the most dangerous thing to happen: for a wing to fall off, the controls to jam, the tail to break away, or the engines to stop?'

Immediately a boy at the front raised his hand. 'They're all just as important, sir.'

'Exactly,' replied Mark, 'the failure of any one of those components would undoubtedly eventually cause the aircraft to crash, and so it is, more or less, with these "Y" subjects.' He gestured toward the blackboard. 'Instead of an aircraft being involved we have our society, these criteria are just as reliant upon each other to keep our whole system going. In much of the euphemistically called civilized world these "Ys" are taught as separate subjects, but we on Whyte Island hold them to be vital components of one whole. Now, we in this classroom will be discussing themes which will involve all four "Ys", and I hope it will become apparent, to you younger children especially, how important they are with regard to each other. Now, let's kick off with a vital subject: birth control. How many reasons can we think of for having a stable population. Anyone?'

Another boy threw up his hand eagerly, 'To make sure there are enough homes to fit the population without having to build more, which would mean taking away farm or leisure land.'

'So there are jobs for everyone, and industry's needs can be planned ahead,' volunteered a girl.

'So that in a time of crisis the island would be able to support the population with food, water and power without relying upon other countries,' explained another girl.

'To prevent the transport system and our welfare facilities from becoming clogged up with too many people,' a boy said.

He was quickly followed by a girl with a typically domestic suggestion. 'To stop any woman from having too many children, which might make her over-worked, stop her from enjoying life to the full and giving her children less attention than they need for a healthy life.'

As each proposal was put forward Mark wrote it down in abbreviated form on the blackboard under the heading 'Birth Control.' Eventually, after fresh answers had ceased to come, he summed up. 'I think that, looking at all these suggestions, they all add up to one main word: happiness. If a population free for all were allowed to occur, therefore, unhappiness for the greater part ensues, especially as it becomes a terrible trap; particularly when it occurs in a wealthy country. Can anyone tell me why?'

A girl of about fourteen a few rows in front of Andrew put up her hand, and the answer she subsequently gave made him realise she was more intelligent or else humane than any of the prime ministers of his own country. 'Because wealthy nations were often naturally rich in minerals for power usage and making things, they could then set up manufacturing industries. People at home and abroad bought the factory products which caused the expansion of industry in old and new firms, these employed people in offices and workshops who, through their spending, created more industries.' The girl paused briefly, then went on. 'They took holidays, bought cars and jewellery, and moved into bigger houses, often having bigger families and living on borrowed money. Over the years the populations in rich countries grew until they were too large to be merely supported by farm production until everyone, almost, became dependent upon a healthy industry.

'Each rich country relied upon people spending money so that taxes could be levied to pay for public services and servants, and specialists who were not altogether necessary, solicitors, psychiatrists, estate agents and advertisers, for instance, had lots of work. Export and import to and from other countries both rich and poor increased until the world became reliant upon such wealthy nations. So while trade grows, everyone spends money in one way or another, but sadly articles last longer than they take to make, so eventually when everyone has purchased a particular item like a car, they won't want another one for years.

'So factories begin to close, then another and another, and as they shut they put people out of work who then can no longer afford big houses, to run cars, go out or do anything, and so they begin to affect the leisure industries who in turn close down. Even worse, many of the unemployed will probably be in debt because of money borrowed from banks, loan companies and through mortgages, and the state not only suffers from loss of different taxes and rates and that kind of thing, but has to pay benefits to stop unemployed people from starving. In the end this can bankrupt a country because money is being paid out but not coming in, and the country is then faced with a lot of homeless, starving and very unhappy people. I think that's all.'

As soon as the girl had finished she was greeted with enthusiastic applause which turned her face red with pleasure and embarrassment, causing her to sit down in some confusion. 'Well done, Charlotte!' exclaimed the teacher as soon as he and everyone else had finished clapping. 'I couldn't have expressed it better myself. I would like to add though that medical services and care for the elderly and the permanently infirm would also suffer, and that both unemployed teenagers and young adults would become a problem.

'In fact, the whole quality of life would begin to suffer; the crime rate would doubtless rise and the class barrier would tend to re-establish itself as those who had gained the most from the trade boom retained their wealth, whilst unemployed people became poorer. This brings me to the next item; can anyone tell me why it's really unnecessary to be rich?'

A girl near the front put up her hand, though somewhat hesitantly, and said, 'Because it's based on the assumption that familiarity breeds contempt. Er... in other words, when someone experiences something nice for the first time, they'll probably think it's wonderful, but the more often they have or know it the less enjoyable it becomes, or rather the less fascinating it is until it can become merely dull.'

'Good,' observed Mark. 'Any more examples anyone, and can the theme be taken any further?'

A boy put up his hand, his reply apparently inspired by the aircraft drawing. 'A person flying for the first time would find it exciting and wonderful, but if they had to do it every day they would become sick of it, especially if they went to the same destination every time. Also a rich person would soon take their wealth for granted and would then take little more pleasure from it. This is shown by rich people who want even more wealth, or kill themselves for some silly reason or other; rich people aren't always happy and often feel insecure.'

The teacher nodded in agreement and observed, 'the rich self-made person has frequently attained their position by enormous drive, perhaps through some aberration in their character which compels them to make money long after they have enough for their needs. On the other hand, the person who has inherited wealth takes it for granted, so that in both cases being wealthy may be no substitute for happiness.

'Incidentally, the clue to real contentment for the individual is that of environment. People are often at their happiest when most of their friends and acquaintances are of the same status as themselves, and they're often at their unhappiest when they feel they're poorer than everyone else. There are cases where people have been quite destitute but reasonably contented because their companions have been just as poor, in fact forming a needy community.

'This helps to explain one of the main aims of our island society. We feel that being rich isn't the answer to happiness for the reasons just stated, but neither is it desirable to be poor. Therefore we endeavour to strike the happy medium 'where everyone, regardless of intelligence, is of similar status, and so we have no jealousy, superiority or inferiority, and no boredom due to over-familiarity. The least person, if there was such a one, on Whyte Island enjoys exactly the same status as does our president. Now, with special regard to population control, who can tell me why there are no other groups or sects of people on our island?'

'Because,' answered a boy, 'apart from islanders voting against them, they could become an embarrassment to our society; everyone here is subject to the same laws and rules. A separate sect would naturally need to have different rules or laws, otherwise they wouldn't be different. Where two or more sects of people are living in the same country, as they are in many parts of the world, it's only necessary for one group to have a higher birth rate for them to gain control of their country, especially where democracy is the method of government. Often a minority group is persecuted whether they were the original natives or not, and often in the name of religion.'

A brief round of applause followed the boy's answer and at the same time Andrew reflected on the reason for the mixture of age groups at the session. He could make a fairly shrewd guess at the ages of the various children by their size and appearance, and from this he noticed the older the age group the more likely they were, naturally enough, to answer; the second year children hardly ever tried to join in, while the first years were merely silent spectators. It was therefore clear that as they grew older the pupils learnt more at each session until they finally gained confidence and were eventually drawn into the discussion. Obviously, they were taught the "Ys" during the course of their studies and the present lesson was just the culmination of what they'd learnt so far, giving them the opportunity to air their views in the presence of children of the other ages.

As the applause died away, Mark followed on with the boy's theme. 'You can all see that in a country where one sect was producing more children than another a dilemma would face the latter sect. If they believed, as we do, that it was essential to control the size of their population for economical or ethical reasons then they would clash with their more prolific brethren. The option would be to risk being overwhelmed and possibly eliminated by the other sect, a process which is actually happening in many parts of the world now. So you children might realise it is taking unnecessary risks to introduce alien sects or races into an established country: it can lead to difficulties quite unforeseen by the originators of the immigration.' He paused for a moment then asked, 'can anyone tell the pupils why we don't donate financial aid to foreign countries, and also why we feel it ethical not to allow another sect or race to settle on our island?'

A pretty young girl who couldn't have been much older than thirteen promptly answered. 'In many of the world's countries, especially those in tropical and equatorial regions, the birth rate is so high that many babies are born with only a few months or years life expectancy. Poor land, disease and the possibility of severe and frequent droughts increase the chances of early death. So not only are the parents irresponsible in having children without a future, but the governments of such countries are also to blame for not teaching their adult populations ways in which to improve their lives. Even worse, government officials in such lands are often useless, often corrupt, putting lots of money which comes their way into banks in stable and wealthy countries instead of helping their poorer countrymen.

'So Whyte Island officials think it is pointless giving money to countries where neither the government nor the people are humane enough to make use of it in the proper way. Our island tried to give advice on contraception and on ways to improve the soil with methods such as creating reservoirs to store plenty of water, crop rotation and the growing of vegetation to improve and stabilise the soil and the building of compost heaps – all important, essential things before a stable society can be built – but generally our advice was ignored.'

The intelligent manner in which the child was presenting her subject so far in advance of her years, was made even more bizarre by the way she then paused and adopted a childlike pose, biting the top of her thumb whilst displaying a perplexed expression on her face, then saying to herself audibly, 'now, what was the second part? Oh, yes. There are some nations in the world which were once powerful, but through various reasons alien people and cultures began to settle in them which helped to ruin them, mostly through overpopulation or civil wars. They also loaned large amounts of money to poor countries which couldn't or wouldn't repay it, wealth which could have been used to help their own poor people who'd once laboured to produce it. These nations were, therefore, often beneficial and protective toward poor countries, but now that they are ruinous themselves they are unable to extend much help. So this is the major reason why Whyte Island must harden its heart toward prospective immigrants, so it can remain relatively healthy and wealthy until such times as our advice can be regarded.'

As the girl sat down she was greeted not only by applause but by much cheering. When the commotion began to subside a little, Andrew whispered to Sandra, 'Although the level of intelligence of the average island child seems to be outstanding, I never expected to hear a speech like that from one so young.'

'I must admit she's exceptional; you might call her a child prodigy. Many teachers have backed her to become a future president, but Charlotte is also a good contender for the job. Possibly, if they lived in most other countries they'd be directing their intelligence to their own ends but, as you could see, much of their brain power is thoughtful toward others.'

'While we're on the subject of charity,' Mark continued from the centre area, 'why don't we require fundraising activities on Whyte Island?'

The answer was slow in coming but finally a boy raised his hand and said, 'because the state takes care of everything for us. A country where the people need to give money out of their own pockets or who have to perform various activities in order to raise money for charities is either living beyond its means, or else is badly run. It's up to the government to ensure there's enough money to cover all needs and services, and it shouldn't have to delegate the responsibility to its citizens because those people are doing something for nothing, while the members of government are paid well for slacking.'

Mark, the teacher, smiled wryly. 'Yes, well, I think you've got the gist of it, Keith. Now, so far,' he went on, 'we haven't involved physiology much. So now for a straightforward question. Why do we place so much emphasis on physical fitness and games?'

A hand was quickly raised and its owner, a girl, said, 'when we take part in sporting activities it helps us to keep our tempers, to remain cool and not to cheat, but the main purpose is so we can keep our bodies lithe, fit and in a healthy condition. A healthy body means it is less likely we'll need a doctor or lose time off from school and later, work. Therefore, a healthy population means a healthy economy.'

'Short and sweet,' commented Mark when she'd finished. 'That just about sums it up, but I might add that physical activity helps to keep our bodies beautiful, and so attractive to the opposite sex.' The discussion, which covered many more subjects, continued until the dinner break, but shortly before he dismissed the class Mark introduced the two visitors. 'Andrew is a sailor on board Whyte

Line ships but he's a mainlander on holiday over here. Now, I'm sure he'd like to know what you all think about your country, so what's Whyte Isle worth to you, children?'

Immediately they all replied in unison, 'everything!'

During a fine meal, once again cooked and served up by children, Andrew enthusiastically talked to Sandra of what he had heard. 'I'm beginning to understand why your society is so successful,' he said just before they rose to leave. 'Unlike mainland schools, you involve the pupils in all aspects of living, explaining how and why everything is intermeshed and dependent one upon the other, and always checking to ensure the lessons have been understood. By comparison our schoolchildren are stumbling in the dark – no wonder they become troublesome if no one bothers to explain things to them and they're constantly subjected to bad examples by mainland society. When you think about it, their teachers aren't much more enlightened.' Although his companion smiled a little she maintained a discreet silence at his criticism of his own country's educational methods.

Owing to the fact that it was the lunch hour, the pair found it unnecessary to visit the office to take their leave for they found the headmistress walking around the grounds accompanied by another teacher. After polite introductions had been exchanged, Mrs Grant said, 'you're off to the summer camp, then? Well, I'll inform them you're coming.' She winked at Andrew in an un-teacher like manner. 'Perhaps they'll have a drink waiting for you – non-alcoholic, of course.' She held a hand out to him. 'Now, young man, I hope you enjoyed your visit to us. If you ever want to come again, don't be afraid to use the phone as there are plenty of other lessons to sample.'

The route to the camp involved the walk back to the station and thence by train the remainder of their journey. He was delighted when, on reaching the station, Sandra took him down the subway to the platform upon which they'd alighted that morning for he realised another section of the island was about to be revealed to him. Whether by accident, or good planning on his companion's part, their train was already standing at the platform with steam hissing gently from the engine.

The unusual flat sided carriages, painted chocolate and cream and painstakingly lined out in gold, seemed far too stately for the rather plain, black locomotive with large boiler and disproportionately small wheels which was about to haul them. Sandra, by now well aware of his fascination for railways, stood patiently waiting while he studied the machine from all angles. He would have liked to exchange a few words with the crew, but both men were busy at their various tasks. Eventually she nudged him, intimating it was time to board their coach and she preceded him into a carriage which, apart from a wooden parcel van, was the first vehicle behind the engine and tender.

'Would you mind if I went and stood in the vestibule?' Andrew asked after they'd found a pair of seats in the relatively crowded train as the train began to slowly move out of the station.

Sandra smiled. 'I wouldn't advise it. We'll be going into the tunnel shortly, and as it's over a mile long with an increasingly steep gradient the engine tends to throw up a lot of grit, so it's dirty and dangerous.' She placed a hand over one eye as an illustration and she'd scarcely done so when, as if to stress her warning, the locomotive whistled briefly, plunged into the tunnel and began to labour and roar mightily; at the same time the carriage lights came on.

The noise was so loud that speech became impracticable and so Andrew's thoughts turned to consider that many a railway fan, or merely an older person, on the mainland would have given a great deal just to be in his place. For he was experiencing a mode of transport which, after a recent long and successful revival, had once more slid into almost total decline due to the recession and the resultant decrease in spending money.

Somehow he was able to put himself in the place of a small boy going on a seaside holiday; part of the pleasure and excitement would be in boarding a train hauled by a steam engine, entering into the tunnel and arriving at the important and busy looking station with the large overall roof, which they'd just left, and seeing other steam trains coming and going.

He vaguely remembered looking at children's books, handed down from his grandfather to his father, containing pictures of youngsters armed with buckets and spades at railway stations of which steam engines, bookstalls and milk churns had been chief components. The illustrations had held little meaning for him then, but now they'd come to life; surely the seaside when attained by a road trip in a private car or a coach could have nothing like the same impact. It made him realise just what the island authorities were trying to do. So much of what had once been interesting and individualistic had been lost on the mainland and much of the materialistic world during comparatively recent times, and the Whyte Islanders were trying to reverse that trend for their own gratification.

His reverie was interrupted by the train suddenly bursting from the tunnel out into dazzling sunshine. At first they roared through a cutting but as the gradient levelled out, the bank on the right had side disappeared so allowing a perfect view of the shimmering sea. The railway had obviously been built on the side of a hill, for on the opposite side the land rose beyond the chalk bank to where numerous sheep grazed, while on the coastal side the down land sloped gently toward the cliff tops. Once on the level the train increased speed effortlessly, rushing past scattered woodland and isolated farmhouses, and once through a station at which a train bound for their late town was standing. Soon the brakes were applied and the train eventually drew to a halt at a station, the buildings of which had been almost entirely constructed of green and cream painted wood.

Andrew felt quite important when he realised, after they'd watched the train disappearing down the straight tracks which seemed to stretch on into infinity, that the stop had been made on their sole behalf. The undulating nature of the landscape was apparent from the fact that the station had been sited upon quite a lofty embankment, the lane from which inclined somewhat steeply down to its junction with a road passing under the railway. However, when they reached the junction Sandra turned to the left, and soon they were climbing past the cottages lining both sides of the road, heading toward an escarpment which dominated the horizon.

As they passed one cottage which, through various signs and notices, proclaimed itself to be a general store Sandra murmured, 'wait here,' and disappeared inside to reappear soon after with a couple of ice lollies. Handing one to her companion she said, 'we'll be needing these, we've got a fair climb ahead.' He was grateful for her gesture but it didn't prevent him glancing enviously at a picturesque little inn which they passed shortly afterward.

Soon they'd left the village behind, the road still continuing upward with birch woodland on either side. Eventually the road diverged, and once again Sandra took the road to the left. This dismayed Andrew more than a little, for their route continued to climb while the other road had levelled off. They'd long since finished their ices and he was beginning to feel distinctly thirsty as there was little wind and the sun shone out of a sky which, though far from cloudless, consisted of an aerial fleet of small clouds which scarcely hid the sunshine at all. The continuous climb was sapping all his energy but he noticed his companion seemed quite unaffected by her exertion.

She must have been aware of his difficulties for she stopped and removed a bottle of lemonade from her shoulder bag and proffered it to him, and henceforth the bottle was passed between them as they continued climbing, each taking a swig in turn. Not a word had been spoken since leaving the store, Andrew because he'd been saving his energy for the climb and Sandra, he suspected, out of sympathy for his feelings.

At last, some half an hour after leaving the village, they came upon a track branching off to their left; here the trees, no longer primarily birches but also oaks and ashes, cast a cooling shade over the path and this feature together with the downward trend of the track made the going much easier. 'We're almost at the camping site now,' she advised encouragingly. 'What did you think of the climb?'

'Pretty hard going,' he replied ruefully.

But his attractive companion laughed. 'That's the first test for our children, both girls and boys. They're expected to run up the hill from the end of the village with quite heavy packs on their backs and under controlled conditions; in other words temperature, humidity and wind force and direction are noted so the physical fitness of each individual can be judged accurately.'

'You mean they're forced to?' he asked incredulously.

'They're encouraged to,' she corrected. 'No one is driven beyond endurance, but all the children know they're expected to give of their best and so they can drop out whenever they like, although one of the accompanying teachers is compelled to keep pace with the more energetic youngsters while the others shepherd the stragglers. I ought to tell you that the summer camps are not only intended as leisure centres but have many other uses; as an appreciation of outdoor life, for instance, to study and respect wildlife, but also as an endurance test, to learn how to live off the land and to understand what it's like to live in a rough and ready fashion. If nothing else, the children learn to appreciate companionship, their society and especially their parents because there's no mollycoddling up here.'

Whilst Sandra had been explaining, the path they followed descended rather more steeply until it finally ended in a great clearing in the centre of which was a significantly sized lake. Beyond, a great wall of grey rock with woodland at its foot rose to the sky. In the afternoon sunlight the scene was peaceful and beautiful; watercraft of several different types studded the lake, a couple of small sailing boats, a canoe and a dinghy were out near the middle while a punt was being poled along close to the bank, and at various spots around the perimeter children were angling. 'About how many kids would they have here?' Andrew enquired as they strolled across toward a big wooden hut surrounded by small tents.

'Oh, roughly seventy-five with around six teachers, and also a married couple who look after the place. The children are all post-green school and come from various island schools.'

'Are there any other summer camps?'

Sandra nodded. 'Three more. Two are on the shores of the main lake, while the other is near Harbourtown.'

'It would appear that water is an essential element,' he observed.

She barely had time to nod once more before leading the way up some steps to the hut's veranda, where she knocked at a glass panelled door and, without waiting for a reply, went in. Andrew, following, found himself inside in a large room almost entirely devoid of furniture apart from large cupboards on both sides of the entrance door, numerous folding tables and benches leaning against the walls. At the far end, however, a writing desk, a chair and an upright piano stood upon a low platform behind which a large blackboard was fitted. On each side was a door and between the two windows on either side of the room various charts, diagrams and pictures devoted to natural history, field and boat crafts were pinned up.

Upon their entrance, a tall blonde man wearing appropriately a checked shirt and faded jeans arose from the desk and came down to meet them. 'Hello, Sandra,' he said cheerfully, taking her hand then, turning to her companion he shook his hand also, adding, 'you must be Andrew. I've been expecting you both. Come on, I've got the kettle on.' He led the way through one of the doors into what appeared to be a kitchen diner.

'Apart from the permanent couple's cottage which is, naturally, private, these two rooms and the storeroom are the only really civilised habitations up here,' Gregory explained apologetically as he handed them a large mug of tea each. 'We try to let the children experience an authentic outdoor life, even to living off items which they catch or pick such as fish, rabbits, mushrooms and berries, et cetera, but nothing outlandish. Mostly, though, we have to provide victuals, hence the kitchen and stores; and then, of course, the weather could turn rough compelling the children to take shelter in the recreation room.

Andrew asked, 'do you keep the place open during the winter months? Because it must be quite bleak up here then.'

'No,' Gregory replied, 'the camp's closed to schoolchildren, but the authorities don't like to leave places lying idle, so it's reserved for the use of naturalists and those who want a real break from civilisation. There are several small dwellings around the margin of the lake which visitors can sleep in, but they dine in the this hut, self-catering of course. It's a wonderful experience, isn't it Sandra?' She smiled enigmatically but said nothing.

Having finished their teas Greg, as he wished to be called, led the way outside. Commenting on the lack of children to be seen apart from those on and around the lake, he explained they were out on various activities. 'We'll meet up with the various groups during our tour, no doubt,' he added. From the bottom of the steps he led the way across to the lake shore pointing out as he did so that the lake was man made being no greater than three feet deep at its maximum and that the level was held constant by a reliable supply and overflow.

'During the winter months when all boating activities have ceased the lake is a mecca for certain ducks and other waterfowl, thus the popularity of the area for birdwatchers; I think Brian and the others over at the main nature reserve would be quite envious if they didn't have so much of their own wildlife to keep them occupied.' Upon reaching the water's edge they turned left and followed the verge until the well-worn path entered an area of trees.

'Originally,' Greg continued, 'this woodland comprised mostly of birches, which is a natural progression from un-grazed heath land for the underlying soil up here is sandy, but now it's been planted with many other tree species so the children can identify them as well as the many creatures which populate them; for the same reason wild flowers, shrubs, fungi and other organisms have also been introduced.'

Shortly after entering the wood the shouting and laughter of excited children could be heard, and before long the trio arrived at an area much thinned of trees where ropes hung down from the boughs of those which remained; logs spanned pits, and nets and log walls represented obstacles, whilst concrete pipes formed tunnels. 'Our assault course,' observed Gregory somewhat unnecessarily, 'is much beloved by almost all of our children, especially the girls. Isn't that so, Grace?'

He turned to a young woman supervising the fifteen or so children who swung, climbed, crawled and balanced on the various apparatus. The girl, despite her mud caked face and tracksuit, grinned. 'I can't get them off it.'

'No bones broken, I hope?'

'Only mine,' she laughed.

'Did you notice the mess she was in?' Greg asked after they'd continued their walk. 'Knowing Grace, she probably fell into one of the pits just to give the kids confidence. Underneath that muck is the most beautiful girl on the island – apart from Sandra, of course.' For which pretty compliment he received an immediate playful slap round the head from the recipient.

The next group of children were busy with archery both at level targets and those requiring upward trajectory which, as their accompanying teacher explained, gave them practice in hitting prey at ground and treetop level. Andrew couldn't help noting how accurate many of them were, but he was also amused to note that each age group had bows to match its size and that they each had their own special distance from the target. As they moved on to the following section he asked, 'how long do the children stay at each pastime, and do they keep the same teacher all the time?'

'Actually,' replied Greg, 'the teachers get together each evening and arrange how much time they're going to devote to each lesson, or pastime as you put it. It doesn't really matter what the children do or in what order, just as long as each child has a fair turn at everything during their stay here. We also find they prefer to keep with their particular teacher all the time. In this way they can identify with each other. There are only from twelve to fifteen children in the care of each adult and usually a very happy unit develops. Each teacher is fully qualified in all the skills practiced here and, I might add, are also more than proficient in first aid and, with all places with a degree of danger attached to them on the island, there's a cleared area for the reception and taking off of helicopters. So there's no problem with rapid medical attention.'

The trail circled the route in a generally clockwise route, but was far from being straightforward, for occasionally it skirted the lakeside, only to suddenly veer back into the woodland. Neither was it devoid of interest and beauty because the path rarely remained on the level for long; often it descended into a cutting where the sides might be sheer, divulging the fact that rocky ground wasn't always far below the surface; or else the sides might slope gently down being grass, shrub or tree clad. Sometimes the path led upward to follow the crest of a ridge or perhaps to surmount a solitary hillock; at one such place all the trees had been cleared away to allow an unimpeded view down over the lake and camping area, a very beautiful sight. 'Was the path deliberately designed like this?' Andrew enquired, adding, 'only, it seems too hilly to be natural for this area.'

'Full marks for observation,' Greg answered with a laugh. 'Yes, it was actually constructed as a joint effort by teachers, parents and children, with a little help from heavy plant machinery of course. It's attractive isn't it? But it was really built, as was the entire area, in the interests of education. At first sight it would appear as though we're merely duplicating the nature reserve, but whereas they're mainly devoted to conservation and leisure activities, our site was designed with the primary aim of teaching survival, with nature study and enjoyment as secondary considerations and this is why our path alternates between lakeside and woodland, low and high levels. Built into this single area of roughly a thousand acres are just about all the inland habitats and soil conditions to be found on Whyte Island, each with its own typical trees, shrubs, flowers, herbs, fungi, ferns, mosses, grasses, lichens, rushes and so on, many of which are native to our island; however, other plants, especially more useful ones, have been introduced.

'By making the path burrow into the ground we can expose deep underlying calcareous subsoil in order to display the lime tolerant plants, by making the path proceed along true ground level we can ensure a neutral soil, again with plants which prefer such conditions, and then at the opposite end of the scale the hills and ridges provide a means of utilising clay and loamy soils, usually acid by nature, for the growing of plants that are extra-sensitive in their soil requirements. In some cases you'll find plants such as birches growing in all sites indicating they're reasonably happy in any type of soil. In this way it's hoped the children will remember more easily where a certain plant will be found, what it looks like and what its benefits or dangers are. Hopefully this method would be superior to having them obtain their information from books.'

'Surely, though, Greg,' Andrew pointed out, 'the children can't be expected to remember all the plants which are to be found here?'

'Oh, no,' came the reply. 'We do supply very good illustrated books on botany and other subjects, but we've proved through tests that it's a great aid if the pupils have seen individual plants, for instance, in their various ecological sites. So visits to the camp might be seen as really just to supplement the pictures and information in those books.'

At one point they followed another path leading directly away from the lake; after a short distance they came to a large oblong area a good ten feet below the current ground level and it wasn't difficult for Andrew to surmise that this was a shooting range, even though it was at present deserted. 'Although we teach our children how to fire various weapons here, this is also one of the main ranges on the island, which is why it's so elaborate.' After Gregory had explained about different weapons used by the children, the means of scoring and why it was thought necessary for the normally peace-loving islanders to learn about firearms, they retraced their steps back to the main path and continued their tour.

They hadn't gone very far before they came abreast of the second small hut Andrew had noticed since they'd begun their walk. This building was of a similar design to the first, but whereas that had been built of logs, this one featured brick walls and a tiled roof; it was a single storied structure with a shuttered window on either side of the front door and a further two at the rear, and there was a chimney at one end of the steeply pitched roof. When Andrew commented on the hut, Sandra suggested they should look inside on his behalf, to which their companion readily agreed. The interior was quite austere, the furniture comprising of four peculiar wooden benches with solid sides. Each was about six feet long and there was one under each window. A long table stood in the centre of the room and there were several coat pegs, along with a number of diagrams and instructions on the walls.

When they were all seated on a bench drawn up against the table Gregory explained, 'apart from being used as dwellings for out of season visitors, they make useful refuges from sudden showers and also as classrooms for learning about the different fauna and flora in the immediate area.' He pointed to the diagrams by way of illustration. 'There are three other huts, making five in all, one built of stone, another of clay lump and the last of flint.' He stood up and walked across to one of the vacant benches and raised the hinged lid, 'These make nice little bunks for the more permanent visitors, with enough room to keep the bedding and other articles in. As I mentioned, the occupants are required to return to the main hut for their meals, but they can boil up a kettle on the fire for drinks and a wash.'

As they left the hut to resume their tour Andrew said, 'you mentioned something about teaching your pupils survival methods, Greg. Don't the authorities feel Whyte Island's got a future, then?'

The teacher glanced meaningfully at Sandra and then replied, 'our people think that with the nervous state of the world in modern times, there might be a nuclear war, in which case if there are any survivors they might possibly have to start from scratch again. Naturally, we hope some of those survivors will be Whyte Islanders and so, by educating our children on how to build homes, to hunt, fish and identify plants for foods, flavouring and medicines, we'll be increasing their chances of making a success of some future civilisation.'

Just beyond the hut, which allowed a fine prospect of the lake, the path veered sharply to the left. Andrew reckoned they were more or less exactly opposite the encampment and surmised, correctly as it turned out, that they were heading toward the rocky outcrop he'd first noticed from a distance. But before they reached it they came across another group of children accompanied by the inevitable teacher. Observing the pleased expression on Sandra's face when she saw the man, Andrew could hardly suppress a pang of jealousy, for although she'd quickly put him in his place when he'd made his crude pass after the sex demonstration, familiarity had become briefly confused with possession in his mind. However, he greeted the teacher pleasantly enough when Sandra introduced him as her partner, and subsequently he regretted his envy, for the man was extremely friendly and obviously dedicated to his vocation.

Despite the arrival of his lover with two men, one of whom was a complete stranger, David went on to finish his description of the medium sized tree under which his little group stood. 'This plant which is not native to our region, has been widely introduced throughout the island because of its edible nuts, comparatively rapid growth and pliable timber.' Whilst he described these and many of the tree's other features, Andrew noticed the children assiduously writing the particulars down in their notebooks.

He and his two companions remained to hear several other plants described in some detail before they resumed their walk, but not, however, before David had drawn his lover to one side in order to engage her in earnest conversation. Andrew noticed her looking anxiously toward him several times before finally shaking her head and rejoining him and Gregory. 'I hope I'm not spoiling anything,' he said to her eventually, 'only I saw you glancing my way when you were talking to your boyfriend.'

Their guide had tactfully drawn ahead by the time Sandra answered. 'David wanted me to stay on till late but I said it wouldn't be fair on you.'

'Don't worry about me,' Andrew replied gallantly, 'I can make my own way home.'

'There isn't any argument,' she replied firmly. 'I came with you and I go with you. David had no right to ask, and he should know better.'

Feeling somewhat confused he was silent for a moment, until an idea suddenly came to him. 'In that case, if I can contact Mr Maynard's home, I'm willing to stay on for as long as you wish, providing there's some grub going, of course.'

Not really knowing whether he should have insisted more forcefully upon leaving on his own he was gratified when she squeezed his arm and thanked him profusely, adding, 'I'm sure you'll enjoy the campfire supper and the singing.' Then she hurried after Gregory to tell him the news.

Although he tried to appear happy enough, Andrew suddenly felt quite dejected. Having messed up his relationship with each of the Maynard sisters, the thought of playing cupid to Sandra and David hardly filled him with joy; he felt utterly downcast, and so his forthcoming unaccompanied visit to the Station Arms held little pleasure for him. In spite of what several girls had by now told him, he doubted if a female companion, especially the auburn haired slave, would be there just for his sake. Recalling what Sandra had said about telephone dating cheered him up a little, but he still couldn't rid himself of his feeling of self-doubt and intrinsic loneliness. If his companions were aware of his mood neither showed any sign, but they all remained silent until a clearing in the trees revealed the rock face toward which they'd been heading.

Even though he'd more or less become accustomed to sudden surprises on Whyte Island, the vision of half a dozen children aged from about twelve to fifteen roping up to tackle a cliff face rather bemused him, despite the fact that a female teacher was obviously about to take the lead. Although the cliff appeared less formidable than from a distance, tending to slope back from the vertical and being well supplied with ledges, it still represented a challenge to people so young. A further group of children stood nearby, from where they'd be able to watch the ascent in detail. Gregory made no attempt to approach the teacher, obviously considering she had enough to concern herself with without being bothered by introductions to a stranger. Andrew, though, couldn't refrain from making his feelings known in an undertone.

Somewhat to his surprise it was Sandra who answered. 'Although you might not think it, it's actually perfectly safe because it's nowhere near as difficult or dangerous as it seems, and no child is made to take part, but I've never heard of one refusing; have you Greg?' He shook his head, and she continued, 'And there has never been a serious accident. All the pupils receive a thorough briefing in the classroom before they go and, of course, in addition to Barbara, some of the others in each particular group will have climbed the cliff before.'

'Do they have to return by the cliff?' Andrew enquired, thinking a descent would be far more intimidating.

'Only after they've been up at least twice before, and only if they're quite happy about it; there's an easy path down otherwise.' The three joined the group of children staying behind and together they watched the ascent. Apart from some whispering and a few nervous giggles, the latter doubtless emanating from novices, the climbers were observed in silence. It soon became obvious to Andrew, by the size of some of the climbers and by the instructions occasionally called from above or below, that the least experienced children were sandwich between those who'd already climbed before.

It fascinated him to see how the line of climbers altered position in relation to each other; at times two children would be close together only to part, perhaps to join the child immediately above or to be joined by someone below. He thought it was reminiscent of a caterpillar making its way up a leaf, except that often the progress was in a sideways direction while another section might still be climbing vertically. Eventually the summit was attained and the last climber scrambled over the top.

As he and his two companions turned to leave, Andrew, after wishing without irony a cheerful good luck to the waiting children, observed, 'I suppose mountaineering is taught in order to instil team spirit and confidence into the youngsters?'

Gregory answered, 'yes, mostly, although we don't look upon scaling an easy cliff as mountaineering as such. But as you're probably aware by now, Andrew, we live in a fair and unselfish society; this means every person has the same chance in life whether at work or play. So when a child is being educated she or he is offered the opportunity to participate in everything; we feel that being able to experience activities like climbing, swimming, boating, even flying, allows a child to find out for themselves what she or he likes or wishes to do. Probably most of these children won't want to climb again after experiencing it a number of times.

'There is, however, a less obvious reason for encouraging our pupils to take part in potentially frightening or dangerous activities, and that is to prevent empty bragging. Many youngsters, especially boys, often put on a show of bravado when the right people or situations aren't present to call them to account, but are found wanting when real courage and steady nerve is required. Such bravado is, naturally, usually a symptom of hidden insecurity and so any child disposed to demonstrate that trait on Whyte Island would soon realise1 that they'd be expected to put their courage to the test. So most youngsters soon learn to present a modest exterior because it isn't unknown for a slight, apparently timid girl to display more courage and endurance than a well built over confident boy. Of course, it also helps a withdrawn child to discover facets of their nature which they were unaware of.'

No further groups were met with on the remainder of their walk, which was undertaken at a much slower pace. The path continued along the foot of the cliff face for a considerable distance, and from the way the eminence rose sheer and at times even overhung the trail, it became obvious that the section used by the children was one of the safest and easiest. 'Presumably the more precipitous parts of this cliff are used fairly often by experienced climbers,' Andrew suggested.

Gregory, glancing up at the heights speculatively replied, 'I suppose they do represent a bit of a challenge in places, but I doubt they're high enough for most climbers. Now, if you were to visit the gorge downstream from the dam on the main lake you'd find crags two or three times higher than these, and that's where many climbers foregather, so they tell me.'

Hearing Sandra laugh Andrew turned to her. 'He's kidding you,' she exclaimed. 'Greg and his wife Grace, whom you've recently met, live for climbing. Actually, there are some rare birds of prey, a particular species of crow and alpine flowers to be found up there, just as there are here, so they're both prohibited areas. But as Greg well knows there are also large parts of the dam, pun intended, cliffs open to the public.'

Gradually the outcrop became less high and steep. At one point, a large stream of water spouted from a crevice half way up the cliff to fall, in a graceful curve, into a rocky pool and then hurried away along a well-worn boulder strewn channel in the direction of the lake. Close to its exit from the foliage-lined pool, a stone built bridge carried their path over the stream; nearby, a matching stone hut, every crack and crevice apparently packed with flowers and small ferns stood. 'What a picturesque site,' Andrew remarked in some awe.

'And all with the compliments of the island authorities,' Gregory said.

'You mean it isn't natural?'

'No' replied Sandra, 'this is an outlet from the main lake, constructed to keep the summer camp's lake full of fresh water. Later on when it nears the coast it's purified and serves as a water source to the towns and villages by the sea. Building it was a major feat of engineering because between this point and the main lake the water's contained in a pipe a considerable depth below ground level. As you said, Andy, it is attractive, and while it remains above ground it's been designed to look natural.'

After remaining on the bridge enjoying the scenery for several minutes and watching some small dragonflies, or damselflies as Greg identified them, flitting about they continued their circumference of the lake. For the remainder of their walk the path skirted the reedy margins of the water's edge for much of the time, but on one occasion it traced the outline of a creek half hidden by rushes, willows and alders; here, the sudden muffled beating of large wings together with a harsh croak announced the departure of a heron; and shortly after Andrew glimpsed a brilliant blue and green arrow speeding at head height along the watercourse, which he immediately recognised as being a kingfisher. Eventually they reached an open space where, beyond a small wooden bridge spanning another stream, the lake's outlet, the summer camp stood.

On the way over Gregory explained that it would be at least an hour before all the children returned from their different activities and the there'd be a lecture on survival for half of them while the remainder organised the evening meal and built a fire. 'So would you like to attend the lecture?' he asked. They both nodded. 'In that case,' he went on, 'your time's your own for the next hour or so as I'll have a little organising to do. Might I suggest you do a little fishing while the lake's comparatively free? As you can see there's a choice of craft, and you know where to get the bait and tackle from, don't you Sandra?'

While she saw to the fishing arrangements Andrew made his telephone call. Much to his embarrassment the voice of Helen replied, although, in retrospect it was hardly surprising at that time of day. 'Oh Helen,' he said with more confidence than he felt, 'I hope you had nothing planned but I'm over at one of the summer camps and Sandra and I have been invited to stay on for a barbecue.'

There was a pause, then she said without emotion, 'what time will you be back here?'

'Sandra reckons about ten thirty.'

'Alright,' came the laconic reply.

'Listen,' he went on hurriedly, 'I'm sorry about last night.'

'What for? It was the time of the month, that's all.' There was a brief silence, then she added gently, 'I enjoyed myself thank you.' Then she put the phone down.

Women! Andrew thought as he left the hut. What on earth was wrong with her? He suspected subconsciously he shouldn't have mentioned Sandra; anyway, he considered as he walked down to where his companion waited beside a dinghy tied to a small jetty, he might as well enjoy himself now and perhaps he'd be able to sort something out on the morrow. As he came closer she asked if it was alright and when he nodded and told her who'd answered, she asked, 'how was she?'

'She sounded a bit short.'

'Probably just the time of the month,' she replied dismissively, and he couldn't help smiling at the ironic coincidence.

By mutual agreement Andrew took the oars even though he'd protested he couldn't row. 'I'll tell you what to do,' Sandra urged, 'but as a sailor you ought to be ashamed of yourself.'

Eventually, after some shaky progress during which he narrowly missed catching a crab on several occasions, they reached the centre of the lake where they soon baited their hooks and cast out. He marvelled at the deft way in which she found the exact depth, and she quickly caught her first fish which she subsequently placed in a keep net; although it wasn't long before he also got a bite he was nowhere near as successful as his companion who usually managed to catch two to every one of his. Despite the shallowness of the water it was much too murky for the bottom to be visible, but he didn't mind as he considered it added to the attraction of angling if the fish weren't visible. After catching his third fish, which was so small that at Sandra's instigation he threw it back, he asked, 'is your fishing season the same as on the mainland?'

'I doubt it,' she replied, 'because we haven't got one. For a start, due to our low ratio of people per land area, our rivers and lakes aren't under as much pressure from anglers as yours are. I don't know much about your fishing laws, do you?' He shook his head. 'But we're permitted to retain a certain poundage of what we catch if we want to, and the minimum weight of each fish is quite high. We have to keep a log of where we fished, what species we caught, their quantity and weight, and how much we retained. In this way an official record is kept which gives a good indication of population levels; from this it's been found that regular year round angling has no detrimental effects on fish stocks. This log keeping is all done on trust as fishing permits aren't required; anyone can get out their angling gear and fish when they like, though there are some places where it's forbidden to fish, mainly in dangerous areas or on designated wildlife reserves; also, after we had a fatal accident, no one's allowed to fish alone. But apart from that, as long as fishing tackle isn't discarded but disposed of in a responsible manner, anyone can fish where they want.'

'So none of your fish species is endangered?' Andrew asked in wonder after witnessing Sandra reeling in a fine bream.'

'Only those which are outside the island authorities' control; some of the fish originating from the sea aren't getting to our estuaries through over-fishing by some foreign states which should know better. But when you consider our fresh water fish aren't under threat from poaching or water pollution it's hardly surprising they're thriving.' She checked her watch. 'Well, I reckon we've caught more than our quota. When we've packed our gear away, weighed our catch and released those we don't want, it'll be time for our lecture.'

By the time they'd reached the bank a good number of children were back from their lessons, and so they were surrounded by an interested group as the weighed each fish which Sandra diligently noted in her log book. He couldn't help feeling envious of her when he realised the onlookers' highest praise was for the ones she'd caught, but this was incidental for neither she nor he laid claim to any particular fish. While she dispatched the fish they were to keep, he took the remainder to the lakeside and watched them swim away and, on his return, he was given the dead ones to take to where the food was being prepared. Sandra awaited him on the hut's veranda, and together they went into the lecture.

Andrew found the talk extremely interesting for there must have been few items regarding the subject of survival which were not touched upon; details as varied as the construction of huts similar to those on the camp trail, the hunting, killing, skinning and cooking of game were explained in depth, in addition to the making of clothes, cultivation of land and growing of crops. Although Sandra's partner David wasn't present, two other teachers were, one of whom he recognised as Barbara, the woman tutoring the climbers, and these, together with Gregory, took it in turns to explain the various skills required in the serious business of survival. Before the lecture had ended the aroma of roasting meat had begun to permeate the air, and so it was with a growing appetite that Andrew joined his companion and the pupils as they left the room at the appropriate time, ready to tackle any food offered to them.

Although the sun was still quite high in the cloudless sky it was beginning to lose some of its power to light and heat, spreading instead a golden glow over everything; it looked as if it was going to be a perfect evening. Various birds, including nightingales, were singing and swifts flew high overhead occasionally screeching, whilst their companions in aerial display the swallows and martins dived over the lake. Somewhere near the cliffs a ubiquitous owl hooted briefly, no doubt in anticipation of a night's hunting, as a flock noisy jackdaws descended to roost among the treetops. 'Beautiful, isn't it?' whispered Sandra who stood beside him on the veranda, and he could only nod in agreement.

But the spell was broken by Gregory who, being the last to leave the main hut, now pressed a pair of mugs, mess tins and cutlery upon them saying, 'you'll be needing these; come on, this way.' He led them to where several rows of great tree trunks lay in the form of a square in the middle of which a large bonfire blazed, and with a barbecue on one side out of its direct heat; the latter was scarcely to be seen for the number of chattering children who, under the supervision of several teachers, were intent upon cooking, doling out or receiving food. On the barbecue spit a large unidentifiable carcass was being slowly turned by a young lad who stopped long enough to allow slices to be removed every time a customer presented themselves, the carver being an efficient young girl.

When Andrew had been ushered up for his share he was surprised at not only being given several generous slices of meat, but also subsequently a portion of filleted fish. At first he thought this was in recognition of his and Sandra's angling efforts until he noticed that a youngster behind him also received a piece. With his companion he made his way over to one of the logs where children were already eating, and they were both soon enjoying their ample and delicious meal. Apart from the fish and the meat, which she assured him was mutton, there were roast potatoes and minted peas, with blackberries and cream for dessert, together with a great mug of tea.

'The vegetables, fruit and herb were quite possibly grown and stored on the campsite,' Sandra remarked while they washed their utensils in the tub of hot soapy water provided up in the hut's kitchen unit, 'and you know where the fish came from, though it would have been caught yesterday, as freshwater fish need to be soaked in salty water for a day, at least, to take the muddy taste away.'

'What about the sheep?' he joked. 'Was the site responsible for that?'

She smiled. 'It was probably donated by a local farmer, but you can be sure some of these kids would be able to deal adequately with most aspects of shepherding.'

Shortly after returning to where they'd eaten their meals they were joined by David who, after a brief greeting, sat down to consume his meal in silence. Andrew presently noticed many of the children were going over to their tents and returning with various musical instruments, those of the stringed variety predominating, and soon from different parts of the square came muted sounds of instruments being tuned and songs being practiced. Eventually, when the last person had eaten their meal, washed their mess tin and returned to their seat, Gregory rose to his feet. 'Where did we get to last night?' he asked. A hand was enthusiastically raised from the second line of logs to Andrew's left. 'Alright,' said Gregory, 'let's hear what you can do.' Immediately came the sound of a mandolin as the child played himself an introduction to be followed, after a few bars, by his sweet soprano voice singing a mournful song about a girl who yearned after her dead lumberjack lover.

This was the beginning of a highly entertaining evening for Andrew; he'd never before heard such a variety of music played upon so many different instruments in such a generally talented fashion. Even the manner in which the concert was managed was unique, for after the first child had finished his performance, someone started off a song which everyone seemed to know, so that soon the air was ringing with joyful melody. This set the pattern for the evening's entertainment, for immediately the last notes had died away another child began playing and singing, to be followed once again by a popular song, but this time with a robust chorus.

Between such songs Andrew heard a great number of musical instruments, usually accompanied by a song; occasionally more than one child took part as if the players had rehearsed beforehand. He recognised instruments such as six and twelve string guitars, banjo, ukulele, violin, harmonica, concertina, harp and even bagpipes. Once, a girl stood up to play a lilting jazz tune on a clarinet accompanied by another girl on a banjo and a boy who tapped drum sticks upon a coconut shell, the result being wonderfully melodious. The pieces sung and played ranged from classical music to various types of jazz, folk, rhythm and blues, and pop songs, a teacher sang an unaccompanied operatic aria and a pupil played some almost faultless Spanish guitar music, while sea shanties were the favourite for chorus songs.

So enthralled was Andrew by the concert that once, when he turned to make a remark to Sandra, he was surprised to find neither her or David there, but immediately forgot the fact when he became lost in the music of the next performance. How long she and her partner were away for he couldn't tell, but when he next became fully aware they were seated near him again. As the dusk surrendered to darkness and the flames of the campfire, growing more vivid, threw sparks high into the air, the singers became more relaxed, the shrieks and laughter grew louder and more frequent, the singing and playing surer.

Large flagons of ginger beer and lemonade together with glasses were brought out, making it appear even more of a party occasion. To the visitor it seemed like the beginning of a non-alcoholic bacchanal, but whether or not it became one he wasn't to find out, for just as one of the chorus songs came to an end and the first notes from a concertina became audible he felt a tapping on his arm and Sandra whispered loudly in his ear, 'Half an hour to our train; we'd better be going.'

Causing as little disturbance as possible to the revellers they both stole away after saying goodbye. Before starting up the track toward the lanes, Gregory came over to ask if they'd find the way alright. Taking the question as a mere formality Sandra laughed and produced a powerful torch, adding, 'there's plenty of moonlight to see by, anyway.' After thanking him for everything, they shook hands with him and began the long walk back to the station, the sound of music following them for a considerable distance.

'Where on earth did all those instruments come from?' asked Andrew after he'd praised the children's talents. 'Surely they weren't expected to run up the hill with those on their backs?'

'No,' was the amused reply, 'the loribus would have brought them up, suitably labelled of course.'

'I wish that bus was here now to take us down the hill. I feel quite tired all of a sudden.'

She laughed in astonishment. 'Haven't you got any stamina? I thought the women in your country were supposed to be the weaker sex. Shouldn't you be offering to carry me down?'

Finding conversation a good defence against torpor, he was quick to take advantage of the opening unwittingly provided by his companion. 'Have you ever been to the mainland, Sandra?'

She replied quite vehemently. 'No, and if you'll forgive me for saying so, I don't particularly want to. I've heard of several people who've visited or stayed there and I'm afraid few have had anything nice to say about it. People over there seem to be too self-centred, and it's very much a case of living on one's own personal merits. I could go on about it all the way to the station but it would be unkind to you.' Despite all his protestations to the contrary, that he wouldn't mind, she refused to talk any further about his homeland.

Still fighting against tiredness, Andrew brought up a fresh subject. 'If children of that age can make such good music, it should be fantastic at the Station Arms tomorrow night.'

Sandra agreed. 'Yes, it will be. David and I go fairly often. If it wasn't for his stint up at the summer camp we might well have been going there too. Anyway, I hope you enjoy yourself and that there will be a girl waiting for you.'

Silently hoping the same, but still doubtful, he said, 'Sandra, do you mind if I ask a rather personal question?'

'That depends upon what it is. Try me.'

'Well, you mentioned that David, like the other instructors, spends a month each year up here on average. But you're going home now; so, er, what do you do about...'

'Sleeping arrangements?' she finished for him, noting his embarrassment. 'We don't get as much time together as we'd like, but we don't do too badly. He gets days off and sometimes in the evenings we stay together in the village or usually we share a tent in the camp. It's only temporary because when I've passed my exams I'll be sharing a tent with him on a more permanent basis.'

Not knowing quite how she'd receive his next query he then asked, 'who does he share his tent with when you're not around?'

To his relief Sandra smiled. 'You're thinking of his female opposite number. Well, no doubt her partner isn't far away. But as I said yesterday, lovers are loyal over here. I trust him just as he trust me with you.'

Andrew thought for a moment, then said, 'I'm not sounding you out, because this is just a hypothetical question, but supposing I managed to seduce you between here and the station. I mean, it's a beautiful night, made for romance, and you're a beautiful young woman. So what would you do?'

'Afterward?' When he nodded she went on. 'Women, although men usually prefer to think of us as all having the same character, are just as individualistic as males. So although we've got a reputation for being irresponsible and easily led, this isn't necessarily always the case. However, there are obviously girls and women who have a low resistance level, and that is why island girls have been trained to be more accountable for their actions, just as our males have been brought up to not to try and seduce us, especially when we're already spoken for.

'What I'm leading up to is this: the only way you're going to get me into those trees, apart from force, and good luck to you if you're thinking of taking me on, will be because I really want to go. Therefore, because I want you then it follows that I wouldn't want David anymore; so as soon as we'd done what we wished to do, then it would be my duty to go back up this hill and tell my lover that our partnership was over.' She paused, then asked, 'so what do you suppose he'd do about it?' He shook his head. 'He'd do nothing. Perhaps he'd be a little upset, because we've been going together a long time, but he'd put himself in my place and reason that if I'd wanted to preserve our relationship I wouldn't have made love to you.

'Have you ever tried keeping a cat on your lap when it wants to leave?' He nodded, vaguely wondering where this question was heading. 'It's a pointless exercise, isn't it? Our lovers' philosophy is like that; every islander knows it, so there's little ill will when a relationship breaks up. David probably wouldn't mope much after losing me. He'd immediately contact the computer dating service and would soon be involved with a temporary or, perhaps, permanent lover. There is one way in which he might become angry, however, and that would be if you subsequently failed to take me on as your permanent lover, because that would mean you'd wrecked a perfectly good relationship for your own selfish sexual gratification. In the early years of our society quite a number of people, occasionally entire families, were exiled for failing to act on that ethic. So don't ever go poaching over here, Andrew!'

By the time Sandra had finished explaining they'd reached the station, where they didn't need to wait long before the lights of their approaching train became visible from afar. He'd been surprised to find about twenty people already waiting, and then he remembered being told that almost every station served a place where some form of entertainment could be found, and he vaguely wondered what the village's speciality was.

The comfortable seat and the gentle swaying of the coach had a soporific effect on the young man and try as he might he couldn't ward off increasing tiredness, and his last memory was of seeing his companion smiling indulgently at him. He was eventually woken by Sandra shaking his arm. 'I thought you might like to freshen yourself up with a wash as we're almost at Harbourtown. I wouldn't like to think of you falling asleep on the bus ride, though I doubt you'd end up in the depot.'

Suitably refreshed he stood with Sandra at the bus stop. 'What happens now?' he asked. 'I mean, will you be showing me around any of the red establishments?'

She shrugged. 'I've no idea. No plans have been formulated as far as I'm aware. You'll have to ask Mr Maynard, I think.'

'Well, whatever happens, will you be my guide again?'

She laughed in surprise. 'Goodness, what's so special about me? I think you're a bit of a butterfly, the flower you're at is the only one for you.'

Their attention was drawn by the arrival of his bus. He said seriously, 'I mean it.'

She shrugged. 'We'll see, though I'm not really a free agent. By this time tomorrow night there'll surely be a new flower to claim your attention, anyway.' She turned away. 'Be seeing you,' she called over her shoulder.

Andrew, boarding the bus, replied, 'thanks for everything.' She raised a hand in acknowledgement and walked off into the darkness.

Sandra had hit the nail right on the head he considered as the bus started off. He felt sure she considered him insecure, and maybe he was: he seemed to fall for all the girls he met – Helen, Linda, the slave girl, Sandra – or at least to need them. Without being fully conscious of it, an idea had begun to form in his mind. It all depended on his programme on the morrow. If nothing had been planned for him he would, perhaps, try to contact an available girl through the computer dating service and see if he became overaffectionate with her.

To his relief there was a light on in the Maynard kitchen and so, out of consideration, he tapped lightly on the back door, wondering as he did so who was going to answer. For his own peace of mind he hoped it would be Charlie. However, it was Linda, characteristically clad in a revealing nightgown, who opened the door. 'Hello, Andrew,' she said quietly but cheerfully, a warning finger to her lips. 'They're both abed, but I've waited up like a dutiful matron.' She led the way through to the kitchen saying, 'I've just made some cocoa. Did you have a nice time?'

Andrew answered her as briefly as possible but then observed, as she placed a mug on the table before him, 'shouldn't you be wearing something a little less suggestive? I can see all your charms.'

She smiled. 'You've seen them all before and, I might add, experienced them.'

'Maybe,' he replied, 'but that doesn't mean I've be sexually satisfied for the rest of my life. I still find you… stimulating.'

'Well, come Thursday you can have me again, or else won't want me, as the case may be.'

'And what about last night's lover?'

Linda smiled without humour, then abruptly picked up her mug of cocoa and turned to leave. 'Don't forget to switch the lights off,' she said as she left the room. Sometimes, Andrew silently addressed himself, you're a pain in the neck.

He was awoken the next morning by the sound of pouring rain. A glance at his clock told him he still had a couple of hours before he need get up, and prior to lapsing back into sleep he definitely decided he would try the computer, for unless Charlie was considering taking him somewhere he would almost certainly be left to his own devices.

Once again he was awakened by Linda knocking upon his door, and with a reaction which surprised himself he asked her to enter, as he wished to talk to her. Immediately the door opened to admit her and she tactfully closed it behind her. 'Yes?' she enquired gracefully, looking down at him without a trace of reproach.

'I'm sorry if I upset you last night. I seem to be making a habit of putting my foot in it with you and Helen.'

She studied him for a moment and then said, 'I don't understand you, Andy. I must have explained it to you lots of times. Look.'

She untied the belt of her pink dressing gown and shrugged the garment off her shoulders. Naked, she stood before him and began to turn slowly round, saying as she did so, 'I've just got a standard, mature young woman's body. It has all the necessary features; better than some women's maybe, but not as good as others'; and I foolishly pride myself on being able to use it.' She tapped her head. 'It's up here where it counts, intelligence, personality and genuine love. Intelligence we'll give a miss; personality – well, I should think most island girls are far nicer than me – and as for actual love, well, I like you a lot but that's as far as it goes.

'I want you to have someone, hopefully on the island, who's more intelligent than me, with a nicer personality and who will really love you; a girl with a face and body which would knock mine for six, someone who really knows how to use the latter.' She bent down and retrieved her dressing gown; as she put it back on she urged, 'but please stop thinking of me as your personal property. I don't mean to turn you on and I promise I won't wear revealing clothes while you're around in future. I admit it was thoughtless of me; I like to feel comfortable and free, but I wasn't trying to tease you.'

Andrew, his mind now elsewhere after her display of nudity, asked thoughtfully, 'is your father booked up for today, do you know?'

Understandably surprised at this sudden contrary question she answered, 'I think so; why?'

'I'm probably jumping the gun, but if he's got something to do and you're still standing in for that teacher, then that leaves Helen to look after me and I think I ought to keep out of her way.' He gazed shrewdly at her, then added, 'Sandra says I need only phone the computer to get a date, and I thought perhaps I'd give it a try for today. If I get a girl, should I ask her to come to the Station Arms tonight?'

Linda sat down on the bed with a thump, narrowly missing his left leg. She looked up at the ceiling, gave an audible sigh and murmured, 'remind me never to play poker with you.'

He smiled with a mixture of relief and anticipation, but decided not to pursue his victory, being content to allow her to extricate herself as best she could. With a partial smile she then said, 'of course, I don't know whether dad's got any plans for you, but if you are at a loose end then a date for the day might be a good idea, although I should leave this evening free. I might change my mind and come along with you.' Both knew the other wasn't fooled but neither said anything more on the subject. Linda suddenly jumped up. 'If I don't watch out I'll be late. See you downstairs.' And she quickly left the room.

During breakfast, after Andrew had told the family about the previous day's events, Charlie said, 'Perhaps you'd like to stay in today and rest, unless Helen can think of somewhere you'd wish to visit together, but it's a pretty nasty day and looks like remaining so. Unfortunately, I've got a meeting to attend.'

Before Helen could speak, Andrew answered. 'Actually, I was thinking of phoning the computer dater. I'm sure your daughter's got enough to do without bothering about me.' To his perplexity Helen, who had been distant but polite, flashed him a look of extreme annoyance which made him wonder whether he'd missed his chance with her again, but he went on. 'Could someone show me how it works after breakfast?'

Linda volunteered at once. 'It's easy. But don't forget to explain you only want a girl for the day. You won't want to disappoint a lovesick female, like Helen.'

'I don't think that's very funny,' snapped the recipient of the remark. 'Leave me out of your stupid jokes.'

'Yes,' interposed Charlie, 'don't tease your sister, Linda; you were taught to know better than that.'

Completely unabashed Linda ate her meal, chatting to whoever wished to listen, and immediately upon finishing her tea she said, 'come on, Andy, I'll show you how it's done.' Out in the hallway, she quickly found the number. 'Now, the machine will ask you for your name, address, your telephone numbers, gender, age, et cetera, then it'll ask for your requirements which you'll need to keep brief. Some women will be unattached and probably looking for a more permanent relationship, but others, for reasons best known to themselves, will just wish to while away a few hours which might or might not include sexual activity. But you should ask for an attached girl – that way you can be more certain that no sex will be involved.'

'But I might want sex,' Andrew objected.

Linda winked and advised, 'I should save your strength because you might meet someone at the Station Arms, you never know. Anyway, attached women provide a useful service by temporarily partnering men who might be lonely otherwise; of course it could be the other way round, but because these people are attached, sex won't come into it.'

'But why use attached people then?'

'Because sometimes suitable unattached people aren't available, and therefore an attached partner is better than no partner at all. This is getting complicated, but what it amounts to is that the authorities don't want anyone to feel lonely – it's unhealthy. But just phone.' She checked her watch. 'Oh dear, I'll have to dash.'

'But what happens after I've phoned?' he pleaded.

'They'll call you back; it might be the computer to give you a number to contact or it could even be your date. Cheerio.'

Before picking up the phone, Andrew pondered on whether he should ask for a temporarily unattached girl, but finally he decided to take Linda's advice, most fortunately as it turned out. The telephone call went surprisingly easily, though he was taken aback when a very feminine voice answered; he gave his details and requirements without any problems and after replacing the receiver returned to the kitchen. Of Charlie there was no sign, but Helen was at the sink washing up. 'Where's the tea towel?' he asked of her.

'There's really no need,' she answered. But he insisted and she just shrugged and handed the cloth to him.

'What's wrong Helen?' he asked after they'd worked for several minutes in pregnant silence.

She turned and faced him. 'The only thing wrong, as you put it, is what I told you last night on the telephone.'

'Then you don't mind me phoning for a computer date? I mean, I haven't ruined any plans?'

She gave a flat laugh. 'No, I'm afraid I've got enough to do as it is. Besides...' but she was interrupted by the sound of the phone ringing. 'There's your girlfriend,' she finished.

Andrew went and lifted the receiver with some trepidation, but it was only the computer. 'Ring five-six-six-four,' the female voice said, 'Gillian is waiting to hear from you.' Then the line went dead. Before he forgot, he wrote the name and number down on the telephone pad and then studied his reflection in the mirror hanging on the wall above the phone. A mixture of excitement and doubt rose within him, and he grimaced at himself; just like contacting a call girl he thought, and smiled at the unintentional pun. His eyes challenged him from the mirror. 'Go on,' they seemed to indicate, 'don't keep her waiting; it's what you wanted.' He tapped out the number.

'Yes?' said a woman's voice.

'Is that Gillian, please?'

'Wait a moment, please,' came the reply.

A few moments later another, livelier, female voice spoke. 'Hello?' it said.

Trying to sound decisive, Andrew replied, 'Gillian? My name's Andrew, I got your number and...' he floundered.

But the voice at the end of the line came to his aid. 'Where do you live? What's the nearest town?' He told her. 'You know the railway station?' When he said he did, she went on. 'Just around the corner from there is a coffee bar, it's the only one in that neck of the woods. I'll be in there about ten o'clock, alright?'

'There's only one thing,' he said, and the girl waited patiently. 'I'm a stranger to the island and so I don't know my way around, especially on a day like this.'

She laughed. 'Somehow I didn't think you were a Whyte Islander, but don't worry, Andrew, I know a few places we can visit, even when it's wet. See you, then.'

He grinned to himself in a self-satisfied manner as he put the receiver down but glancing at his watch brought him back to reality. There wasn't much time to lose if he was going to be there on the dot. Returning to the kitchen he apologised to Helen for abandoning her, but she merely shrugged; before leaving the room he said in a fit of gallantry, 'I wish it was you, Helen.'

Still busy at the sink, she paused and looked at him. 'Do you?' she asked dryly. 'I wonder.'

He gazed at her in return, then replied, 'I like you a lot, but you're very difficult to understand.'

Unexpectedly, she suddenly smiled. 'Perhaps you will one day.'

As was his wont, he'd completely underestimated the ability of island transport, and even of his own legs, to move him from one place to another rapidly. He'd therefore found himself in the vicinity of the stated venue some twenty minutes too early and so, having identified the coffee bar in question, had drifted back to the station forecourt where he was now passing the time watching the movement of trains with some fascination. He was beginning to wish he hadn't phoned for a date, for although it had stopped pouring there was still plenty of cloud about and the wind was

182

strong and blustery which carried the occasional drop of rain to his face. Despite the island's propensity for suddenly revealing fascinating surprises he doubted whether much could be made out of a day like this.

'Hello,' a voice behind him said brightly.

He turned round to see a very attractive brunette standing before him; he was so startled that all he could say was, 'I'm sorry but I've got a date, I'm waiting for someone.'

The girl's eyes and lips smiled back at him as brightly as her voice. 'I know,' she answered, 'I'm Gillian. I saw you go past the café.'

Without knowing why Andrew, suddenly feeling devilish, decided to test her reactions. 'I was hoping for someone attractive,' he said with a solemn face.

Not a flicker of emotion passed across the girl's features. She just stared back at him and then said, 'sorry.'

'You're beautiful instead,' he replied.

Instantly Gillian laughed out loud. 'I don't know where you come from stranger,' she eventually answered, 'but I think I'm going to emigrate there.' Then more seriously she added, 'you're not supposed to say things like that on an attached date. We're just meant to be company for each other, that's all. I don't know about your partner, but mine would be most annoyed.' She opened her shoulder bag, and from a purse withdrew a money note. 'Here's my contribution to the outing,' she said offering it to him. However, despite all her efforts Andrew adamantly refused the money, but she showed she could be equally as stubborn for she walked over to an adjacent drain grid and, standing over it with the tightly folded note in her hand, she threatened, 'if you don't accept it then I lose the money and you lose me.'

Faced with such an ultimatum he could only acquiesce, but in accepting the money, said, 'alright, but on the condition that you take charge of the day's entertainment. So lead on, MacGillian.'

From that moment on a complete bond united the two, so quickly had they come to a mutual understanding that henceforth they were more like lifelong friends than members of different genders who, a mere few minutes earlier, had been complete strangers. Both agreed to give the coffee bar a miss and Gill, as she preferred to be addressed, took him to the lounge of a nearby pub; the room, which was practically empty at that time of day, was decorated in Edwardian style consisting entirely of different shades of red. Gill's plain green dress, revealed when Andrew helped her off with her grey raincoat, matched the decor perfectly. After seeing her seated at a table for two in a secluded corner he went and fetched her a sherry, choosing a beer for himself.

During their subsequent conversation she told him she was a nursing sister. 'I suppose that means you haven't got any other jobs?' Andrew asked.

'Everyone, except Charlie Maynard, the president, mothers and carers and those under tuition has secondary work, but I particularly like all kinds of gardening.'

'Just like Mr Maynard; although, of course, it's just a hobby to him.'

'I know,' Gill stated, 'I've worked with him. But how did you know?'

'Oh,' Andrew said nonchalantly, 'I'm staying with him.'

She didn't seem particularly impressed but observed with some feeling, 'I hope you realise how fortunate you are; he's a great man.' Then she asked, 'How do you get on with his daughters?'

Andrew explained his problems in that direction as if to an elder sister, even going on to his feelings about the slave girl and Sandra. Gill gazed shrewdly at him, 'I bet you'd marry me tomorrow given the opportunity, wouldn't you?'

'Yes, I suppose I would,' he agreed ruefully.

'Poor lad, you're love starved. Don't worry though, you've only been here: ten days, isn't it? You've just got off to a bad start, that's all. You've got on well with Linda, Sandra and me, Helen's being awkward so we can leave her off the list, and it looks as though you made a good impression on that slave girl; so all you need is the right opportunity. I think you'll be a marvellous catch for some appreciative girl; island men are, by comparison to you, quite blasé about girls and sex, which is a good thing really – it's better than being sexually frustrated and therefore untrustworthy. But I can't think why a mainland girl hasn't snapped you up a long time ago.'

He gave an ironic laugh. 'With them it's a vicious circle. You've got to make a nigh on perfect impression the first time or you usually don't stand a chance: you need to be a mind reader; but if you fail too often then you lose confidence, so that even when a girl does show interest you think, "What's the point, she's only going to leave you on the first or second date"; thereby delivering a blow to one's ego. Apart from Helen, who's different anyway, all island girls apparently seem to invoke confidence. But you really care about me, don't you Gill?'

'Of course I do. A person who's mixed up regarding the opposite sex is a liability to themselves and others. But now you can take heart; if you don't score tonight, although I think you will, just pick up the phone and ask for an unattached girl. Sooner or later you're bound to find a consort because you're such a nice man, but think of the pleasure and confidence you'll gain during the act of seeking her.'

'Well, I hope she looks like you, Gill.'

'And Linda, Helen, Sandra, the slave girl...' His companion counted on her fingers, and they both laughed.

By the time they left the lounge there was little each didn't know about the other; Andrew, especially, had rarely felt happier or more relaxed. 'Where to next,' he asked.

'I think on a day like this a visit to our botanical gardens and the aquarium would be very suitable. It isn't far.'

He couldn't help but feel amused at the mention of an aquarium after his exploits over the previous days, and he vaguely wondered if Gill was making gentle fun of him; also he wasn't sure a visit to some park, no matter how attractive, on such a wet and windy day was all that good an idea. But once again he needn't have worried, for Whyte Island furnished yet another pleasant surprise for him.

Gill led him through the gates of what, from the outside, appeared to be an ordinary park, large grassy areas, trees and shrubs within a great square of railings; but, once inside, a path went steeply downward in a series of wide, shallow steps. Before him Andrew noted the path separated two imposing buildings; the one on the right was obviously a huge greenhouse tall enough to contain mature trees, and from the outside a mass of foliage could be readily seen. But the opposite building was entirely different being long, wide, low and constructed from honey coloured stone. There were no visible windows in the walls, although from the top steps the almost flat roof had been built of glass, which a good number of gulls appeared to find perfectly acceptable as a resting place.

Upon their reaching the buildings' ground level, Gill took him along the side of the stone structure to the far end where still more steps led down to an entrance door. 'Prepare yourself for a shock,

Andy,' she said before entering.

Upon going inside his first impression was that he was actually underwater, but he instantly realised he and his companion were actually standing in a rounded, clear glass, or plastic, tunnel, for on either side the water reached almost to head level. What made the effect so startling was the fact that both side walls had been painted to represent a seascape; on the left hand side a coastal resort seen from several miles out had been cleverly portrayed, while the opposite side showed a flat horizon with clouds and a distant ship, given perspective by a small scale buoy in the foreground upon which was perched a model gull.

On bending down to look beneath the surface, Andrew noted that the buoy even had a weed covered chain which attached it to the bottom. Apart from a few stones, shells and a variety of crustaceans, the ridged sandy seabed was featureless, seeming to stretch away into infinity in the somewhat murky water. A person could easily imagine they were really standing at the bottom of the sea, for not only were numerous fish of many different species swimming about but the seabed was alive with flatfish, starfish and other bottom loving creatures.

The shoreward side of the aquarium was a complete contrast, as here the bottom comprised of rock which was bedecked with various seaweeds, winkles, limpets, anemones and even some human jetsam; once more the wonderful effect of infinity had been achieved. Looking ahead Andrew noticed the great tube gradually sloped downward, and that where they were actually standing was the only visible part above water. 'It's marvellous,' was all he could say.

Gill smiled in proud agreement, and after they stayed watching the smaller inhabitants of the reef, the tiny fish, seahorses and octopods for a while, she urged, 'Come on, this is only the start.'

The supposition that the left had side was the coast and the opposite the open sea was continued down the length of the aquarium which was literally one massive tank. As the tube submerged below water level it was no longer possible to see what was above the surface, but rocks, the bottoms of cliffs, mud and sand banks gave a constant repetition of coastline, while the right hand side always seemed as if it went on endlessly. Here, though, the monotony was relieved by a few small reefs, and several marvellously scaled down wrecks which managed to look extremely realistic despite the fact that the various plants and creatures which inhabited them obviously couldn't have been miniaturised. The way in which the aquarium had been devised, together with its denizens, fascinated him and he frequently paused to gaze at each fresh vista, leaning on the waist high metal rails running along either side of the tube, as he did so.

After allowing Andrew enough time to get the feel of the place Jill began to explain everything she knew about it. 'All the creatures and plants in the tank are native to our coastline and are, as far as possible, in the correct ratio. This makes things quite difficult because, in nature, everything preys upon something else, so therefore different species disappear faster than others; some of the larger fish, for example, are extremely voracious. So it's a case of frequent replacement of many of the creatures. On the other hand some of the big fish thrive too well, and then they have to be netted and either released or killed. Look at that one for instance.' A grey form, barely visible in the murk on the seaward side, suddenly turned toward their tube revealing itself to be a shark about six feet long as it passed overhead on its way to the shoreline side of the tank. 'That's probably due for release in one way or another,' Gill commented.

'As a matter of interest,' Andrew mentioned, 'why don't we see any fish being curious about the glass? I mean, in many aquariums a lot of the fish appear to be just as interested in the visitors as the visitors are in them. Also, wouldn't it be dangerous if the glass broke? Apart from the small stretch by the entrance the tube has been completely under water so far.'

'That's easy to explain. As far as the fish are concerned, we're just a cable or something lying on the seabed, and that's because the glass is tinted, though I don't what colour it is from their side; but it's also strong enough to withstand pressures far greater than the water, or the fish for that matter, could impose. However, in the unlikely event that the glass did break a safety measure has been incorporated. These perforated metal grids,' she pointed down at the floor of the tube, 'cover another tank with a volume capacity equal to this one, so if water did get into this walkthrough it would quickly drain below. Of course, a major breakage wouldn't be amusing but it's doubtful anyone would be seriously hurt. One other point is that actual seawater is being continuously pumped in and discharged again so that impurities can be removed but microcosms, invaluable as food for the smaller creatures, are always circulating; but if the water level suddenly dropped drastically the automatic supply valve would shut itself off.'

A little further down the tank a small shoal of quite large fish, which Gill identified as herrings, emulated the shark by coming in from the gloomy right hand side and passing overhead, where their bodies could scarcely be seen due to the glare of daylight. In following their progress Andrew's eyes were drawn to the coastal side of the tank where the wall had now been fashioned to represent the foot of some cliffs; here considerable erosion had been deigned to have taken place, for there was a high degree of overhang, and great boulders rested on the sea-bed, one of which almost touched the glass tunnel. The effect was quite stunning for fish and other small creatures swam through the shafts of daylight which penetrated the depths, and in the many crevices and on the great rocks anemones of differing colours, sea urchins and other shellfish clung where crabs and octopuses dwelt.

'These cliffs,' explained Gill, 'aren't only intended to add more interest to the aquarium by making it seem as though the coastline is respectively near and then far away, but at this point the storeroom and workshop have been constructed. It looks very realistic doesn't it?'

'And very attractive,' he added.

Shortly afterwards the half-round tunnel joined a wide section with a flat ceiling, and here five pairs of park benches had been positioned back to back. Preceding him to a vacant bench, for they weren't the only patrons of the aquarium, Gill explained, 'we often come here and spend ages just looking at the fish. It's so peaceful and not dangerous like real diving can be.'

Andrew, mentally pricking up his ears, asked, 'do you go aqua-diving then?'

'Oh no,' she replied in amusement, 'I'd be much too scared.'

'Somehow I don't associate nurses with fear.'

She eyed him curiously. 'How so?' she asked.

'Well, because of all that blood and the operations, and also because of the responsibility and having to deal with sudden emergencies. I'd find that…' he emphasised, 'frightening.'

'Nursing staff soon get used to it, but it helps to have a flair for the work, of course.'

After a pause he said in a conspiratorial fashion, 'I suppose your health service isn't in the same sorry condition as the mainland's?'

His companion, who had been gazing at the fish before them, turned and stared at him with a puzzled frown. 'What a strange thing to say, Andrew. Of course it isn't. As a one hundred per cent welfare state our health service would be one of the last island institutes to suffer, and I'm sure you haven't seen any shortages in other areas over here, have you?' He shook his head as she went on. 'With our strict population control policy we haven't got large numbers of unemployed to finance to the detriment of our hospitals, schools and other essential services; and our authorities won't allow a constant flow of settlers from abroad to swamp our living standards.'

She might have continued but for the arrival of a little girl, too young for school, who ran up to the glass and banged it in an attempt to attract the fish. 'She'll be disappointed if they can't see her,' whispered Andrew, and he glanced round to see who the child's guardian was. Approaching their area was an elderly but sprightly man obviously well past retirement age; in his left hand he carried a walking stick which he seemed to use more as a mascot than as an aid to steadiness. A sudden thought came to Andrew as he watched the old man say something to the child and then take her by the hand. 'That's very odd,' he observed half to himself, as the ill-sorted couple moved away down the aquarium.

'What is?' enquired Jill.

'Seeing those two has reminded me of something which is completely missing from Whyte Island, and as a nursing sister you're probably one of the best people to explain the phenomenon to me.' She raised her eyebrows and waited. 'I can't recollect having seen anyone in a wheelchair, whether young or old, or an elderly person tottering along on walking sticks or a frame, in fact, now I come to think of it, anyone physically or mentally disabled.'

Gill said solemnly, 'I don't think I should tell you if you don't already know, because you mainlanders have some weird standards in comparison to us. But let me put a proposition to you: supposing you had an old horse which you could no longer ride and couldn't afford to keep, would you have it put down, or would you just turn it loose to fend for itself?'

'You know the answer to that.'

'Well, as far as we're concerned your government and, to be fair, others globally, apparently prefer to take the latter course; they haven't attempted to influence their populations to live within the means which their respective states can provide, and the results have been bankruptcy. Therefore people are compelled to fend for themselves, just like our imaginary horse, and we don't think that's right.'

'So you kill off your unwanted people?' Andrew stated, anger suddenly rising within him.

'I think that's rather too dramatic a way of putting it,' Gill replied calmly, raising a hand to prevent him from interrupting. 'Let me explain. Any person, regardless of what age they are, who isn't able to look after themselves, is of no practical use to the community, or feels they no longer wish to live, often after the loss of their partner, has one of two choices: either they agree to be exiled or else they can be painlessly euthanised. Now I know that sounds dreadful,' she went on hurriedly, 'but allow me to continue. If they choose to be exiled then they're sent to one of several nursing homes on the mainland, all of which are staffed by local people. These homes are of the highest quality, often far superior to similar private and national establishments over there which, I believe, often have a reputation for being callous and abusive to their charges. Ours are, of course, entirely free to the residents and I can vouch for their quality because I'm one of several people who regularly go over to inspect them.'

'You seem to have overlooked one thing,' he interposed, still hostile, 'Many helpless people, the very old and young, the feeble-minded, are unable to decide for themselves, so what do you do about them? Euthanise them?'

She shook her head. 'The onus rests upon their next of kin. Unfortunately it's a difficult choice for them to make for more than one reason; you see, if they choose to have their dependant exiled then they'll have to go too. They'd then usually go and live near one of our businesses on the mainland where there's always a job for them.'

'I suppose that's so they can be close to their relatives?'

Gill looked grave. 'Only partly. But mainly because our authorities believe any family which has been forcibly parted from a close relative would tend to become, to put it mildly, disgruntled; so rather than risk such an occurrence the family must leave.'

This statement with its implication made Andrew even more angry, and without realising he began to raise his voice. 'Let me get this straight – if they value their child's, their mother's, their mentally ill sibling's lives they have to leave Whyte Island? But if they condone the murder of that person then they can stay, is that it?' A middle aged couple a few benches down, the only other people now in the section, glanced round wildly on hearing his loud voice then stood up and walked away.

She stared at him in disbelief, her face growing pale. 'You talk to me of murder?' she eventually replied with quiet vehemence. 'What about the homeless in your country, forced to roam about in all weathers, sleeping rough, ignored and unwanted by almost everybody; the babies with bronchitis or pneumonia being raised in damp, vermin infested flats, their parents or parent scarcely able to afford to feed them; the young and not so young who should be looking forward to a bright future, injecting themselves with filth because their present is too horrible to face? I could go on indefinitely about other forms of living death. We might kill our weak in comparatively small numbers, and my partner and I, Mr Maynard and his daughters and everyone else on our island will some day come into that category, but you kill your fit wholesale and often slowly and painfully. The only difference is that your method comes under the guise of being natural.'

She rose abruptly and walked quickly over to the metal rail where she stood staring into the aquarium. Left alone, Andrew sat thinking, feeling acutely embarrassed by her tirade; her argument had made his appear absolutely ridiculous. By comparison with most of the rest of the world the island's practice of euthanasia seemed positively humane. Full of remorse, he stood up and hurried across to her; he could see she was almost in tears, and he was tempted to put an arm about her, but instead he gripped the rail with both hands. 'I'm sorry,' he explained, 'it was a thoughtless, stupid remark to make. Please continue explaining. I promise I won't interrupt or criticise again.'

'Are you sure you want to hear?' she asked, turning to him. He nodded, and with some reluctance she preceded him back to the bench. 'I expect you'll be wondering why we don't allow our less fortunate citizens to reside on the island in special homes, nursed by competent and caring staff? And the answer is that if we did then it might be detrimental to our happy carefree society.

'As a nurse I can assure you that tending people who are only temporarily ill can be disheartening enough at times, but it's positively soul-destroying when it comes to nursing the terminally ill, the insane, geriatrics or children who are never going to lead a full and independent life. Anyone involved in such work isn't going to be able to shut out the experience immediately they leave the hospital, or institute, at the end of their duty, unless they're completely insensitive.

'It's this fear that medical staff will not only become demoralised by their work, but will pass on their unhappiness to their family, friends and our society in general, which makes the authorities unwilling to accommodate our less fortunate citizens; and, naturally, the same precept applies to the relatives of these people. Keeping alive fellow human beings who are unable to care for themselves might at first sight be a noble and humane act, but it's also a somewhat hypocritical one on the part of the relevant legislators, for you may be sure such people wouldn't be prepared to nurse helpless people themselves even on a semi-permanent basis. Faced with tending an incontinent relation they would eventually either delegate the responsibility, or else bring in euthanasia.'

Gill stood up, and she and Andrew continued their tour of the aquarium. 'Actually,' she said thoughtfully as they stood where a mud bank sloped down almost to the glass, 'this euthanasia business is nowhere near as bad as it would at first seem. Our environment is far more hygienic than yours usually is, our water, air, soil and food is purer and generally free of chemicals, and therefore our standard of health is quite high, as is our accident record. The result is that there are relatively few candidates for exile or euthanasia. We carry out pre-natal scanning programmes so any deformed babies can be aborted, and we have regular comprehensive medical checks on all our people in order to discover early signs of dangerous diseases.'

She checked her watch and murmured, 'we'd better get a move on soon. We've still got the greenhouse to see, and I've arranged a little surprise in there for you.' She studied his face for a moment as if to gauge how much he'd learnt and perhaps accepted regarding the island's society, because she then said, 'I suppose you've heard about the way in which we use psychology to improve our social standard?' Andrew nodded. 'Well,' she went on, 'people born on Whyte Island have been raised to look upon euthanasia as being a noble act if the circumstances are right. You remember, no doubt, about the story of our mutual hero forebear Major Wheatley whose statue is to be found in several mainland cities? How he and his companions were being pursued by natives and he, being wounded, elected to guard single-handed a narrow defile through which his comrades subsequently escaped. How, when a relieving force came to seek him they found his body decorated by his enemies in honour of his courage. We too are willing to give our lives freely for the common good. If I should suddenly become crippled, develop an incurable illness or become mentally ill permanently, then I would expect to be given a pill or injection which would instantly and painlessly end my life; the same would apply if, at the end of my time on earth, I began to waste away into senility. I would also be willing to allow the administering of the dose to my parents, my future husband or child under similar circumstances. The average islander would have no wish to be a burden to their country or fellows, and we've all got a wonderful precedent to follow.'

Andrew asked bluntly, 'who?'

'Well, it's common knowledge over here, but it could be embarrassing if you haven't been told, so you've got to promise me you won't mention it to anyone.' He agreed, and she continued. 'Alright. Several years after Whyte Island was founded Mrs Maynard, our president's wife, was diagnosed as having contracted an incurable disease.' The young man gasped, but Gill went on. 'The idea of euthanasia had already been established here and so there wasn't any going back, but neither Charlie or Marion would have wanted it any other way, so Mrs Maynard became one of the first to set an example. Of course Charlie and Helen would've taken it very hard but Linda, fortunately, would've only been a baby at the time. In the long run it was probably for the best, because the disease in question is often slow and messy.'

Andrew was greatly affected by this information, and it must have shown in his face for Gill said gently, 'Look, I know all this death business has come as a bit of a shock to you but to us it's perfectly normal; we're trained to be fatalistic. But just consider all the benefits which living on Whyte Island brings when compared to other countries. People of all ages and both genders can walk anywhere at any time without fear of molestation, there's no loneliness, sexual frustration, poverty or favouritism. There's plenty of entertainment open to all, beauty and friendship, and everyone's got a job, several in fact, and a guaranteed home. Above all, we've got access to the best health care. All that adds up to a lot of credit against a little debit. Don't forget that in your own country there are intelligent, able-bodied people wasting away because there's no work for them.'

'I know,' replied Andrew, 'my dad and younger brother are two of them.'

'I'm sorry to hear that, but not particularly surprised; but please cheer up, and let's enjoy the rest of our day out together. Alright?' Against all his inclinations he was forced to smile; all that his attractive companion had said was true and as a result he was just being a bore. 'That's better,' she said, smiling in turn, 'come on, let's inspect the rest of the aquarium.'

A little further along, on the coastal side, was the mouth of a very realistic cave, the floor of which was covered with polished pebbles in a variety of colours giving a very pleasing effect, and this was followed by an area representing a sandbank. Although the tank was of great length, he was impressed by the way the different types of coastline were skilfully merged into each other, for there wasn't a single place where the variation was so drastic that it looked odd. On the seaward side a large stone convexity, tapering out at the base, had been built upon some rocks to represent a lighthouse, and nearby an old fashioned anchor was lying.

'Tell me, Gill,' he asked as they watched a jellyfish swim past, 'why are some places on the island free but you have to pay to visit others?'

'It's a bit complicated, but usually where a place is thought to be educational, such as here, it's generally free. But if it's purely for amusement then a charge is normally made; this is really a gentle hint not to go too often, so allowing others to have a fair share. Of course, in many places the computer is used to apportion shares correctly. Take this aquarium for example – because it's devoted to sea creatures from around our coastline it's frequently visited by school parties of all grades who study the creatures, plants and environments in detail, and this, incidentally, is why there are so many kinds of coastal areas, so therefore it's free.

'But the layout of this place has been so successful, apparently, that they've decided to construct two more aquariums of similar design though in other parts of the island; one is going to be dedicated to native freshwater fish and plants, and will actually simulate the various habitats in a river including the current. I believe it's already being built, and it'll no doubt be considered educational and so will be free. But the third is to be for tropical fish and so it'll probably provide more scope for water-scaping with extra varied and beautiful plants, creatures and habitats, a real fantasy world without limitations, in fact. That will be of less educational value, naturally, and would doubtless be classed as entertainment, so a small charge will almost certainly be levied.'

During their conversation they'd been slowly walking along, though they often stopped to gaze at the fish or at an outstanding piece of scenery, but eventually they reached the end door. 'Remarkable,' Andrew exclaimed as they climbed the steps outside, 'but I'd like to see what your people could do with the other two aquariums though.'

Gill agreed. 'When you think about it the sea in temperate climates is probably the most restrictive of the three environments; you can only do so much with a seascape.'

'That aquarium couldn't have been improved upon, though,' he objected.

'Perhaps not, but see what you think of this.' A short step across the windswept space between the two buildings had brought them to the door of the greenhouse; inside was a glazed lobby, and yet another door, which Gill immediately opened. The sudden warmth, humidity and sweet earthy smell took his breath away after the cool, fresh breeze outside. 'Welcome to the jungle,' Gill laughed.

Once more the island's flair for exotic arrangement had carried all before it. Confronting Andrew was indeed a jungle; everywhere there was green foliage, branches and half hidden trunks of large trees, but very little to remind a visitor they were actually inside a building. He'd expected to see all the plants, from diminutive flowering shrubs up to mature trees, positioned in beds with viewing paths arranged between in geometric order. Having once before visited a large tropical greenhouse, he'd also expected such paths to have metal gratings set in them as in the aquarium, but this time with the primary purpose of allowing warm air to rise. However, these paths were neither straight nor grated, but instead wandered freely and were made from packed earth. The network of paths, he subsequently discovered, frequently crossed one another thereby permitting visitors to take many different routes as well as enabling them to examine individual plants from various angles.

There was an amazing variety of species on display from tall deciduous and palm trees, down through smaller trees and shrubs to ferns and flowers, the latter mostly of the shade loving varieties for, as Gill had indicated, it was truly a miniature jungle, the wide spreading foliage of some of the larger trees and shrubs allowing little light to penetrate below. As they wandered about Andrew was reminded of the garden at the house in which Linda and he had stayed exactly a week ago, for although these paths were only on one level they, just as in the rock garden, were cunningly hidden from each other, occasionally by large rocks, but more often by the bushy plants which formed much of the lower vegetation.

On many of the paths it wasn't unusual for Gill and he to have to push their way past plants which had been allowed to encroach across their route. In places where the floor was scarcely visible due to the foliage he considered he wouldn't have been surprised if he'd glimpsed a snake or lizard. It therefore came as something of a shock when, on pushing past a shrub, he caught sight of a bird which, he realised in the few seconds before it darted off into a bamboo cane brake, was definitely not a temperate species. 'Did you see that beautiful little crimson bird?' he asked in astonishment.

'No,' Gill admitted, 'but there are some tropical birds in here; about forty I believe, of some five or six different species, also some exotic though harmless insects, and also lizards.' She went on to explain that it happened through a natural sequence. 'Some zoos throughout the world began building ever larger aviaries through which they built paths for visitors, stocked them with various plants and constructed different features such as rocky areas, ponds and waterfalls to add interest. So it was only a matter of time before tropical greenhouses combined with aviaries to produce what we have around us. We just copied the idea, but it's worked out very well because there appears to be a natural balance, as everything seems to control everything else; personally I think it would be sad to see so many plants without some sort of wildlife amongst them.'

Some time later Andrew observed, 'the only thing missing is somewhere to sit down.'

His companion smiled and replied, 'I think I can promise you a seat after we've had a good look round.'

'I could do with a bite to eat as well.' But Gill merely smiled again.

The interior of the greenhouse was so vast that, together with the meandering paths, the lack of markers by which he could calculate their position and the concealing of the sides and corners by foliage, Andrew became entirely disorientated. Eventually, after examining numerous leaves, fruits, flowers and seeds, and reading an equal number of identification plates which invariably displayed masses of information and complicated, usually meaningless, names he asked, 'Where are we?'

She smiled. 'Not far from one of the spiral staircases, so we might as well roam about the tree tops if you're agreeable. It's quite fascinating up there.'

At the foot of the green painted ironwork, when Andrew motioned his companion to precede him, she flashed him a shrewd look and observed, 'I wonder if you're being a gentleman or just acting arch.' He was too naïve to comprehend her remark and it wasn't until they were well up the stairs that, being weary of the interminable climbing, he glanced up to see how far they still had to go. The sight which confronted him made him realise what she'd meant, and so he quickly lowered his gaze with some embarrassment. For the remainder of the ascent he kept his eyes averted, wondering as he did so why he'd enjoyed taking advantage of Linda under the same circumstances, yet felt confused with his present companion.

'You're a gentleman,' she announced as he joined her on the catwalk. She smiled when he confessed that he'd accidentally looked up her skirt, but she shrugged dismissively. 'I don't mind – you wouldn't have seen any more if I'd been on the beach, it just appears more sensual, that's all. But as a gentleman, once you'd got away with the glimpse, it would've been polite not to have mentioned it.'

Thinking it best to change the subject Andrew glanced about him. 'How far up do you think we are?'

'Thirty five to forty feet, I should imagine. I know it's somewhere around there.'

He could scarcely believe they were so far from ground level for the mass of foliage surrounding them gave no indication of their height; of necessity the catwalks, or what could be seen of them, were straight, but they were some distance away from the aluminium framed glass walls, and in between was the vegetation of the various trees. So dense was the foliage in places that it partially obscured the route. Leaning on the railing next to his companion, he gazed down onto the sea of leaves and palm fronds and subsequently, on their tour round the catwalks, he was to discover it was virtually impossible to see the ground floor due to this mass of greenery.

Andrew found it strangely beautiful wandering amid the huge tropical and subtropical plants. Even at this height many trees towered above them, and he noticed there was still plenty of height and space into which the tallest trees could continue their growth. While he was gazing up at the roof he enquired, 'I suppose those pipes are for watering the plants?'

Gill nodded. 'I think you'll find that most nights see a tropical downpour; not much fun for the small inmates, I don't suppose, but quite normal for their genuine environment.'

Her concern had been aroused by the sight of a predominantly dark green plumaged hummingbird whose feathers shone with iridescence as it hovered before a large orange flower. Up among the tree tops birds were much in evidence, lured by the brightness cast even on this cloudy day and by the many blossoms, some of which were borne by various trees, others having arrived on creeping, climbing plants whose origins were to be found far below. The relevant authority must have toured the planet in their quest for suitable specimens, for the most flamboyant colours on display were only rivalled by the various heady perfumes emanating from the blooms. Many of the creepers weren't content to confine their attention to their host plants but crossed over to the catwalks, twisting and turning around the handrails and stanchions; others obviously found the ironwork more preferable as a climbing aid as they seemed to have made their way up independently.

Through skylights left open during warm summer days, but meshed to keep some birds in and others out, bees, hoverflies and other flying insects passed, drawn by the scented flowers and the promise of nectar. Many more entered the greenhouse than ever departed, for different species of bird, all with gaudy plumage and mostly long tails, perched upright on separate branches making frequent sallies against unfortunate bees and other insects, which rarely missed.

'Well, shall we continue?' enquired Gill, turning to make her way along the catwalk where the blossom and, therefore, the insects seemed to be extra abundant.'

'Wait,' cried out Andrew behind her, 'won't we get stung?'

She stopped walking and waited among the flowers, hoverflies apparently swarming angrily about her, until he came closer. 'Anyone can tell you're a mainlander,' she exclaimed in obvious amusement, 'these fellows,' she went on, swatting half-heartedly at the colourful flies, 'are completely harmless, they're all bluff. But the bees, which could sting,' she emphasised, 'are far too busy to bother about us; even the wasp, which doesn't normally appear in any number until late August, generally only stings accidentally.'

Gingerly making his way toward her he paused and pointed at a large dark-coloured fly hovering menacingly a few inches from his face, seemingly intent upon inoculating him with several grains of painful irritant. 'Isn't that a hornet?' he asked nervously.

'Hornets,' she answered with a smile, 'are orange-brown striped, the size of queen wasps, uncommon and peaceable. That is just another silly old hoverfly; they come in all sorts of guises and will intimidate you all day if you let them. Come on.' Feeling rather small and foolish at his attractive guide's information, he decided to put his misgivings behind him and was once more soon lost in admiration at the beauty of the vegetation upon every side.

'There are three things missing which every good rain forest requires,' Andrew declared during their tree top tour, and he added immediately, 'No monkeys, no noise and no massive brilliantly coloured butterflies and moths. But,' he continued hastily, 'it's all very wonderful and interesting despite that.'

'You don't want much,' Gill laughed, 'Small birds and buzzing insects are one thing, but howling, shrieking monkeys would soon make short work of this place, as would the flycatchers with the Lepidoptera, and water and the occasional leaf wouldn't be the only things dropping from above.'

Regardless of the descriptive plates on the relevant plants, thoughtfully provided above as well as below, Andrew had little difficulty in identifying many of the fruit-bearing trees including date, coconut, fig, banana, lemon and orange, though he was surprised to see the latter three fruits were no other colour but green. 'I thought you were a sailor,' his companion chided gently when he mentioned this fact, 'as far as I'm aware they only change to yellow in temperate climates.' He was glad, after her mild criticism, she didn't add the words "even our schoolchildren know that".

Much too soon, as far as he was concerned despite his increasing appetite, they completed their circuit of the lofty walkway for he'd have been content to stay for much longer but Gill, after glancing at her watch, urged him to descend to ground level. 'There's still your surprise to come yet,' she explained.

As he stepped down the spiral staircase, a different one from that by which they'd ascended, Andrew gradually became aware of a subtle change in the smell of the greenhouse; as the sweet, overpowering perfume of the blossoms gave way to the smell of damp humus, the aroma, quite unexpected, of cooked food became distinctly obvious. He also thought he could hear the distant sound of cutlery touching china and the muffled tones of a number of people in conversation. 'Don't tell me there's a restaurant in here,' he remarked once they stood at ground level, 'Is that your surprise?'

Gill nodded, 'And I've booked a table just to be on the safe side, though I doubt there'll be many patrons.'

The restaurant was situated in an area directly in the centre of the greenhouse which Gill had obviously studiously avoided and, as she had intimated, was far from full of customers. Upon their arrival at the periphery of the canopied square they were immediately approached by a waiter and shown to a table for two. 'Well, this is a new experience,' Andrew observed enthusiastically as he sat back and examined his menu, 'I expect you had to shift heaven and earth to get us in here.'

Gill shook her head. 'As you can see, during weekdays there aren't usually many people around, and besides there are plenty of other dining places locally with equally good decors, would you believe? In the evenings, though, it definitely comes to life; it's really eerie then and has a special ambiance.'

'Would there be coloured lighting?' he asked casually.

'Yes, why?'

He smiled. 'It just seems that everywhere I go there are coloured lights.'

Looking puzzled she asked, 'don't you like them? We love colours and music and variety in our lives.'

'I was only kidding,' he replied and changed the subject. 'I don't know what to have; I suddenly don't fancy fish. I don't suppose they do fried monkey?'

Gill laughed. 'Hardly. I recommend the chicken salad, and a

glass of Sauterne with ice cream and coffee to follow; that's what I'm having.'

Upon giving their orders and waiting a surprisingly short time, Andrew was amused by the sight of the waiter emerging from the tropical foliage and pushing a service trolley over the earthen floor. 'I'm glad you didn't take the euthanasia too much to heart, Andrew,' she said as they began their meal.

'I must admit it did come as a bit of a shock, but I'm beginning to realise that different countries have their own ways; every nation needs to educate its people to its own moral standards. So I can't really condemn Whyte Island's principles because, as you indicated, my own country's leave a great deal to be desired.'

Lowering her voice quite unnecessarily, for no one else was within earshot, Gill declared, 'I think it would be in your best interests to accept our standards unconditionally.'

Sensing intrigue in her voice, Andrew asked, 'why?'

'Once again I shouldn't really tell you, but I'm sure I can trust you.' She took a sip of her wine, thereby unconsciously adding to the effect her words were about to have. 'I don't suppose you realise it, but you're almost certainly going to be offered Whyte Island citizenship which, I must add, automatically means you'll be required to renounce your true nationality and accept everything our authorities and constitution wish you to do.'

Her companion was shocked, 'why me, and what for?'

Jill smiled with sympathetic concern. 'Whichever way you look at it, it's quite a compliment to you. From the moment you became an employee of our island a careful check would have been kept on you; in short, in all aspects you appear to have passed with flying colours. The authorities like you! You asked me what for, and the simple answer is that somewhere on Whyte Island a man of similar age to you has probably recently died.'

'Would you like anything else – sir, madam?'

Andrew looked up in confusion to see the waiter standing by them. Gill said, 'Yes please. could we have another glass of your excellent Sauterne and more coffee?' When he'd gone she explained, 'the authorities are so determined that every person should have a companion of the opposite sex that they've devised this method as an insurance, so every alien employee is a prospective partner for a Whyte Islander.'

'Wait a minute,' he cut in, 'do you mean to say there's a woman over here I've got to marry, like that slave girl I told you about?'

She smiled again. 'Does that sound like Whyte Island policy? Of course you haven't, you'd be treated like any other islander. If you wanted to you could live with all the unattached women over here; one at a time, of course.' Andrew couldn't refrain from grinning at this last remark as the waiter served them their order.

Afterwards, Gill asked, 'didn't you ever wonder why you'd been invited here on extended leave, or why you'd been shown so much of our way of life and our various institutes?'

'Yes, of course I did, especially after experiencing the wall of silence regarding the island aboard Whyte Line ships, but it didn't occur to me there might be an ulterior motive. Besides, I didn't like to ask Mr Maynard and the girls, or anyone else for that matter. I just assumed everyone was being friendly.' She smiled in reply, and for the remainder of their time in the restaurant they were both silent.

When the waiter had come and gone again, leaving a bill which both amazed and pleased Andrew, he asked his companion, 'is it customary to leave a tip at any time?'

Gill shook her head vigorously. 'Goodness, no; it'd be an insult to him. You'd be calling him a menial.'

Confused, he replied, 'I didn't think there was any class consciousness on the island.'

'Of course there isn't, but he may well be someone in a senior position in his main job, and as he doesn't know you're not an islander he'd think you had a sick sense of humour.'

As they stood up to leave Andrew, remembering Monday evening, asked, 'is this one of those places where you might have to do the washing up?'

She shook her head again. 'No, that doesn't apply to this kind of place, alright?'

At the park gates Gill glanced at her watch and then turned to face him. 'It's nearly five o'clock and time for the parting of the ways.' She held out her hands, and in taking it he reflected it was the first, and probably the last, time they'd had physical contact.

With a lump in his throat he replied, 'Thank you for giving me a nice time, the hands of the clock went round far too quickly, and thanks also for your hint about possible island citizenship.'

The irony of what he'd first said was entirely lost on him, but she simply said, 'I hope you have an even better time this evening.'

Still with her right hand in his, she cupped his right hand with her left in a warm gesture. 'If, as Sandra thinks, there is a girl there for you, I want you to introduce me to her.' Releasing his hands she delved in her shoulder bag, and writing her phone number upon a piece of paper, she handed it to him. After saying, 'if you have a mobile I'd be inclined to warn your Helen you're coming,' she turned and walked off.

Left to his own devices once more, Andrew thought briefly of going to see his old ship again, but the sudden departure of his attractive and interesting companion left him in a mental vacuum, and all he felt like doing was walking to allow his confused thoughts an airing. So after phoning Helen that he'd probably be back about six he decided that, as the rain had ceased, the wind had dropped considerably and gaps were beginning to appear in the clouds, he'd take the path back to the Maynards which Linda had introduced him to on the occasion, he thought ruefully, of his last making love to her.

As he set off his thoughts, once more, were in a turmoil, the loneliness which was never far below the surface of his character had returned with a vengeance at Gill's departure and all he wanted to do now was to be alone and miserable. But the optimistic, adventurous side of his nature, urged on by his several island female companions' assurances, encouraged him to believe the folk club would turn up trumps; once again, however, self-doubt encouraged by disappointments on numerous mainland social occasions assailed him. But he suddenly remembered Jim and Carol whom Linda had introduced him to, they were friendly and cheerful enough and if all else failed their company, together with the music, if it was anything like that played at the barbeque, would be more than adequate to ensure him a pleasant evening.

So intent was he on his thoughts that, apart from a feeling of nostalgia when he came to the place where the small path diverged toward Linda's and his late love nest, he recalled little of his stroll. For not only had he purely selfish things to think about, including whether he ought to accept island citizenship – if, as Gill declared, it was offered to him – but also the morality of euthanasia was bothering him. One thing he was sure of, he wouldn't mention these two subjects to anyone, certainly not the Maynards, unless they were raised first.

When at last he reached the lane he checked his watch and was amused to note that, despite his leisurely and largely subconscious pace, he was exactly on time. The family were only awaiting his arrival before beginning dinner, Helen having taken advantage of his phone call to prepare and cook him an especially small meal in order, Linda informed him, to ensure he had time to digest it properly before starting out for the Station Arms. 'You also chose the dishes especially, didn't you Helen? So Andy wouldn't be too upset by all the beer he was likely to pour on top.'

'Thank you very much,' Andrew naively commented as the elder sister flashed him a look of embarrassment, 'this fish is superb.'

As usual she'd done an excellent job, boiled fish with a delicately flavoured sauce, creamed potatoes and finely chopped mixed vegetables. The dish gave him a cue to talk about the aquarium and latterly, the greenhouse both of which he congratulated Charlie on. Linda, though, was far more interested in his companion. 'What was she like, Andy?'

'Intelligent, interesting and attractive. In fact a typical Whyte Island girl I should say, from my experience.' Remembering his unintentional slight of her that morning he stared across at Helen and added, 'I was wondering whether I could persuade another typical island beauty to come out with me tonight.'

Instead of answering she stood up, collected the plates and left the room, leaving a dismayed young man to look askance at his remaining companions. Charlie chuckled. 'Most people would be doubtful about describing me as intelligent and interesting, but even fewer would think me attractive, so I'm afraid that leaves me out.'

Linda was also amused. 'I'm not going to be your second choice,' she joked. 'You're on your own.'

Much later on he asked, after getting ready and sat relaxing with a cup of coffee, 'what time do you think I ought to set out?'

Both girls agreed that eight would be ideal. 'But I wouldn't take a bike if I were you,' Linda advised, adding after an affected pause, 'you might get too tipsy and fall off.' Even Helen, now a little more affable, smiled at the remark.

By the time he left the cottage the wind had dropped entirely and the sun, though fairly low in the sky, was shining brightly; he'd promised himself he'd take his time over the walk, even dawdle, but despite his vow he couldn't prevent himself from hurrying for, due to the steep gradient, every time his concentration lapsed he speeded up. Eventually, he simply gave up trying; he was much happier now than when he'd first taken his leave of Gill, the main reason being that he been amused by the way Linda especially had treated him like a prize cockerel before a fight. In the time between the end of dinner and his departure the sisters had refused his offers of help in the kitchen. Linda, instead, had ushered him into the lounge, made him sit down and had brought him another cup of coffee. 'We don't want you tiring yourself out,' she'd said with a wink.

There weren't many people at his destination. On a bench outside were seated two couples who greeted him cheerfully as he was about to enter the main door, and after purchasing a pint of beer from the landlord who obviously remembered him, he sat down on the bench which he and Helen had previously occupied. There were only three customers in the main bar, a couple who, after giving him a cursory glance and a raised hand of greeting from the man and a smile from his girlfriend, went back to their conversation; the third person was a rather lonely looking girl in a far corner who was of similar size to the slave girl, but even from where Andrew sat he could see she was dark haired.

As they looked across at each other she smiled and gazed down at her drink, probably waiting for her regular boyfriend or a computer date, he thought. Glancing round the room to pass the time he noticed a guitar case lying on top of the piano, and what also appeared to be a banjo case leaning against the wall by the door, proving that at least some musicians had arrived. Without thinking he stared across at the girl again. To his gratification she was studying him, but once more she averted her gaze. As he took a sip of his beer he heard a train approaching the station; it subsequently stopped and after a few minutes restarted with a short whistle. It was a sound he was scarcely conscious of, for he was working himself up into going across to speak to the girl.

Weighing up the pros and cons before making his move, he felt sure he would be reasonably well received and also that, should she already have a boyfriend, then he wouldn't be particularly annoyed when he showed up. On the other hand he doubted she would venture out on her own without good reason, especially when she could have arranged a computer date, so that if he did approach her he might be interfering where he wasn't wanted. Eventually he decided to look once more at the girl and if she was still staring back at him he would go across to her, for she might be someone whom Linda had set up for him. He realised, though, that he would have to act quickly before the bar became too crowded and therefore too noisy.

So once again Andrew glanced over to where the girl was seated; their eyes met across the room, and this time she didn't look away but stared back in a challenging fashion. He began to rise to his feet, but he was too late; the significance of the train's arrival hadn't dawned upon him before as he'd naturally assumed people would be turning up gradually in couples, but now it came to him forcefully as the noise of many loud voices, happy and excited, passed by the windows and then came through the open doorway. Looking round he saw a large number of people enter the room, the foremost of whom was Jim. 'Andy,' he cried out enthusiastically as he saw him, 'glad you could make it. What are you drinking?'

By this time Andrew was facing him, but out of the corner of his eye he saw the girl also rise and, carrying her glass and shoulder bag, she made her way through the throng toward the door. As she passed them Andrew, who had returned Jim's greeting and was now telling him what he'd have to drink, glanced at her; in profile, he thought, she seemed remarkably like that little slave girl of a week ago, apart from the colour of her hair. Jim also watched her, though in a disinterested way, as she went by. 'Have you been here long?' he wanted to know. 'Who have you brought with you?'

As he explained that he was alone he felt really sick at heart as he saw the girl leave the public house. He was quite sure now she'd been waiting for him, especially as she'd seemed quite annoyed as she went past; and he was certain she wouldn't be returning.

'That's too bad,' Jim exclaimed, 'couldn't you have persuaded Lynn or Helen to come?' Andrew shook his head as his acquaintance put an instrument case on the adjacent table. 'Look,' he went on, 'Carol's ordering the drinks so I'll go and tell her what you want. I'll introduce you to the others when we come back, alright?' Some of the others Jim had entered the bar with were known to the young man from the jazz club and so he exchanged words with both women and men quite familiarly. Most of them seated themselves on the continuous bench running round the walls of the room primarily in the vicinity of Andrew's table, as it appeared to be their headquarters; almost all of them carried instruments, some of which ended up on the table alongside Jim's. 'Do you play or sing?' one girl asked Andrew. As he shook his head he heard his name being called, and upon looking round he saw Carol beckoning from the door way.

'Someone wants to see you outside,' she explained as she handed him his beer.

'Who on earth?' he wondered aloud.

'Go and find out,' she advised with a smile.

Feeling completely bewildered and in a daze Andrew walked through the open doorway and automatically turned his head to the left where the bench and table were situated; of the two couples who'd been there when he'd arrived there was now no sign. Instead their place had been taken by the little red haired slave. 'Hello!' she said, looking up at him with a half-smile on her lips. 'Remember me?'

For several seconds he was lost for words, then he mumbled, 'I could hardly forget you.' Placing his drink on the table he sat down beside her and in an unconscious gesture which surprised himself, but apparently not the girl, he took her hands from where they lay in her lap, lifted them to his lips and kissed them.

'Presumably that means you've changed your mind about me,' she observed wryly, replacing her hands back in her lap but with his hands held firmly within them.

'You know,' he stated, overwhelmed by her presence, 'when you were drying me I was dying to kiss you.'

'From what I could see of you,' she laughed, 'it wasn't just kissing you were thinking of.' She paused, then added thoughtfully, 'I hope your passion was assuaged.' Andrew began to reply but she raised a hand to prevent him. 'I don't want to know anything about it,' she said firmly, 'but what I do what to know is, are you coming out to play?'

He squeezed her hands tightly, both now returned to her lap. 'I can't think of anyone else I'd rather play with, because you're my dream come true; but why me? I don't deserve you.'

Once again the girl laughed then, half closing her eyes in a simulation of evil, she raised her hands to hold them like claws before his face. 'I'm a female rapist intent on forcing you to share your masculine attributes,' she whined.

A couple en route to the bar stared at them in some surprise, and his new companion immediately dropped her pose and began to laugh. Andrew would have liked to join her but was too confused by what was happening to him, and in fact was a little embarrassed by her apparent silliness. He took a drink of his beer and waited for her to stop. 'I'm sorry,' she said eventually. 'I'm not making a very good impression, am I? The answer to your question won't be very satisfactory because it happens to be that I don't know. When I first laid eyes on you I was instantly attracted to you, I was newly free and you fitted the bill; so here I am. But you shouldn't belittle yourself Andrew; you are attractive to women.'

Behind them came the sound of a guitar being tuned up. 'As you know my name could you tell me yours?'

'Julie,' she replied.

'Well, Julie,' he began, taking hold of her hands once more, 'will you be my companion and guide while I'm on the island?'

She nodded. 'For as long as we care for each other, which I hope will be forever.'

As if thinking of it for the first time he asked, 'How did you know I was going to be here, alone, and available?'

But Julie said, 'if you finish your drink we'll go for a walk, then all will be revealed.'

On the way up to the lane Andrew confided, 'I'm glad you appeared on the scene when you did. I tried out the computer dating service today with an attached girl, and the girl I was with at the roman villa had promised to renew our acquaintanceship if I didn't meet anyone tonight,' he squeezed her hand, 'and when I was in the bar earlier there was a girl on her own who was about your size. I was going to chat her up, but she left before I could do anything about it.'

'The reason why that girl was like me,' she commented as they reached the junction with the lane and turned right to cross over the bridge, 'was because she was me.'

He stopped dead in surprise. 'What? But she was a brunette. Besides, she wore a brown coat, and yours is green.'

'Ah,' she cried triumphantly, 'I was wearing a wig, and this coat is reversible. As a beautician I love dressing up and any old excuse will do; as my lover you'll be in luck because you'll have a whole train of different females to sleep with.'

'But why did you come in disguise?' he asked, mystified.

'I just wanted to make certain you were alone. If you weren't I'd have been able to slip away without compromising you.'

Standing there facing her Andrew was filled with heart-aching desire. 'I'm glad I wasn't with anyone,' he whispered. Her nearness to him was testing his passion beyond his control and so suddenly taking both her hands in his, he pushed them firmly though gently behind her and then pulled her body tightly against his. Her lips met his in willing abeyance as they simultaneously thrust their tongues into each other's mouths, and for Andrew nothing else mattered but the sensation of this beautiful girl's body pressed up against him, and the proof of her regard for him in her lively, questing tongue.

Unwilling and unable to stop himself, he felt physical passion rising in him, and obviously Julie did, too, for she began trying to pull her hands away from where he held them locked against the small of her back; yet, paradoxically, she continued to probe every feature of his mouth with her tongue. No please, he thought, let it last forever. But greater still was his wish not to hurt this wonderful creature and so, reluctantly, he slackened his grip so enabling her to remove her hands, but to his astonishment and delight her freed hands weren't used to push him away; instead, with great force she threw her arms about his neck so that her elbows became locked around his nape. The difference in their respective heights meant she was now forced onto the tips of her toes; to Andrew it felt as if she wanted him to penetrate her through their clothing, for she was thrusting herself against him with all her strength.

Suddenly her tongue left his mouth, and she removed her lips; pressing her right cheek against his she whispered hysterically in his ear, 'I love you, I need you, I want you oh so much.' But then, with true feminine contradiction, she pleaded, 'please let me go!'

Bewildered, Andrew withdrew his arms and she stood before him, tears beginning to trickle down her cheeks, looking utterly miserable. "Not another island girl I've made cry", he thought, as he fumbled for his handkerchief, puzzling as to just why she was so tearful. Like a lost little girl she allowed him to dab away at her wet face. 'I'm sorry,' she said at last, 'but I shouldn't have done that. It was cruel.' To Andrew this confession meant only one thing, she'd been leading him on; probably she still missed her boyfriend.

Doubtless a mixture of unhappiness and confusion showed on his face, for Julie stepped up to him and put her arms about his waist. 'I'm hurting you,' she said maternally, 'What I'm trying to say is I'm getting us both excited and it's still mother nature time.'

Upon seeing him still looking confused she translated, 'It's still my time of the month.' He was still too astonished and relieved by this frank admission to reply. 'Come on,' she urged, 'let's walk as far as the river. I've still got some explaining to do.'

As they strolled down the lane in the gathering dusk, arms about each other like long term lovers she told him how, when Linda and he had shown up at the Roman villa, she'd immediately desired him which was something that had never happened to her before, and that was why she'd displayed her body to him, and when that hadn't worked she'd made even more blatant gestures. 'Linda could see what I was doing and by her obvious amusement she tacitly told me I could make a play for you. But truly I was absolutely bewildered by your lack of interest and your behaviour when you eventually confronted me. You told me how beautiful I was, yet you rejected me! Then, when you began to demonstrate how insecure you really were by talking about not letting me go if we got together, I finally realised you must be a mainlander.

'I could see you really wanted me, yet you didn't wish to start something which you couldn't finish, but I'm afraid your unselfish act made you even more desirable to me – that and your jumping in the creek with Linda. So when she came out and explained everything I was well and truly hooked on you. Of course I wanted to have you immediately, but I had this damned thing coming up, and just like one of your mainland brides, I wanted to be ready for you. So I phoned up Linda and she suggested I came down here tonight, by which time I should've finished, but I was late starting. I'm sorry.'

Giving her waist a squeeze Andrew observed, 'you island girls are amazing; even the most promiscuous girl in my country would hardly be so frank on a first date.'

'We just like to get this sex business out of the way as soon as possible. To us it's hypocritical pretending a heterosexual relationship is going to be platonic at first, because partners know that sooner or later they'll be going to bed together. It must put a terrific strain on a relationship when one party wonders when they should make a sexual pass, and the other wonders when they will. It's such a waste of time, especially when they could end up being incompatible.'

'In what way?' They had reached the beginning of the river bridge, and Julie guided them down the gravel path leading to a towpath along which convenient park benches had been sited. So far they'd seen no one else, though Andrew suspected that later on the riverside would become more than a little crowded.

'Take us two, for instance,' she replied after they'd seated themselves and she'd snuggled up to him. 'So far we're getting on alright, but our first and subsequent intimacies might prove disastrous, as might our residency together, but at least, unlike your average mainland couple, we won't have wasted a lot of time if we aren't compatible.'

Taken aback by her assumption that they were going to be living together, he whispered, 'then you really do love me, Julie?'

He felt her head nod against his shoulder. 'Let's say it was fifty-five per cent passion, but I know very well the odds will be going to rise when I've known you a bit longer.' She paused, then said, 'I hope, when you've finished unbuttoning my coat, you'll restrict yourself to putting your arm about my waist; otherwise you'll be getting a judo lesson.'

'But I do love you too, Julie,' he admonished.

'Maybe you do,' she conceded, 'but I'm not giving you an aperitif without the main meal. When you come to bed with me it's going to be private, comfortable and the full works, as well as unhurried. However, I'm quite willing to give you a real aperitif if you want one.' She rummaged through her shoulder bag which was lying on the bench next to her, but first she withdrew the dark-haired wig and before Andrew could prevent her she'd placed it on his head. Suddenly she became deadly serious. 'I'm a secret lesbian,' she confided solemnly, 'and I'm compelled to dress men up before I can make love to them. Kiss me, beautiful.' She pressed herself up against him, and once more he felt her soft lips against his; one of her hands ran through his pseudo-hair whilst the other fondled an imaginary breast.

For a moment he was utterly shocked until he felt Julie's lips trembling with mirth. Giggling uncontrollably she sat back and stared at him. 'I love you,' she said at last, 'you're a perfect straight to my comedienne. Keep it on, it suits you,' she urged as he began to remove the wig. She returned to the bag and eventually removed a bottle. 'A present for you. Can I have a swig first?' Without waiting for an answer she undid the top and upended the bottle, after which she handed it to him. Not noticing the label in the half-light he took a great gulp and was startled when his throat caught fire; the last thing he'd expected her to be carrying was a bottle of rum, he thought, as he coughed and spluttered, much to her further amusement.

'We ought to be getting back,' she said when she'd cuddled up to him again, 'you don't know what you're missing. It's fantastic.'

'It can't possibly be better than being here with you,' he replied. He took another swig and returned the bottle to his companion. 'When am I going to be allowed to bed you then?'

He waited patiently while she had her drink, then she stated, 'I'll see you on Friday. That way, if we like each other, you can stay the weekend because I'll be free.'

Having immediate visions of living in the Roman villa, Andrew asked, 'where do you live, sweetheart?'

The term jarred in his mind as he uttered it, but Julie seemed to appreciate the endearment for her body tensed as soon as she heard it. 'You know the harbour at Laketown?' He nodded. 'Well, I've got a nice little flat, complete with balcony, which goes with my job, and it overlooks the harbour. But don't worry, I'll meet you at the station.' She hesitated, and warned, 'And you needn't think I don't know where your hand's creeping; I'm not joking!'

'I only want to feel you,' he mumbled.

'I don't care,' she answered firmly, 'besides, it wouldn't tell you anything about what's under my bra. After having six children to suck, my nipples are dark and in line with my navel, and my breasts are red raw and permanently blue veined.'

'They didn't look like it in your slave garments,' Andrew observed dryly.

'Actually, I was lying,' she replied removing his hand from the inside of her coat. 'I was describing my right breast; I kept the left one dry as a souvenir.'

'You mean the right one isn't right and only the left one's left?'

'Something like that,' she agreed, giggling.

'Julie?' he murmured gently. Raising her head from his shoulder she gazed at him enquiringly, 'thank you for entering my life.' He covered her mouth with his and once more their tongues caressed and explored, but in a much slower fashion than previously. When he thought she was in a semiconscious state he removed his right hand from hers and insinuated it gently onto her right breast; to his delight the only response this move elicited was a series of moans and an increase in passion as he alternately fondled and squeezed the soft yet firm flesh through her clothing. Both lovers lost all sense of time for neither wanted to desist, and Andrew had no idea how long they remained in embrace, but he reckoned it must have been an all-time record for when at last they parted, panting, it was almost dark.

'You bastard,' Julie exclaimed, 'that was my sore point.'

'Just checking,' he answered, 'you seemed alright to me.'

She laughed. 'It's a very special bra,' then added, 'you can stay here all night if you wish, but I'm going to listen to some folk music.'

Half way between the two bridges Andrew confessed, 'you're probably the most beautiful girl I've ever seen, Julie, let alone been with; you're certainly the funniest and one of the friendliest. What I'm trying to say is that I'm love and sex starved as well as being lonely, so you're in the position of being able to break me completely.'

He felt her hand, resting on his waist, pull against him. 'You know,' she stated, 'before I saw you, love at first sight was a woman's magazine or romantic novel ploy, but now I know it really exists; so therefore you've won ninety per cent of the battle. If you kept me chained up in a damp dungeon I might go off you a bit.' After a brief silence she went on thoughtfully, 'Linda was very fond of you and she gave me the impression she wanted to hang onto you, she also mentioned her sister had been very keen but had suddenly dropped you.'

'It must have been quite a conversation,' Andrew murmured, taken aback by these revelations. Julie, however, merely smiled. 'Of course, I wanted you at first sight as you did me, but I couldn't bear the thought of losing you when my leave ended or else taking you back to the mainland, even if you were willing to go; a quandary which one of the Maynard girls was kind enough to point out to me.'

She laughed. 'Well, no doubt they had good intentions, but that would have been our problem. Thank you for trying to put me off you, though. I loved that!' And she gave him a quick kiss.

This time a solitary couple was seated outside the pub entrance which was now illuminated by a wall lamp. Andrew was certain they were staring at him in surprised amusement as Julie and he approached, especially when the pair glanced at each other and smiled. He mentally shrugged the thought off as being his imagination, but when they stopped at the bar to buy the drinks, the publican also looked at him in an odd manner.

His lover, though, prevented him from opening the door into the actual barroom. 'It's good practice to stay outside while there's singing going on, even though it's only a chorus number,' she explained. When the song had finished and the applause had died down she opened the door and they entered. Andrew wasn't ready for the sight confronting him. Every inch of the wall bench had been taken as had all the chairs, and people were even seated on the floor. The tables, where they weren't occupied by musical instruments, were packed with glasses and bottles, and a smell of sweat hung in the air.

As they stood in the doorway he noticed all the faces, which had turned in their direction upon their arrival, change from curiosity to surprise then break into smiles, then suddenly everyone began laughing.

When the commotion had died down someone shouted, 'Give us a song, Julie.'

But the girl, after an amused glance at her companion, staggered into the cleared centre of the room. 'Alas, I cannot,' she cried, striking the pose of Victorian womanhood outraged. With left forearm against forehead and right arm fully extended, slightly bowed, index finger pointing accusingly toward Andrew, she went on. 'I have been half ravished by this mad transvestite.'

Immediately, Jim leapt to his feet and drew himself to his full height. 'What?' he roared, 'Arrest him men.' And he, too, pointed at Andrew.

But Julie, however, quickly went down on her knees before Jim and clasped her hands in supplication. 'Stay sir,' she implored, 'for he has stolen my heart.'

'Oh, in that case,' Jim exclaimed, apparently deflated, 'he can buy me a pint of bitter!' At this everyone burst into gales of laughter.

Julie rose to her feet and went over to her companion; with love and happiness on her face she removed his forgotten wig and, scarcely giving him time to put their drinks on the nearest table, drew him into the centre of the room. She held up her hand and everyone went quiet, 'This is Andrew, he's a mainlander, he's been here a week and he's mine.' As she spoke the last words mayhem broke out, cheers, foot stomping and applause rent the air.

Finally someone yelled, 'can you sing?' She looked at her lover enquiringly, but he was forced to shake his head. 'Show him how, Julie.'

'Something appropriate,' prompted Carol.

Without hesitation she took Andrew's hands in hers, gazed into his eyes, and began to sing; despite his confusion he heard every word clearly. The song was about a young maid who lamented the loss of a much-loved partner. It was clever in that common garden plants with punning names were mentioned, and appropriate because the name of the present month was referred to. The tune was hauntingly beautiful and Julie, with her clear, sweet, unwavering voice, did it more than justice. When she'd finished, and before the clapping began, she quickly kissed him.

Somehow he eventually got her away from the attention of everyone in the room and, after retrieving their drinks, they began to sit down on the floor near Jim. But Carol stood up. 'Here you are Julie. Oi, you,' she addressed her lover. 'Give Andrew your seat; they're both honoured guests tonight, and I don't want to see him going near that bar.'

As Jim presented him with his chair he laughed and told him, 'you wouldn't think my arm aches through flogging her daily, would you?'

To Andrew the remainder of the night had a dreamlike quality; his new found love was always by his side surreptitiously holding his hand, and his glass was always full, but there was little opportunity for conversation because someone was always singing, playing, or both. The music of the previous evening, he soon realised, had just been a preliminary – mere amateurism to what he was hearing tonight. He hadn't realised there were so many beautiful melodies, so many fascinating words and stories in the world of folk, that there could be so many accomplished singers and instrumentalists of both genders in one room. There had been many different musical instruments at the summer camp, but here they seemed innumerable.

All too soon for Andrew the last song, sung by everyone from start to finish, came to an end, and he found himself outside with his arm about Julie in the company of Carol and Jim, and inhaling the sharp, sweet air so familiar to the night time drinker. 'Listen,' said Jim, 'are you going back with Julie?' He shook his head sadly. 'In that case you can come on the train with us. It'll save walking up that hill.'

Carol, with sound common sense, put in, 'our train goes before Julie's, and they want to be left alone.'

So it was that Andrew found himself seated with his lover in a remote part of the station. He had tried unceasingly to persuade her to let him escort her home, but she'd remained adamant. 'Patience, my love,' was all she'd say in reply.

With the clarity of mind which intoxication sometimes brings he said, 'you've left me with two problems. How am I going to get through tomorrow and most of Friday without you? And what will happen to us if I remain a mainlander?'

Pulling his head against hers she kissed him tenderly. 'In answer to your first query, why not go home to see your parents?' she suggested eventually.

As they watched the tail lights of the Harbourtown train disappear into the distance and the headlamps of Julie's train approaching, Andrew asked without thinking, 'were any of your former boyfriends there tonight?'

The answer was immediate and nonverbal for he received a violent and unrestrained slap across the face, which caused brilliant flashes to appear in his right eye. As if to demonstrate his remark, though tactless, was forgiven the girl then took his right hand and placed it over her left breast, holding it tightly there. 'What did you do that for?' he enquired in a hurt manner.

'You've got my brain,' she replied vehemently, 'my heart, my soul, my body and all my love. You've got my present, and my future if you want it. But my past is my own.' She paused, 'No, look, the train's almost here. You can have my past and I'll take the rest back. Is it a deal?'

Understanding what she was saying Andrew yelled, 'no, no, no; definitely not.'

Julie kissed him as a way of sealing the contract and they both stood up. As they walked along the platform she said, 'Linda's got my address and phone number. I'll meet you at my station at seven p.m., but give me a call when you're about to board the train.' From the open window of the vestibule door she added, 'we'll talk about your other problem in bed. Give my regards to your people.'

Andrew considered himself as masculine as the next man, but as he watched his lover's train steam off into the night a tear ran down his numbed cheek, and long after the red rear lights had disappeared he remained on the platform. The result was that as he started back to the cottage both the station buildings and public house appeared dark and deserted, as if it they'd been a part of some fantastic dream.

In retrospect he never knew how he got back home that night, for although he was far from drunk he still managed to undertake that long walk entirely oblivious of his surroundings. For the second time that day his mind was in utter turmoil; once again he'd been abandoned by a beautiful friendly girl, and this occasion was far worse than the first, for to his loneliness was now added sexual frustration. Even the knowledge of now having a perfect lover couldn't quite make up for his present desire for sex and companionship, but apart from Julie's stinging slap, his only physical souvenir of the evening's adventure was the remains of the rum she'd pressed upon him, which he vaguely remembered taking the occasional gulp of.

When he reached the cottage he was compelled to let himself in as the place was in darkness. In the kitchen was a note addressed to him, signed by Helen, informing him that he could make some coffee if he wished, hoping he'd had a nice time and that his companion had been up to standard. Post scripted was a message from Linda, the first word of which was underlined, and read that if he came home that night to make certain he drank a glass of water. Obviously made maudlin by the drink he'd imbibed, the sight of the sisters' signatures and their well-meant messages caused him to weep, much to his disgust. Later, before retiring, he turned the message over and wrote that he'd like to be woken early as he wished to see their father.

Just as on the previous morning he was aroused by a knock at his door and by Linda's voice calling to him. 'Can you come in for a moment?' he answered.

'Did you meet her?' she enquired as she sat down on the bed.

'Oh yes,' he replied enthusiastically, 'and I loved her blonde hair, even though I don't usually go for short haired girls. And those green eyes of hers!' The girl, caught off balance, looked puzzled but Andrew placed a hand on her forearm. 'I just want to thank you with all my heart. She's beautiful, friendly, funny, intelligent, but above all she says she loves me and, well I know it sounds childish, but I love her in return.'

Linda shook her head slowly in wonder. 'I've never heard of

instantaneous love in real life before. But what I don't understand is why, in that case, you're here and alone.'

'Because her period hasn't finished yet.'

Still looking nonplussed and entirely unaware of her own recent duplicity on the subject, she observed, 'personally, I've never found that a problem; there's more than one way of making love.' She stood up abruptly, possibly realising she'd left herself open to criticism with her statement. 'Anyway, I'm glad you're fixed up at last, but really I was only a go between.'

'You were much more than that, but in a way I wish I'd known what was being planned because I've felt really lonely and confused since I last made love to you.'

She smiled. 'You've got your Julie to thank for that; it was her idea to keep you in the dark. After all, you more or less told her you didn't want her, and I suppose she thought if she left you to cool your heels and then sprung herself on you it would make you change your mind. And I certainly wasn't going to spoil her plans, but she's worth looking after if she wants you to experience the full enjoyment of her whole body. But how did you get your sore eye?'

After Andrew explained, she couldn't conceal her mirth. 'I told you not to do it. It's taken for natural over here that virtually all lovers have had previous attachments; and the best way of all in coming to terms with any jealous feelings is to ask yourself if you could subsequently bear to see your sweetheart in the company of your replacement. If you couldn't, in your Julie's case, you'll just have to live with her previous experiences.'

An expression of relief appeared on his face. 'I'd always thought you had wisdom far beyond your years, but that advice is the best yet. I genuinely thank you very much and I certainly will watch what I say in future.' His expression changed to concern. 'Look, I don't know how to put this without seeming oafish, but if I've hurt either you or Helen in any way I want to apologise.'

Linda bent down and planted a kiss on his forehead. 'That sounds like a leave taking. However, as far as I'm concerned you've got nothing to apologise for, and I don't really want to speak on my sister's behalf. But I will say this – she's been issued with the same set of playing cards as the rest of us girls; if she doesn't wish to play them then it's up to her. Julie did choose, and she won you, so go to her with a clear conscience. Incidentally, when are you going to consummate your love?'

He told her, adding that on Julie's suggestion he'd be hoping to go home in the interim. Walking over to the door she paused and turned to look across at him. 'I'm really happy for you, and I hope you both enjoy your relationship. I know her quite well and she's an all-round lovely girl, but if it doesn't work out make sure you learn everything she teaches you!'

'How did you get on last night, lad?' Mr Maynard said, asking the inevitable question during breakfast. Andrew explained, but avoided all mention of his lover much to Linda's obvious enjoyment. 'I understand you want to see me about something,' Charlie asked when he'd finished, adding, 'in private?' The younger man, after a furtive glance at Helen, nodded.

'When I mentioned about my visit to the folk club last night I deliberately left a lot out,' he began when they were both seated in the lounge. 'In fact, I met a beautiful girl and we fell in love.'

'That's extremely unusual on a first meeting,' Charlie commented.

'She's asked me to tea on Friday evening, but until then I thought I might pop over and see my family if you don't mind.'

The ghost of a smile crossed Mr Maynard's features, but all he said was, 'I'll sign an exit and entrance permit for you. It's a pity you couldn't have given us more notice as there might be a plane going over, but I'm afraid you'll have to make do with a vehicle ferry. You've got some money for mainland transport?'

Andrew nodded and continued. 'I'm afraid there's something worrying me, Charlie.' Mr Maynard waited expectantly. 'Because I love this girl I naturally won't want to hurt her; so what will happen to her, to us, when my leave is over and I need to return to sea?'

To his surprise and relief the smile on the other man's face broadened, just as a benevolent chess player's might in recognition of an extremely shrewd move on the part of an opponent. He took a drink from his cup of coffee and then observed, 'her name is Julie, isn't it?' Put like a question, it was really a statement of fact. His next words were an echo of Gill's. 'From birth or domicile every Whyte Islander has their activities, progress, ability and personality recorded, and this, rightly or wrongly, also applies to employees of our island. In brief, Andrew, in your case it means the authorities are extremely pleased with you. If they weren't then you wouldn't have been permitted to set foot on our island, and I think you've seen enough of our society to understand why. Therefore, since you've been allowed to come here and, naturally enough, been able to meet the people, it follows that you might wish to form a liaison with one of our women. In your case, I believe that if it were a matter of deciding between losing one of the island's girls or gaining a mainland boy then we would decide upon the latter choice.'

Andrew's face broke into smiles of relief and pleasure at these words, but Charlie held up a hand in warning. 'What I've said is entirely unofficial, mind, and you'll have to wait for an official invitation; you'd also be required to take a series of examinations to ensure you're suitable for our society and sign a statement saying you'll accept Whyte Island citizenship unconditionally. At the moment you've got four weeks of your leave still to run and you haven't yet experienced all the island has to offer; there are some activities here which you might not like or think bizarre, and our customs are, as you know, unique with regard to the rest of the world. You'll need to undergo virtually everything germane to becoming one of our citizens, just as all our adults have had to. But because Julie and you say you love each other then it will seem natural to everyone that you'll want to set up home together.' To his surprise Charlie winked at him as he spoke these words. 'If you do so, can take everything our authorities throw at both of you, and are still happy together at the end of your leave,' he continued, 'then no one is going to attempt to part you.'

After considering for a moment Andrew said, 'Mr Maynard, I don't suppose you'll like what I'm going to say, but it means a lot to me. You or the authorities haven't set Julie up to persuade me to become a Whyte Islander, have you?' He went on hurriedly, 'only I couldn't live without her now.'

Charlie stared at him with amusement before shaking his head slowly in amazement. 'Actually, lad, we were under the impression we were going to do you a favour by offering you citizenship, but it appears as though it's the other way round. Andrew, lad, we wouldn't even consider using anyone to entice you or anyone else into our society; we don't raise our children up so we can use them as our tools, they're encouraged to think for themselves. Julie wants you because she cares for you, so make sure you're worthy of her. I'll wager you one thing, though – after experiencing the love and companionship of a Whyte Island lass, you'll never want to leave us.'

He stood up, as did Andrew, and the latter said, 'you've made me extremely happy, Charlie.'

But Mr Maynard replied, 'thank your Julie; we don't like to deny our children anything they want if it's beneficial for them. Between you and me, I was hoping you'd be taking Helen off my hands. Now, is there anything else?'

'Just a little thing really. Is there anything against importing items into the island?' Noting the puzzled expression on the president's face he explained, 'only I thought I might buy some jewellery or perfume for the three girls.'

Charlie was silent for a moment, then he burst out laughing. At last he said, 'you're a fine nominee Whyte Islander. Shop here, lad; show some patriotism to your intended new country. Wait until you return to Harbourtown if you must buy my girls keepsakes. There are lots of items to choose from and at more than reasonable prices. But don't you dare get me anything or I'll shout bribery and return it to you forthwith!'

Andrew experienced little difficulty in crossing the narrow strip of water between the island and the country of his birth, for Charlie had immediately and easily arranged his passage on a vehicle transporter. As he'd stepped aboard, the captain had called down and invited him up to the bridge; now, having cleared harbour, he asked, 'what are you going over there for? It's terrible.'

The young man smiled. 'I know. I'm a mainlander.' In order to cover the captain's embarrassment he went on to explain how he was on leave from the *Whyte Hart* and had been invited to spend it on the island; if the officer was aware this fact meant his passenger was likely to become an islander he didn't mention it, but merely asked if he'd enjoyed himself. The subsequent conversation then naturally turned to the sea, ships and foreign lands, the captain having formerly been the commander of several Whyte Line ships, but had retired due to "domestic considerations". Just before they berthed the captain wished him a happy leave, but his face showed surprise when Andrew answered, 'I'll be coming back tomorrow.'

Julie's idea that a visit to his family would pass the time away succeeded beyond his expectations, and if he'd needed confirmation that his entire future now belonged on Whyte Island then the events over the following hours were to more than underline the extent of his alienation. In retrospect Andrew realised that in view of the enormous contrast between the two societies, he could scarcely expect to feel otherwise.

From the station, where he purchased an extremely expensive ticket, he attempted to telephone home but found he couldn't get through and so was unable to warn his family of his imminent arrival. The only thing to be said for the train was that it was fast and, Andrew thought cynically, this was probably due to the driver wanting to get home for his dinner. But it was in a terrible condition with grimy windows, and had presumably not been cleaned after its previous journey, for plastic beakers, discarded wrappers and other such litter were scattered everywhere.

There weren't many passengers, and this suited him down to the ground for all he wished to do was think of his lover and to long for the time when he was heading back in the opposite direction, but he'd hardly seated himself and placed his holdall on the fitted table when a man of middle age came and sat opposite. Despite Andrew's attempts to discourage him the newcomer insisted upon making conversation and when the man asked him if he had far to go something in his mannerism made Andrew lie; and so he was able, when the train began to slow for a station, to make his escape.

'Damned people,' he muttered to himself as he headed for the rear coaches; eventually he came to a compartmented vehicle and, drawing back the first door without checking, he was concerted to find it contained a girl of about Julie's age seated alone by the window. As he entered she contrived to send him a look which managed to convey a mixture of suspicion, disdain and boredom, and she pretended not to hear his subsequent cheerful greeting. Being prejudged a seducer or a rapist didn't please Andrew too much, but he didn't really have anything to complain about as it meant he was virtually alone, which is what he wished for, and so the girl's evident rudeness gave him the excuse to ignore her for the remainder of the journey. To his amusement he later noticed her gazing at him with curiosity and interest in the window's reflection as he occasionally glanced out at the passing scenery from the far side of the compartment. If only she were an island girl, he thought; he would then have found the time and inclination to talk to her.

From the station to his home wasn't far and, as it was a fine day and he had little to carry, he decided to walk. There had once been a time when he'd enjoyed this stroll, the anticipation of a reunion with his parents and brothers, or visiting his old haunts, and the possibility of meeting the girl of his dreams making it especially attractive, but for a variety of reasons the pleasure had gradually evaporated as the maze of houses and roads had become seedier with the extensive recession. Since he'd accepted early retirement his father had lost much of his zest for life; his elder brother had, like himself, fled the nest to find work in another country; while his younger brother, born just too late, had failed to make a career for himself. His poor, unfortunate mother had taken the breakup of her family very badly, and despite all his attempts to amuse her during his leaves, she now always seemed peevish and insular.

There had been a time, too, when he'd returned from his voyages, no matter how long the duration, with presents from different lands; but when he doled them out he began to feel that little by little they were less appreciated until they actually became disliked, and he eventually realised his family thought he was patronising them. Obviously he was being well paid while they had to scrimp and save just to survive, so, unwittingly, they were smoothing the path for his eventual abandonment of them and the mainland.

As he knocked on the front door and waited for the sound of footsteps he wished that just for once he'd be greeted with something approaching enthusiasm. 'Oh, hello Andrew,' said his mother, 'back again are you?'

'I tried to phone,' he told her retreating back.

'Oh, it's been out of action for weeks,' she replied over her shoulder, adding, 'your dad's in the back room watching the racing; there'll be a cup of tea along soon.'

Over the evening meal, during which the conversation was dominated by his mother's complaint about the new neighbours and how they'd been such good friends until without warning they'd suddenly turned nasty, his father asked, 'any plans for tonight, son?'

It was a question Andrew dreaded. Loyalty made him want to say he'd like to stay in and keep his parents company, but experience had made it impracticable; he had no wish to spend the evening in front of the television watching the soap operas and quiz shows his mother invariably favoured and which she wouldn't be dragged away from. 'I thought of looking in down at the local, dad; would you like to keep me company?' But his father, he knew, never borrowed and wouldn't be treated. 'What about you, Billy?'

'Nah, I'm going out with me mates.' Despite all his studious casualness, Andrew was aware his brother had inherited some of his father's pride, but Billy, suddenly enthusiastic, went on, 'why don't you go down the new disco? It's loaded with sexy chicks, or so I've heard.' His mother glared at him when he spoke the last sentence, but it was just water off Billy's back.

Knowing the ropes only too well, Andrew took on board plenty of liquid refreshment down at the local before attempting the discotheque. He felt quite self-conscious sitting alone in the fairly crowded bar with no one to talk to, but he had no choice for any of his former acquaintances still living in the area would doubtless be either married, sitting at home penniless, or both. So it came as a relief when his wristwatch told him it was high time for him to try out his brother's observation.

He had little compunction about trying to form a casual relationship with a mainland girl, for at best she would be little more than a pale substitute for Julie and, besides, he knew from bitter experience that wanting a girl and actually getting one were two different things. Finally, as a mainland male he wished to bid a memorable farewell to the females of his native land. To this end he went into the pub's toilet and purchased some protection thinking wryly, as he did so, that to count one's chickens before they hatched automatically guaranteed an infertile clutch.

After buying a ticket which made him feel sure the disco was part owned by the railways, Andrew gained entry; it was a venue he knew well for it had once been the town's ballroom. Now, it was scarcely recognisable for it had changed from being a well illuminated, spacious and reputable room with a resident orchestra, and the occasional rock group putting in an appearance, to a dingily lit area with flashing lights and extremely loud thumping music controlled by a man in a glittering suit standing over his various keyboards, selecting audible and visual effects at lightning speed. As a result the place was noisy and crowded.

Had he not gone there with one aim in mind Andrew wouldn't have contemplated going near it, but he quickly realised Billy had been perfectly right – the place had a definite surfeit of "chicks", though whether or not they were particularly sexy he couldn't tell merely by looking at them. He knew very well why there were so many unaccompanied girls; the management was only too aware that women attracted men, and the two sexes naturally generated a lot of money when they went in search of each other, so by the simple expedient of charging the women a derisive entrance fee they primed the coffers into spewing up gold. He also knew the management didn't care whether the fleeced men could or couldn't afford the cocktails which the pick-ups drank like cups of tea, and he wondered idly how many men were staying at home minding the children whilst their wives were earning a little side money.

Mentally cursing his culpability he began his search for a fallen angel. But to his great disappointment he experienced some difficulty in achieving his goal. He soon found out the reason for his lack of success – he would approach a girl and ask her for a dance, whereupon she'd enquire as to whether he had a mate. 'Sorry,' she'd say when he gave his answer. The modern girl was apparently so nervous of being assaulted without recompense that she wouldn't venture out without a partner of her own sex. In complete contradiction to this attitude Andrew discovered another stumbling block to his quest for sexual satisfaction, for when he did manage to find a spirit willing to risk a fate worse than death he, was invariably asked what make of car he owned within a few minutes of beginning to dance. Bemused, he could only assume rape was bearable if it was undertaken on the back seat of a car, or far from where there could be any help or witnesses.

Eventually, just as he was on the verge of admitting defeat, he found a girl who was neither interested in his friends or in his motoring ability – in fact she didn't seem to be interested in much at all, least of all him – but at least she was quite pretty and, unlike most of her sisters, sported a sensible hairstyle and costume. Another point in the girl's favour was her appreciation of the masculine body, as Andrew quickly discovered when he took her in his arms on the dance floor. But it wasn't until he'd plied her with considerable amounts of fancy gin and tonics that she began to talk in more than monosyllables, then a chance remark of his which complimented her on her appearance instantly opened her eyes to the good taste of her companion. From that moment on he experienced no difficulty in charming the girl and eventually manoeuvring her out of the discotheque well before closing time. If he noticed the man who, in one of the bars, had glared at them then he thought nothing of it for it was impossible not to catch peoples' eyes in crowded places.

'It isn't far,' said his partner as they walked along with their arms about each other, 'and there's a nice dark alley nearby.'

'Can't we go to your place?'

'God, no,' was all she said in reply.

Compared to Linda and Julie the girl's lovemaking skills were non-existent, but Andrew was easily able to make the usual progression from mouth to breasts and thence to the top of her legs without any false modesty on her part. He was just arousing her to a passion when she whispered breathlessly, 'Stop.' After calming down a little she murmured, 'before you go any further I think you'd better pay me.'

Taken by surprise he echoed, 'pay you?'

'Well, I've got to find the mortgage money, and feed the kids.'

'I'm sorry,' he replied, all interest gone, 'but I didn't realise. I don't pay for sex.'

To the girl's credit she neither said or shouted anything as he walked off down the alley, even though she must have felt bitterly disappointed on at least one account. He'd almost reached the road when the figure of a man stepped out and barred his way. 'Have you paid her?' he asked conversationally.

'I don't pay for sex,' Andrew repeated.

The stranger moved up to him. 'Thought you could get it for nothing, didn't you?' his voice was rising and taking on an angry tone. Suddenly he threw out an open hand and hit Andrew on his left shoulder, saying as he did so, 'That was my wife.'

Something suddenly snapped in his victim's brain, a vivid picture of Julie rose before his mind's eye and a hundred emotions sped through him. Using the wiles and practices learnt in his self-defence exercises, he half turned to go and then with horrendous speed and fury he drew back his right arm and let fly; even before the assailant began to collapse he received a further violent blow midway between his solar plexus and waist which sent him reeling backward against a wall where he fell in a heap. Still in a fog of intense anger Andrew lashed out with his feet, kicking again and again at the prone form and only vaguely aware of the sound of rapidly approaching high heeled shoes and of a female voice repeatedly calling, 'Colin! Colin!'

He felt a hand pulling at his shoulder. 'Please,' the girl cried, 'you've hurt him enough.' Then her tone changed as passion for Andrew and latent love for her husband conspired to save the motionless figure. Bending down to examine him she eventually looked up at his adversary. 'If you're quick you can still come

226

inside me.' She stood up. 'No one's ever brought me that far before, and I like a man who can fight!'

Suddenly fully conscious once more Andrew stared at her with a mixture of disgust and disbelief; he pressed a banknote into her hand. 'Forget it,' he replied. After walking a few yards down the road he paused and looked back; beneath the street lamp where the man had fallen the girl knelt, her husband's head cradled in her lap. 'What's your name?' he called softly.

She lifted her gaze from her husband's face. 'Julie,' she answered.

'He's unworthy of you, Julie!'

'I've fallen in love with a girl on Whyte Island,' Andrew imparted in a matter of fact manner during breakfast.

The silence which followed was broken only by the sound of metal on china, then his mother finally said bitterly, 'I suppose that means you'll be living over there from now on.'

'It isn't quite as easy as that. I…'

But his explanation was interrupted by his father. 'I don't know what's so special about that place,' he observed dryly, 'that they have to pick and choose who they let in. Why don't they all clear off down the Antarctic if they want to be left alone?'

His wife turned to their son. 'Couldn't you have found a nice local girl?'

Recalling his experiences of the night before he said nothing, but Billy, waiting patiently for an opening, asked, 'what's she like, Andy?' And he drew an hour glass figure in the air with his hands.

Andrew's mother, refusing his offer of help with the breakfast things with the words, 'it's women's work,' gave him the excuse to quit the house and so walk off his anger. His father's remark, coming from a person who'd once been so understanding and broadminded, had touched him to the quick; apart from the unwarranted attack on the land and the people he was beginning to love, his mother's semi-insinuation that he was deserting them merely for the want of finding a local girl had irritated him, and as for his brother's crude reference to his Julie – well, Billy had at least shown an interest in her.

Their house still sported the appendage "Grassbanks", named after his father's best winner, on a carved wooden block hanging from the porch, but Andrew considered the horse's name should have been, more appropriately "Indifference" for no other could more accurately describe the mentality of the occupants. 'Oh Julie, Julie, Julie,' he called silently, 'love me, and give me the good fortune and strength to leave this land of fools permanently.' All the bad experiences which had happened to him since leaving the transporter were quite common on the mainland, but his faultless leave on Whyte Island had served to emphasise their importance in his mind, besides which he seemed to be experiencing all these unfortunate occurrences together in one brief stay. But a final tribulation, perhaps the worst of all, was about to collide head on with him in the local park, to which he was now proceeding.

In the old days, as a toddler, he'd taken some of his first unsteady steps there as had his brothers before and after him; he remembered his mother taking him down on many occasions to feed the large number of wildfowl which suddenly congregated at the least expectation of food. Of how he'd cried when, with unsteady aim and low height, he'd failed to clear the hurdled fence with his thrown crusts and they'd bounced back at his feet, whereupon his mother would pick him up to allow him to increase his range and turn his tears to laughter as the birds squabbled and fell over each other in their excitement.

Now, seated on a bench overlooking the lake and what remained of the hurdles, his heart felt heavy as he surveyed the water, for apart from one or two coots, only a pair of mallards probably half wild and leading a nomadic existence from one reasonably peaceful area of water to another, were visible well away from where he sat. Not far away, where a wire wheel, a handle and a shiny piece of black metal, the remains of a pram, stood proud above the surface, a webbed foot and a white feathered body accorded stark evidence of the folly of allowing air guns to be sold to bored youths brought low by the recession. Near the lake's edge was a pair of blackened stumps, the sole remnants of a board which once carried the pictures and details of ten species of exotic waterfowl, former residents of the lake and now shot out of existence.

To Andrew's right, as he sat there lost in thought, the path curved away behind a thicket of laurels. Up till then he'd been the only person in the vicinity, but now he heard the patter of rapidly approaching feet and upon glancing up in the direction of the bushes he saw the figure of a little girl aged about three running toward him. Reaching the far end of his bench she pressed her hands against its arm and stared at him with amused interest; she was a pretty little thing with curly blonde hair and big blue eyes, but she'd no sooner arrived when her presumed mother appeared on the scene, clearing the short distance between the thicket and the bench at lightning speed.

He could see the toddler was an exact miniature of her parent as her mother rushed up, and he opened his mouth to compliment her on her daughter's beauty, but the woman, flashed him a look of malevolent hatred which might have caused a tiger to tremble. She grabbed her child and shook it until it screamed, punctuating the words, 'keep away from the nasty man,' with a heavy slap round the head.

Long after the child had been dragged away shrieking, Andrew continued to sit on the bench in a state of shock, his eyes moist with pain and anger. As full consciousness began to return he heard himself mumbling. 'You bloody cow,' over and over again; rage, strong enough to equal that of the previous night, overwhelmed him and he wanted to race after the woman and hit her, shake her and shout, 'I didn't do anything! I was sitting here minding my own business! I don't molest children!' Sudden resolve came to him and he jumped up, but instead of chasing after the mother he made for the park gates.

Arriving back at his home, he went straight up to his room and began packing his bag with his mother, by his side, repeatedly demanding to know what was wrong; even through his fury he was well aware he was burning his bridges for he knew he was upsetting his parents, yet on the other hand it was by no means certain there would be an opportunity for him on Whyte Island. So he couldn't decide whether to just take back the stuff he came over with, or to strip the room of his property; finally, despite his mother's interference, he took the more personal items as well as some extra clothes, and so he took his leave of his family with a loaded suitcase in addition to his holdall. At the gate, his mother asked anxiously, 'when will you be back?'

Without stopping, Andrew called over his shoulder, 'it's a bit late for you to be concerned about that, but never I hope.'

Fortunately for him he was just in time to catch the relevant train and, therefore, he was able to board an earlier vehicle transporter which, by a curious coincidence, was the same one he came over on. During the train journey he'd been so upset that he was entirely unaware of everything going on around him, and now on the vessel he still wanted to be left alone with his thoughts, so it was a source of some annoyance when the captain noticed him. 'What's up, mate?' he asked. 'You look really browned off. Hey Jim,' he called to a deckhand, 'bring some tea up to the bridge, would you?' And turning to Andrew he confided, 'we've still got twenty minutes before casting off.'

Over the mug of tea the young man confessed, 'I don't know what's wrong with me; I never used to be soft but on Wednesday night I wept, and today I had near hysterics. The first time was when I said goodnight to my new found girlfriend, and the second was not long ago when I was more or less accused of being a child molester.'

The captain chuckled. 'Don't worry, you're just a victim of two opposing societies. I think I'd cry like a baby if I'd spent a lot of time on Whyte Island and then had to experience this place. I shouldn't really tell you this, but the mere fact you've been allowed on the island means you're almost certain to be asked whether you'd like to become an islander, and your self-called softness is a point in your favour for it shows you've got a heart and a soul.' After taking a gulp of tea he raised a warning finger in the air. 'Mind you,' he grinned, 'you mustn't be too soft, because you'll be required to sign a declaration you'd be willing to defend the island to the death if need be, like the rest of us.' He was silent for a moment, then said, 'I suppose you know all incoming baggage has to be searched? But if you want to hurry back to your girlfriend you can leave your gear on board and I'll see it gets to where you're staying.'

It was a measure of his faith in island people that Andrew concurred whole-heartedly with this suggestion. 'So where do you live?' urged the captain. When he was told he whistled appreciatively. 'What a berth: two sisters, one a brunette, the other a blonde; all you need now is a redhead.'

His passenger smiled. 'I've got the redhead.'

They both laughed, and then the captain rose to his feet. 'That's better,' he exclaimed, grasping the young man's shoulder firmly. 'Never keep your troubles to yourself, not on Whyte Isle at any rate. See these mugs are washed up, won't you?'

Unencumbered by any luggage, Andrew was resolved to carry out his plan of buying gifts for the three girls, and so he strolled down Harbourtown's high street until his eye was caught by a jeweller's shop window. Inside it was smart and modern, and scarcely had the entrance bell stopped ringing when an equally smart and modern assistant appeared. To his knowledge he'd never set eyes on her before, but as soon as she saw him she exclaimed delightedly, 'hello, Andrew,' and she went on to explain that she been at the Station Arms. 'Oh, you are lucky,' she continued, 'we all think the world of Julie, and she's one of the loveliest girls on the island.'

Understandably pleased, he replied gallantly, 'you aren't so bad yourself.'

The assistant blushed noticeably. 'Anyway, what can I do for you?' she beamed. 'Your word is my command.'

The young man told her, but was surprised when she answered, 'we don't sell much real jewellery here, instead we usually hire it out. Mostly we design, manufacture and export it, and we also repair watches. Another thing is that we don't work with precious gems or metals as it's considered to be ostentatious.' What a word to use in a jewellers he thought as the girl continued. 'However, I think I've got something which would suit your Julie perfectly – it'll go with her hair and pale skin really well.' She brought out a small leather case and opened it proudly; displayed upon a white satin cushion was a beautiful necklace consisting of a fine gold chain from which were suspended five emerald teardrops, and within its circumference were a pair of matching earrings.

'It's fantastic,' Andrew exclaimed, 'but I couldn't possibly afford it, could I?'

The girl showed him the price tag – it was ridiculously low. 'You see,' she explained apologetically, 'if the jewels were authentic it would cost a fortune.' She paused, allowing him time to consider whether or not he wanted the set, then she continued. 'What usually happens is that when a woman is invited to a ball or similar function she hires her jewellery to match her outfit; that way she has access to countless items without owning a single piece.' Noticing his look of disappointment she went on quickly. 'But don't worry, it isn't unusual for a man to present his consort with a piece of jewellery. I think you'll find Julie will love this item.'

'You've convinced me, and in that case it'll do perfectly, but don't let on you chose it, will you?'

The girl smiled. 'I didn't choose it; I only showed it to you.'

He was equally pleased with the presents for the sisters which the assistant also helped him to select. For Helen he bought a pendant in the form of a bird, which the girl identified as a goldfinch made in authentic colours, and for Linda he chose a diamond studded bracelet. Before leaving the shop he observed, 'I suppose the ban on selling authentic jewellery is so as to prevent snobbery developing.'

The assistant nodded. 'Also, zigzagging would stop being a pretence and become reality.'

'Zigzagging?' he echoed in bewilderment.

As if realising she'd made a mistake, she replied hastily, 'Oh dear; you'd better ask your lover about that.'

As he travelled in the bus back toward the cottage, Andrew felt in a far better frame of mind than when he'd left his home; anticipation of his meeting with Julie and what was to come afterward together with the captain and the jewellery girl had cheered him up considerably. But he couldn't help wondering what zigzagging was; it sounded really bizarre.

When he reached the cottage he found Helen alone and busily ironing a pile of washing in the kitchen. 'Hello,' she greeted him cheerfully, 'you're back early; did you have a nice time?'

'Unfortunately I didn't,' he replied candidly.

She switched off the iron. 'I'm very sorry to hear that. Look, while you were away I started to do some thinking, and I want to talk to you; so I'll make us both a hot drink and then we'll go up to my study where we won't be disturbed. Do you mind?'

Andrew smiled and shook his head, but really he was most annoyed at her invitation; he'd already unsuccessfully tried to contact Julie from Harbourtown but even though she was apparently away from home he was determined to see her as soon as possible, and so he'd merely called in at the Maynards' to shower and change his clothes. Helen's buttonholing of him was therefore far from welcome, but he resolved to be patient and to listen to what she had to say.

She was visibly moved by his account of his experiences on the mainland which, apart from certain modifications regarding Julie's namesake, he gave in full. Looking quite upset she eventually murmured to herself, 'I thought so.' Glancing at him as he sat beside her on her bed she said aloud, 'from what you've just told me I think I've misjudged you.' Waving aside his protests to the contrary, she continued, 'you're much more sensitive than I ever realised. When the lover I told you about left me I was badly hurt, but even so there was a part of me which hoped that one day someone would come along to take his place.'

She paused, obviously trying to put her next words as tactfully as possible. 'Several young men from the mainland have stayed here, but I never really got to know them because Linda immediately beguiled them; that explains why I was so distant with you, I knew you'd been intimate with my sister and so every time you'd made a pass at me I assumed you were just trying to add me to your list.' She studied her hands which rested in her lap. 'I could imagine you boasting to your friends about how you'd had two sisters; but what I didn't take into account was that you, like most men, could sleep with one woman but really desire another. When I did realise it, it was too late, Julie was on the scene and I was compelled to take part in Linda's conspiracy of silence.' Andrew watched a tear roll slowly down her cheek as she continued. 'You remember when we came back from the reserve and were listening to the nightingales in the lane? I was silently begging you to take me into the woods; despite Julie, you could have done what you wished with me.'

'If only you'd said,' he commented, continuing with typical masculine tactlessness, 'I wanted nothing more: but it's too late now.' She broke down completely at these words and Andrew put an arm about her shoulder and positioned her head beneath his chin.

He could feel her tear soaked cheek against his throat as she wailed, 'Julie and I must be sisters under the skin because I can understand her loving you at first sight. I've nothing against her but I hoped you wouldn't hit it off, but now my chance has gone.' She lifted her head and gazed at him in silent pleading; her cheeks, red flushed and matching the tip of her nose in colour, contrasted with the paleness of the rest of her face. Andrew was unable to refuse her mute entreaty, and slowly and gently he lowered his mouth to her waiting lips.

At first Helen, with her arms folded tightly around the back of his neck, was content to press her mouth firmly against his but then, insidiously, she forced her tongue between his teeth; deliberately, he realised, she then leant backward pulling him with her until they were both lying on the bed and in the position for intercourse as her legs were now wrapped about his. In a frenzy of passion she moved her body while her lips worked against his and her tongue probed every part of his mouth; very much against his will he felt himself responding to her sexuality and he began to grope for the hem of her skirt.

But he immediately realised that if he were going to satisfy her he would need to disentangle himself; so somehow he managed to stand up and, after gazing down at her for a moment he roughly removed her skirt and lower underwear. He was beginning to feel irritated because what he'd considered to be an act of charity toward her was now beginning to take on the aspect of a rape, for instead of helping him she had lain passively whilst he'd undressed her. Hesitating for a second to glance at the mat of dark brown hair which, framed by her navy blue sweater, dark suspenders and stocking tops, contrasted so vividly with the surrounding pale flesh he bent down, lifted her legs and manoeuvred her lower trunk further onto the bed. After unzipping himself he climbed on the bed, pulled her legs apart and began to lower himself on top of her, but at the last moment she closed her legs and turned over onto her side. 'I haven't got any protection!' she cried.

Angry with frustration Andrew shouted, 'Well, I have.' And he began to fumble inside the breast pocket of his jacket. As he did so, Helen slipped out from beneath him, sat on the edge of the bed and hastily pulled on her underwear and skirt.

Open mouthed he stared at her as she stood up and turned to face him. 'No,' she said, 'I'm not going to allow it. You're Julie's, and she won you fair and square. I should've taken you when I had the chance, but I'm not going to poach someone else's property now. It isn't done on Whyte Island.' Barely giving him the opportunity to render himself decent she pulled him off the bed and began propelling him toward the door. 'Go to her,' she cried wildly, 'don't wait for anything.' Remorselessly she pushed him out of the room and in the direction of the stairs, and Andrew, realising resistance was pointless, went meekly. Half way down the flight of steps she called after him, 'no, wait. I'm going to take you to the bloody station, so wait by the gate while I write a note for my dad.'

'But what about my stuff?'

'Don't worry about that now,' she snapped, 'I'll send it on.'

Andrew felt as though he was an errant child being taken to

school by his mother as Helen escorted him along the lane with his left hand clutched tightly in her right. After progressing about a third of the way in silence he suddenly said, 'Don't be annoyed, my love; because no one's really to blame. Forget me and find someone else; you're really beautiful and I reckon men will fall over themselves trying to date you.' He almost added, "If you open up to them", but instead said, 'If you let them.'

Immediately, she stopped and faced him. 'I don't want anyone else,' she blazed. 'I haven't given you up, you know. I wish Julie and you no harm; in fact I wish you every happiness, but I'm going to wait exactly one year for you. If you and she part during that time then I want you to contact me, and then you can have what you narrowly missed having as much as you like. But if I don't hear from you I'm going to surpass Linda in promiscuity.' Then she began pulling him down the hill again. On the village station platform, when they saw the distant plume of smoke heralding the arrival of his train, Helen embraced him, and with tears starting in her eyes she whispered, 'I'm no witch, but I sense that some day soon you and I will be together again. So remember what Julie teaches you and then teach it to me.'

Understandably confused by the sudden turn of events but secretly doubtful he'd ever get the opportunity of bedding his present companion, he replied, 'I will, but would I still be on the island in a year's time?' With tears now running freely down her cheeks, she nodded; removing herself from his arms she turned and, without a backward glance walked off down the platform.

Despite the number of buildings in the vicinity of Laketown harbour with attached balconies Andrew experienced little difficulty in locating Julie's flat. The front door was positioned between two shops and as he raised his hand to ring the bell a woman passing by kindly informed him that he should walk straight in. Inside, he found a narrow passage leading to a short flight of stairs at the head of which was a small landing containing the door to the flat he sought. A further set of stairs led, he presumed, to an apartment above. The answer to his ringing was, in his excited state of anticipation, far too long in coming; but when the door finally opened he was confronted, not by Julie but by a handsome young man of about his own age.

For Andrew, tired and distraught due to a whole series of abnormal events, being faced by a man when he'd expected to see the girl he loved and craved for, was the last straw. The word "treachery" screamed in his battered mind, and without a word he turned on his heels and rushed down the stairs as fast as he could; the fact that the young stranger had red hair and shouted his name after him failed to register in his brain. All he wanted to do was to get back to Helen as quickly as possible and bury himself in her welcoming arms.

If he'd been on the mainland he'd have almost certainly been killed or seriously injured for as he emerged from the building he dashed straight across the road without checking the traffic, and in the event he narrowly missed colliding with a cyclist. Striding out determinedly, he swiftly drew away from the scene of his intense disappointment but then, into the fog of his outraged mind, came the sound of a familiar voice calling his name repeatedly; he was aware from the voice's gradually increasing volume that he was slowly being overtaken, and his eyes moistened as pride told him to keep on going while common sense begged him to stop and give the girl a chance to explain.

Suddenly Julie's voice was directly behind him, and he felt her hand pulling roughly at his arm. 'Look at what you're doing,' she screamed at him. Caught off balance by her injunction he stopped and glanced down at the spot indicated by her pointing finger. 'This road's tearing my stockings to shreds,' she exaggerated, 'now pick me up this instant and carry me back to our flat.' Like a sleepwalker rudely awakened, Andrew automatically obeyed, and when she lay cradled in his arms her face suddenly broke into a smile. 'You man, me woman,' she whispered and, taking advantage of his helplessness, she kissed him passionately while the breeze blowing off the lake whipped her auburn hair across both their faces. 'You are a fool, Andrew,' she murmured fondly when she'd removed her mouth, 'island girls might be sensuous, but we're not up to sleeping with our brothers.'

'Your brother?' he echoed in wonder.

'Yes. At the moment he's an engineer on one of the steamers over there,' she motioned over her shoulder with her head. 'Go on,' she urged, 'start walking.' Heedless of the bemused looks of passers-by, unaccustomed to such scenes of blatant affection she continued. 'All this morning I've been boring, and that's the operative word in your case but with two "Os", my parents with details of you. My twin brother got to hear of it and he dropped in for a cup of tea and a chat; I wouldn't have let him open the door to you for the world, but you weren't expected.'

Overwhelmed by relief at her explanation Andrew replied, 'darling Julie, I'm very sorry for my ridiculous behaviour but I had a really bad time at home, and like a storm tossed wreck I headed as quickly as possible for your haven. I tried to phone you.'

Smiling happily and tightening her grip about his neck she replied, 'I haven't been back long because I've been shopping as well. I've bought you another present, but rather more physical than the previous one.'

With a lump in his throat, he observed, 'how could I have so little faith in you, Julie? I really don't deserve you.' But she merely laughed.

At the roadside door of her residence Julie's brother stood waiting and obviously pretending nothing out of the ordinary had occurred. 'I see you've got your hands full, and in more ways than one,' he grinned as they approached, 'so I'd better not try to shake hands, but my name's Jeremy.'

'I believe you know mine,' Andrew returned. 'Sorry if I made a fool of myself.'

But Jeremy shrugged in dismissal. 'You'll probably wish you'd kept on going before too soon,' he smiled with a wink. 'Anyway, I'd best be getting back to the boat, we're due out soon. Send me a signal if you require help with that minx, and I'll see you both tomorrow.'

The girl in Andrew's arms remained silent as she watched her brother walk away, then she suddenly called out, 'I don't know why you're bothering; they don't need you, you useless sod.' However, he didn't bother to acknowledge the insult.

'You look really tired and worn out,' Julie said with genuine concern as her lover carried her up the stairs, 'Are you hungry?' He shook his head. 'In that case you're going straight to bed.'

'Only if you're coming with me.'

Smiling, she replied, 'just you try and stop me, but positively no sex until you've had a snooze. A tired lover is of no use to me. You can put me down now.' She pushed open the frosted glass panelled door which had been left ajar, and taking him by the hand drew him into the flat. 'I'm going to give you a brief tour first so you know where everything is, then a shower and so to bed.'

They were in a small passage containing four doors and, at the far end, a small window; opening the first door on the right she said, 'this is the lounge,' Peering in, Andrew noted a high ceilinged room of moderate size with pale pink emulsioned walls, very dark furniture and a set of French windows. 'They lead to the balcony,' she told him. Before leaving he noted a dove grey fitted carpet, a modern chandelier and an individual lamp set in each wall. Taking him on to the next door on the same side of the passage Julie showed him a compact but adequate kitchen fitted with every modern convenience; a table and four chairs stood in the centre and there was a single ample window over the sink. On the table two mugs, half full of brown liquid, as well as a bulky paper parcel tied up with string, stood.

'Come on,' she urged, and she opened the door opposite. 'This needs no explanation,' she observed as he surveyed an obvious toilet/ shower room. 'And now,' she announced grandly, 'for the most important room in the flat.' Opening the last door, which was back near the entrance, she ushered him into the bedroom, a room considerably smaller than the lounge but still bigger than the kitchen and bathroom combined. In the middle stood a very comfortable-looking double bed; the remainder of the furniture comprising a chest of drawers, dressing table and wardrobe although not matching in style, were all painted white against a darker pink wall colouring. A single lounge chair upholstered also in white, was positioned in each of the far corners, with two tall narrow windows between overlooking a street outside; completing the contents of the room was another fitted carpet, though red this time. 'Haven't you got any luggage?' Julie asked, suddenly aware of its absence.

Andrew shook his head and told her about leaving it aboard the vehicle transporter. 'I was in such a panic to see you, sweetheart,' he added; then adopting a serious tone, he continued, 'I've got some confessions to make.'

She held up a hand, 'I don't want to hear them yet; unless they affect your love for me?'

'No they don't,' he admitted, 'but I think you should listen.'

'You've come to me for comfort when you're so obviously upset, and that's all I care about at the moment. Now, that parcel on the kitchen table is for you, and so if you'd like to take it into the bathroom with you, you can take your shower and return here suitably adorned; but knock on the door before you enter, won't you?'

When he'd unwrapped the package Andrew found it contained a royal blue dressing gown and, as he began to try it on, a pair of similarly matching slippers fell to the floor; much to his surprise both garment and footwear were a perfect fit. Before he left the bathroom after he'd folded his outer clothing up and piled them on the conveniently sited chair, and thrown his underwear and socks into the laundry basket, he transferred his lover's gift and those of the sisters' to a pocket in the dressing gown. Julie invited him to enter as soon as he'd knocked, and he found her seated on the bed clad in a matching green dressing gown and slippers. 'One for regality and the other colour for naivety,' she joked after he'd hugged and kissed her in gratitude for her thoughtfulness. 'Now you can take my presents off and jump into bed while I get some whisky. That'll put you to sleep.'

Before he slid between the sheets Andrew pushed her present underneath one of the pillows, and shortly afterward his lover reappeared carrying a tumbler almost full to the brim; after taking a mouthful she handed over the glass as he sat up in bed. 'Drink it all up; but not too fast,' she added, 'neither of us wants you to have a coughing fit.' He'd been looking forward to seeing her body, but he was to be disappointed, for after taking the heavy tumbler from him she drew heavy curtains across the windows so plunging the room into deep gloom. 'No peeking,' she commanded as she disrobed and slipped into bed on his left hand side. With the warmth of the whisky seeming to permeate the length and breadth of his body, Andrew felt wonderfully content and satisfied as she gently eased herself into his arms. 'If you felt my body all over,' she murmured intimately in his ear, 'I'd scream… in my loudest whisper.'

He had no real need for Julie's quaintly worded invitation, for his hand was already moving in the direction of her breasts. 'Oh, my love, you feel beautiful,' he murmured after he'd turned partly over on his side the more easily to fondle her and as his palm gently grasped the soft plumpness, and his fingers traced the outline of her prominent nipples; she also murmured, but with pleasure, as he then pushed his hand further down her body until he reached the little bush of hair which indicated the proximity of her most intimate area, and she moaned in quiet passion as he probed further. 'Can't I?' he pleaded.

She was excruciatingly silent for a long time, then whispered, 'no, you must sleep, but first it's my turn to explore you. Oh, you poor man, all ready for action,' she teased, 'but you're just as I remember you.' For several more minutes she probed, pinched, pulled and tapped gently with her fingers all over his torso, an activity which Andrew, even in his increasing tiredness, found to be extremely arousing to the appropriate senses. 'You are hairy,' she exclaimed at last in delight, adding, 'lift up.' Her right hand trying to push its way beneath his neck provided him with the hint he needed, allowing her to cradle his head on her forearm. 'Put your hand down here; that's wonderful, now close your eyes and I'll sing to you.'

He cupped one of her breasts with his other hand and turned his head to kiss her gently on the mouth. 'Julie,' he breathed, now barely awake, 'there's only one thing more beautiful than your hair, face and body.'

'What's that?' she smiled.

'Your mind!' Softly she sang to him and stroked his hair until he fell into a deep slumber.

In the twilight of half sleep, much later, he seemed to hear knocking coming from the direction of the outside door, of his companion leaving their bed and the muffled sound of whispered conversation, then he lost consciousness once more. When he finally awoke he could feel his loved one's head resting on his chest and, by her regular breathing he knew she was asleep; longing to study this beautiful creature who obviously loved him dearly, he carefully eased himself from the bed without disturbing her and, guided by a thin strip of light he reached the curtains and noiselessly drew them back. Fortunately, the panes were covered by net curtains, otherwise his nudity from the knees up would've been only too evident to anyone passing by.

As quietly as possible he got back into bed where, after propping his head on an arm, he gazed down at the sleeping girl for a long time while full of admiration for the perfection of her face, and wondering at the golden red softness of her hair which his fingers now gently caressed. Lifting up a burnished lock he studied it then pressed it to his lips: he couldn't understand why this living work of art should not only be interested in him, but be content to be actually sleeping with him, should be loving him.

Unable to contain his curiosity any longer, he carefully pulled back the bedclothes until her breasts were revealed; just like everything else about her he'd so far seen they were beautifully faultless. Whenever a naked woman lay on her back, as he well knew, her breasts were rarely ever shapely, invariably becoming flattened, but even so it was obvious that his sweetheart's were going to be beyond criticism; they were milk white with only a few pale blemishes, and her nipples were small in diameter, but standing proud, shaped like miniature cones and of a delicate rose pink hue. He smiled to himself as he recalled her grotesque description of her bust and bent his head to kiss, with his tongue, each nipple in turn.

'People who don't say they love them, shouldn't be taking liberties with women's bodies,' Julie observed in an undertone. Before he could reply she went on, much to his surprise, 'I don't want to go to the toilet, do you?' Sitting up suddenly, like a child doing something naughty, he shook his head. 'How do you feel now?' she enquired with concern.

'Wide awake, but a little groggy,' he answered.

She sat up and smiled. 'Are you hungry yet?'

Quickly he replied, 'only for you.'

'So I noticed, but don't expect me to cook 'em,' she said dryly. 'Anyway, I suppose I'd better satisfy my newfound urchin. Open the top drawer of the smaller bedside cabinet and inside you'll find a tube.' He followed her instruction and handed her the item. 'Come up here where I can reach you,' she urged after squeezing the contents out onto her palm. 'You've got a one track mind,' she laughed as she spread the jelly on him, 'now climb aboard sailor, and do your duty.'

'But shouldn't I sort of... arouse you first?' he exclaimed, remembering the blue school demonstration.

'That won't be necessary on this voyage to exotic lands,' she muttered, even more amused, 'as you will shortly see.'

'Oh, Julie, I love you so much. You're so beautiful,' he whispered when at last he lay inside her.

But she stopped him with a kiss. 'You might not know it, but there's a science to this sort of thing. I've waited twenty two years to do this with someone I deeply love and I want this experience to last. Now, don't take any notice of what I do, but as soon as you begin to reach your peak stop dead. Pretend there's a venomous snake in the bed, and don't move; I know it'll be difficult for you, but if you do as I say then I can guarantee you an experience you'll

never forget. We call this compassing, by the way. Go on then.'
Beside himself with excitement and impatience Andrew began to
thrust into, and then out, of her body, but immediately Julie stopped
him again. 'Do you want to give us both pleasure?' she asked
gently.

'Of course I do, darling.'

'Well, press hard up against me and gyrate your pelvis instead,
and take your time. Keep kissing and talking to me, as I will with
you. Try it, it's so much nicer.'

Taking her advice he began again, thereby quickly realising that
until then he'd been a rank amateur when it came to physically
satisfying women; their lips met, mouths opened and their tongues
danced together, suddenly she tore her mouth from his. 'I love
you,' she urgently gasped in his ear, 'you're so handsome, so
strong.'

Taking her voice as a cue, he told her, 'You're so beautiful, so
soft, so kind, so warm. I need you so much.'

Alternately they kissed and whispered, their voices
intermingling, becoming more incoherent, but neither cared; then
Julie began to pant, then to moan and squeal until she finally
screamed in agony as though her lover had pierced her with a red
hot poker. 'Oh, thank you, sweetheart,' she exclaimed when she'd
calmed down, 'that was wonderful, but please don't stop.' Shortly
afterward though, in abeyance to her instructions, he was
compelled, very much against his own inclination, to finish. 'Keep
still,' she reminded him. After several minutes, still locked together
in intimate embrace with her legs entwined about his, she said, 'I
think it's safe now. Well, here comes the difficult bit for you as a
novice. I'm going to straighten my legs, and we've got to roll over
on our sides without coming apart, so to speak.'

With some difficulty this manoeuvre was finally accomplished.
'Now, that's more comfortable, you were beginning to get a bit
heavy, my darling Andy. But I'm ready to hear your confessions
now.'

With great difficulty, due to his desire to continue on to his
climax, he told her about his relationship with Helen including
every detail of their attempted lovemaking earlier that morning. He
couldn't understand why he was being so explicit, because he felt
sure he'd be putting his relationship with the girl he adored in
danger, but there was something about her which encouraged him

to be candid. 'I suppose you want me to get dressed and go now,' he finished miserably.

'On the contrary,' she replied, nibbling at his earlobe in order, he presumed, to reassure him, 'I'm full of admiration at your honesty. But I think you're a rotten bastard.'

'I wanted to make love to her just to comfort her,' he pleaded.

To his astonishment she retorted, 'when you had her on the bed you should have forced yourself into her if need be; it's cruel to arouse a female and then not satisfy her. You know, when you were asleep she came here; she must love you as much as I do to bring all your affects this far. As long as you came to me afterward I wouldn't have minded you consoling her; but it's too late now.'

'Did she say anything?' he asked, distressed by Helen's unselfish act of kindness.

'She asked me to take care of you, that's all. She wouldn't stay, though. If you've got any more confessions they can wait until the next stage.'

'Which is?'

'Just move in and out. There isn't much else you can do, but I'll let you enjoy the sensation without interfering too much. So off you go.'

'First kiss me, Julie, in my mouth.' With the length of their bodies, from head to feet, in mutual contact Andrew experienced some difficulty in moving the relevant part of his torso, but he soon discovered that his relative lack of freedom was no bar to pleasure for the resultant physical sensation was far more subtle than that obtained from the previous position. Simultaneous with his lover's tongue beginning to explore his mouth, her free hand began to caress, scratch and probe every part of his back within reach of her arm, and the subsequent feeling was so pleasurable that he began to have a vision.

He was riding through a dense forest, he couldn't see the horse he was seated upon, he only knew he was riding and leaves and twigs were scratching at his back, he only knew he was riding; at length he came to a village, an ancient village, people were there, staring at him and waving, he wanted to ride on, but he daren't, he mustn't. He stopped moving. But Julie continued to kiss and caress him for a considerable amount of time afterward. 'Thank you, darling,' he announced when she'd removed her mouth from his, 'that was fantastic.' And he told her about his vision.

'What a coincidence!' she giggled, 'I'm about to ride you and I hope to be staying on till the end. Anyway, have you got anything else to tell me?'

When he'd finished explaining about her namesake and husband on the mainland she was obviously upset. 'What's wrong, sweetheart?' he asked.

'Oh, Andrew, can't you see how cruel your society is in forcing women into prostitution, and so make it necessary for husbands to endorse it? That girl might easily have been me or any other island woman. Stories like that make me overjoyed our government is so intelligent; fancy allowing adults to have as many babies as they wish and then not foreseeing one day there might not have enough jobs available. Or don't you think they cared? But you shouldn't have hit her husband.'

Stroking her face and hair, he answered, 'I know I shouldn't have, now; but I was so angry when he pushed me. I felt really frustrated and disappointed, I wanted you like mad at that moment. Aren't you angry at me, though, for desiring another woman?'

She shook her head. 'I love you even more now for being so frank, but really the fault was mine for sending you away. I couldn't sleep for worrying about, and needing, you on Wednesday and last night. But you must promise me never to lust after another woman because that'll mean you don't want me anymore.' She suddenly began to giggle, the tremors being transmitted throughout Andrew's body, but most effectively into his still erect member, which somehow seemed to make their intimacy even more personal than actual intercourse. 'You poor thing,' she exclaimed at last, 'what an opportunity you've missed; I could've been your third conquest in two days!'

But her lover, as gallant as ever, immediately replied, 'all I want is you, I don't care about anyone else, and our being locked in love and passion only increases that wish.'

When Julie had suitably rewarded him for his outstanding statement, she said, 'time to make the next move, and in a moment you'll see me in all my glory. It's quite difficult, especially this part.' Once more they changed position, until she was lying on top of him, then slowly and cautiously she raised herself up until she was kneeling astride him. 'Do you like me now?' she prompted as he gazed up at her.

'You're everything I didn't dare dream about,' he exclaimed in admiration, 'such a gorgeous pair of breasts I never saw before.'

'And I bet you've seen plenty, you rogue. Take hold of them, then,' she urged.

'But I want to look at them for eternity and a day.'

Julie took his hands and placed one over each of her perfectly shaped breasts, 'so you shall, my darling, but later. Don't forget to tell me when to stop, will you?' After grasping hold of each of his wrists she then began to move her hips.

Andrew found the feeling indescribable, for not only was he enjoying the pleasure her movements imparted to him, but he could also fondle her breasts and study her face. For most of the time she kept her eyes closed, but when she opened them she invariably gazed down at him and smiled. He watched her closely, waiting for the first signs of an approaching climax, and when it finally came he immediately transferred his hands from her breasts to her shoulders then pulled her down on top of him as she shrieked in surprise; roughly he rolled her over and, still connected to and facing her, he pushed himself up onto his arms and did rapid press ups above her. Fortunately, for his position was rather uncomfortable, he soon reached a climax after which he fell onto her like a bird shot from the sky. There, after a short period of recovery, he began to whisper over and over again that he loved her and to kiss her passionately both on the lips and orally.

'Thank you, sweetheart,' she breathed, when at last they lay still. 'I'll award you a million out of a million for that, minus one for bad behaviour. You frightened the life out of me, it was so unexpected.'

'I'm sorry darling, but I couldn't stand the suspense anymore; I just wanted to finish, and you can take that as a compliment.'

'It's a pity, really, I think you would've enjoyed going west.' Andrew, baffled, frowned. 'North, south, east and west,' she explained, 'that's why that particular ride is called compassing.' Close to exhaustion they lay locked together in silence for a while, eventually Julie voiced a thought, 'I wonder how much you love me; would you want to do all the sensual things with me it's possible for women and men to do together.'

He chuckled. 'Until I was confronted by them I really couldn't say.' Whilst he'd been lying there he'd begun thinking he still didn't really know what he had to offer her that Whyte Island men couldn't supply; but if he questioned her too closely he ran the risk of getting another slap round the face, or far worse. Suddenly he thought up a ruse; she'd questioned the extent of his love for her, so he'd question hers. 'But how much do you love me?' he emphasised.

'More than anything,' she replied with great conviction.

'Enough to let me tie you up?'

For a moment she remained silent, staring up at him with an expressionless face; at last she answered. 'If you tell me what on earth you want to do it for then I might let you.' Andrew began to redden with embarrassment as she waited patiently for his explanation, for he realised he had only the truth to reveal, and that wouldn't do at all. But suddenly she came to his rescue, because she gently pushed him off her and then sat up. 'I know,' she exclaimed enthusiastically, 'we'll get dressed, have some lunch, you can then go out and pretend to be a sex maniac. Then you can rape me.'

Astonished by this suggestion, he could only stammer, 'But I don't want to hurt you.'

Giggling, she replied, 'don't be silly, darling, you won't hurt me. It'll be fun.'

He shook his head. 'I only wanted to tie your hands.'

With much amusement she told him where he kept her stockings, but when he began to tie her hands in front of her she giggled again, turned over on her face and crossed her hands behind her. 'If you're going to do something, do it properly. Only a rank amateur would tie a person's hands in front of them.' When he'd got back into bed again and had helped her to turn over, she asked, 'is that it? No legs, no mouth?'

'I don't know what you expected me to do, but I'm afraid I've deceived you. I want to ask you about your boyfriends.'

Instantly Julie's expression changed. 'You can just untie me, get dressed and clear off,' she wailed, 'I knew I shouldn't have trusted a mainlander.'

Tears of anger and frustration sprang into her eyes, but Andrew pulled her to him and held her tight. 'Listen, my love,' he whispered with compassion and running a hand through her auburn tresses, 'I want to be consoled, that's all. I want to be assured I'm not really a nine days wonder, that you won't tire of me. And I can't understand why your previous lovers were stupid enough to let you go.' He slid his hand down her back and clutched one of her bound hands. 'You're so beautiful and perfect in every way. I love you so very, very much, darling and I know I always will. I just couldn't live without you. But please put me out of my misery and tell me what you see in me.'

Greatly appeased by these words Julie smiled through her tears; without realising Andrew had uttered the kind of phrases she longed to hear, for almost every woman yearns to be loved, needed and admired. 'My poor sweetheart,' she exclaimed, love, almost akin to that of a mother for her first child, welling up inside her, 'you really are insecure. I've already told you that I can't explain why I love you; I just do. And I don't think I'll tire of you because, believe me, it's out of character; I'm not a frivolous person in that way. But I can easily explain about my previous boyfriends: they weren't up to scratch; like most Whyte Island girls I choose who I want to share my life with, and unless I really love a man I'm not prepared to consider him. I know I love you because I can't get you out of my mind, and I was trembling like a kitten while I was waiting for you to show up.

'But I think you're taking our affair a little too seriously at the moment because we might very well prove to be incompatible, and we'll need to prepare for that possibility. However, you must get one thing straight; you'll never know who my former boyfriends were and I shall never discuss them with you and that's going to be a rule in our relationship. So either forget them or forget me!' she paused for effect, then said, 'now, will you help me to sit up?' When he'd done so she went on, 'you can tie and gag me if you want to play a game, or else release me and let me get on with lunch.'

This strange offer furnished him with another plan. 'Alright,' he said, 'if you really don't mind then I will.'

'When you do my mouth,' she advised, 'if you want to be authentic push a rolled up stocking half way down another, or else tie a knot in the middle.'

'You seem to know a lot about it,' he observed as he made a knot.

'I've had some practice,' she answered mysteriously.

'Right,' he exclaimed, 'now bend your head forward so I don't catch your hair, close your eyes and open your mouth.' As soon as she'd done so he dropped the stocking, rummaged beneath the appropriate pillow, opened the lid of the jewellery box and clipped the necklace about his lover's neck. Instantly she opened her eyes, and much to his surprise her hands appeared from around her back and began to finger the item of jewellery. With a squeal of delight she leapt from the bed and ran over to the wardrobe where she examined herself in the full-length mirror on the inside of the door.

'Oh, darling, it's beautiful,' she cried with joy. But Andrew was thinking the same thing about her long, shapely legs and the profile of her breasts.

'That isn't all,' he told her, and leaving the bed he came across to her and clipped on the earrings.

'Oh, thank you,' she breathed, and turning round she hugged and kissed him in a delirium of passion and gratitude. When, eventually, their mouths finally parted Julie said, 'as a token of my appreciation for all you've given me since you came, or even before that, there's a lovely little game I want to show you; it won't take long and we'll then dine.'

Taking him by the hand she led him back to the bed where, after seating herself down on the edge, she positioned him before her with his back toward her; before he had time to consider her next move she had his hands behind him and was tying them together. 'It's only fair, sweetheart,' she explained in a reasoning tone, 'you did it to me; besides, I won't hurt you and it's only a little fun.'

Having finished her task she stood up and faced him. 'You won't get out of that in a hurry,' she taunted, 'what's it feel like being at the mercy of a naked woman?' He felt one of her hands touch an appropriate part of him, and she laughed, 'I don't need a verbal reply to that question, obviously. Now, did you bring those contraceptives with you?' When he told her where they were she kissed him with an ardour which generated great indignation within him, though he couldn't understand quite why. Upon telling him not to move she went to fetch the items she'd enquired for, but from the doorway she glanced back at him and smiled, 'There's many a raped woman who'd love to be where I am now.'

Andrew, feeling ridiculous, a little angry and somewhat uneasy about what might happen when she returned, attempted to free himself while she was away, but finding it impossible he only became more irritated. But she was soon back and, after kneeling before him and fitting one of the condoms, she stood up and roughly pushed him backward; he staggered until the backs of his legs came into contact with the bed and then he fell backward onto the bedspread. Julie then went for a stocking and bound his ankles. By the time he'd raised himself into a sitting position she was over by the chest of drawers pulling on a black skirt. 'You're not going to leave me like this are you?' he called over with genuine concern.

She paused in zipping the garment up and stared at him. 'I'm certainly not!' she replied indignantly, and coming across to him she picked up the unused gag, stuffed it into his mouth and secured it at the nape of his neck. 'But it is an idea,' she teased gazing down at him with satisfaction, 'or I could stay and torture you. So I'd cause no trouble if I were you and just lie there like a helpless little babe.' In silent fascination he watched her putting on a white brassiere and matching blouse then, after tying her hair back in a ponytail, she turned and faced him. 'The perfect mainland secretary,' she announced, opening her arms wide and pirouetting slowly, 'skirt, blouse, bra and no knickers.' And with that observation she left the room, and subsequently Andrew could hear her presumably readying a meal in the kitchen, leaving him with the problem of what might happen next.

There was absolutely no point in his attempting to free himself as he'd already satisfied himself that he was at her mercy, and now even the option of calling for help was denied him, so all he could do was follow her advice, lie still and await her will in as comfortable position as he could find. After far too long a period she re-entered the bedroom with a large towel over one arm and carrying a tray of food. 'Move over and rest your back against the headboard,' she commanded without ceremony, 'it's din-din time!'

'Perhaps you'd like to explain what you're playing at,' he enquired without humour when she'd given him the ability to speak after spreading the towel on the bed and the tray upon it.

'You're still my prisoner,' Julie reminded him, 'and I can still re-gag you. So kindly cooperate, otherwise...' She pinched his noise until he had to breathe through his mouth, 'see? So speak when you're asked to.' She then sat on the bed in a similar position to him on his right and fed him with chips and sausages which she alternately fed to herself and saying, "one for mummy',' "one for daddy',' "another little chippy, baby?" and other similar puerile terms until they'd consumed all the food before them and washed it down with lukewarm tea. Before removing their lunch things she re-gagged him by the method she'd threatened, and left to attend to the domestic chores, leaving him to ponder on what next awaited him.

When at last she returned she called from the doorway, 'pudding time, little one,' but she had nothing with her and instead collected cushions from the bedroom armchairs which she strewed on the bed when she reached it. There then followed a lot of manoeuvring as she positioned him on the bed to her satisfaction, saying nothing to him in the process but humming away quietly as she did so; the result was that he found himself in a prone attitude, his head upon a pile of cushions on her lap as she sat with her back to the headboard, legs straight out in front of her.

'You're my beautiful little baby, and babies don't talk do they? ''Cos mummies get angry when they do, don't they?' she whispered in an extremely patronising fashion, and began removing one of her breasts from out of its bra cup until it was pressed against his face. 'So don't annoy mummy, otherwise she'll leave you like you are all night, and it's scarcely four p.m. now.' With that quaint threat, she removed his gag and, as his lips had nowhere else to go but against her nipple for she held his head tightly against her breast, he had no alternative but to take it into his mouth. 'Go on,' she coaxed, 'test your imagination, see how many ways you can please me, as I'm about to please you.'

Such an experience was totally beyond any of his previous sexual encounters, as it would no doubt be for most of the other human males on the planet; for many different emotions began to spread through his mind trying, it seemed, to compete against one another to be foremost in his thoughts. Should he be angry because he was being forced against his will to do something so bizarre; should he be happy because a gorgeous girl wanted him to arouse her; should he feel humiliated because she'd made a helpless slave of him, had overpowered him, because she'd degraded his masculinity; ought he to hate, or adore her? These, and an innumerable number of fancies, formed a cocktail of emotions in his mind which were both satisfying and frightening. But most powerful of these combined feelings was the fact that they were an entirely a new experience which couldn't be understood or calculated against; like the emotions of person left tied to a stake by natives in a totally hostile environment and with no hope of help. No one could understand how they'd feel unless it happened to them. But at least, Andrew thought, my predicament is pleasurable and all is not lost.

So he began suckling her, using his tongue to tease her nipple, biting it gently just short of causing pain, rubbing his nose against that part of her breast available and sucking at it to test how much he could draw into his mouth, and his mind was concentrating on other ways of using his initiative when he felt a fresh sensation. Her hand was clutching his sheath and beginning to manipulate its content. "No, no", he wanted to shout out, 'that well's empty, it'll distress me if you try to draw from it!' But with her other hand pressing his head hard against her bosom, allowing only enough space for his nostrils to take in air, it was impossible to communicate with her and so he was powerless to prevent the exquisite torture she was causing him. Sucking at her breast and having to endure her impossible expectation of him seemed to last an eternity, but finally she stopped her mild exertions and loosened her hold on the back of his head.

If he'd hoped his ultra-sensual ordeal was over, then he was sadly disappointed, for Julie was still in playful mood by her standards, and so when he cried out, 'you bitch, that was beyond bearing!,' she gave him a weak slap on his head and replaced his gag.

'You naughty little baby, mummy said don't talk. Now I have to punish you.' Immediately she pushed his body off her lap and crawled over him to the other side of the bed; there she pushed, dragged and pulled him until they were positioned in exactly the opposite position to where they were before. On this occasion she brought forth her left breast thereby allowing her brassiere to hang uselessly beneath her bosom; once again she quickly removed his gag and forced his lips against her nipple which he was compelled to take into his mouth for want of an alternative occupation.

But much to his relief she ignored his penis as such and instead turned her attention to the surrounding area by exploring it with her finger tips, moving them relentlessly and rapidly as if in desperate search of something. They never stayed in one place long but were not averse to returning repeatedly until the entire sensation became extremely pleasing to him but with much less stress; this time he wanted the experience to go on for ever and somehow he must have communicated his pleasure through her breast because she began whispering to him in a loving fashion.

By the time she'd allowed his head to become disengaged from her breast he was in a much better temper, and even when she'd manhandled him off her and positioned him lengthwise in the bed with the bed clothes covering his torso, he felt little indignation. But it was only after she'd put a on a c.d. of soothing classical music, removed her clothing and climbed into bed alongside him that she deigned to remove his gag, but still left him bound.

'So what do you think?' she asked in an innocent voice, as though nothing in particular had occurred.

'Well, I thought you'd gone insane and I assumed you were attempting to make me the same,' he replied with as much indignation as he could summon, 'I feel like marching out of this flat and never coming back!'

'Don't you mean hop?' she giggled after resuming her exploration of his nether regions, 'you're hardly in a position to hurry anywhere. Never mind, you'll be able to take your revenge some time this weekend; I'm looking forward to being raped, and I expect to be shown as much mercy as I've just shown you.' Then she began exploring his ear with her tongue and nibbling at the lobe, adding further to the distraction she was already causing him.

'I'm beginning to think you're deranged,' he observed.

'Well what's wrong with that? But I'm different, though, because I know when to stop.' Upon his frowning, she went on hastily, 'I can see I'll need to explain what I'm doing; I've won the battle to get you into my bed but the campaign must continue to keep you there. I may have gorgeous hair and a beautiful body as you claim, and I might have a lovely temperament but I must take care, as every woman ought, not to let my attributes be taken for granted by my lover. You might not believe it now, darling, but unless I can keep you entertained then one day our mutual love might sour and one of us might begin to look elsewhere for company. If you like, you could say I was showing off my talents to you; I want you to realise that there's more in me than just being a perfect effigy and that I'm never going to be a "ho hum" kind of partner who thinks, "oh dear, he wants another screw, better put up with it and let him have it'.' When you want it, then my goodness, I'm always going to ensure we're both going to enjoy it!'

She ended her explanation by leaning over and giving him a passionate kiss and adding to its ardour by using her active hand in squeezing his scrotum. 'I also want you to learn,' she stated after removing her mouth from his, 'that no parts of our bodies are off limits to the other, so that we can soon consider ourselves as halves of one whole, I'd like us to have no secrets from each other from now on and no false modesty. There's only one rule I'd like us both to agree on and that's when the bathroom is occupied for any other reason than having a shower then it's banned to the other lover; there has to be some privacy for the sake of propriety and a constant air of mystery. If we agree on the points I've made then we'll soon always be lovers, friends and inseparable companions to each other with not a trace of self-consciousness between us. Do you agree?'

'After the way you've been treating me,' Andrew answered ruefully. 'I'd be better advised to return to Helen, but I suppose I might as well stick around and see how we get on. Is there any chance of your untying me?'

Julie smiled, rolled him over on his side to pull him against her and fiddle with the knots on his wrists, but she was just teasing him. 'None at all, I'm afraid. I prefer you like that, I find it exceptionally exciting, and you've got a lovely bottom.' During her digital exploration of his back she enquired, 'did you have anything more to tell me about your mainland horrors?'

Despite the distractions her fingers were now creating to his lower spine, he managed to tell her about his family's indifference toward him and of his mother's complaints regarding their new neighbours. 'Goodness,' she cried in astonishment, 'don't mainlanders know how to communicate? It was extremely rude of those neighbours not to tell your mother what was annoying them with regard to your family and I don't blame her for being upset; it would be like being tried and condemned in one's absence.'

'The only trouble is sweetheart,' he answered, still disturbed by her questing touch which was now concentrating on his upper back, 'that it seems an unwritten law on the mainland that you don't complain; it often aggravates the problem.'

'Well, it seems ridiculous to me. How on earth can you be friendly with your neighbours if you have no idea what's troubling them? As for your family's lack of interest in you: that really is sad. As you probably noticed during your school tours, a lot of care is taken in teaching us how to socialise adequately with each other, and people are much nicer if they know others are interested in them.'

'Unfortunately,' Andrew pointed out, 'many people in my country are so self-centered that if you do show an interest in them they very rarely reciprocate.'

'That just goes to prove your education policy must be more than a little inept.'

'I'm really enjoying what you're doing, sweet Julie, but I expect you've noticed I'm starting to knock on your door, and I've nothing left to deliver.'

'I'm well aware of both your observations,' she replied and pushed him over onto his back again. 'Lift up your head.' When he complied she pushed an arm beneath his neck and together they lay side by side.

'If you knew I was dry, why did you continue trying to make me climax and what was the reason for the sheath?' he asked with some reproach in his tone.

'Because my darling sweetheart, I was trying to create as many sensations as I could for you, to transport you to the realms of a fantasy world; I know very well from the appropriate school lessons that once a man's seeds have been expelled it takes a while for them to be replaced, and also that to continue to, let's say, milk him for more produces a rather erotic but uncomfortable affect that, together with the other emotions I was subjecting you to, gave you, I hope, a very pleasing and bizarre ride. As for the contraceptive, well, I turned it inside out so the lubricated coating would prevent your skin chafing. I wanted to send you as close to the verge of discomfort as possible without causing you pain. I definitely knew what I was doing.

'Now, is that everything you have to tell me about your mainland trip?'

'I have, but it made Helen cry, so I don't suppose you'd want to hear it?'

'Try me; because I'd like to know what you said to upset her.' So he told her about the toddler and her mother in the park, and of how its description caused Helen such anguish. 'I can understand the woman being concerned for her child and she could have been more discreet about her feelings,' Julie said, 'but treating you and her daughter in the way she did was unforgivable. There's definitely something wrong with the way they bring up their youngsters, and they've got no idea on how to produce a caring, friendly society. As for poor Helen, like she said she had no idea you were so sensitive and I'm sorry she's missed her chance, but if she hadn't I would've lost my darling Andy.' And she briefly pulled at his far shoulder in emphasis.

They lay together contentedly in silence for some time, apart from his occasional requests to be freed, listening to the music until the disc came to an end. Julie then got out of bed and untied his feet without explanation except to state it was time for a shower. Standing beside her while she tested the warmth of the water, still as naked as she was but with his wrists still fastened behind him was more than a unique experience to him, especially as he would be a helpless participant in whatever she was planning.

As soon as she was satisfied she entered the shower and helped him to follow, whereupon after allowing them both a good soaking, she shut off the water and began soaping him down by using her hands in a manner which ensured she visited every part of his body with the exception of the soles of his feet. Taking some shampoo from a convenient shelf she then washed his hair and afterward rinsed him down with fresh water. Meanwhile Andrew couldn't stop gazing at her beautiful face and body with her hair plastering her head, face, shoulders and the upper parts of her breasts, arms and back.

Her glistening skin made her appear extra sleek and slender, and so she seemed to be a sea sprite or water nymph escaped from some allegorical painting of times past. Every movement she made presented him with a new erotic pose which was guaranteed to engender rising passion within him so that Julie, having stooped to wash some remaining suds from one of his legs, naturally noticed the evidence of his discomfort and, having rolled the sheath off, she knelt down and pleased him while simultaneously picking at the stocking which bound him.

'Do exactly the same to me,' she urged later, standing with her back to him and her wrists crossed behind her, 'and this time don't let me free myself.' So he did what she urged and enjoyed every extended minute of it including doing that which he'd never done before and, because he was beginning to recognise his new lover was the only female he ever wanted, he did his very best to ensure her maximum gratification. As soon as he stood up he pulled her roughly against him and kissed her with his mouth open and was overjoyed when she immediately responded so that their tongues entwined in a real lover's embrace.

After he'd dried them both thoroughly he took her by an arm and guided her toward their bed where he sat her down, hunted around for the gag and tied it in her mouth then he knelt at her feet and bound her ankles together. Standing her up again, he peeled back the bed clothes, helped her lie down and covered her over; before joining her he crossed to the drawn curtains and pulled them back to allow the now fading daylight to enter.

She had her back to him when he joined her, so he cuddled up to her with the full intention of merely enjoying her warmth and proximity, of pondering on the great good fortune which had led to his path in life meeting hers and, hopefully to continue as one until a far off time took one of them into eternity to be joined, eventually, by the other. But then, hadn't she averred they'd be as one, that nothing they could do physically together could be considered off limits? He didn't wish to disturb her for she was lying peacefully and, as he was in a position to please her, he hoped, he manoeuvred himself and pushed into her. Since leaving the bathroom she'd astonishingly made not a sound of complaint but had remained perfectly agreeable to everything he wished, but now she began to object, though she soon became as quiet as before when he did nothing further, but merely lay still with his arms about her.

Recalling Linda's advice he began whispering in her ear about how much he loved her, complimenting her on her looks especially specific areas, and how much he enjoyed being inside her and of how sweet, kind, gentle and adorable she was. That he never wanted to be with anyone else ever again and that he hoped years of loving companionship together lay before them. For her sake he tested his power of initiative into thinking of as many compliments, and other niceties, as he could in as truly a heartfelt tone as he was able to muster. Meanwhile, he fondled, tweaked, probed, explored and squeezed as much of her body and face available to him, for which he was rewarded with many quiet moans of pleasure emitting from her stifled mouth. Only once, when he was overly attentive to a certain area of her lower region by rubbing it too much, did she protest by urgent grunting, until he desisted.

Andrew meant to release his sweetheart as soon he'd finished pleasing her; but as he was fondling one of her breasts, with his face nuzzling into her hair, he fell asleep and he only awoke when the room was lit by early morning daylight streaming through the windows. His first thoughts were for his lover for she'd accidentally been gagged and bound for hours on end and she might well have suffocated, but she was still warm and he could clearly hear her steady, relaxed breathing. Nevertheless, he quickly removed her gag in something of a panic; though he freed her hands at a more leisurely pace for he had made his knots over tight. He had to leave the bed to untie her feet and, having done so, he went to inspect her. She was still sleeping peacefully so he continued to the kitchen where, after some searching, he found all he needed to make two cups of coffee with some biscuits, placed them on a tray and put them down on the convenient table by her head.

'Wake up, sweetheart,' he quietly called as he gently shook her from his kneeling position beside her, 'I've made some coffee.'

To his relief she immediately opened her eyes and smiled at him. 'Gosh,' she exclaimed, 'I'm as stiff as a board and my mouth is so dry. Don't tell me I've been tied up all night, and gagged!'

He was all contrition. 'I'm sorry, darling; one minute I was amusing us, and the next thing it was morning; it was so sudden I was still inside you, though it was a rather timid thing when, with difficulty, I removed it. I hope I didn't offend or hurt you because you seemed to be trying to say something.'

By now she'd managed, with some difficulty and silent facial expressions of pain and discomfort, to sit up in bed and had had a sip of coffee and was now waving a half-eaten biscuit about in dismissal, 'Oh, that,' she emphasised contemptuously, 'that was nothing; it's entirely legitimate, couldn't be anything else unless the authorities were willing to climb into every couple's bed! No, I was fussing because you weren't protected; there are lots of nasty germs in there and I didn't want my only true sweetheart catching some disease or other. Also, without lubrication, you could have made us both extremely sore and, finally, what goes up must come down and I didn't want you making a mess of the bedclothes. But, in the event, the last two objections weren't valid as you didn't do anything. So, darling, you can go in there as often as you like, but from now on do use protection!' She moved over sideways and patted the vacant space beside her. 'Sit beside me, love, then we can have the tray on our laps.'

He was only too happy to comply where, after transferring the tray, he stroked her hair, kissed her lips, tweaked each nipple and pushed his hand beneath the bedclothes. 'I can't believe all this beauty is mine to share,' he murmured, lovingly.

'And I can't believe all this is mine.' She aped him in words and action. 'But if you think I'm about to turn over so you can complete your list with this tray on my lap, then you can think again.'

'I do hope you didn't stay awake for too long after I slept,' he mused after he'd drunk some coffee and eaten a biscuit.

'I did actually,' she replied, 'for about an hour or so.'

He was shocked. 'Weren't you uncomfortable? I'm so sorry, I really didn't mean it!'

'Tit for tat,' she shrugged dismissively, 'after all I left you trussed up for quite a while, and you were awake all the time. But yes, I wasn't too comfortable, and pins and needles in my hands were a bit of a problem, but I daren't move because you were still inside me and I had no wish to harm you. But it was a nice sensation, thank you, and I could still feel you long after you'd deflated.' She turned her head and gazed into his eyes. 'You shouldn't worry too much about female discomfort, Andy – we've evolved to endure much more physical pain than men. In the days before any type of anaesthetics, I think you'll find far more women died giving birth through lack of hygiene than due to pain. I'll metaphorically bet I can withstand you lying on top of me, even though you're heavier than me, than vice-versa.

'Actually, darling, I rather enjoy being rendered helpless as long as I have complete faith in the person whose placed me in that state; it must be something really primitive within me, like the natural wiles of women helping them to live alongside their more powerful, aggressive fellow males. The drawback in our relationship, at least, is that whenever you bind and gag me, or do something similarly erotic, you won't be able to do it again until I've done it, in one way or another, back to you. That way it'll be fair and will act as a governor against such games getting out of hand or occurring too often; it's also illegal to leave helpless partners alone for too long which, technically, you've just done to me, and especially without checking they can breathe sufficiently or are in any way liable to permanent injury.' She shrugged. 'It's all just a case of common sense, that's all.'

Andrew observed enthusiastically, 'in that case, sweetheart, I'll look forward to our relationship even more, if that's at all possible, because I must confess I enjoyed being your captive only a little less than your being mine, because you are a slave girl after all, and

I love and adore you so much that I'm only too willing to obey any of your and the island's rules to the letter. You know I'd never really hurt you in mind, body or spirit if I can help it; I always want to please you!' She put her arms about his neck and bent her head to kiss him passionately as soon as she heard his later words; and there were tears in her eyes when he removed the tray from their laps. 'Don't forget your brother's coming some time today and, as it's just gone five, we might be lucky and get a little more sleep,' he advised, 'but I'm dreading seeing Jeremy again after all I've been doing to his only sibling.'

Julie began giggling as he slid down into the bed as far as the bottom of her breasts. 'So what beverage are we having this fine and sunny morning, sir, mild or bitter?' Andrew, now thoroughly acclimatised to his lover's sense of humour, chose the latter to which she replied, 'in that case, sir will need to enter the bar entirely and climb over the barmaid,' at which she rolled over onto her left side and stacked a pair of pillows against her right breast. Knowing by now what was expected of him, he lay down on her left side with his head level with her right nipple and began sucking at it.

After about five minutes he raised his head to peer up at her and called out indignantly, 'barmaid, this pump's dry!'

'Oh sir,' Julie answered, 'it's been like that for some time, try twiddling the knob.'

'And, pray what does that do?'

'It turns me on; go on,' she urged in a normal voice. Taking her as being serious he took her nipple between the fingers of his left hand and turned it back and forth with the occasional slight tug for good measure; the effects of his effort were not long in coming for she began to sigh and shudder until she said in a hoarse voice, 'You'd better stop now, I'm becoming aroused now and, as you say, we'd better be fairly bright by morning.'

Removing the pillows from under his head, he wriggled upward until they lay side by side on their backs with their arms about each other. 'Jeremy will no doubt be bringing his girlfriend with him,' Julie announced, 'but you needn't be embarrassed, lovers often pass sensual games about from one couple to another, and my brother and Natalie have had some of mine and I've had some of theirs. So just bear that in mind when they call and you'll be perfectly relaxed; just don't say anything at all about all we've been doing since you arrived. No one, by the way, cares about what happens between lovers in private on Whyte Island, the mere fact that each set of lovers continues to live with each other is taken as proof that all's well between them. It's so easy for us, for instance, to break up and quickly find new partners whether temporary or permanent, that neither of us has to put up with the other if we no longer like their ways. That's why I want our relationship to work, as I hope you do.

'Anyway,' she said, changing the subject, 'Now our bodies have been thoroughly introduced, don't you think we ought to examine the contents of each other's minds, our preferences, what hobbies we fancy, et cetera, which, I hope, we can come to agreement on if they are too opposed to that which one of us likes or dislikes. What, from my viewpoint, life was like for you in the Whyte Line? You can even tell me about the girls they laid on for you if you wish, because I'm not envious of your past.'

So, completely relaxed and contented, primed by his wonderful lover's calming and physical presence and the intimate atmosphere which the room seemed to create, he quietly described everything he thought pertinent about himself; and when he'd finished she told him about her family, childhood, employment and many other similar details. And so, within half an hour or so, each knew more about the other than many mainland couples knew within the course of a lifetime living together. But without either being aware of the fact, during their conversation they were gradually becoming ever more weary until they finally fell asleep in close embrace within minutes of each other.

Andrew was awoken in the morning by the sound of water splashing on the pavement beneath the window; getting out of the bed as quietly as possible, he drew back the net curtains and surveyed the scene outside, the sky was a leaden colour and continuous heavy rain was falling. Climbing back into bed after checking it was still too early to contemplate getting up, he was quite pleased at the bad weather because he hoped it would mean the cancellation of her brother and his girlfriend's visit. He no longer had any real misgivings about meeting them after his lover's explanation, but it was just that he wanted: to have the beauty whose bed he shared all to himself a little longer. As he cuddled up to her she muttered something and altered position toward him; gazing at her with love overflowing inside him, he wondered if he could ever fail to appreciate her and decided that it would be impossible.

'Oh dear,' Julie said when, much later, she awoke and became aware of the rain. 'This afternoon I was hoping to be able to hire a couple of bikes and visit my parents because it's such a lovely ride, but it looks as if we'll have to go by train instead. She turned and smiled at him. 'Meanwhile, I suppose you're patiently waiting for the premises to open up again; well, hand me an apple so we can sweeten our breath.'

Later, after they'd showered together, and Julie had unpacked his cases in search of a change of underwear and fresh socks, he cooked breakfast and she put all his clothing and other gear away in the appropriate places. 'It seems incredible, darling,' he mused during breakfast, which she'd had the graciousness to compliment him on, 'that I saw you for the first time only exactly ten days ago, and only really met you a mere three days since, yet I feel as if I've known you all my life.'

Julie sipped some coffee and then smiled. 'That's because we haven't wasted time on all this courtship business and, of course you know my body intimately now.' She then added, as if she were asking him the time, 'so, are you coming to live with me?'

'Don't be silly sweetheart!' he exploded, 'of course I am; if you'll have me.'

'You don't think I'm a dirty bitch then?'

'I'd much rather have a dirty bitch, if that's what you are,' he replied with a grin, 'than a clean prude, just as most people would prefer a merry devil to a staid saint.'

His lover smiled with obvious relief, 'I thought you might say that somehow. Well, if you're definitely going to move in you'd better phone Mr Maynard and tell him. In the meantime I'll make a start on the breakfast things.'

Andrew was fortunate enough to catch Charlie who, with Julie's connivance, suggested they both call in on the morrow to discuss arrangements for the move. 'Could I speak to Helen for a moment?' he eventually asked. When she answered he said, 'I want to thank you very much for bringing my stuff over personally. 'Look,' he continued, 'I don't know what to say, except I'm sorry for the way things have turned out .'

There was a pause, then she asked, 'are you happy?'

'Yes. Very.'

'Well, that's all that matters, isn't it?' she answered without a trace of bitterness.

Andrew replied, 'I think I ought to warn you that we'll both be coming over tomorrow because Julie's asked me to move in with her.'

To his surprise, Helen said with extreme enthusiasm, 'oh, Andrew, I am pleased for you, and don't worry about your visit because I won't make a scene. I'll have the remainder of your stuff already packed for you if you wish.' And she rang off.

'You women are all mad,' he exclaimed as he walked into the kitchen.

Julie, poised in the act of putting a plate away, smiled in surprise. 'What have we done now?'

But he just shook his head in dismay and observed, 'I don't understand you, that's all.'

Natalie, when she arrived an hour or so later with Julie's brother, was a black haired girl with a straight fringe across her forehead and greenish eyes, all of which gave her a rather solemn, sinister appearance; in fact, though, she was a cheerful, friendly person with an ironic sense of humour that Andrew quickly warmed to. 'It's a pity it's such a bad day,' Jeremy commented when he'd draw up an armchair and pulled his lover onto his lap, 'we might perhaps have made a day of it and gone somewhere that might've interested Andrew.' He took a swig from his bottle of beer, one of which Julie had handed round to each of them.

But Natalie said, 'Don't be so ridiculous, you idiot.' She winked across at Andrew who, following her brother's example, had Julie on his lap. 'They don't want us with them all today, not on their first day together. Maybe, but only if they're willing, we'll have plenty of time to go out as a foursome in the future.'

Taking a gulp of her beer, Julie remarked, 'yes, that'd be alright occasionally as we do share some of the same interests, but that'll be if we're all in favour. Though for the moment, Andrew and I do want to get to know each other a bit better.'

Over the next few hours they played cards, during the course of which Andrew discovered much more about each of his companions than mere cross conversation could reveal; for the inevitable banter, mock accusations, false boastings and complaints brought out a hint of the true personalities of each of the participants. Inevitably, Jeremy was the most belligerent and had more to say than the rest of them, while his girlfriend made subtle fun of him with endless criticisms which engendered admiration for her from Andrew at the skilful way she walked the line between going too far and not far enough. Julie, however, merely gently chided her brother, while her lover took a neutral's part in playing as well as he could, though not with the astuteness of his companions, and just enjoying the amusing activity he was witnessing.

'So how do you like it over here?' Natalie asked him when they'd tired of cards, and Julie had made them all coffee and sandwiches.

'It's out of this world but still in it,' Andrew quipped, 'I think it's great! I was over on the mainland for a brief visit until yesterday morning and everything appeared to go wrong over there, which just seemed couldn't possibly happen here.'

'Frankly I'm not surprised – from what we've heard, it can be something of a nightmare,' Jeremy said.

'I meant to tell Julie about this when we were alone, but somehow we were always occupied,' mentioned Andrew, and a secret smile which passed between their guests wasn't lost on him, 'but I'm sure she won't mind...' He glanced at his lover, who was back on his lap, but she showed no sign of objection. 'MrMaynard told me that if were both happy together by the end of my leave then I'd be offered the chance to become a Whyte Islander!'

If he'd been expecting his companions to express unbounded joy at his revelation then he experienced an anti-climax, for Julie merely lovingly drew his lips down onto hers and shortly afterward said, 'we didn't expect anything else, darling; they won't allow any doubtfuls on our island. You obviously meet all their criteria, which is why you're sharing this flat with me. But becoming a citizen is a very long way from being invited to become one, while you're here you'll still be under probation to ensure you aren't pretending to be near perfect, and there'll be several difficult examinations and statements of intent to pass which I'll have to thoroughly help you with. However, even after becoming a Whyte Islander you'll still be subject, like all of us, to permanent exile if you misbehave badly enough.'

'She's quite right Andy,' agreed Jeremy, 'those exams are real terrors, but we all had to take them before we could really call this island our home, but I'm sure you'll find it all worthwhile; and I doubt you could find a better teacher than my sister, even though she's rubbish at anything else.'

'I don't know about that,' he replied, 'but she's a reasonable…,' and he paused deliberately to encourage them to think the worse, 'coffee maker!'

Julie slapped him hard on the back. 'You pig,' she laughed.

Both Natalie and Jeremy rose, the latter saying, 'well, it's time for us to no longer outstay our welcome.' He shook Andrew's hand. 'It's been nice to meet you, and I hope we can all have some good times out together,' he looked over Andrew's shoulder at his sister and emphasised, 'occasionally.' Returning to her lover he advised, 'She's not a bad girl if you keep her chained up at night, especially during full moons.'

While he was saying goodbye to his sister, Natalie came over to Andrew to hug him and with her cheek briefly pressed against his, she whispered huskily, 'it's been lovely meeting you, Andy.' The scent of her overpowering perfume lingered in his mind long after both visitors had gone.

'It's just as well you've got a decent coat now,' Julie mentioned as they stood in the doorway of the building they lived in, staring out at the pouring rain, 'anyway, we needn't get too wet, the bus stops just over the road and the driver shuts off the engine and has a bit of a rest, so we won't need to press the panic button. Anyway, what did you think of my brother and his girlfriend?' Andrew told her he liked them both and how amused he was at their mutual, if one sided, banter during the card games. 'Natalie's one big tease as far as he's concerned, she loves to plague him but manages to placate him at the same time; my brother can be a little over serious occasionally but she often gently lets him see the light side of life. They're deeply in love, just like most other long term island couples; they support each other, as we'll also, hopefully, continue to do.' And she squeezed his hand.

In the event, the fact it was a rainy day turned out to be an advantage for it gave each an opportunity to explore their companion's personalities in more detail. The rain in no way spoilt their journey, for it was a brief dash to the waiting bus, and they were subsequently soon dropped off in the station forecourt. Julie had already explained that her parents lived in Newtown, and so he was looking forward to a nice long train ride in her company. Despite being a Saturday, the train was only half full due, his lover surmised, to the inclement weather and so they easily found a double seat at the end of a coach with a partition opposite instead of a facing seat, so allowing them as much privacy as was possible in an open coach. Julie sat by the window and she willingly cuddled up to Andrew when he sat down.

'You neglected to tell me what other jobs you've had, darling,' he commented at one point in their following conversation.

'It's a bit of a joke really, because I often find myself being something of a beautician, but this time I over frequently find myself beautifying the countryside. Groups of us roam along the lanes pulling out grass and unwanted plants from banks and verges, and replacing them with wild flowers, ferns, seeds and the like.' She nudged him and winked saucily, 'plenty of opportunity to romp in the woods and cornfields.' Then noticing the expression of anguish on his face she continued hastily, 'I was only joking, darling.'

Andrew hugged her tightly. 'Don't tease me in that way. I can't help feeling jealous, because you're the best thing that's ever happened to me and I'm scared stiff of losing you.'

'If you keep telling me you love me, that I'm attractive, and persist in being kind and considerate then you won't lose me; the danger would arise if you began taking me for granted, but I'd give you plenty of warning beforehand, so don't worry!' She paused, then asked, 'when you toured the schools, did anyone tell you the children were encouraged to confide in their teachers if any of their schoolmates misbehaved?'

He thought for a moment. 'Yes, I believe they did.'

'Well, here's one of the payoffs. Having got you to live with me, if any person, male or female, heard of, or saw, me being unfaithful they'd quickly hot foot it to you and let you know.' She kissed him briefly on the cheek. 'That's why I dragged you out before everyone at the folk club; I wasn't just proving to you that I loved you, I was also letting some of my acquaintances know – giving you an assurance ticket as it were.'

'Supposing you were unfaithful, what would happen then?'

She smiled understandingly. 'It's practically unknown for that to happen nowadays, but I'd almost certainly lose all my friends and that'd mean it'd be politic for me to find some new places to frequent. I wouldn't be banned or anything like that, but everyone would be cool toward me and it would get about that I couldn't be trusted. But,' she kissed him again, 'that rule also applies to you; so don't go finding substitutes while I'm away in the evenings.'

Andrew sighed with relief. 'I never thought I'd be pleased to hear about telling tales. But don't worry about me, I couldn't find anyone to match up to you, sweetheart; I wouldn't even try.'

Due, no doubt, to the windows being double glazed he could have easily have gazed out through the clear glass, but for once he was completely indifferent to the passing countryside and so was only half aware of the grey skies and the colourless scenery flashing by; all his attention was taken by his gorgeous companion, who was saying, 'I feel really sorry for spouses in your country who accidentally discover their partners have been deceiving them. Presuming their neighbours were laughing at them behind their backs must be almost as bad as the treachery perpetrated by their assumed loved ones.'

Andrew shook his head in sympathy. 'The divorce rate on the mainland is horrifying, as you doubtless know, darling.'

'What's wrong with your people,' she asked, suddenly sitting upright and staring at him while a wrist rested upon his shoulder. 'Aren't your psychologists aware of the underlying reasons and the eventual effects: that broken marriages produce a high proportion of confused children? Those kids often become confused adults who subsequently manage to mess up society; they make great psychiatrist cannon fodder, but create hell in so many different ways for their fellow citizens.'

She shrugged her shoulders and grimaced in a mixture of amazement and contempt. 'Do you know, our simplest children leave school knowing more than your psychologists apparently do? Our divorce rate is just about nil; I expect you know couples over here need to live together for several years in reasonable harmony before they're permitted to become parents, and because we receive more than adequate education in the social sciences and there are none of the domestic worries attendant as in mainland marriages there's much less that might go wrong. As I've just explained, there isn't any philandering; nor hang ups regarding sexual activities as I'm sure you'll readily testify.'

She relaxed and cuddled up to him again; giggling she said, 'those things we did last night; these bloody moralists: you can imagine them saying filthy, dirty, obscene. Like I said, it's approved practice in island relationships and it might warrant all those descriptions, but it helps to keep our relationships together; it stops husbands from seeking the sexual thrills from mistresses and prostitutes which are no longer available to them in the marriage bed if, indeed, they ever were on offer; and making love, not mayhem, prevents kids from hanging around on the streets at their wits end in not knowing what to do with themselves.

'I was testing you last night, Andy darling, and you passed your examination with flying colours. I've got lots of other erotic games to show you, and even straight forward lovemaking can become more exciting if dressing up, different types of music, and various lighting colours are employed. I meant to show you the wall lights in the lounge and bedroom last night but I'm afraid you had an alternative idea; in the bedroom, one is red, another is green, a third blue and the other is orange. The lounges are of a lighter shade, but both sets are remote controlled and can be used singly or in a combination. Whichever is chosen the effect can be remarkable, especially when they're programmed to change over automatically during romantic situations, and,' she added, rolling her eyes suggestively, 'that's when things can really get passionate. So I can promise you our relationship will never become dreary; which, I think, is probably one very good reason why your mainland divorce rate is so high, I wouldn't be surprised if many of your divorcees just became bored with their spouses.'

'I hope you'll remember, darling,' Andrew cautioned, 'I'll need time to acclimatise to your ways; don't forget, the mainland girls I've been with aren't the heart and soul of lovemaking, they don't normally exactly make things easy for their male friends where sexual relationships are concerned?'

Julie went into a giggling fit, crying out, 'oh dear, Andrew,' when she'd finished, 'you sound just like an old time virgin on her wedding night: "Be gentle with me, please",' she mimicked. 'And I thought I was in love with a dirty young sea dog! Don't worry sweetheart, I'll go easy on you.' She gave him a light kiss on the lips, but he immediately grasped her firmly in return and embraced her passionately; after a few moments, however, she tore her mouth from his. 'Steady on,' she gasped in embarrassment, 'we'll get thrown off in a minute. You mustn't be so demonstrative in public, it's rude and thoughtless!' Disengaging herself from his grasp she began to straighten her clothing in time-honoured fashion, then she took hold of his hands. 'Tell me,' she asked, 'that irate mother in the park: are many mainland women nervous like her?'

Her lover, bemused by the strange moral standards so recently demonstrated, and confused by her sudden question, took a while to answer. The train, having just come to a halt at some station or other, began to pull out as he replied, 'you know I wouldn't deliberately hurt a fly, don't you?' Julie nodded earnestly. 'Well, those bitches over there... No, that isn't fair: some of them,' he emphasised, 'treat you like a criminal. I've been standing in a shop waiting to be served when a woman who'd left her handbag near me on the counter gave me a dirty look and snatched it away; I've started to go down an empty subway when a couple of teenage girls preceding me have begun to run, as though I were a threat; and I've walked along urban and suburban streets and noticed approaching women cross the road in order to avoid me. That's what really hurts,' he exclaimed bitterly, 'knowing they don't care about a person's feelings. When it happens to me I'm too dumbfounded to say or do anything, but afterward I feel like shaking them and even doing what was apparently expected of me.'

In unconscious contradiction of her prior admonition Julie took him into her arms and began to stroke his hair maternally. 'Poor, poor Andy,' she soothed, 'but you must remember those women were obviously concerned or even frightened; they might well have been victims once, or knew, heard or read about people who had been. However, they could've been much more circumspect. But you can see why I wouldn't contemplate living over there.'

By mutual consent they changed the subject, and Andrew, who had already been informed about his lover's favourite pastimes began questioning her about them, especially with regard to horse riding, sailing and fishing. 'That's usually what the typical mainland sexy pin up pretends to prefer,' he observed with some amusement, 'but I hope you'll let me share them with you.'

'I'll gladly introduce you to them, but I daresay we'll find some others which we'll both enjoy; after all, we've still got a great deal to learn about each other's preferences. During my school activities I experienced most of the pleasurable hobbies Whyte Island has to offer and we can try them together, until we find something we both love.'

Julie's erstwhile home was situated about a third of the way along an avenue which ran between the station approach road and the blue school; a modern style, semi-detached house, it faced the school park and the cliffs beyond. As they walked up the garden path still in the pouring rain, his lover asked, 'you know that game we played, when I pretended to suckle you and did other things, darling?'

Astonished and mystified by the untimely reference, Andrew replied uncertainly, 'yes?'

'Well,' she answered, ringing the door bell, 'my mum taught me that.' And she began giggling uncontrollably. In a desperate attempt to stop her he began to shake her but she immediately threw her arms about him and kissed him avidly. And so it was while they were in this position that he first set eyes on his sweetheart's mother.

'Obviously,' he heard a mature female voice say, 'some people never tire of sex.' Startled, he turned his head and saw a grey haired woman, though still with plenty of hints of her former redheaded status, and an attractive face standing in the open doorway; fortunately for his peace of mind she was smiling broadly.

'Hello, mum,' Julie said calmly as soon as they'd drawn apart, 'I was just telling Andy about how you taught me that baby game.' She turned to her lover. 'You really liked it, didn't you darling?'

'Julie,' he exclaimed, flushing with embarrassment.

'Don't mind her,' the woman advised, stepping back to allow them entry, 'she's always teasing. I'm just as broadminded as she is, so if you enjoy sucking our daughter's breasts then good luck to you. We wouldn't have made her if we bothered about silly little things like that.' When they were in the hallway she held out her hand. 'My name's Jean, and welcome to our house. I must say Julie's completely taken with you, and I think I can see why.'

Now much placated by her reassuring words, Andrew shook the woman's hands and observed, 'I can see where your daughter got her beauty from.'

Immediately Jean laughed and called out, 'John, I'm just going to run off with our Julie's young man.'

From an adjacent room came the reply, 'well, would you pour my tea out first?'

This auspicious start was to presage all Andrew's subsequent dealings with the Lucas family for, just like his lover, the other three members were kind, caring, friendly, tolerant and rarely serious for any length of time. From the very beginning they welcomed him with open arms, looking upon him as a new member of the family who could do no wrong. He was astute enough to recognise that Mrs Lucas especially, accepted him because he was so obviously loved by her daughter, but in time she came to discover those qualities in him which Julie admired and adored so much and from then on he was treated as though he were her son. But from the very first they all took an interest in him, which was disconcerting after his own parents' and brother's attitude toward him.

Julie and he hadn't been in the house for much longer than an hour when Jeremy arrived. 'Oh, no!' cried his sister as he walked into the lounge, 'not you again. Haven't you done enough to try and spoil my relationship with Andy?' And so began a belligerent afternoon tea; to Andrew it seemed as though sister and brother lived just to insult each other, and their parents did little to prevent the slanging match. For the guest, knowing it was all in fun, it was more than a godsend because he was able to relax even more in the shadow of the repartee flying between the siblings. At first he'd been extremely embarrassed by his lover's reference to their sex game in front of her mother, but now he realised she'd been deliberately putting him at his ease by showing him her parents wouldn't mind about their relationship.

The rain continued unabated all day, but it failed to spoil their visit for the five of them played cards and many other games, enlivened by bantering conversation and background music from the CD player. Once, Andrew commented, 'it's a pity it's wet in a way, as I'd have liked to look round Newtown.' And he explained about his trip to the blue school, and how Sandra had recommended the town as well worth a visit. 'Not that I'm not enjoying myself here, of course,' he added hastily.

His companions all smiled at this remark and Julie's father, a somewhat quiet but dry witted man, said, 'I don't think that's much of a problem; why not go tomorrow? The weather should have improved by then, and you can both sleep here tonight.'

Andrew glanced across at his lover, he liked the suggestion but not at the expense of her bedtime absence; however, she smiled back encouragingly. 'But we haven't got anything to wear,' he protested.

'Knowing my sister,' interposed Jeremy, 'you won't need any bedtime attire.'

'Oh, shut up,' exclaimed the butt of his remark, 'if you were as sexy as me then your Natalie would be here!'

'As you well know, she's at work; besides, she's already had enough of you today.'

'When my two children have finished,' Mrs Lucas interjected, 'I would like to hear Andrew's answer.'

He'd already come to a decision. 'If you don't mind having us, we'd be only too pleased to accept your kind offer, Jean.'

Much to his relief, there was no question of Andrew having to sleep alone; and that night in her old bedroom Julie remarked, 'if I wash our underwear before I come to bed we can go straight on to the Maynard's.'

'Will it dry in time?'

'Of course,' she answered, 'spun dried, then in the airing cupboard.'

'In that case, I'll wait up with you.'

'Oh, no,' she insisted, winking, 'there's only one dressing gown and that's mine, so you can wait for me in bed.'

While he awaited the return of his lover he kept the table lamp on and passed the time in studying in much detail her former bedroom. At the back of his mind lay her brother's almost hidden reference to her lack of virtue, and although he knew he was being foolish it was beginning to rankle more than somewhat. So, despite his realisation that he was once again attempting to tread upon dangerous ground, as soon as she reappeared, he declared, 'I'm really enjoying our visit to your parents, but I wish Jeremy hadn't mentioned about your not wanting a nightdress.'

Julie laughed and came over to sit on the bed. 'He was only kidding. I bet you've had more lovers than I have. Being jealous of me is extremely complimentary, but I do wish you'd bury that green-eyed monster because it could destroy us eventually. Get used to the idea that if you want a virgin on Whyte Island you'd better go along to the blue school and try to book a fourteen year old or younger; even then it'd be a lucky shot because girls graduating from blue schools generally prefer to team up with boys of a similar age.' She stood up. 'Now, if you like I'll go and sleep in the other bedroom; I'm sure my mother won't mind if you stay here till Monday morning, then you can pop along to the school and sort yourself out a little playmate for future reference.'

By way of an answer Andrew threw himself across the duvet, grasped her by the back of her legs, and pulled her down on top of him, and while she struggled, shrieked and giggled he smothered her face, hair and even her dressing gown with kisses while his hands groped wildly and indiscriminately at her body. When at last they lay silently together Julie said, 'I want to come to bed dressed like this, then you can unwrap me.'

But he shook his head. 'No, I won't let you. As soon as you climb into bed I'm going to ravish you; but you'll have to be as naked as I am. This is your parent's house and we shouldn't be playing sex games while we're in it.'

She giggled, sat up and removed the dressing gown. 'Is this alright? You are silly at times, darling; it wouldn't have been much of a game anyway.' She slipped in beside him. 'Whatever we do,' she whispered as she drew him into her arms, 'we'll mess the sheets up.'

'Presumably,' replied Andrew, turning the light off, 'your mother knows the facts of life.'

He was awoken early the following morning by Julie. 'Want to do it again?' she asked.

Later, as they lay in each other's arms, he whispered, 'You're a nymphomaniac.'

She stirred in contentment. 'No I'm not; it's just that you're a wonderful lover; besides, I love you more than ever now, if that's possible.' Puzzled, he asked why. 'Because you wouldn't let me come to bed in my dressing gown; I was beginning to wonder whether you had a forceful mind of your own. Besides,' she added quickly before he could interrupt, 'you also showed you respected my parents, and I liked that.'

'Sweetheart,' he answered, 'I've not only got to get to know you, but also the island's social code; so at the moment I'm compelled to steer the narrow path between forcefulness and compliance with your wishes. You're my teacher now, but I think I can promise you that when my lessons are over you'll find me more than man enough for you.'

Rolling over on top of him she kissed the tip of his nose. 'You're not doing too badly now, darling; but like any good teacher I'll tell you if you ever go wrong.'

There were only four of them at the breakfast table, for Jeremy had gone back to his own home, and so the meal was consumed in a far more peaceful atmosphere while the mid-morning sun shone brightly through the patio windows. 'We'd have liked to accompany you to town,' apologised John Lucas, 'but I'm afraid I have some gardening to catch up on, and Julie's mother will also be busy; so perhaps some other time.'

Andrew, having noticed the small, neat front garden and also the large rear one, laid down to lawn with several fruit trees and bordered by a pair of hedges with a brick wall, ivy clad, at the far end, realised gardening wasn't one of John's main pastimes. So he merely smiled and said it really was a pity they couldn't all go together.

'I think it ought to be mentioned, Andrew,' Jean informed him, 'that John and I have rarely seen our daughter happier. It's our greatest wish that you should become a citizen of our contented island and one day, perhaps, we could call you our son-in -law.'

'Oh, do be quiet, mum,' begged Julie, just as embarrassed as her lover.

But Mrs Lucas continued. 'Until that day arrives we'd like you to think of yourself as our rightful son.' She paused for a moment and then added, 'so you'll have two families to care about you.'

Andrew immediately jumped up. 'I think I've left something upstairs,' he muttered, and fled the room.

Newtown certainly lived up to Sandra's rosy description; Andrew could scarcely believe it was a bare fifteen years old, for everywhere there was a timeless quality about the place. Lanes and alleyways abounded and led to fresh vistas of buildings displaying different architectural designs, and also to numerous squares, each one peculiar to itself. The first one they came across was mainly grass covered, but the next was entirely paved apart from a young oak in the centre which, as Sandra had implied, gave its name to the square, a third was shaded by trees and shrubs through which paths wound, and another comprised an area of cobblestones containing a fountain; some were raised above the surrounding ground level, and others were sunken. These latter ones, Julie explained, were specifically designed to allow moisture-loving trees to thrive, 'They have a slight camber toward the centre to collect rain water,' she explained.

Always, as a backdrop to these squares and allowing a different aspect to each one, there were the buildings, usually three storeys high and varying not only in their architecture and fabric but in colour also, the plaster faced structures being particularly favoured with a variety of hues. Mostly these were of pastel shades, but here and there a bright, bolder colour seemed to cry out for attention.

As Julie and he sat on a bench in a square containing a large number of flower beds, unmindful of the occasional spray blown from a nearby fountain, Andrew commented, 'there are certainly a lot of pigeons about.' They were idly watching a group of the birds strutting about on the path in front of them in the warm sunshine.

His companion laughed. 'Newtown chickens, you mean. There used to be thousands until some bright spark had the idea of harvesting them; pigeon breast as a main or side dish is a popular speciality of the area, and it's cooked in quite a large number of ways. The rest of the bird goes for pet food, fish bait and fertiliser.'

'You islanders are so practical,' he observed, not in the least put out by her information.

She poked him playfully in the side. 'And you mainlanders are so impractical. If, by the way, you're going to become a citizen of our contented island,' she made fun of her mother, 'then you'd better start thinking like one. Are you ready to continue with your tour yet?'

As they strolled out of the miniature park Andrew said, 'I've only got one real complaint about Whyte Island girls, and that is you're all a little too informative. When you were explaining about the pigeons it sounded as though you were an official guide.'

Julie instantly proved she could be equally as candid. 'That's because we consider the mainland to be a very backward country; all island children are taught to take an interest in their environment, and so they learn a large number of various facts during the course of their lessons. Therefore, when they meet a newcomer to the island they naturally assume they'll wish to be told everything they might think interesting; after all, if you're in receipt of a lot of information there isn't much point in keeping it to yourself, is there? You are interested in my explanations aren't you?' He nodded, and she laughed. 'That's just as well, because you're going to hear them anyway.'

Jostling and being jostled by the good natured Sunday crowds who shopped and wandered down the streets, lanes and alleys was a wonderful experience for Andrew as it added to the atmosphere which the town engendered. The buildings, which tended to dominate the mainly narrow thoroughfares almost to the point of shutting out the overhead light, served to trap the aromas of coffee, freshly baked bread, cooked food, fresh fish, beer, perfume and such like. And each time his lover led him round a corner he discovered a fascinating new scene; he lost count of the number of shops she took him into, and no one seemed to mind when, after examining old books, paintings or various antiques, she invariably said, 'lovely, but we're only looking.'

They had four cups of coffee, together with freshly baked crusty rolls containing savoury or sweet fillings as the mood took them, in as many busy cafes, and three sets of alcoholic drinks in an equal number of public houses; and each venue displayed an individuality in its décor which was truly remarkable, the bars, especially, appearing far older than their true age implied. On several occasions Julie met up with people she knew, but apart from introducing them to her companion and after the briefest of conversations they were soon on their way again for, as she told him afterward, 'there'll be plenty of time in which you'll be able to get to know them, but at the moment I want you all to myself.'

Eventually, to gain respite from the hustle and bustle of the streets, she led him into the pseudo-church. Andrew was well aware of what could be accomplished when old-style architecture was copied by modern craftsmen for he'd visited several churches and civic buildings on the mainland which, while seeming quite ancient, were relatively new. He was therefore not particularly surprised at the building's interior; but even so, the construction of this sham church had been masterful in being an accurate representation of a medieval house of worship.

Comprising a lofty nave with a north and south isle, there was an abundance of stained glass windows with an extra-large and magnificent one behind the beautifully dressed altar; almost every other feature of a church of the period was present except for the large numbers of pews, only a few rows near the chancel being in position. The remainder of the nave's floor area was quite empty, but both aisles were full of glass cases containing all aspects of medieval life; bulkier items too large for inclusion in cases lay on long tables or were stacked against the walls.

'Isn't it rather sacrilegious having a church when you don't intend to use it as such?'

Andrew observed while they were examining a most ornate piece of armour.

Julie shook her head decisively. 'It can hardly be sacrilegious if no one on Whyte Island is religious, can it?' she pointed out. 'But people don't need to be religious to appreciate antiquity and beauty; when you think about it, often the best examples of both are to be found in churches. Anyway, a town the size of this one couldn't possibly be without a church, it'd look ridiculous without one, and besides it serves several useful purposes: as you can see, it's a museum, and they often stage exhibitions, concerts and medieval banquets here; and last, but not least, it's an ideal place to come for a little peace and quiet. Oh, yes, I forgot, musicians often come here, and to other churches on the island, to practice; as you can imagine the acoustics are magnificent in such places.'

'Are the banquets anything like the Roman feast?'

She smiled, as if in recollection. 'Very similar and just as elaborate, except they don't throw in a free bath; everyone is dressed in period costume, there's authentic food, medieval music and conversation, jugglers, acrobats, a fool and all that kind of thing; people are even expected to throw their leftover bones over their shoulders. If you promise not to seduce a peasant wench I'll book up for us, otherwise the official invitation might be too long in coming.'

Andrew, glancing about to check no one was watching, pressed his lover up against a glass case, touched an appropriate part of her anatomy and whispered, 'but I prefer to keep abreast of Roman affairs.'

'You'll get us both shot,' she giggled in reply. 'Come on, I want to show you something which helps show why we don't have religious teaching over here.' She then took him on a tour to inspect the various memorial wall plaques. 'Now these are all genuine, bought from redundant churches on the mainland – see how elaborate many of them are?' He nodded, and they continued their inspection until they'd returned to where they began. 'Did you see how they were virtually all dedicated to the rich and the powerful in the areas from where they were collected? Even where battles or campaigns were mentioned in war memorials the common soldiers came last in the lists, if they were mentioned at all. Yet the Bible states, "all men are created equal", but obviously the church doesn't practice what it preaches, and you've just seen the most blatant proof of that!'

'Are there still some in actual island churches, though?'

'Come on, let's sit down; my feet are killing me. And yes, I think you'll find the interiors of most, if not all, our churches have been left intact. We like to be reminded of how things used to be and they're useful for teaching our youngsters on how controlling the church and state used to be over ordinary people's lives.'

'But isn't Whyte Island controlled by your government?' Andrew objected, when they were seated in one of the pews, 'just like any other nation to one extent or another?'

'Well,' Julie replied with a smile, 'we prefer the description "managed" to "controlled" because we're a true democracy and every person has a right to change the constitution if they can find enough supporters. But because no one ever does tends to prove everyone's happy with the way things are, so we don't have any dissenters. In the old days, though, everyone knew what happened to those who challenged the status quo, and it often wasn't very pleasant.'

Her lover entirely satisfied with her explanation changed the subject by saying, 'one thing puzzles me about your shops. I can understand the presence of necessary stores such as for food, clothing and household requisites, but what about shops which supply non-essentials or long lasting goods, like pictures or furniture? Surely they don't receive much custom, so why are they here in this and other towns in such number?'

'Can you imagine how dull towns would appear without such places? But I get your point; you want to know how they manage to justify their existence when profit isn't the motive. Well, like many things over here they have several uses, and I've just mentioned one. However, another is they help provide a variety of jobs for a lot of people. As you doubtless noticed, such shops weren't exactly overcrowded with customers, and so they're ideal as a means of providing a quiet occupation where little skill is required. It's the type of employment given to farm workers and others who spend a lot of their time outside, because it ensures the greatest amount of contrast to their main profession. Such people rarely get much time to communicate with the average person, and so it allows them to maintain their social skills and gives them something to think about when engaged in their predominantly solitary agricultural or other tasks.

'But another reason for having non-essential shops,' Julie continued, 'is so everybody can obtain variety in their personal property. Take furniture as an example, supposing we'd decided our lounge suite needed changing; we'd then go along to the nearest relevant shop, choose something we both fancied and then had it delivered. The shop would remove our old furniture, renovate it where necessary and then offer for sale a replacement to the next customer who might like it; and all at minimum cost to ourselves, because the idea isn't for the shop to make a profit, as yours do, but to provide satisfaction and diversity for the customer.

'Our shops are also showcases for various household items manufactured on the island, some of which may be purchased, although most are intended for export, and so the public are able to keep a check on the variety and standard of workmanship in our products.' She stood up. 'Now, shall we go up the tower? You can see for miles, and there's a fantastic view of the town as well.'

As they climbed the spiral stairway Andrew called up to his sweetheart, 'the day I first kissed you, darling, I went up a similar staircase, except it was iron, with that Jill, but I looked to my front then.'

Julie's laughter echoed round him. 'I wonder where you're looking now?' she taunted.

'At the most beautiful pair of legs in the world, and the gateway to paradise.'

'Don't be silly,' she called back, 'legs is legs, and as for the other thing: it can also be the exit to hell for too many people around the globe.'

'Hopefully, though, not that particular one,' was his rejoinder.

'Now,' his lover advised him when he'd joined her on a large flat area allowing access by way of an oak door onto the tower roof, 'if you step out quickly you might catch a glimpse of a peregrine or sparrow hawk winging away, as they're often seen perching up here waiting for a juicy pigeon or some other luckless bird to pass by below. Go on' she urged, 'I'm not trying to be rid of you!'

Andrew did as she wished, and was rewarded with a glimpse of large bluish grey bird perched on top of one the crenulations before it disappeared below the tower; he raced over to the edge and was in time to see it gliding down to a tree in one of the parks. 'Another good reason for having a church,' Julie, now standing beside him, observed, pointing at their feet to where a mess of bones and feathers indicated the prowess of the raptors in keeping the pest problem under control.

'From your description it sounded like a peregrine,' she mused as they stood gazing about them. They could indeed see for miles, and below them the town was shown in as similar a detail as that on a street plan. 'You'll not be surprised to learn,' his lover commented, 'that the architects built this tower first so they could use it to survey the kind of settlement they had in mind.'

Andrew was surprised at the large size of the place but could only stare in admiration at the good job which had been accomplished. Turning his attention to the adjacent landscape which, however, was only slightly lower than the height of the tower, for the almost totally surrounding chalk cliffs blocked off much of the view, he could only see the windbreak forming forest and some chalk down land between. But from one side of the square tower he could view the harbour section and the sea beyond quite well, but even this view was restricted.

When he voiced his disappointment at the lack of distance evident, his lover called across to him, 'come over to this side, this should make you change your mind.' She pointed in a direction he'd missed once he'd joined her, and there, through a large gap between two sections of rolling down land, was a patchwork of fields, hedges and copses stretching into distant obscurity; there must have been a fairly strong breeze blowing from which they were protected in the town, for scudding clouds cast ever moving shadows over the landscape adding to the interest and intrinsic beauty of the scene. 'I should think you could almost see across the whole width of our island from here,' Julie commented.

'You know, love,' Andrew remarked when, having crossed over to the opposite side of the tower just prior to descending, they stood gazing down at the maze of buildings, through fares, squares and trees below them, 'a scene like this is now more or less unknown in my own country. It's as if all the tiny remnants of the past in all our cities and larger towns were joined together, unspoilt by high rise flats, office blocks and endless acres of suburbs.'

'That's why it was built like this, no doubt,' she replied, 'to remind us of how the mainland used to be; but like this church, it's all sham. With regard to your mainland, though, all that destructive building is simply caused by population levels getting out of control. It can't be stopped due to economic reasons and can only end in disaster eventually; so you be a good boy, pass all your exams and then you can stay here with your ever loving Julie without a care in the world!'

Glancing around to check they were still alone Andrew asked, 'in that case, will I be shot if I kiss you in the midst of all these people?'

His sweetheart smiled. 'Well, if you get caught don't forget to name me as your last request. But you'd better hurry up, I'm sure I can hear the secret police rushing up the stairs!' Eventually she said as she removed his hand, 'you only mentioned a kiss; that's going to cost you one hell of a dinner.'

'One thing I especially like about Whyte Island, darling,' Andrew observed when they were on board a train once more, but this time bound for Harbourtown, 'there aren't any louts about trying to intimidate the boyfriends of attractive girls when they're out and about, especially on public transport.' Before she could comment he continued. 'Occasionally, on the mainland, you'd meet up with a group of blokes who'd be jealous, presumably, because you had a girl when they didn't and start swearing or making obscene remarks; you'd then be left with the choice of trying to ignore them or else taking them on with the certain chance of being beaten up. If you merely tried to reason with them they'd almost certainly torment you even more.'

'So what did you do?'

'I'd ignore them, though it hurt almost as much as being courageous.'

Julie gripped his wrist in a gesture of approval. 'You did the right thing,' she declared. 'To begin with, you possibly wouldn't have seen them again, so heroics might have been wasted; then, as there would've been more of them than you, that would've made them more cowardly, so more aggressive, like a pack of hyenas, and you'd possibly been badly mauled; but most of all you owed your allegiance to your companion. If you'd attacked them you'd almost certainly have lost, that would either have meant leaving your girlfriend defenceless against them, or anyone else who happened along, especially if you were far from home having all been thrown off public transport due to having caused a nuisance; she'd also be compelled to choose between nursing a lame duck or abandoning you to look after herself.' She smiled. 'Judging from what I've heard of mainland females, most of them would decide upon the latter course of action.'

'Thank you,' he replied.

But she hadn't finished. 'Your society's rotten, Andy. You are over here to partner a girl because the island is one male short; but it could quite as well have been the other way round. That, however, shows how much my society cares about its people; if your administration had a similar scheme then each of those louts might've had a girl to partner him; not only would such louts have then had less reason to annoy innocent people, but their girlfriends, if they'd gut any guts, would've been a stabilising influence upon them.' She cuddled up to him, and added, 'besides giving them other things to do.' She sighed and continued, 'I can think of half a dozen reasons why such a thing couldn't happen to you over here, and if you paid attention during your school visits, so could you; but not least of all would be kicks in the baby farm from yours truly.'

Andrew laughed. 'How poetic,' he observed wryly.

When they were seated on the bus taking them up the hill to the Maynards', Julie resurrected the subject of the louts. 'They wouldn't only have been tormenting you because you were with a girl, darling, but also because of your ability to obtain an attractive one. Deep in their hearts they'd probably have been in awe of women and so they'd resent you for having the ability to go out and get a good looker; I'll expect they would've been in their early or middle teens. But you can understand why our authorities train and encourage us girls to go out and pair off with the opposite sex, because in the long run it's for our own good.'

'I get great pleasure when I see men admiring you, and they do it all the time,' he stated, 'but I'm glad that's all they do.'

They arrived at the cottage practically on time; but before they knocked Julie whispered, 'watch what you're saying, don't upset Helen.' Andrew had been considering their visit more of a chore than an enjoyment for he still felt somewhat guilty at what seemed to him to be his rather cavalier departure from that friendly home; but he hadn't been on the island long enough to know it had been expected of him, and so he was greatly relieved when his lover and he were welcomed as honoured guests.

Charlie Maynard was much taken by Julie. 'Surely this must be the brightest jewel in the island's crown,' he exclaimed. 'My dear, you're really beautiful. How on earth did you net her, Andrew?'

'It would be truer to say,' he replied, 'that she netted me, with Linda's connivance, but I'm still not sure why.'

His lover, ever ready to be humorous, said in a stage aside, 'he still doesn't know we're planning to heap the tortures of hell on his head.' Andrew couldn't help feeling a little annoyed at her apparent disrespect, but Charlie seemed to like her all the more for it.

When they were all seated in the lounge with their coffee, Mr Maynard announced, 'shall we discuss the more serious business first? Then we can enjoy the remainder of the evening.' Upon receiving general agreement to this suggestion, he went on. 'There isn't really any problem about your staying somewhere else, lad; you've had tours of some of the important establishments, and that virtually leaves just the red training colleges.' Turning to Julie, he asked, 'which one did you attend, my dear?'

'The one with a beautician's course on its curriculum,' she answered with a smile.

'I thought I recognised you,' he beamed, 'you were one of the girls who introduced zigzagging to our society!' Andrew glanced at his daughters in bewilderment upon hearing this strange expression again to see what effect the term had on them, but he was somewhat disconcerted to note they were gazing at his lover with little interest. 'I hope it wasn't too much of an ordeal for you,' Charlie finished.

'Well, it was quite uncomfortable and scary, especially in not knowing when it was going to end, but that was the whole point, wasn't it? All in all, though, it was a strangely satisfying experience.' She looked over at her sweetheart speculatively. 'I'm waiting to see how Andy takes to it because I really don't want to lose him.' She paused, and then seemed to come to a decision. 'Charlie, I don't wish to be forward or out of turn, but when Andrew returned from the mainland he was very upset by certain experiences over there. I must tell you I love him dearly and so, absolutely without his knowledge, I've written a letter to our government...'

'Julie!' her lover cried in shocked embarrassment.

'... asking if they could bring forward all his examinations, I was hoping I could prevail upon your daughters to countersign it, just as my family has done.'

Andrew had a lump in his throat and felt his eyes begin to water as Charlie, also visibly moved, glanced across at him. 'I did hear something about your being upset,' he stated. 'You've more or less burnt your bridges over there, haven't you lad?' As he nodded in reply he saw Helen hold out her hand to Julie for the letter: she perused it briefly, procured a pen, and signed it. Linda did likewise.

His lover then said, 'I'm going to try to get the folk club people to sign it as well.'

But Charlie Maynard took the letter, sealed the flap and put it in his pocket. 'That won't be necessary,' he declared, 'but you realise I can't get involved; I'll see it gets to the right place, though. What I can do is to hurry the zigzagging along. Don't worry, Julie, I'm sure Andrew would walk through hellfire for you. I know I would.'

Looking at the three girls in turn, the younger man thanked them profusely and then did something which was to have dire consequences, for he suddenly became aware of the sisters' gifts in his coat pocket. Linda subsequently unwrapped her present with much gusto and was obviously pleased with her bracelet, but Helen opened hers with some uncertainty; she withdrew the little brooch and studied it briefly. 'It's a parting gift,' he blurted out, sensing something was wrong, 'just to thank you for having me and being such a wonderful hostess.'

She immediately stood up and, unconsciously emulating him, she rushed for the door, saying as she went, 'I'm just going to put it on.'

As soon as she'd gone Julie turned to him, eyes blazing with anger. 'I hope you did that through sheer ignorance,' she accused coldly before standing up and following after Helen.

Andrew, his face hot with embarrassment, glanced from Linda to her father. 'What should I do?' he enquired uncertainly.

She shrugged, and advised, 'nothing. Pretend you didn't notice.'

Charlie said, 'they'll get over it sooner or later.' He paused. 'Whatever you do, don't apologise, though; it'll only make things worse.' The two girls were gone for some time, and during their absence Charlie continued to outline the position with regard to his guest's new address. 'So you see, lad,' he finally said, 'you're only a telephone call away if something turns up; and you might receive permission for Julie to accompany you to the colleges. I can think of few islanders more fitting.'

When Helen did eventually reappear, Julie stood in the doorway and beckoned to her lover with a forefinger. 'You unfeeling bastard,' she exploded after dragging him into the kitchen, 'that kid's been crying buckets. What on earth compelled you to do it? You know she loves you as much as I do. I feel so guilty that I'm considering dropping you and leaving you to her.'

Confusion suddenly becoming replaced by annoyance at being

blamed for what he considered to be his well-meant gesture, he replied angrily, 'I'm not a piece of luggage to be handed about at will. You're the only one who has first call on my affections; I love only you, Julie. Look, I didn't know I'd upset her, I'm only an ignorant male unused to the niceties of life. I don't know how to handle women! All the time I spent in my own country most of the girls paid me as much attention as they would to a sewer and now, when I come over here I find myself in great demand.'

'Alright,' she answered, still angry, 'I'll think about it. Now, we'll go back in there; don't mention what happened, and behave yourself.'

Fortunately, the remainder of the evening passed reasonably well. Helen managed to put on a brave front and even thanked Andrew for the brooch, saying how beautiful it was, and seeming to take great delight in it as she frequently glanced down and admired it. He couldn't help wondering at the complete transformation in her: from an apparently self-possessed woman she'd become a little girl and he could only hope the change was merely temporary. His sweetheart, however, remained cool and distant with him, and all he could do was wait patiently until she began to show him affection once more. She wasn't averse, though, to singing several songs at his request, all of which went down very well with the Maynards who applauded her sweet voice vigorously. Eventually, they said their goodbyes, Andrew laden with a borrowed case containing the remainder of his gear, and after shaking hands with Charlie he kissed both sisters on the cheek, though Helen displayed little emotion at this fond farewell.

It was dusk when they left, but still light enough to make the use of a torch unnecessary, and by mutual though silent consent, Julie and he made their way down toward the village at the foot of the ridge, neither spoke or attempted to touch the other; finally she asked in a small voice, 'are you still sulking?'

'No, my darling,' he replied patiently, 'I'm waiting for you to be friends again. If you're still angry with me then I won't try to make you change your mind, because it would obviously be against your wishes.'

Immediately she snatched the suitcase from his grasp and dropped it on the ground. 'Andy, you're impossible!' she shrieked as she stamped her foot.

He turned and faced her. 'Look. Those people up there have

been very good to me, so I bought the sisters a present each as a mark of my gratitude; so what did I do wrong? I tried to be thoughtful but all I accomplished was your hatred.' His use of the final word wasn't without a certain amount of guile, and Julie rose to the bait eagerly.

'I don't hate you,' she wailed, 'but Helen loves you. When you gave her that brooch you were as good as telling her in front of us all that she couldn't have you, but to take the gift as a consolation prize.' She put threw her arms about him. 'I'm sorry I was ratty; I realise now it was your upbringing and lack of experience which was at fault. You're too nice a man to do such a thing deliberately – I see that now. Do you still love me?' she asked plaintively. His reply remained unspoken but left her in no doubt of his feelings in that direction.

'Darling,' she said further down the hill, 'would you ever consider us living with my parents? Because I'd like to change my job at the villa and that would possibly mean giving up the flat.'

Andrew, nonplussed by the question asked, 'but surely you like the job?'

'I love it, but I love you more. I don't think it'd be fair on you if I keep it up as I'll be working from 2 p.m. to 11 p.m. most nights. My parents have got two empty bedrooms, and I know you like Newtown and I also know they'd love to have us.'

'I wouldn't mind in the least; but what might your new job be?'

'In all modesty,' she replied, 'my skills are in great demand, so there'd be little problem about obtaining a position in Newtown, and more importantly, sweetheart, we'd be able to spend our evenings together!'

After a few minutes thought, he answered, 'look, I suggest we don't do anything too hasty. For a start, it's by no means certain I'll be able to stay over here; but if I am, what job would I have? I fancy trying the railways, which might mean unsocial hours and which, therefore, might also mean you'd have changed your job pointlessly.' He stopped, put down his case and drew her into his arms. 'Lastly, my love, we've just had our first, bad quarrel. I didn't think it would ever be possible, and I detested being ignored by you. So do you really think our relationship has any real future?'

Without being entirely conscious of the fact, Andrew had turned the tables on his lover and put her in the role of defender of their romance; to her his words apparently held a scarcely veiled threat.

Lifting her suddenly tear-stained face to his she pleaded with a vehemence which he found startling, 'Don't say that, Andrew, I didn't mean to hurt you; I love you so much!' And she promptly burst into tears. From that moment on Julie did her very best to ensure their relationship, doomed though it was, continued smoothly, and she succeeded admirably almost to the very end.

They slept in late the following morning, Julie's excuse being that she wanted to be fit and lively for her evening's work, but much to Andrew's consternation she adamantly refused to allow them to make love. She permitted him to kiss and fondle her, saying at one point, 'oh, yes, my love, that's nice; you can do that as much as you like.' But when he attempted to share her pleasure he was quickly rebuffed. Eventually when she realised he was becoming frustrated, she whispered suggestively in his ear, 'I want us to play a game later, and I'd like you to have plenty in store.' He could only look puzzled at this enigmatic statement.

After breakfast, she suddenly exclaimed, 'get your coat on, we'll go and see the waterfall.'

Almost before he'd had time to think, Andrew found himself being whisked away in the direction of the dam. It was another warm and pleasant day with the inevitable breeze blowing off the lake, and he felt himself in paradise as they rode along on the open top deck of one of the white buses. He could hardly take his eyes off his companion for, just as with Linda's shorter fair hair, the slipstream blew and tossed Julie's long golden-red locks all about her face and head, and as she talked, smiled and laughed he thought her the most beautiful creature on earth. Although she was quite content to allow his arm about her shoulders, she wouldn't permit him to kiss her because they weren't alone on the upper deck, but he suspected she was really only teasing him.

The dam's lower viewing platform was reached by a seemingly endless number of steps. 'Look at that lovely rainbow,' she cried like an excited child, 'and at those beautiful mosses and ferns – you wouldn't think there could be so many shades and variety.' The noise was deafening as they leaned on the parapet and studied the great volume of water falling from high into the large cauldron of boiling foam which was the beginning of the river.

'Come on,' Andrew said at last, 'we're getting soaked by this spray. We'll go inside and you can watch me enjoying a drink.'

His lover pulled a face. 'Can't I have one too?' she pleaded.

'Well,' he considered, 'if I'd been allowed to have my way with you...'

Laughing, she slapped him, 'I'd have thought my body worth more than a mere drink.'

Over a glass of wine each, seated by a plate glass window overlooking the falls he mused, 'no pun intended, but I thought those steps were a bit steep.'

She was quick to understand his real meaning and gestured over her shoulder, 'don't worry there's a couple of lifts round the corner by the bar; you wouldn't expect the poor staff down here and in the generator rooms to have to carry their necessities up and down, would you? But youngsters like you and me are supposed to consider taking lifts as being sissy. We have to keep fit; and talking about fitness, I'll have to enrol you for weekly sessions in my local gym.' Upon his groaning, she continued. 'It's what island citizenship is all about. It isn't all just bedroom athletics, you know!' she giggled.

Later, having finished their drinks, Julie studied her lover thoughtfully. 'Are you ready for our game now,' she asked at length.

'What; here?' he asked in surprise.

Grinning, she replied, 'no, you fool; it'd cause a sensation if we did it in public.'

'Now' Julie said when they were back in the flat, 'I want you to go outside, bear right and a few doors down you'll come to a nice little pub; it's all fishing nets and things inside, so you can't miss it. Have a refreshing pint of beer, and try to convince yourself you're a burglar and, most of all about how you're going to bluff your way past the person who opens the door to you by not causing her undue alarm.'

Deliberately, for effect, she then slowly dropped four nylons into his lap one after another, adding with a smile, 'To prevent the said housewife from fighting back and screaming blue murder.'

'Listen, sweetheart,' he stated, picking up the nylons and offering them back, 'I don't fancy this, I might harm you.'

Laughing, she observed, 'don't be silly, love, it'll be great fun; and in the most unlikely event you do hurt me and I can't speak, I'll do this.' She shook her head three times, then nodded thrice. 'Go on,' she urged, at his hesitation, 'I trust you; and don't worry, I'll co-operate and if you make it all as realistic as possible, and I mean that,' she emphasised, 'then I'll treat you to a special evening when I return tonight!'

As he sat alone, mercifully undisturbed, in the public house, Andrew, having become resigned to what he thought of as his lover's idiosyncrasies, mulled over the problems she'd presented him with, to wit: how to gain entry and overpower her in a convincing manner and without harming her in the process. Finally, after deciding on a plan, he made his way back to the flat.

To his consternation, the door was opened at his summons, not by his loved one but by a slovenly young woman with blonde hair piled up on top of her head, an over-made up face, untidy dress and an air of indolence. She leaned against the door frame with a lit cigarette between her lips and asked, in a bored tone, 'yeah?'

Completely confused by the unexpected appearance of a stranger together with the unfamiliar role he'd undertaken, he muttered, 'er, I must have the wrong flat. Sorry,' as he turned to go.

The woman sighed audibly. 'Andrew,' she announced in a resigned manner, 'you have NOT got the wrong flat. Now go down those stairs and start again.' And she closed the door once more.

After he'd done his foul deed, he let himself out of their flat and wandered across to the lake's harbour where he idly examined the quayside area with all its paraphernalia and watched one of the pleasure boats set off on one of its limited cruises. Next he strolled over to the water's edge and gazed around the horizon of the lake's perimeter until he began to lose all sense of time; originally he'd merely intended to give his lover a taste of what it'd be really like to be in a similar position to that of an unlucky housewife. Until, suddenly recalling she'd formerly told him it was illegal to leave a person unattended when left in such a manner, and checking his watch, he dashed back to the flat in order to release her. For the second time recently he was panicking that he hadn't interrupted her breathing, for he'd double gagged her this time.

As soon as he let himself in he was relieved to hear her muffled mixture of complaint and frustration coming from the kitchen where he'd left her bound to a chair, and she gave him a distinctly unamused stare as soon as she became aware of his presence. 'I didn't want you to be that authentic!' she chided him in an ill-tempered fashion as soon as he'd removed the thick scarf covering her lips and had pulled the filled up stocking from between her teeth, 'and no, don't bother with my wrists. Thanks to the way you trussed up my ankles to the chair leg spacers, I've been left with unbearable cramp in my feet and legs.' So stiff was she when he'd totally released her that she sat in the chair for a considerable time afterward, but her peevish complaining continued. 'Twenty five minutes you left me, and each second seemed to take an hour. Where on earth did you get to? And don't expect me to clear up after you. I could hear you rummage around in my drawers and throwing things about!'

Andrew who stood leering down at her, struck when the opportunity was provided by her, 'You seemed rather to have appreciated me rummaging round in your drawers earlier, before I started turning the place over. I wish I'd left you how I found you now, then I could have stuffed the fish and chips I bought, in your moany mouth every time you opened it.'

Julie whom, he was rapidly discovering couldn't be serious in the face of something even mildly amusing, smiled at his remark and replied, 'I must admit the ravishing part was far beyond my criticism but the agony bit was rather too much. Never mind, I couldn't help admiring the way you threatened to leave me trussed up in a position guaranteed to ruin my marriage if I didn't comply with your demands, though leaving me wearing only my underwear and the bottom half of my dress to cover my modesty below my waist, with just my bra on above, was hardly likely to improve my wedded bliss. But I note that when you threw me on the bed, you didn't take any risk that I might kick you where it hurt but spread my legs in a way which ensured complete safety to yourself. Beforehand, though, prior to your untying my ankles, when you put on protection, did you mean to do what you did or was it mere clumsiness?' When he nodded she asked, 'did you like it?'

'Very much,' he replied enthusiastically, 'but as you'd called for authenticity then you'll appreciate I was in a rush to get my thieving over and done with and get away without being caught and so if you hadn't been writhing and groaning away on the bed I would've ignored you. Therefore my raping of you was pure selfishness and lust on my part, otherwise I would have ensured you gained some pleasure from it, which is why everything I did was at top speed!'

'Don't worry, darling,' Julie cried, getting rather unsteadily to her feet, throwing her arms about his waist and kissing him, 'you did everything perfectly, like a real, professional villain. We women are supposed to like being bowled over, you did just that and I loved it, even the chair torment!'

Later, after they'd consumed the somewhat cool fish and chips with gusto and tomato sauce, and Andrew's sweetheart had got ready to go to work, they sat down together and he asked her, 'why exactly did you want me to do what I did to you? When I glanced up to see you struggling on the bed, you somehow seemed so sexy and desirable, so helpless; I just had to have you. You turned me into an animal when all I ever wanted to do was to be kind and loving toward you.'

'You did enjoy our game, though? You certainly seemed to.'

'Much to my disgust at the time, I did, but now I feel nothing but contempt with regard myself.'

Placing a hand over his she murmured kindly, 'ad to say, darling, we're almost all a mixture of saint and sinner to one degree or another. Look how paranoid your women over on the mainland were, from your own experiences; yet we on Whyte Island are well aware of all the films and the television programmes which feature terrible violence, many of which tend to make women, and girls of all ages, the main victims of all kinds of terror and brutality. Such media offerings are enjoyed by both genders which, as far as females on our island are concerned proves there's something primeval about enjoying violence combined with sex, as long as it's controlled and we can trust and have faith in those who supply it to us: our loving partners.

'So we offer ourselves up for their and our own pleasure. I'm one of the females, however, who insists that, tit for tat, we reverse roles each time in the victim-aggressor games; and as you know, you can take that rule or go and find someone else! Though at least, over here, it's only for amusement, and we women can walk alone anywhere on our island without molestation, but elsewhere in the world sudden violence toward our gender and children isn't merely confined to entertainment. So, sweetheart, enjoy our games in future, and if you can improve upon them or think of new ones, then do so by all means so we can add to the pleasure and variety which brings interest, love and affection to our mutual relationship.'

Whist they dealt with the dirty dishes Julie explained her tension release theory. 'Take a mainland couple, for instance, beset with all those pressures existing over there, both internal and external; these often mount up slowly like gas in a cylinder, ready to explode and resulting in wife beating, baby battering, mental breakdowns, drunkenness and similar types of domestic problems. But if they indulged in the type of games we enacted this afternoon it obviously wouldn't make the pressures vanish, but it would go a long way toward easing them.' She held up her hands to display the chafing marks her wrists. 'These beat a black eye and a ruined marriage any day; besides, I think it's much more fun even, in retrospect, being temporarily forgotten.'

Her lover observed, 'after what you said to Charlie Maynard yesterday I'm beginning to think I know what zigzagging is.'

But she merely smiled; nudging him conspiratorially she whispered, 'we're changing roles tomorrow, that's the rule of our house, or should I say flat? You'll be the victim, and I'll make you squeal alright!'

Despite all her protests Andrew insisted upon accompanying her to the ferry. 'What am I going to do while you're away?' he asked mournfully.

'Goodness, I'll only be gone a few hours. First you can clear up the mess you made, apart from one locked drawer the contents of which will, in time, be revealed to you, I've got nothing to hide, so you can browse through my belongings to your heart's content in the process. You can play some CDs, look through my books, go for a walk or a bus ride. Anything.'

'I won't come across any love letters?' he asked candidly.

Deckhands were patiently waiting to remove the gangway as Julie quickly embraced him. 'It's all done by phone,' she replied, 'besides, we don't usually go in for souvenirs over here. Oh, don't bother to cook anything for tonight, we'll be having a Roman supper, fringe benefits.'

Back in the flat Andrew put on a series of discs. His lover's taste in music was quite catholic, but tended to folk and also to original jazz, and as he listened with pleasure to the latter he idly wondered if he'd been anywhere near her during his first night's entertainment on the island. Going over to the bookshelves he scanned the titles – books on sex, philosophy, psychology and sociology predominated, many having been written, he was sure, by Whyte Islanders. Their presence did much to explain his loved one's knowledge and propensity to lecture him on those subjects. Romantic works of fiction were notably few in number; not surprisingly, he mused, for by comparison his sweetheart's love life must have been far more exciting than anything an author could dream up.

Taking a pile of books he went back to his comfortable armchair and, apart from cooking himself a simple snack at the appropriate time and standing on the balcony for a while in order to survey unnoticed the busy urban scene, he spent the remainder of the day and evening perusing the contents and listening to more discs. Much to his surprise he found the non-fiction works quite fascinating, and they went a long way toward helping him understand what the island authorities had been aiming at.

However, after beginning on one of several books devoted to sexual practice, reading a couple of descriptions and gazing at a few explicit illustrations, he felt compelled to return all those dwelling on the subject to the shelf from whence they came; such literature, he decided, was not meant to be absorbed when one was without one's lover. When he wasn't reading he lay back in his chair and thought with affection of his sweetheart; a moment of jealousy quickly passed upon his contemplating Julie's rubbing down dry naked men during the course of her slave duties, for he realised much the same service, and even worse, was required of nurses, and their lovers or husbands presumably had come to terms with the situation which he was now in. Thinking of nurses made him remember he'd promised to call Gill as soon as he knew when he'd been definitely fixed up with an island girl, but he decided to leave that problem with Julie. Eventually, after glancing across at the wall clock for what must have been the hundredth time, the hands told him his sweetheart's arrival was imminent.

Love and need for that girl, he mused as he donned his coat, is so intense that it's painful; he turned off the light and left the flat, excitement mounting within him as he crossed the dark, silent and deserted street. The ferry was just manoeuvring into the tiny harbour as he arrived on the quayside, and he waited impatiently while the boat was docked and the gangway positioned. Julie was one of the first passengers ashore, accompanied by two other girls whom he vaguely recognised as her companion slaves at the villa; she went straight up to him as soon as she saw him and put an arm about his waist, facing her colleagues she announced, 'these pair of work shy wasters are Christine and Maureen. This is Andy.'

As he took the hand of the blonde, she asked, 'would you care to elope with me, love?' Assuming he'd made yet another conquest, he was just about to make a suitable rejoinder when she continued, 'that way I won't have to listen to her saying "Andy this" and "Andy that" all day long.'

'Yes,' agreed her dark haired companion, 'I was expecting to find a heart-stopping prince on a snow white charger at least waiting, or else someone with a pair of wings on his back.'

His lover giggled and hugged him defensively. 'I ought to warn you two that my man is so highly sexed he's likely to ravish me now, and then any other female in the immediate vicinity.'

Both girls promptly chorused, 'Oh yes please.' But belied their retort by moving off into the darkness; one of them called over her shoulder, 'don't tire yourself out because I'm not going to pay for your night time fun, tomorrow.'

After replying with an apt insult Julie, oblivious of who might be around, embraced her lover passionately; he felt her cold nose against his cheek before she whispered into his ear, 'I love you so much my darling, I've missed you so. Promise we'll always be together.' And she pressed her lips tightly against his.

'That proves my point,' she exclaimed as they crossed the lamp-lit cobbled road with their arms about each other.

'What does, my love?'

'Without thinking, my work mates automatically endorsed my rape threat, even though it was only a joke. Most women, caught off balance, would probably give a similar reply, so proving the thought of enforced sex is by no means displeasing to them; providing it's undertaken by the right man, of course.'

'Do you really talk about me a lot?' he enquired, changing the subject.

She gently bit his ear lobe. 'You mustn't be surprised if I do, my sweet; you were the only man waiting for his lover on the quayside tonight.'

As Julie put her shoulder bag on the kitchen table, she asked with obvious concern, 'what did you have to eat today?' She unwrapped the parcel of food and began to dole the contents out onto a pair of plates.

Andrew finished pouring a couple of glasses of wine. 'I was too lovesick to eat,' he lied, 'so I went for a walk, and I saw this beautiful girl and....'

In an instant she had a heaped spoon beneath his chin. 'Would you prefer it down your collar, or your trousers?' she threatened with a malicious leer.

'What would you like us to do now?' she asked after the last of their somewhat unusual meal had been eaten, for she'd positioned herself on his lap and fed them both with her fingers on the morsels which comprised the repast, between sips of a superior tasting wine.

'Go to bed,' he suggested, 'because I want to lie in your arms, deep inside you, and tell you how gorgeous, kind, sexy and intelligent you are, and how much I adore you.'

She nodded her head slowly and smiled in agreement. 'Sounds like a fairly good idea to me; but first I want to clear away the dinner plates while you have a shower, after which if you'd like to get between the sheets au naturelle, then I will join you after I've also bathed.'

When Julie reappeared he was pleased to note she was wearing her Roman tunic, had her hair dressed in a ponytail and was carrying a bowl of fruit in the crook of one arm. Deftly she rearranged her lover so he lay parallel with the headboard of their bed, but still covered over, lifted his head onto her lap after she'd seated herself upright and slid a pillow under it. 'Now, my sweetheart, this time I'm not your captor but your slave. Open wide.' Dangling a grape just above his mouth, she quickly removed it when she felt he was about to take it, and instead popped it into her own mouth where she sucked it with evident pleasure; then she lifted his head to hers and transferred the fruit into his mouth.

In this fashion they shared all the fruit; sometimes she consumed the item without offering it, but usually he was the recipient, though only after the fruit in question had passed between her lips and been thoroughly rolled around inside by her tongue. Often she'd drop the morsel in his waiting mouth, still moistened with her saliva as a change from being passed orally, but whichever way she chose he always took her unusually supplied gift eagerly. To Andrew it was just another form of lovemaking between them.

Finally, while he rearranged himself lengthwise in the bed she picked up the light controller, put on the red tinted wall lamp and cancelled the main light, then she slid down the bed to lie alongside him. 'This,' she murmured, 'is the actual tunic you saw me wearing when we first met. We have three and I've been keeping a check on this particular one in the hope that one day you'd take me in it, and that's the only hint you're going to get tonight!'

To Andrew, lying naked beside a dressed woman in bed was yet another fresh erotic innovation brought to him by his sweetheart's store of games to relish and physically enjoy, so he lost no time in fondling her both inside and out of her clothing. 'I wore lower underwear when you first saw me,' she explained at an appropriate moment during his exploration; and shortly afterwards he began to make love to her. 'I see, or to be more accurate,' she whispered when he lay still, 'felt that you took my advice seriously; it's wonderful having you inside me especially when you do it like that. So what were you saying earlier about telling me what you liked about me?' she urged after a moment's pause.

During the night he was vaguely aware of his lover leaving their bed and of the toilet distantly flushing; but he was far too tired to think anything special about it and was soon asleep once more.

'Wake up, darling,' Julie was calling him, shaking him, 'we've overslept, it's past ten a.m..' As he struggled to sit up he considered that after another night of passion it was hardly surprising they'd slept late, between them they'd brought a new meaning to the expression "hat-trick". Though he was taken aback when he noted she was fully dressed. 'Look!' she cried excitedly, 'we've got a letter, the first one addressed to both of us, but you can open it.'

Inside the envelope was an invitation card giving details of a weekend card party at a certain country house; the dress was to be formal, but day clothes might be worn upon arrival. 'But I don't like playing card games, you saw how useless I was at them, anyway,' he groaned, still half asleep.

'Nonsense,' his lover admonished, as she sat down on the pillow next to him and tapped the card enthusiastically. 'Anyway, that's got nothing to do with it,' she exclaimed, 'look at the border, it's crimped.'

She was right; the information was enclosed within an oblong design which, although attractively intricate, contained a definite zigzag pattern. 'But what does it mean?' he asked with a frown.

'I'll tell you while we're having breakfast,' she replied, adding in an offhand manner, 'oh, don't bother to dress just yet; you can have a shower right after we've eaten. I'll bring you your dressing gown.'

'You see, darling,' Julie explained between mouthfuls, 'in order that every Whyte Islander can experience such entertainments as banquets, balls, parties and various displays, everyone receives a certain number of invitations each year, and sent out by the main computer. They can be really gorgeous occasions and often involve the wearing of period costumes, or other guises. I love them and I could go on all day about them.' Her eyes sparkled as she ate a mouthful of porridge; she picked up the card and examined it absentmindedly. 'They're all compulsory, though,' she continued after she'd finished eating, 'you can delay going if you don't feel well, but sooner or later you have to attend. They're ideal as social levellers and ensuring people aren't left out of such entertainments. However, every invitation card has a border round it; if it's straight, then it merely means nothing special is going to occur; if the border has a sort of curved or wavy pattern set in it then some kind of display is going to be put on as a diversion, a sword fight or something.'

'Like they have on our television,' Andrew commented.

'I expect so,' she replied uncertainly, but went on, 'if, though, the pattern has got sharp angles to it, like here,' she tapped the card, 'then I'm afraid it's a case of audience participation. It usually begins with attendance at some sort of social gathering, but not always.'

'But you won't tell me exactly what it involves?'

His lover considered long enough for him to realise she was teasing him; finally, however, she shook her head. 'No, I couldn't,' she stated decisively.

As he washed the breakfast things a thought suddenly came to Andrew. 'Darling, would you have really let me go back to Helen?'

'If I had I would've always regretted it,' she paused in her drying up to glance at him. 'A lot of stupid things are said in anger,' she reminded him.

'But you wouldn't mind me writing to her?'

'Of course not, love,' she laughed, 'but what about?'

'I think it ought to be to ask her to rescue me. But really to try and explain.'

'Yes,' she nodded in agreement, 'that would be a very good idea, and I think you really will need rescuing after today.'

It was an enigmatic statement he wished not to have explained, but having finished his task he walked over to the kitchen door. 'I'm going for my shower now, pet.'

Julie looked at him. 'But you'll be getting dressed in the

bedroom, won't you?'

Smiling to himself and not bothering to wonder at her rather pointless query, he continued on his way. 'Of course,' he called from the passageway.

Andrew wasn't entirely surprised to find his lover awaiting his subsequent arrival in the bedroom. 'If you promise to do as I ask without question,' she said as she rose from the bed and came toward him, 'I'll show you what zigzagging's all about; I think it's a shame you should have to wait until it actually happens.'

'Alright,' he agreed reluctantly as she undid the belt on his dressing gown and then removed the garment, 'but I don't believe you. Jeremy's quite right, you really are a minx; however, you put yourself in my hands so...' He shrugged dismissively.

Without taking any notice of what he was saying, she led him over to the bed, made him sit on its edge with his back to her and then sat down behind him. 'First,' she explained as she tied a knotted stocking in his mouth, 'they prevent you from communicating orally; usually they employ sticking tape, but as you've just eaten I think a nylon would be better, it'll stop you from swallowing your tongue and making you sick.'

Her next move was to position him in the middle of the bed until he was lying on his back. 'Of course, they use a wooden table, not a bed,' she continued, 'and they take a hand and fasten it down to the nearest table leg. Like this. And then the other hand. And finally... the feet, like so.' When she'd finished he lay crucified on the bed, each arm firmly secured by a stocking to the adjacent leg below the bed frame with his ankles bound together and tied via a piece of long twine to both the bottom legs. And as he stared up impotently at his lover she gazed back in obvious satisfaction at her handiwork and he rapidly became increasingly apprehensive about what she'd do next. What she actually did only increased his uncertainty, for she began to giggle until eventually she was laughing uncontrollably, 'Oh, darling,' she spluttered at last, 'you look so funny; I've always wanted to know how a sailor stands to attention in the presence of a superior!.'

She continued to stare at him in amusement for some time until she finally managed to calm down. 'You'll have to forgive me for the next bit of zigzagging,' she apologised with excessive politeness, still smiling, 'only I haven't got the genuine article so we'll just need to imagine it. They spread meat extract on you, like this,' and she began massaging every part of his exposed body within reach in a most intimate and suggestive manner as she pretend to rub the supposed liquid in; he automatically winced when she came to a delicate piece of his anatomy but noticing, she exclaimed, 'don't worry, sweetheart, that's my most precious possession, I'm certainly not going to harm that!'

Eventually, when it seemed to Andrew as though she was going to continue teasing him forever, she ceased; but it was only to be a brief pause in his torment for she then informed him, 'what they do next is to place this massive clear plastic cover over you, and then they introduce about thirty blowflies, you know: green and bluebottles, into it. It's ever so nice, as you can imagine.' And by way of demonstration she knelt beside him and delicately traced her forefinger nail over his belly in a meandering fashion; she paused to study his face to gauge the effect of her action, and said, 'I should say that was a fair representation of the sensation, but multiplied thirty times.'

And she began again, but in a different area of his body. If he found the massaging almost intolerable then Julie's latest assault on his torso was unbearable, and he began to struggle at his bonds in a vain attempt to escape while tossing about in discomfort, mumbling incoherently as he did so.

But his beautiful tormentor, apparently regretting the fact she was being too successful, soon ceased but then began a different form of provocation; for she stood up on the bed and, when she saw she had his full attention, she slowly began removing her clothing. The next hour or so were utter frustration for him as she imperceptibly brought him to the peak of sexual desire by kissing, fondling, caressing and whispering suggestively to him.

She employed a seemingly endless number of ways of teasing him to distraction including allowing her the tips of her auburn hair to trail across his face and, in a similar fashion, also her desirable breasts. He tried, on numerous occasions, to ask her to stop or to satisfy him, but he only succeeded in making ridiculous noises; and then, just as he was about to reach a climax without her physical aid, she glanced at the bedside clock and suddenly exclaimed, 'Oh, dear, look at the time! I'll make us both a cup of coffee and then I'll have to dash off; thank goodness I'll be able to have something to eat in the villa. Don't bother to get up, sweetheart.' And to his consternation she began to get dressed.

He thought her a cruel bitch as he watched her leave the room, and began to hate her, but he knew he'd detest her as much as a starving person could a potential provider of nourishment. With much difficulty he glanced at the clock and was shocked to see that his illogical lover would need to be on the ferry in little more than half an hour. Could there be anything worse, he wondered, than being taken almost beyond the peak of sexual arousal, only to be abandoned by the girl who took you there or, even worse, to be unable to satisfy yourself?

Even though it was so late, however, Julie still hadn't ceased tormenting him for when she reappeared she was actually carrying two mugs of coffee and, treating him as though he wasn't in a mute, immobile state, she advised, as she placed a mug next to the clock. 'Don't let it get cold. I don't know what you're going to do while I'm gone, possibly some housework like you did yesterday.' She left the room once more, but soon returned with a book. 'Just got time for a quiet read,' she muttered to herself and sat down in an easy chair by the empty fireplace with her back to the bed. As he lay helpless a slow feeling of doubt began to percolate in his mind; staring at the clock again he realised his lover might be mad enough to leave him in situ until she returned home.

Andrew was therefore dismayed, though not particularly surprised when, after about twenty minutes of silence she stood up and put on her coat; before she left the room she put on a CD and the sound of church organ music filled the air. 'I thought it might be apt,' she declared brightly, coming over to the bed to grasp the appropriate part of his anatomy in her right hand, 'how punny. But there's no point in you standing up for your rights, is there?' Still holding him, she leaned over the bed and slowly ran her tongue along his lips. Then she withdrew, and by the door she told him, 'don't bother to meet me tonight if you've got better things to do.'

As soon as the door closed to be followed by the front door shutting more noisily behind her, he began to work at the stockings again, despite the realisation it would be a hopeless task, and thinking as he did so that his lover would've made an excellent boy scout in some ways. Finally desisting, he began to wonder how he'd be able to withstand the dreary, frustrating hours which lay ahead, how he'd cope with the cold which evening might bring and for how long he'd be able to control his bladder. Another drawback to his immobile state was the bloody music she'd left him to endure; he despised such pieces.

Fortunately he wasn't too uncomfortable, and she'd left a fair amount of slack in the nylons, thereby allowing considerable movement to his limbs, though not enough to be of real value to him; but his main concern, apart from his, thankfully, rapidly declining sexual frustration, was the loss of dignity which his situation imposed; supposing she brought someone, perhaps her companion slaves, home with her? It was an action she was quite capable of, he realised with a mental shudder.

And so he lay wondering, worrying and feeling utterly ridiculous for over twenty five minutes until, much to his astonishment and, latterly, consternation, the bedroom door began to open slowly; fortunately, he was very relieved, yet surprised, to discover his visitor was just Julie. Somehow she'd managed to change into a simple green cotton dress which buttoned up at the front, and she'd pinned up her delicious red hair in a way which always made her look elegant; together with the garment's matching white collar, sleeves, buttons, polka dots, and short hem she gave the impression of an innocent young girl only just past puberty, a vision which, together with her wide eyed surprise at discovering him trussed up, apparently for the first time, caused him, much to his alarm, instant arousal.

She immediately exclaimed in evident horror, 'oh, you poor darling!' and she rushed over to the bed. Staring down at him she asked with obvious concern, 'what have they done to you?' She paused, as if undecided about what she ought to say or do next, but if her captive was expecting an early release he was disappointed for she bent down and removed her white knickers; holding the item aloft she observed, 'I know this won't compensate you for the harm that's been done you today, but as a virgin I'll do my best!' And as she threw her underwear across the room, she climbed onto the bed and with an ease which amazed him, she quickly straddled him.

Any other human female in the world, Andrew mused later, would probably have left it at that, would simply have satisfied him; but not his Julie, for every so often she'd stop moving her hips in order to make some adjustment to her appearance. The first thing she did was to undo the top two buttons of her dress and force her right breast from its white brassiere cup; later, she unpinned her hair and allowed it to fall about her shoulders; her next move was

300

to display her remaining breast and finally, after undoing all the buttons and letting him view, with some discomfort on his part despite an extra pillow supporting his head, her small amount of bodily hair, she dispensed with her little dress altogether.

Twice more she stopped, moaned and shuddered while an expression of pain and anguish appeared on her face, but after each spasm she went on gamely, her sole objective, seemingly, being to satisfy her sweetheart; finally she squealed with delight as he reached his long awaited climax and threw herself down on him. Groping wildly at the knot which secured his gag, she managed to tear the stocking away and urgently pressed her mouth to his, immediately she inserted her tongue and began to manipulate it in an excess of passion.

'Shouldn't you be at work?' he asked ingenuously when he was at last able to speak.

Julie sat up and stared down at him in something akin to surprise, tears began to well up in her eyes as she began to giggle; clambering off him, she subsequently laid her head upon his chest and, as her gorgeous hair tickled him, her body began to tremble with laughter. His chest was soon wet with tears and saliva as her laughter turned to shrieks of mirth and, not knowing quite why, Andrew presently felt compelled to join her in her merriment. Eventually, after several false starts, she managed to scream out, 'I got up in the middle of the night and put all the clocks forward two hours, even your wrist watch; so I didn't go to work, I just went in the kitchen and got lunch ready.' And she went into paroxysms of laughter once more.

Prior to untying him she turned the CD player off. 'Good job I subconsciously put some music on instead of the radio; the regular time checks would've undone all my preparations,' she observed with a smile.

'What would you have done if I'd wet the bed in your absence? Because I really thought you'd abandoned me.'

'Don't worry, my love, I wouldn't have run screaming home to mummy; anyway, there's a moisture proof membrane guarding the mattress, so the only real damage would've been to your ego. Besides, I love you too much to leave you tied up all day.'

As soon as she'd released him he grabbed hold of her with some ferocity. 'And if I didn't love you so much, I'd hate you for what you did to me!'

But Julie wasn't in the least put out by his reaction. 'It came to a satisfactory conclusion didn't it?' she asked innocently. 'The next time we do it I'll throw in appropriate soft music, subdued lighting, perfume, alcohol, sexy costume and exotic dancing, and then you won't know what's hit you; what we did just now was a mere aperitif. One thing you can be sure of my dear, sweet, handsome darling,' she promised as she held his head against her breasts and stroked his hair, 'our relationship will never become dull and boring; I think you're worth hanging on to and that's why I did it.'

As his lover had intimated, it was only to be the beginning of many such erotic adventures she arranged at his expense; she loved to immobilise him, and then tease him by being patronising, irresolute, coquettish along with many more poses; but Andrew soon learnt to enjoy and endure such humiliation with fortitude, safe in the knowledge that, sooner or later, she'd satisfy his frustration to the best of her not inconsiderable ability; he was also aware that, within a day or two, she'd allow herself to submit to his revenge with little real complaint, in any way he wished.

But although they displayed great initiative in the manner and variety of their games they never allowed them to get out of hand; the emphasis was always on discomfort not pain, teasing not torment and implied rather than actual mental and physical cruelty. For each lover automatically understood that ill treatment would eventually lead to retribution from their erstwhile victim. In a strange way, as Andrew was to discover, the games served to strengthen the bond between his sweetheart and himself for, as Julie had suggested, they really were a means of releasing tension besides being extremely erotic and exciting for both assailant and victim. Gradually, over the period of their relationship, their love of idiosyncratic romping accelerated their desire for each other's company as he began to relax entirely in her presence for they now had secrets to share, and he began to understand he could do very little that she would disapprove of. Thereby a lifetime of marital coexistence had been compressed into a relatively short period.

Andrew barely had time to dress and eat lunch before escorting his lover across to the ferry; on the way over, he said, 'yesterday, I amused myself reasonably well but I doubt whether that form of occupation could satisfy me indefinitely, so have you got any other ideas? Charlie suggested you might tour the red establishments with me, but until that's fixed up I'll be at a loose end. I miss you a great deal while you're away, and I'm worried about becoming lonely and bored.' She tried to reply, but he went on hastily, 'I don't want to try computer dating because you're the only girl I'm interested in; and, anyway, I'm not going to risk jealousy breaking up our perfect relationship.'

Julie transferred her arm from his shoulders to his waist. 'The first thing to do,' she stated, 'is to separate afternoon from evening. So this afternoon you could visit the local school and brush up on martial arts, for instance. No,' she suddenly said, 'I've got a better idea; when you return from seeing me off have a stroll around until you come across the town hall, go in and tell them your problem; they'll give you plenty of literature, and we can go through it and discuss the options tomorrow.'

When they reached the gangway his lover, much to his surprise, pulled him up it. 'I've arranged for you to come over for the trip,' she explained, 'Jeremy, of course, knows the captain, not that it made any difference.'

Using his experience of seafaring, Andrew chose a suitable spot on the upper deck for sheltering from the somewhat strong wind which was causing rather a swell, and Julie and he leaned against the safety rail and gazed out across the lake. 'Of course,' she observed, referring to the problem of his loneliness, 'you could receive your citizenship within weeks and then, as you said, we could come to some arrangement; but I'm certainly not going to allow us to be apart more than necessary, so unsociable hours for only one of us is out. But don't worry, my love, the present set up will only be temporary.'

Andrew, who'd wondered if she was as accomplished as the women he'd fought with onboard the Whyte Line ships asked, 'just how good are you at self defence, darling?'

He knew she wasn't kidding when she replied casually, 'I've got most of the top awards. In a bare room with you, both of us devoid of weapons and clothing, I daresay I could throw you about indefinitely until I got bored and tired, then I could kill you painlessly in a couple of seconds. For a quick job I'd knee or kick you in the testicles and then finish you off. I suppose I'm about average for a Whyte Island girl.'

Andrew grimaced, but commented, 'no doubt it's more useful than learning a foreign language at school. But aren't you rather assuming I wouldn't be able to defend myself?'

Julie turned and stared at him with interest. 'What sort of awards have you got then?' He shook his head to admit his lack of any. 'Well, then,' she answered, 'besides, men with their balls are always more vulnerable in unarmed, unprepared combat than women; it's agility rather than strength which pays off in the end, as well as the confidence to take on someone more powerful than oneself, which frequent practice, together with ability, brings.'

Quickly changing the topic once more, he asked, 'why do you need to go to the villa so early?'

She left the rail and pressed herself against him, putting her arms about his neck she explained, 'well, we have to help with the cooking, tidy up and do other domestic chores, then we have to make ourselves up to look authentic. I love the job, but I love you so much more. If it meant being longer with you I'd work down a sewer.'

He kissed her gently and lingeringly for this remark. 'Julie, my sweetheart, I'm scared I'm going to wake up from this beautiful dream at any second.'

Giggling, she threatened, 'I could remind you this isn't a dream.' And he felt one of her knees lifting one of his recently mentioned organs.